THE UNDERCOVER AGENT AND THE LYCAN

HANNAH HITCHCOCK

Copyright © 2024 HANNAH HITCHCOCK

All rights reserved

The characters and events portrayed in this book are fictitious. Any similarity to real persons, living or dead, is coincidental and not intended by the author.

No part of this book may be reproduced, or stored in a retrieval system, or transmitted in any form or by any means, electronic, mechanical, photocopying, recording, or otherwise, without express written permission of the publisher.

*To a long suffering friend whose idea it was to write a story.
They encouraged me and helped me to develop my potential.
This dedication is to say thank you. I wouldn't and couldn't
have completed this without you.*

And also for Simon, for indulging me

Author's Note

You are about to read Morgan's story of self-discovery. Be warned, darkness and graphic references are rife. Recommended for those who can withstand the evil acts committed by bloodsuckers.
18+ years of age advised.

You can now follow the author on Instagram
@author_hannahhitchcock

CONTENTS

Title Page
Copyright
Dedication
Epigraph
Playlist
Prologue — 1
Chapter 1 — 2
Chapter 2 — 10
Chapter 3 — 21
Chapter 4 — 34
Chapter 5 — 47
Chapter 6 — 60
Chapter 7 — 72
Chapter 8 — 83
Chapter 9 — 97
Chapter 10 — 109
Chapter 11 — 121
Chapter 12 — 132
Chapter 13 — 142
Chapter 14 — 158
Chapter 15 — 169

Chapter 16	180
Chapter 17	194
Chapter 18	204
Chapter 19	214
Chapter 20	229
Chapter 21	242
Chapter 22	253
Chapter 23	265
Chapter 24	278
Chapter 25	291
Epilogue	304
Afterword	307

PLAYLIST

This Is The Beginning - Ely Eira

Nightcall - London Grammar

Numb - Linkin Park

How You Remind Me - Nickelback

Good Riddance (Time of your life) - Green Day

Empire State Of Mind (feat. Alicia Keys) - Jay-Z

Freak On A Leash - Korn

Thriller - Michael Jackson

Beautiful Things - Benson Boone

In The Stars - Benson Boone

Bring Me To Life - Evanescence

Luminary - Joel Sunny

If The World Was Ending - JP Saxe

All Of Me - John Legend

PROLOGUE

Dear diary, sorry I haven't written in a while. The funeral was awful. It was damp and smelly in the church, maybe from all the rain we have had lately. I've never been to a funeral before. There were lots of songs that everyone seemed to know the words to. I didn't. Aunt Winnie said it was more a blessing of passing than a traditional funeral, as Mum and Dad weren't religious. Everyone kept looking at me and whispering. If only they hadn't gone out that night. Why couldn't they have just stayed home with me and had pizza like the week before? At least they died together; quickly upon impact the police officer had said. According to Aunt Winnie, the other driver was a drug addict who had ploughed straight into them, driving across the dual carriageway. I vow here and now to never touch drugs. They ruin lives, families, my family! It's a little over a two-hour drive to Aunt Winnie's, I'm going to live with her now in Great Yarmouth. It won't be so bad, at least I have a focus now, I know what I want to grow up to be. I'm going to be the best badass policewoman there ever was. My life will have a purpose! I'm going to hunt criminals and put them behind bars!

Signed 11-year-old Morgan Hudson

CHAPTER 1

The Briefing

Morgan sat alone on the maroon Chesterfield leather sofa in the small waiting room, outside Chief Special Agent Steve Rush's office. It had been newly painted a crisp white and the smell of fresh paint lingered in the air. Awards and medals adorned the wall and a few potted plants added a boost of colour to a very clinical room. Martha, the Chief's secretary could be heard tapping on her keyboard just outside the door, which created a soothing rhythm for Morgan to drift away into her thoughts.

Morgan was told at short notice last Wednesday, that she would be going deep undercover, handed a USB flash drive and told to take the rest of the week off work to organise her affairs. She loved undercover assignments they were thrilling!

She had done two before. In the first, she had posed as a bank clerk to expose a counterfeit money scam, when she was assigned to the National Crime Agency. The second, was when she first earned her place in the Drugs Squad, posing as a sex worker to gain access to a drug smuggling operation in Portsmouth.

Back at her studio apartment in a converted old warehouse, she grabbed her pet carrier down from the top of the wardrobe and searched for her black cat Hermes. He usually liked to hide under the bed, so Morgan crouched on all fours but he wasn't there. He wasn't really her pet as such, he just appeared one day five years ago, the day she moved into this apartment and he never left. Hermes was already wearing a name tag and she had taken him to the vet, but he didn't have a chip.

Scanning round the bedroom before she closed the door, she saw a glimpse of a tail behind the curtain; got him she thought triumphantly. She packed her suitcase, emptied her fridge and took out the rubbish. Then she locked her front door and drove her rental car the one hundred and thirty miles to her Aunt Winnie's in Great Yarmouth.

It was obvious that Aunt Winnie was thrilled to see her, as she parked on the grass adjacent to the static caravan. Aunt Winnie was a classic hippy straight out of the 70s, totally carefree and in touch with nature. She often walked around barefoot, cleansing the caravan with sage every full moon and foraging in the local woods for herbs and plants, which she made into pickles and oils. She believed that she had a sixth sense. She could usually predict when it was going to rain and the changes in the season. Aunt Winnie shirked the traditional patriarchal attitudes of society, living her whole life in a communal setting, sharing food and living mostly off-grid.

She was a redhead like Morgan's mother, but whereas Morgan's mother was preened to perfection from head to toe, Aunt Winnie was the complete opposite. She let her hair grow wild, rarely brushing it and always wore mismatched multi-coloured clothing, with various patches to cover any holes. Morgan looked nothing like her Mother or Aunt Winnie except for her eyes; they all shared the same emerald green eyes.

Morgan had struggled to lie to her Aunt, about her undercover mission, but orders were orders. She had told her Aunt that she was working undercover in the UK and would have limited contact until her assignment was over and to only contact each other in an emergency. Her Aunt was the only one close to her that knew she worked for the National Drugs

Intelligence Unit as a special agent. Everyone else just thought she joined the police department at eighteen and moved down south.

She had a lovely break with Aunt Winnie, the weather had been glorious. They had brownies for breakfast, barbecued every mealtime and watched old movies all night. It was just like the old days when she came to live with Aunt Winnie. Her room was exactly the way she left it when she moved out eight years ago. The simplicity of life in the caravan on the commune was a breath of fresh air from the hustle of London life and the complexity of going undercover.

Upon her return yesterday to London, she had spent all day with the mockingly named 'glam squad'. Usually, they dressed down the undercover agents, adding wounds, tattoos and hair pieces. They also gave lessons on how to age the face or hide personal tattoos, but today Morgan was getting the full beauty treatment. Women paid a lot of money in London for the amount of treatments Morgan had done. Her long hair had been trimmed, with layers and a full fringe added, dyed a dark chestnut brown and chemically straightened. Her short-bitten fingernails were manicured and painted black. She had been waxed everywhere that grew hair and semi-permanent black eyeliner and pink lip colour applied. Along with full instructions on to how maintain a casual sultry look. Morgan gritted her teeth at the thought of waxing again, why do females do that to themselves? If it wasn't meant to have hair on it, your body wouldn't grow it there. Morgan had concluded that when the glam squad weren't working on transforming undercover agents, they were assigned to a classified torture division.

Morgan wasn't one to become embarrassed easily, but she did see a smirk slide across the beautician's face, when she uncovered Morgan's secret tattoo of a prowling black panther, usually hidden by hair on her lady parts. A rebellious teenage act which in part she regretted, but she still embraced the panther as her spirit animal, drawing on its spirit energy to be fierce and courageous.

Abruptly the door from reception to the waiting room opened and Chief Special Agent Steve Rush marched in, greeted Morgan and unlocked his personal office. Morgan automatically stood to attention and followed the Chief inside, closing the door behind her. Steve was a tall, fiery-red head who could often be heard shouting, but in the three years Morgan had worked for him he had always been fair, and she respected him. As he sat behind his desk he gestured Morgan to take a seat.

"Your assignment is to infiltrate the Lucas crime gang and provide indisputable evidence to take down the drug cartel. As you're aware, this is the third costly undercover operation and so the Commissioner has this morning personally signed off on any means necessary mandate. The mission is on a need-to-know basis and therefore not to be communicated with your colleagues, for fear of a breach in the department.

The opening of their third bar in Nottingham, due to open in time for fresher's week, gives you the perfect cover to pose as a University student needing a job. The latest intelligence says it will be named Wild, the address and other details are included in this latest report. We've embedded as much of your personal life as possible into your undercover alias, your new name will be Morgan Ann Fletcher, twenty-six years of age, with your birthdate. You grew up in Great Yarmouth with your aunt, as your parents died in a car crash. You have been saving for University by working in bars and have just started a Physiotherapy BSc Hons degree at Nottingham University. Your dream is to be a sports physiotherapist and travel the world."

Handing Morgan a plain well-worn purple rucksack Steve continued, "Inside you will find your new identification, laptop and University schedule. You will attend all lectures without fail and maintain a 2.1 average. The tech analyst team have created your social media profiles, the passwords are stored in the Notes app on your new iPhone, commit these to memory and delete them. I suggest that you study the background events the team have created. The iPhone is updated with the latest technology; it will use Face ID to recognise only you, but will purposely fail to recognise you. Code 252518 will unlock Morgan Fletcher's phone, whilst 911229 will unlock your agent account. You are to check in daily, pass back intelligence and receive orders."

Reaching into his top pocket he handed Morgan a key, "Here is your house key, you will be living in the downstairs front room of a shared house with four other students at 11 Elmsthorpe Ave, you will make friends with your housemates and classmates but remain undercover at all times. Have you got any questions?"

"No sir," said Morgan in her usual confident military manner.

"Then leave all personal belongings in your locker, and take civilian transport to St Pancras train station to catch the three-thirty-five to Nottingham. Be vigilant,"

But before dismissing her Steve added, "I put you forward for this Morgan, you're my best female operative, don't let me down." He signalled for Morgan to leave.

Special Agent Morgan Hudson was now Morgan Fletcher, a first-year physiotherapy student. Who, truth be told was a bit irritated that her boss had referred to her as his 'best female agent' when quite clearly she was his best agent period! As she was about to prove.

The train had been fairly empty, so it had allowed Morgan time to get to grips with her new phone and examine her social media accounts. The tech analysts really are good at their job she thought. If she didn't know that the pictures were photoshopped, she could have sworn blind that they were real; although she would never lick a shot off someone's armpit, undercover or not!

Morgan took the first taxi cab in line at Nottingham

station and took the short journey to Elmsthorpe Ave. She stood on the threshold of number 11, an extended 1930s semi-detached with two suitcases, a hold-all and a rucksack. Morgan took a deep breath, inserted the large Yale key into the lock and opened the door. On the right-hand side of the narrow hallway, she could see the door to the room which was to be hers.

As she slid the smaller silver key into the room lock, a friendly voice shouted, "Hi there, I'm Molly." Morgan turned towards the staircase to see a petite blonde waving frantically. She was wearing denim shorts and a white boobtube with her hair in pigtails. Morgan took a deep breath, and answered "Hi, I'm Morgan, isn't this so exciting!" Molly proceeded to relay, that she had moved in at midday and Morgan was the last house member to arrive. The other three were male and it had been decided that everyone would go out to a local bar in town for food and drinks, to get to know each other. That left Morgan nighty minutes to shower, unpack and see the clothes which had been assigned to Morgan Fletcher.

As she entered her room she surveyed the contents. Luckily the room came fully furnished. She had a wardrobe in the far right alcove and a dressing table in the other, a medium-sized TV was mounted to the chimney breast opposite a double bed and the large bay window had a view of a beautiful old oak tree. Everything was magnolia including the soft furnishings, apart from the carpet which was dark grey and very worn.

With true military precision, everything was unpacked and hung in the wardrobe in twenty minutes. But standing in front of the garments in just her underwear, Morgan was flabbergasted at how different Morgan Fletcher's style was, to her own. Gone were the tracksuits and trainers she usually wore. Morgan was faced with the option of a short denim skirt, short shorts, or ripped skinny jeans and every colour of crop top imaginable. Morgan would concede that she did have a perfect hourglass figure. This was due to her dedication to her fitness regime. But did the ops team think this mission was to be finished in a month flat and therefore she wouldn't need any winter clothing or anything that might cover her midriff? Skint student or not, she was going shopping for some suitable jumpers at the first opportunity.

She settled on ripped jeans and a black cropped T-shirt. Luckily she had arrived in her own trainers. She opened the wardrobe door fully and stared in the full-length mirror on the back of the door and smiled. Show time.

The bar was an interesting place. The walls were cladded with wood and the seating was luminous orange. The waitresses wore orange hot pants and clearly, the hiring policy stated that you had to have enormous fake breasts. Morgan chuckled to herself, it was a good job the Lucas family didn't run this bar, or she wouldn't have been assigned the mission. The food was delicious though, as the whole party tucked into varying degrees of spicy chicken wings and deep-fried gherkins.

Her male flatmates were George, David and Phil. George was an Aerospace engineering student who was tall with a rugby player physic. David and Phil were both studying Accountancy, both of average height with glasses. All three were mature students, although Phil was definitely the oldest of the three. Molly was also studying accountancy but was definitely the youngest housemate, clearly straight out of public school. Molly said her father was making her do the course so she could manage her inheritance better, but she had no intention of completing it and was instead here to party. She had missed out on halls accommodation because she had to go through clearing and 'Daddy' had paid a substantial contribution to the University for her to be accepted.

The guys all seemed pleasant enough, uncomplicated intellectuals and unpretentious. Morgan imagined it would be easy to befriend them, but Molly, befriending Molly was going to be more of a challenge. Morgan had never been described as a girly girl or a party girl and Molly was quite frankly the epitome of both. On the commune, Morgan had grown up with lots of children, of all different ages, but she had always felt an outsider. Perhaps, because she had only met them when she moved in with Aunt Winnie at eleven years old, or maybe because she went to a mainstream school, whereas most of them went to school on the commune. She had never had a close best friend as a youngster and this had continued into adult life. She had made her career her whole life.

She assumed she would meet a partner at the gym or at work and nearly did once. A gym instructor had asked her out for a drink after a kickboxing session. She thought they had a great night, but then he never asked her for a second date and after one painful will he or won't he speak to me at the end of the next session, Morgan booked onto a different class so she never had to see him again. No one at the training academy or the office had ever asked her on a date, or shown any interest. She aced all her theoretical classes and trained twice as hard in the gym as any of them. She figured they were all too intimidated, or maybe they thought she fancied women.

The meal turned into drinks and the gang didn't stumble back home till midnight. But as Morgan curled up under the covers, she congratulated herself on a great first day.

CHAPTER 2

*The Hunt Begins, But
Who's The Prey?*

Today was Saturday and lectures didn't start until Monday. This gave Morgan the perfect opportunity to scope out getting a job at Wild and to fix the midriff wardrobe malfunction. But first things first, a quick 5k run, the same way she had started every morning for the last eight years. Exploring the surroundings would be fun and necessary if a quick escape was ever needed. The sun was shining and it looked like it would be another glorious day.

Morgan started with a light jog past a row of identical semi-detached 1930s houses on her street into the next street, all indistinguishable from one another. It seemed to be student central, as all the houses looked like houses of multiple occupancy and parking spaces were hard to come by. There were a significant amount of alleyways and lower brick walls if a quick exit was ever needed. She mentally planned her escape from the bay window in her room, to an alley in the next street and into the nearby playing fields.

Morgan slowed down as she approached the last few streets before Elmsthorpe Ave and turned past Faraday Road. She checked the timetable at the bus stop and learned that bus route 36 would take her into town. She decided to catch the nine o'clock bus. That would give her time to stretch, shower and change.

The main bathroom was on the second floor. It was a simple white tiled room, with just a shower-bath combo inside. The toilet was in a separate room next door. Morgan had never come across this before but thought this was a clever design feature; to prevent waiting in line in the mornings. Molly was fortunate to be on the third floor in the converted attic and had her own en-suite, something Morgan was definitely jealous of.

Staring into her new wardrobe she contemplated what to wear. Background intelligence had said the scene in Nottingham was eclectic. But based on the premise that Wild was aimed at alternative music, wardrobe had ensured there was a slightly punk rock element to the fashion choices she was now presented with. The jewellery options were very different to Morgan's usual taste and she looked at the spiky dog collar in disgust. However, the clip-on fake nose ring was interesting and didn't hurt as she clipped it on. She had always procrastinated about getting some piercings, but after having the tattoo was too scared about the pain and the regret.

Standing in front of the mirror now at her new reflection, she was pretty impressed with the transformation from her usual mousy brown wavy locks and zero make-up approach. She selected a slashed AC/DC T-shirt, a short denim skirt and Dr. Martens. After peeking out of the curtains to assess the weather, Morgan grabbed a cropped pleather jacket from the back of the door. She wrapped a red tartan shirt from the wardrobe around her waist, hoping that would prevent her from flashing her knickers to anybody.

Before turning to leave she looked one last time in the mirror at the complete ensemble and knew she was missing something, but what? Not that dog collar! Looking at the dressing table she noticed a box of hair crayons. Why not go wild? After all, it was time to stand out and be noticed. She opened the new box of hair crayons and added streaks of electric blue into her newly dark locks. Impressed with their vibrancy she left the room and ran for the bus stop on Faraday Road.

The bus dropped Morgan off in central Nottingham and it took no time at all to find the large shopping centre, which Molly had recommended the night before. She perused several stores before purchasing two jumpers. One a loose knitted purple/black striped jumper and the other a black hoodie with white skulls. She had a sneaky suspicion they had been in the Halloween fancy dress section, but she didn't care.

The bar was only one street away, it would be easy to scope it out on the premise of a shopping trip and see if staff were setting up. Out of habit more than anything, Morgan weaved her lucky rabbit's foot key ring between her fingers as she walked through the alley to the next street.

Morgan was in luck! A big delivery truck was outside with the side curtain open. A rather rugged man, in jeans and a white tank top with shoulder-length brown hair, was carrying two large kegs at a time into a cellar trap door. The uniformed delivery driver was stacking crates of tonic water on the street. Placing her shopping bag on the ground by the stack of crates, Morgan picked up a crate of tonic water and walked towards the open bar door. "Where do you want these," she called over to the man lifting the kegs. He turned and tilted his head slightly as if assessing if she was a friend or enemy. "On the bar," he replied.

As he turned she recognised him as Fenik LeLoup, he had more stubble now than in the photos she had previously seen of him, but his piercing bright blue eyes and long hair were instantly recognisable. He was a close associate of the Lucas family who was to be the Nottingham bar manager. He was often photographed with different members of the Lucas family and was definitely in the inner circle.

Morgan continued back and forth until Fenik had waved off the delivery driver and the delivery was safely inside. As

Fenik went behind the bar and started stacking away the crates he asked, "So what can I do for you?"

Leaning over the bar to respond, Morgan cheekily answered, "Well I'm hoping I've proven myself useful and could prove more useful to you if you would give me a job."

Quick as a flash Fenik responded, "Yeh, why not, I like a woman with initiative, come back Thursday at eight for a trial."

Before Morgan walked out the entrance, she flicked her hair back over her shoulder and turned to ask, "So who do I say hired me?"

He chuckled, "It's a trial and the names Fenik, I'm the manager, and who did I just hire?"

She smirked as turned around to leave; her flirting had gotten her desired response. "Morgan." She shouted. As casually as that, she had landed the job and got her way in!

As Morgan left, a shadow emerged from the stairs. Striding across the bar after coming up from the lower level was Tristan Lucas.

"What did the foxy minx want?"

Fenik smirked, "A job," he replied.

Slightly annoyed that he had to speak again, Tristan sarcastically added, "And?"

"She's coming back on Thursday for a trial; we need all hands on deck for the start of freshers. Why?" Already knowing the answer as it was written all over Tristan's face, he added, "Do you like her boss?"

With a sly smirk as he walked back downstairs Tristan shouted back, "Does a wolf like to hunt a fox?" And if you don't know the answer to that, the answer is yes.

Safely locked in her room, she activated Morgan Hudson's phone account and typed, *'I start work at Wild on Thursday'* and pressed send, two blue ticks appeared and then the message vanished. Morgan waited for a response but there wasn't one, so she locked the phone again and left the room to enter the communal kitchen/living room. It appeared that a well-done would be too much to ask for.

Molly and Phil were playing a Mario Kart game on the TV, so she settled down on the spare leather sofa, opened up a magazine from the coffee table and began to read. Having lived in the caravan from the age of eleven, Morgan didn't find it strange to cook, eat and watch TV all in one room, or that a door led off from the kitchen to a toilet.

The kitchen cupboards were old and battered, varnished in a dark brown but you could tell they were good quality and must have been expensive a long time ago. The back wall of the room was full with cabinets and each room was assigned one for personal pantry items. A much newer small island housed the electric hob with enough space for two bar stools. The large shabby fridge freezer looked out of place set in front of the back door. It made access to the outside impossible, but it was a practical addition to the kitchen. The extension took up the entire outside of the property so a back door was pointless anyway. There wasn't any natural light in the room and the bulbs only gave a dim glow. The walls were a plain magnolia and three brown leather sofas formed a u shape around a large TV.

Morgan thanked Molly for the Primark tip and small talk began between the housemates. The other housemates had arranged to walk to the local supermarket in an hour. The plan was to get an Uber back and go for drinks again in town. In the spirit of joining in and following orders, Morgan obligingly joined them.

The start of the week passed in a blur, having never been to University before Morgan found it enthralling. She loved to learn and several instructors at base camp had referred to her brain as a sponge. Her University class was large at roughly forty-five students but everyone in the class was eighteen years old, straight out of A-levels, so making friends as a mature student seemed unlikely.

Regardless, Morgan fully immersed herself into the student lifestyle as ordered. Socialising in the student union and drinking in the evening, predominately with her male housemates. David had a passion for cooking and had even taught her how to make carbonara on Tuesday; the accountant in him was clearly evident as he reeled off all the ingredients, the price of each and calculated how much per portion the meal came to. He offered to cook dinner for everyone Monday to Wednesday if they paid him the cost of the ingredients and everyone had agreed.

By midday, Thursday lectures were over and Morgan was planning her approach for the evening ahead. The last two failed missions had centred on the Leicester nightclub managed by Tobias Lucas, the oldest son of Vincent Lucas. Whilst it was believed that Vincent was still heavily involved in the family's criminal activities, he rarely showed up at the nightclub and surveillance had concluded that he did most of his business dealings at home. Now in his early seventies, it was believed that he was passing the reigns over to his sons and they would be easier to infiltrate.

However, the last two missions, one a seduction attempt and one a friendly bartender, had both failed and worse, the agent posing as a bartender had been found dead a week after going missing. The autopsy revealed it was a drug overdose. Stakes were high to get this right. Morgan had decided that a cheeky, helpful bartender wasn't going to be enough and whilst she was prepared to play the long game; as she did have cover for three years as a University student, she wanted this over quickly to prove to everyone that she was a great agent.

She had decided that she had two options and was going to see how the first few weeks played out before deciding whether to seduce Fenik, the bar manager or Tristan, the younger son. Personal preference leaned her towards Tristan, with his jet-black short hair, sculptured stubble and smart-suited fashion sense, he reminded her of a movie star on the red carpet and after all, he was the son of Vincent Lucas. She was more likely to get into the inner circle if she was dating the boss's son. But she couldn't be choosy, so her decision to lure in Tristan would have to go undetected by Fenik. Just in case, Tristan rejected her and she had to switch her affections.

Background intelligence on Tristan showed that he was never photographed with the same girl more than once, so seducing him was going to take all her cunning and wit. She had aced her profiling class during training and determined that to attract such a playboy, she would need to play hard to get. By becoming unobtainable, she would drive him wild.

But first things first, she needed to catch his eye. Morgan stared at her wardrobe and thumbed through the rail, finally settling on black tights that appeared as if she was wearing suspenders, black denim shorts, a Led Zeppelin crop top T-shirt and Dr. Martens. She added her now favourite add-ons; electric blue hair chalk, a nose ring and matt red lipstick. It would be cold when she finished so she grabbed her pleather jacket and carried it over her arm. She was feeling confident and determined, as she ran for the bus stop.

It was a short walk from the bus stop to the bar and as Morgan approached she saw Fenik standing outside, smoking with Tristan by his side deep in conversation. Time to put her plan into action! Unconsciously she played with her key ring in her hand as she put it in her jacket pocket and sauntered up to the entrance. Both men turned towards her as she approached, so she put an extra sway to her hips. She smiled suggestively at both Tristan and Fenik before the perfect opportunity arose to put plan A into action.

Tristan's trouser zipper was undone. This she thought, would be enjoyable. Locking eyes with Tristan she lowered her gaze to his manhood and bit her lip. His gaze was fixated on her and she could tell she had grabbed his attention. Morgan relished in bursting his bubble, by casually telling him that his zipper was open, as she walked past them both into the bar. Behind her, she heard Fenik roar with laughter.

Fenik followed her inside and instructed her to put her personal belongings in a lock box behind the bar. Prior to handing over her jacket, she slipped her phone off silent mode and placed it into her back pocket. She was now recording live to HQ.

After a quick briefing and introduction to the other bar staff, Fenik left Morgan to work on the entrance bar with Jono and Nathanial. There was a steady stream of people from eight o'clock onwards, most grabbed a drink at the entrance bar and made their way down the spiral staircase to the floor below. Along with the small entrance bar, there was a mezzanine level set away from the entrance, raised up by four steps and this was being managed by Fenik and three others. The bar had a country smoking lounge vibe, with deep red leather upholstery, dark wooden panelling and antler wall lights. The lights above the bars were large dangling Edison bulbs, which cast a soft glow around the large room.

When she could, Morgan entered into friendly chit-chat with Jono and Nathanial. Nathanial was nineteen, a second year at Nottingham University, 5ft 10 with fair hair and a lot of ear piercings. He had chanced his luck like Morgan and asked Fenik for a job.

Jono was approximately mid-twenties, roughly the same height as Morgan at 5ft 6, but wide and must live at the gym with those biceps. He had fair hair too and was covered in tattoos, with some visible at his neckline and a small one over his eyebrow of a tribal pattern. He usually worked at Pulse, the nightclub in Loughborough ran by Tobias Lucas, but he was helping out in Nottingham for the launch. Morgan made a mental note to check HMRC records to run background checks on all the staff.

By ten, both upstairs bars were heaving, but as Morgan kept watch on the back staircase, a large proportion of people were still filtering downstairs with very few coming up. How big was downstairs? She decided it was time to find out.

By now the music was so loud Morgan had to lean

over and shout into Jono's ears to make herself heard, as she asked him where the toilet was. He pointed downstairs and gesticulated for her to go. She crossed the bar floor and made her way down the spiral staircase, but was puzzled as she entered a fairly small room with only a handful of people sitting in armchairs at tables. She saw three doors; one labelled staff only, directly opposite the stairs which she believed would lead under the bar to the cellar. The other two doors were the male and female toilets. She crossed the floor and tried the staff-only door, but as she suspected it was locked.

To keep to her cover story, she entered the female toilets and looked around at the bank of stalls, but they were empty too. As she started to make her way back upstairs, she surveyed the room looking for a hidden door and then she saw it. The wall with a bookcase pivoted opened, as two giggling girls made their way into the toilets. Morgan conscious of the fact that she had taken longer than she should have to visit the toilet, carried on walking upstairs and started serving again behind the bar.

A little before midnight, Fenik switched places with Jono and offered Morgan a fifteen-minute break in the staff room upstairs, pointing towards the larger bar. She thanked him and proceeded over. Invisible from the entrance were stairs going to an upper floor behind the second mezzanine bar. Hoping she would be alone, she climbed the stairs and surveyed the top floor. She was presented with three doors, one plain, next to another one which displayed a brass crest of a wolf head in the centre of the door and one on the opposite side of the hall with a sign saying Flat 114A.

She opened the plain door first as it was closer, it clicked open to display a smallish magnolia room with coat hooks, a small kitchenette and a couple of Ikea tables and chairs; this was clearly the staff room. She grabbed a glass from the draining board and ran the tap to fill it up. Scanning around the room there were no obvious cameras, but she couldn't rule out hidden ones. Morgan was intrigued by the ornate door, surely that was an office and the other must be an apartment.

As she was weighing up the pros and cons of investigating it right now, her phone rang bellowing out the theme tune to friends. That was Aunt Winnie's personalised ring tone, it had been Morgan's favourite TV show when she was a teenager and it had been on repeat when Morgan first lost her parents, teaching her to laugh again.

But why was her Aunt ringing her at midnight? She answered the phone quickly, as the sound of Aunt Winnie's worried voice boomed out of the phone, "Are you ok? What are you doing? I can sense you're in danger." Morgan was used to this strangeness and over-protectiveness from Aunt Winnie. After all, she had no children of her own and her sister and brother-in-law had died suddenly, changing the course of both their lives.

"I'm fine honestly, don't worry," Morgan responded.

"I wish you would let me know what city you're in at least," begged her Aunt.

"I can't do that but I promise you I'm fine," Morgan replied and noticing the time on her phone she ended the call with, "I love you, bye." Morgan washed her glass out and made her way back downstairs to finish her shift.

As the clock struck two, the lights turned on and the music which had been progressively getting more comical changed to children's nursery rhymes and Morgan let out a little chuckle. Jono, Fenik and what must have been a bouncer from downstairs, dressed all in black, appeared in the entrance bar to usher out drunken partygoers. The change in music was clearly a tactic to clear the bar out quickly.

Fenik thanked all the staff, then he threw Nathaniel and Morgan a large black T-shirt each, with a wild logo emblazoned on both sides in white. Fenik welcomed them both to the team. They were to bring their credentials tomorrow and would discuss a rota then.

Morgan ordered an Uber and loaded the dishwasher as

she waited. Not once did she see Tristan appear, but as she waved goodbye, Tristan watched from the top-floor office bay window, as he contemplated how he was going to snare his next conquest.

CHAPTER 3

Treat Them Mean, Keep Them Keen

Morgan was so glad that lectures on a Friday didn't start until one, it allowed for the perfect lie-in. She really had lucked out with her timetable. She was at University from nine until four, Monday to Wednesday, nine until eleven on Thursday and one until six on Friday. It would give her just enough time to travel home, eat dinner and change before heading back out to Wild for an evening shift.

Morgan remained in bed until eleven before putting on her running clothes and starting her daily 5k. The weather had turned whilst Morgan was out running and she was dripping wet when she returned. All of her housemates were out, so she jumped straight in the shower, blasting Pink's greatest hits from YouTube on her phone. After, she proceeded to wander around the kitchen/living room in her fluffy black towel, whilst making a bacon sandwich for lunch. She ate it quickly on a bar stool on the island before heading back to her room to get dressed.

The last lecture of the day ended promptly at six and Morgan rushed out of class to the bus stop. Not being much of a chef and having nothing in her kitchen cupboard to cook, she diverted to the local corner shop on Faraday Road and selected a chow mein Pot Noodle and a Mars bar for dinner before making her way back home. She would need to do a weekly shop tomorrow and stock up on some quick dinners for Friday nights.

Back at the house, the kitchen was empty, so whilst she boiled the kettle in preparation for her Pot Noodle, she grabbed her towel and shower cap for a quick shower before work. By the time she got back downstairs, the kitchen was full of all her housemates making dinner. She poured hot water into her Pot Noodle, leaving it to stew. Morgan disappeared into her room to get dressed; away from the chaos of four people making four separate dinners at the same time.

She applied her sultry makeup using the techniques the glam squad showed her, clicked on her nose ring, applied purple lipstick and added streaks of purple into her fringe and the ends of her hair. She opted for fishnets, black denim frayed shorts and her new Wild logo t-shirt. But as she slipped it on over her head it drowned her in the sheer size of it, it was even longer than her shorts. Whilst she pondered what to do next, there was a knock at the door. It was Molly, carrying Morgan's Pot Noodle.

Upon seeing Morgan's outfit, she instantly scrunched up her face disapprovingly and blurted out, "Here, you left this in the kitchen and George nearly knocked it over, only a little bit spilled. You can't honestly be serious about wearing that, are you?"

Morgan explained that she had been given it the night before to wear at work but shared the same sentiment; that it looked ridiculous. Molly smiled and rushed back to the kitchen, grabbing a pair of scissors before slipping back into Morgan's room and closing the door. "Trust me," she said, "I love a project and did this all the time at boarding school."

Morgan stood as still as a mannequin, while Molly snipped away with the scissors. Molly started on the sleeves cutting up the seam and around to take off nearly half. She then instructed Morgan to remove her arms from the T-shirt and she cut a semi-circle out of the top of the shoulder. Impressed with her work she did the same to the other side and Morgan slipped her arms back through. She then stood for a minute in contemplation, before cutting an upside-down triangle from the rim of the neck to the top of the Logo. She circled Morgan before pinching the back of the T-shirt away from Morgan's body and snipped away to create a slashed effect as if she had been out in the wild and mauled by a tiger.

Morgan opened her wardrobe door to look in the mirror, to make sure the Wild logo was still visible. Molly had done a good job, if anything the logo stood out more now. "Right," Molly said, "How short do you dare to go," lifting up the bottom of the material to check out Morgan's stomach. "You've got good abs why not show them off." She looked at Morgan for approval.

"I'm at your mercy," Morgan responded quite enjoying the excitement on Molly's face.

"Excellent," Responded Molly chuffed that Morgan was appreciating her help. She cut off two wedges from the front of the t-shirt and then sliced up the middle to the bottom of Morgan's ribs, cutting out a further triangle in the middle and then snipped away the excess material at the back. She then showed Morgan how to tie the two pieces together into a little bow at the front. Molly stood back and examined her creation and Morgan turned around in front of the Mirror.

It was a definite improvement and would make a statement. She had enjoyed her bonding session with Molly, maybe they would be friends. Morgan hoped her look would be received well at the bar. She thanked Molly for her help and joked that Molly should switch her degree to fashion as she had a real talent for it. Morgan followed Molly back into the kitchen/living room to eat her dinner and then left for work in plenty of time to catch the seven-thirty bus to town.

Morgan reached the bar just as the clock struck eight and waved to the bar staff as she crawled under the back mezzanine bar and climbed the stairs to the staff room. Once inside she hung up her coat, and slid her phone off silent and into her back pocket as before. She opened the door intending to waltz down the stairs as if her outfit was the standard uniform, when Fenik and Tristan walked out of the other upstairs door.

Morgan immediately turned round to face them to study their expressions in response to her outfit. Fenik was dressed in his usual worn Levi jeans and a standard black Wild T-shirt and had an amused look on his face. He turned towards Tristan who was wearing an expensive-looking thick white shirt with cufflinks, two buttons were undone so a small amount of chest hair was visible and plain black chinos, whose initial smirk turned into a smile. "You didn't think much of the uniform then," commented Tristan.

"I thought I made it look better," She cheekily replied, thankful that they both seemed to see the funny side of it.

"You do," Tristan responded, "but I'd rather not see Jono wearing that." Morgan smiled and both the men laughed as they all made their way downstairs.

Fenik instructed Morgan to start work on the entrance bar again with Nathanial and Summer, who she met last shift but Tristan intervened.

"No, Morgan can join Jono downstairs," looking over at Morgan he continued, "Follow me." Morgan followed Tristan across the bar, down the spiral staircase and through the revolving hidden bookcase door. A DJ playing grunge rock music was in the middle of the room with smoke machines and strobe lighting. A large dance floor circled the DJ but was only about a third full, with most people still sitting in booths around the outside. A small bar was currently manned by Jono and a guy Morgan recognised only from the background intelligence as Jake Kuon, another close associate of the Lucas family. Two men dressed in black; presumably the bouncers were standing at opposite corners of the room. Tristan gestured for Morgan to head over to the bar as he walked in the opposite direction and started greeting people sitting at the booth furthest from the bar. Morgan greeted Jono and he in turn introduced her to Jake, another stocky, average-height guy but with very curly blonde hair.

The downstairs club had a very different atmosphere to the upstairs and as it started to fill up with more and more people, Morgan, Jono and Jake were rushed off their feet keeping up with the demand. Even though it was busy they had some good laughs, particularly at Morgan's expense and her adapted uniform. She had informed Jono of what Tristan had said and challenged him to design his own for tomorrow.

By midnight the downstairs club was rammed full and Morgan hadn't seen Tristan all evening until Jono offered her a drink and a fifteen-minute break from behind the bar. Morgan jumped at the opportunity to stretch her legs and walk around, so she grabbed a Diet Coke and went in search of Tristan. She spotted him as she walked slowly around the outside of the dance floor. He had moved booths now and looked deep in conversation with three men, all of whom she had seen on the background intelligence.

Ronnie and Frankie Cane were identical twin brothers with olive skin and black hair. They both had a long list of criminal charges but none had ever stuck. Opposite them was Matthew Negus, who was instantly recognisable with his large afro and dark skin. He had a clean record as an adult, although an unsealed juvenile record showed he had been in trouble with the law at ten for theft. Intelligence had frequently pictured the four together. They all looked roughly the same age, so Morgan had deduced that they were probably close friends, as well as business associates.

As she got nearer to the booth, Tristan looked up and smiled at her, gesturing with his finger for her to join them. He patted his lap as if offering her a place to sit. Initiating plan A, to keep him keen by treating him mean, she strolled over to the table. Removing her phone from her back pocket, she placed it and her Diet Coke on the table and asked Matthew if he would move around to make space for her to sit.

Tristan clenched his jaw but laughed the situation off as the other men whooped and hollered that he got dissed. He introduced her to the men and they introduced themselves back. Matthew offered her a glass of the Champagne they had on the table which was chilling in an ice bucket and Tristan offered her his empty glass.

"Well if the boss insists," She responded, taking the glass from Tristan and holding it up for Matthew to fill. She locked eyes with Tristan and bit her lip on purpose to watch his eyes move to her lips and then continue down to her breasts before landing back on her eyes. Ronnie grabbed the bottle from Matthew and poured himself another glass, whilst asking Morgan if she wanted to join them for the rest of the evening.

Morgan broke her gaze with Tristan to respond that she better not as her boss might crack out the whip. She got up to leave the table and as she did Tristan responded, "Oh I don't mind."

Smirking, Morgan leaned into his ear, so that only Tristan could hear. She joked, "I don't like whips much. I prefer handcuffs." She glanced back into Tristan's eyes which were now wide and glistening, almost primal with desire. She walked away from the booth and back to the bar to finish her shift, leaving her phone behind on purpose.

Unfortunately, Matthew noticed the phone almost immediately. He passed it to Tristan, suggesting that Morgan had left it behind on purpose, to lure Tristan away from the booth. Tristan glanced at the screen which lit up with a photo of Morgan, three guys and a blonde girl in a bar, easily recognisable to anyone from Nottingham as Hooters. A growl emitted from low in Tristan's throat as he hoped one of these wasn't Morgan's boyfriend. He finished the remainder of Morgan's glass of Champagne and poured another which emptied the bottle. Gesturing he would get a refill to the others around the booth; he grabbed the bucket and headed for the bar.

Making his way over to the bar wasn't easy, the dance floor was full now and several girls tried to dance with him. One even felt up his behind. Usually that would have commanded his attention and he would have stuck around on the dance floor, but he was on the hunt for a better prize.

As he reached the bar it was three deep with customers, so he waited his turn. Jono came to him first and he requested a new bottle of Taittinger Champagne and a fresh ice bucket, before waving Morgan's phone in the air to get her attention. Just as she finished serving a customer and noticed Tristan, a petite blonde in a backless silver dress sauntered over to Tristan, playing with her hair.

She said "Hi," before slipping a note into Tristan's shirt pocket, blowing him a kiss and walking away. Clearly impressed with her directness Tristan removed the note to see a name and phone number. Women throwing themselves at Tristan was clearly a regular occurrence and Morgan wondered whether she was better to cut her losses and attempt to attract Fenik instead.

He handed Morgan her phone and whilst looking her straight in the eyes, he ripped up the paper, sprinkling it behind the bar. He then leaned over to speak directly into her ear and asked for her number instead. Was it just that her profiling was working? That he had chosen her over another gorgeous woman or something else. Morgan didn't know but her insides leapt and she couldn't contain her smile. She asked for his phone and input her number before catching the eye of the next customer and continuing to serve. Tristan swaggered back to the booth, very pleased with himself.

As the lights turned on and the DJ played nursery rhymes again, Tristan was nowhere to be seen. Morgan helped Jono and Jake finish downstairs before joining the rest of the staff upstairs. Fenik fetched a large black diary from behind the entrance bar and signalled over to Nathanial and Morgan to follow him upstairs. Morgan explained that based on her University schedule she wasn't able to work days, so Fenik agreed that he would rota her every Thursday, Friday and Saturday night.

Nathanial had more flexibility in his schedule so he was

happy to be planned in for a mix of days and nights that would change bi-weekly. Fenik handed out more Wild T-shirts so they had enough to last for the week, this time selecting a smaller size for Morgan to take home. She booked her Uber and waited for it to arrive.

Once in bed she activated her agent phone and typed *'I have exchanged numbers with Tristan Lucas, he appears to have taken a personal interest in me. I managed to leave my phone in his company. Did you get any intel from tonight's recording? I will be working Thursday, Friday and Saturday nights at Wild from now on.'* The message disappeared. It was now nearly three in the morning, Morgan decided she would check for a response later and closed her eyes.

Later that morning, Morgan was awoken by a female voice singing and the clattering of pans coming from the kitchen. Morgan checked the time on her phone, it was ten, fair enough she couldn't really complain about noise at ten. Before getting out of bed she checked her agent phone for a response. A message appeared: *'Nothing pertinent to the case received. Well done, keep getting his attention. Steve.'* Well done, Morgan was chuffed with that. She put on her dressing gown and went to investigate the singing.

Standing at the sink with her back to Morgan, using a soup ladle as a microphone, with bright pink headphones on was Molly. She was belting out the chorus to 'Hit me baby one more time' by Britney Spears. Morgan tapped her on the shoulder and Molly literally jumped into the air. Apologising profusely, Molly had gone the colour of scarlet red. Morgan explained how well the outfit had gone down at work and the bet she had with Jono. Molly seemed pleased and suggested that they should all go to this bar next week on Wednesday night.

Once Morgan had showered and changed after her morning run, Molly and George accompanied her to the local supermarket. They didn't have too many bags between them, so they decided to walk home rather than get an Uber. Morgan enjoyed the conversation and learnt a great deal more about her housemates.

George had intended to be a professional rugby player but he broke his back whilst playing. After a lengthy stay in hospital and rehabilitation he had realised his career dreams needed to change. He had applied late for University and missed out on halls.

Molly was a rebellious soul, but full of energy with a positive, generous attitude, she told them lots of funny stories from boarding school and how she always managed to get away with mischief. They spent the rest of the day hanging out together in the kitchen/living room. They took it in turns to play Mario karting on the games console, which George had brought from home for the house to share.

By four-thirty David arrived back from his shift at the local supermarket, quickly followed by Phil who had spent Friday night back at home in Newcastle. Phil was a devote football fan and his dad had managed to get him a ticket to a home game. David offered to make everyone spaghetti Bolognese, so everyone stayed hanging out together in the communal area and the conversation turned to Morgan's job at Wild. None of them were local to Nottingham and hadn't yet been to any bars off campus, but they all agreed to Molly's plan of visiting next Wednesday.

Morgan's phone buzzed and as she checked who had text her, a grin grew wide on her face. Molly being very perceptive immediately teased her, demanding to know who it was. Morgan read the text aloud to Molly, insisting it was just a friendly guy she had met at work and then saved his number. She would reply later as she didn't want to appear too keen. Secretly she was glowing with pride, or was it something else?

Morgan left the room to get ready for her shift and re-read the message again alone. *'Looking forward to seeing what you will wear tonight, Tristan'.* True there was no kiss at the end of the message, but it was very suggestive.

Once showered, Morgan requested that Molly brought scissors to her room to create another masterpiece with her uniform. Molly was thrilled and decided on two different patterns for the two new T-shirts. On the first she slashed the front like a tiger had mauled it and cut into the arms so the fabric hung looping in strings, leaving the back untouched. On the second she cut a big oval above where Morgan's breasts would be and then sliced away thin pieces of fabric in a downwards triangle getting smaller as she got to Morgan's belly button area and then capped the sleeves purposefully fraying a bit of the fabric.

Morgan was extremely impressed with the creations and opted to wear the mauled by a tiger look for tonight's shift. She teamed it with her suspender effect black tights, a black skirt and Dr. Martens. This time she chose a neon pink hair crayon to apply streaks throughout her hair. She thought about replying to Tristan but decided against it, she would keep him keen by being elusive.

Road works through Lenton had caused long traffic delays, so Morgan was ten minutes late when she arrived at the bar. She apologised to Fenik before dropping off her pleather jacket in the staff room and heading towards the downstairs bar, as Fenik had instructed. As she entered the room, it took a few seconds for her eyes to adjust, to the dim lighting and smoke. Morgan saw Tristan and Jake at the bar, howling with laughter at Jono.

Jono had indeed taken on Morgan's challenge and customised his own work T-shirt, ripping the bottom half of the shirt off in a jaunty angle and slashing the collar down one shoulder. To finish the look he had bleached the tips of his hair neon green. He looked ridiculous, but what a good sport.

Overall, everyone she had met at the bar were really friendly and clearly up for a laugh. It pained her to think that they were involved with drugs and murder. The thought brought her back to reality and she started serving behind the bar.

Tristan joined them on the staff side of the bar helping himself to a Jack Daniels and Coke before squeezing past Morgan. He placed his hands on her hips and leaned into her ear. He explained that he would be busy in his office upstairs this evening, but he would see her later.

As Tristan had brushed past her hair, he had caught her scent and she smelled amazing. It took him by surprise, just how much he wanted to be near her. He decided to ensure his business meeting finished early, so he could spend the rest of the evening with Morgan.

The bar was the busiest it had been yet, being a Saturday night and Morgan was rushed off her feet. She kept herself as vigilant as she could be, especially when collecting glasses. On a couple of occasions she thought she saw Matthew Negus receiving money from people, as he sat in the booth furthest from the bar.

On one occasion a group of giggling girls leant over the bar and asked her to get Jono for them. She then saw Jono point over in the direction of Matthew and the girls disappeared. Her mind wandered to thoughts of Tristan and what he was doing upstairs.

It had just gone one-thirty, when Jono's phone rang and after ending the call, he asked Morgan to take a bottle of Champagne up to Tristan's office. Hoping she might walk in on a business deal, Morgan hurried upstairs with a bottle of Tattinger in an ice bucket.

Out of politeness and her training as an agent, she knocked and waited until she heard Tristan's voice shout enter. Inside the small windowless room were two red leather sofas either side of another ornately decorated door, which she believed must lead to an office. A solitary large potted fern was in the corner of the room and an autographed Meat Loaf poster hung on the left wall.

Tristan was stretched out on one of the sofas and Morgan noticed two glass flutes laid out on a low glass coffee table. Morgan placed the Champagne on the table unsure of what to do next. Was he trying to seduce her, or was she reading this situation all wrong? So she opted for, "Did you want me to open this for you?"

Immediately initiating charm mode, Tristan replied, "The Champagne is actually for us. Why don't you join me on the sofa?"

Did he really think that she was that easy to seduce? How many other women had fallen for that line? Morgan could feel the anger and disgust rising like bile in her throat. Trying to hide the disdain on her face, Morgan responded, "If you want to get to know me, you need to do better than this." With that, she turned around and left the office, without even acknowledging the broadening smile on Tristan's face. He loved the thrill of the chase and Morgan was fast becoming an exhilarating hunt.

He followed her downstairs to the mezzanine bar as a painfully familiar song started playing. The bar was now full of students linking arms and singing along to the words. This song had been played at Tristan's brother's funeral. It had been his brother's favourite song. The motto behind the catchy lyrics resonated stronger now than ever. Everyone will die, so have fun whilst you're still alive. Tristan took heed in the significance of those words.

He stood in the doorway behind the bar, watching Morgan as she walked across the crowded room to the spiral stairs. A bunch of drunken male students linked arms with her and span around with her lifting her off the floor. Tristan instinctively went to save her, but saw she was smiling and didn't need his assistance. The next minute her smile changed to defiance, as she slapped the boy to her right on the face and Tristan saw him withdraw his hand from up her skirt. The boy, clearly drunk continued singing along to the song and dancing with his friends, as Morgan descended the stairs.

Then it hit Tristan like lightning, Morgan was completely different to any woman he had ever dated before. He was intrigued by her; she had an air of mystery about her and an abundance of confidence. But it was more than that, he wanted to be near her anytime she was in his vicinity and she had frequented more than one dream, unconsciously as he slept. Maybe she was his soul mate. Tobais, his eldest brother, had tried to describe it to him when he met his soul mate but failed badly.

Years later, when it had happened to Timothy, he said when you know, you know and it would happen instantly. Tristan had never really understood what they meant and although he had casually dated several women, he had never had feelings for any of them. None had tempted him to even ask them to be his girlfriend. He figured he would probably remain a bachelor like Fenik.

Tristan made his way back upstairs; he walked through the first door passed the sofas and through the second door into his main office. He opened the filing cabinet, searched for Morgan's personnel file and began to read, wanting to know everything about her.

Morgan left quickly after her shift finished, not wanting to run into Tristan again. The full moon was high in the sky and it cast a beautiful glow onto the cobbled street outside the bar. She twirled around with her arms out wide, like she had done as child, smiling, before making her way to her Uber on the main road.

Tristan was watching from his office window totally bewitched by her, he decided then and there, he wanted to do more than just seduce her; he wanted to know her and captivate her, just as she had enchanted him.

CHAPTER 4

The Enchantment Begins

  Tristan woke up early on Sunday morning, after a restless sleep. He rolled over in bed and searched for this mobile phone in his trouser pocket. Half dangling off the bed, he automatically scrolled through his recent contacts looking for his brother Timothy's name. Then he remembered the awful truth, he was dead. The realisation hit him like a dagger to the chest, life was precious and he needed to live life to the max. He quickly got dressed in casual jeans and a white T-shirt and headed downstairs to see if his mother was at home.

  He found her washing up the breakfast dishes in the kitchen. She was a petite woman, with Mediterranean features. She spent her life in the gym as a personal fitness instructor. Even at nearly sixty, she could walk on her hands and perform summersaults on the gymnastic bars. She was surprised to see Tristan awake so early.

  He gave her a kiss on the cheek, before grabbing the milk from the fridge and sitting at the breakfast bar directly in front of her. "It's unusual to see you this early on a Sunday, are you ok?"

  "I'm fine, don't worry," he confirmed, before approaching his vexation. "I've always done ok with women, but they've always been a certain type of woman. I've met someone who's different, she intrigues me, but I don't think she's interested in me. How can I persuade her to like me?"

Tristan's mother smiled knowingly, before responding. "Did you know I didn't like your father when I first met him? I thought him arrogant and over confident. Traits you may share, on an initial glance. Ultimately all you can do, is show her your true character, you're loyal, thoughtful and loving. You always have been, even as a pup."

"But how can I convince her of my true nature, when she barely stays in my company for longer than ten minutes?" he challenged back.

"Actions speak louder than words. Show her your true self," She replied.

Still struggling what to do next, Tristan asked again, "But how?"

His mother shook her head in disbelief, "Have you never bought a woman flowers, chocolates, dinner? Ask open-ended questions so that she has to respond and if that doesn't work just talk to her. Make an effort with her friends, she will come around and if she doesn't it isn't meant to be." And with that, his mother affectionately patted him on the arm and left the room.

Morgan spent Sunday catching up on her University assignments and hanging out with her housemates. Juggling an evening job, University and getting to know new people was proving to be a full time job.

Monday morning started far too early when Morgan heard her phone buzzing. Checking the time as she rolled over to inspect her phone, she saw it was 7am. There was no message on Morgan Fletchers phone, so she locked the screen and entered her agent code to see a message from Steve. *'Have you been following the news? There have been two more drug overdoses in the East Midlands area over the weekend and Commander Nicolescu is taking a personal interest. He wants results fast. Push harder. Steve.'*

The message vanished within seconds, as always. Morgan hadn't seen the news over the weekend and she cursed herself for not staying on top of current affairs. She searched overdoses in the East Midlands area on her phone and read the first news report that appeared.

Nothing was described as suspicious, other than the victims appeared to be well dressed and in their mid-thirties, one was a lawyer and the other a HR Director of news for the BBC. Morgan wondered if they were really the type to be partying hard and taking drugs? But then perhaps stressful jobs forced them to need an outlet. They certainly didn't appear to the type to party in Wild.

The day continued on, completely uneventfully until Morgan arrived back home from University to a very excited Molly. Jumping up and down Molly lead Morgan into the kitchen/living room. A huge bouquet of at least two hundred red roses, were displayed on the island.

David, who was making dinner for everyone was completely hidden behind it. Molly was desperate to know who it was from, but assured Morgan that she hadn't opened the card. Morgan didn't need to open the card to know; she smiled and wondered how far she could push him.

Pondering on what his next move might be. She opened the card so that only she could read the contents. *'I look forward to getting to know you Miss Fletcher.'* Molly was eagerly waiting to see the card, so Morgan handed it to her; she pulled a face demanding to know who it was from. Morgan shrugged her shoulders and left the room with an enormous smile lighting up her face.

On Tuesday she returned home to David in the kitchen/living room enthusiastically pointing at a large box, with a Hotel Chocolat logo stamped on the front. She grabbed a knife from the worktop and sliced open the top, lifting out a large black box. She lifted the lid to reveal three draws of luxurious chocolate truffles. David was salivating and after checking the

Hotel Chocolat app on his phone, proceeded to inform her, this was the most expensive box they made; the signature cabinet box and was £190.

Morgan told him to help himself, whilst she opened the personalised message, clearly ordered online as the message was typed. It read, *'Can I take you on a date?'* Morgan thought he had been clever in asking a question because now she needed to respond, if she wanted to appear at least somewhat interested. She picked a dark circular chocolate with a milk chocolate swirl on the top and bit into it, it was heaven in a mouthful; smooth praline truffle coated in bitter dark chocolate. The man had impressed her.

She picked up her phone and typed out *'Where and when?'* Then deleted it, then typed *'Yes'*, then deleted it. She couldn't decide how to play this. Getting top marks in all her profiling assignments and classes did not give her the training on how to attract a mark, whilst playing hard to get. Checking her watch she decided to wait till Molly returned home; the shared calendar on the fridge said she would be back in thirty minutes.

By the time Molly arrived home, David and Morgan were laying on the sofas, watching a stand-up comedy show on the TV, with a glass of red wine in one hand and a chocolate truffle in the other. They had eaten half the top layer already, which was pretty impressive considering David was in the midst of cooking. He had assembled a large lasagne for them all to eat for dinner tonight, which was now bubbling away in the oven.

Molly squealed when she saw the chocolates but declined the offer of red wine. Instead she ran to the fridge to pour herself a glass of white wine and joined them both on the sofa. The first day Molly had met all the housemates she explained that she couldn't drink red wine due to her extensive dental work and teeth whitening processes.

She helped herself to a chocolate truffle and Morgan explained her dilemma and asked for her help on what to reply. "I knew you knew who those roses were from," insisted Molly, before she grabbed Morgan's phone and typed '*I like surprises, surprise me.*' She passed the phone back to Morgan without pressing send. Morgan chewed the inside of her mouth, "Really?" she mumbled.

"It's perfect, isn't it perfect?" Molly questioned David, turning towards him. As he devoured another truffle David responded, "It's differently got an air of mystery to it, if you want to keep him on his toes."

Morgan pressed send and waited for a reply that didn't arrive. During dinner Morgan couldn't help but keep glancing at her phone, but no response. By bedtime she was actually in a little bit of a bad mood and she slept badly that night tossing and turning.

By morning she was practically seething, accidently took a wrong turn and found herself lost on her morning run. By the time she doubled back and found her route again, she was running fifteen minutes late and Morgan hated being late. The sky had almost gone Indigo in colour and the sound of thunder rumbled in the distance before the rain started.

The day went from bad to worse when she missed the bus to University and had to wait around in the bus shelter for an extra thirty minutes. Late, wet and in a foul mood, she entered her lecture and apologised to the professor. He asked her to stay behind after class. He was actually her favourite professor so far, he kept things interesting with little anecdotes and had a school boy chuckle.

She stayed behind when her lecture finished as instructed. Her professor only wanted to explain the next assignment as she had missed that, but staying behind class to chat to him had a knock on effect that meant she was late for the next class and this is how the day continued.

By two-thirty as she waited for her last lecture of the day to begin, her mood had become even worse, and worse still she had no reply from Tristan. She messaged on her housemate group chat that she was having a really bad day and could they postpone their night out to Wild until next week? Molly responded first, confirming that it was no problem at all and proposed they order a takeaway instead.

George, who had clearly forgotten the plan to go out, apologised and said he had made other plans anyway and wouldn't be back tonight. David and Phil were food shopping so offered to purchase some bottles of the same Malbec they had yesterday. Molly messaged back quickly asking them to pick up some white wine for her. At least she could put off bumping into Tristan for another night, Morgan thought.

The thought of how well she was getting on with her housemates cheered her up immensely and by the time she got home she even managed a smile as Phil poured her a glass of red wine.

By six o'clock they were a couple of bottles of wines down and fully into 'Die Hard With A Vengeance'. Molly had declared her love for Jeremy Irons, with his German accent. A debate ensued over whether Die Hard was an action movie or a Christmas movie and a takeaway had yet to be ordered.

All of a sudden the doorbell rang. "I'll get it," Morgan shouted as she jumped over the back of the sofa and walked into the hall. It was dark outside so she couldn't see who was behind the door until she opened it. Her mouth dropped when staring back at her in the doorway was Tristan. He was carrying a bottle of Tattinger Champagne and a large plain carrier bag full of plastic takeaway food pots.

The smell of the food hit her, if she wasn't mistaken it was a Chinese and made her already hungry belly rumble. Then she smelled Tristan, his aftershave was gorgeous, it smelled of sandalwood mixed with lavender. The lavender instantly reminded her of Aunt Winnie and the bushes that grew along the back of the caravan, which she dried and hung in the wardrobes.

His jet-black hair was tousled and spiking up as if he had just ran his hand through it. He was dressed casually in dark denim jeans and a white designer polo shirt with the collar flicked up. His eyes were a crystal light blue, sparkling as they met hers and a wide grin with perfect white teeth appeared on his face as he said, "I thought I would surprise you, I hope you're hungry."

Morgan wasn't quite sure if it was the shock, the smell of the food or how good Tristan looked, but she opened the door wide and allowed him to follow her inside. She opened the kitchen/living room door and introduced Tristan to her housemates.

Mid-debate they all stopped and stared in silence. David spoke first, getting up to shake his hand before slyly adding, "So you're the secret admirer, thanks for the chocolates." Molly let out a girlish giggle and gushed about how nice the flowers were. Phil nodded his head in recognition and then spotting the takeaway bag, asked if there was enough to share.

She didn't know what Tristan was thinking but surely he had realised that she lived in shared housing, given her address and status as a student. He didn't seem shocked; more relieved actually. Tristan said he had more than enough to share, asking Morgan to get the plates and cutlery out as he climbed over the back of the sofa and started unboxing the meal.

Spotting the Champagne, Molly asked Morgan if they had any Champagne flutes in the cupboard. Morgan checked but confirmed that they didn't. As all of the wine glasses were in use, Morgan grabbed five mugs and brought everything over to the sofa area. Tristan laughed, seeing the funny side and popped open the Champagne.

The hours melted away with good food and good conversation. Everyone was laughing and Tristan made a special effort to interact with all of her friends. As it approached ten Molly had fallen asleep on the sofa and David offered to carry her upstairs as he had work in the morning. Getting the hint, Phil offered to help and disappeared upstairs too, leaving Tristan and Morgan alone.

Alone with Tristan after having at least a bottle of

wine and a mug of Champagne, Morgan was feeling brave. Positioning herself sideways on the sofa with her arm on the backrest she leant towards Tristan as she asked, "Tell me something about yourself that no one else knows?" After protesting that there wasn't anything, Morgan bit her lip in thought before she amended her request to, "Tell me something about yourself that I wouldn't have guessed?"

"You first," he challenged her. Thinking how much of herself she really wanted to share, she answered "I've never been in a relationship," it was the truth and the most important lesson of being undercover, was always tell the truth whenever possible and if you need to lie, layer it within a truth.

Tristan didn't even flinch but his eyes intensified gazing into hers responding with, "Me neither." Tristan readjusted his position in his seat and leaned towards her, placing his hand on her thigh. He was looking directly into her eyes and Morgan couldn't help gazing at his perfectly formed lips. His cupids bow was almost heart shaped and his lower lip was perfectly plump. Not only were his lips the perfect shape, they were the perfect colour; a blush pink.

Just then the door burst open and a very angry looking George marched into the room. Instantly realising he had interrupted a moment, he apologised as he bumbled into the kitchen and started filling up a glass with water. With the tension gone, Morgan explained that she had an early start and led Tristan to the front door.

Morgan opened the door for him as he intentionally squeezed past her, winked and walked into the night. Morgan closed the door and slid to the ground. Sitting in a heap on the floor she wondered if she had ever had such a passionate moment and yet they hadn't even touched.

Then reality hit, she had spent the entire evening with him and forgot to turn her phone to record. She cursed under her breath. If she told Steve she would appear incompetent. Morgan tried to justify in her mind the pros and cons of not declaring that the evening took place. Nothing pertinent to the case was discussed; it was just background investigative work. She justified in her mind that she had a certain amount of leverage to relay only important information and she should be trusted to make those decisions. It was settled, she didn't need to tell Steve about this evening.

She quickly got ready for bed and fell straight to sleep but that night she dreamed only of Tristan and the kiss that might have been.

The next day Morgan woke up in a bit of a daze. Had last night really happened? Yes it had! Tristan had impressed her in how normal he was and how at ease she felt around him. The playboy impression she had first had, melted away after spending the entire evening with him. She was intrigued why he acted like a playboy in public, when deep down he was really a sweetheart. She reminded herself of her mission and to stick to the task at hand.

She was a top rated special agent and she needed to focus on the mission. But if Tristan wasn't involved in any criminal activity, he didn't mind her lying to him and potentially imprisoning most of his family and friends, then maybe they had a future. What was she thinking? She rolled over and screamed into her pillow.

She was being idiotic, there was no future in any romance between them. She was focused on her mission, but there were no rules that said she couldn't enjoy her work. She convinced herself that any pleasure she felt was just her taking pride in her work and the commitment to the agency.

She dragged herself out of bed, put on her running gear and switched her iPod to play Eminem's greatest hits. It was the perfect album to loose herself in, away from her phone and the internet, listening to her favourite tunes.

The rest of the day passed quickly, too quickly, it was fast approaching the time for her to get the bus to work. She had now made it a regular routine to apply hair chalk and her nose ring even in the day. Morgan removed her shower cap and touched up her neon pink hair chalk. She reapplied her make-up, applying darker eye shadow than this morning. She selected her original T-shirt creation, matching it with thigh high black socks, black denim shorts and Dr. Martens. She grabbed her pleather jacket as she left the room and headed for the bus stop.

Nathanial arrived at the bar at the same time, so after saying, "Hi," to the rest of the staff, they both headed straight up the stairs to the staff room with Morgan in the lead. As they approached the landing Fenik and Tristan were in deep discussion outside Tristan's office door. Morgan heard Fenik say, "Tell Vincent he needs to get involved," before they simultaneously looked directly at Morgan and Fenik crossed the landing to head downstairs. Morgan apologised in case she had interrupted anything and stayed routed on the landing. She moved aside for Nathanial to enter the staff room and Fenik to pass downstairs.

Tristan didn't seem pleased at what Fenik had said. Perhaps it was at being ordered to involve his father in business matters, or the thought of asking his father for help. Tristan said "Hi," but made his excuses that he would catch up with her later and disappeared back into his office.

"What do you think that was about?" Asked Nathanial, clearly in the mood for some gossip. Morgan explained that she had no idea and they both made their way downstairs. Fenik asked Morgan to join Jono and Jake downstairs again, so she made her way across the bar and down the spiral staircase.

By eleven the downstairs dance floor was full of fresher's in fancy dress and Morgan didn't see Commander in Chief Silas Nicolescu enter the room. He took up a seat at the booth closest to the bar and slowly sipped a large glass of red wine. Jake spotted him first and Morgan noticed Jake nudge Jono and point. Morgan followed the direction he indicated and saw the Commander in Chief staring back at her.

He was unmistakeable, even sat down you could see he was taller than the average man at approximately 6ft 4, he used his height to domineer over others back at HQ with a menacing demeanour. He had a sickly pale complexion, perfectly gelled black hair with a very precisely trimmed goatee. He was well spoken with a non-descript accent. If rumours were to be believed he was single with no children, even though he must be mid 40s given the position he had achieved. He had always given her the creeps.

Morgan's brain went into overdrive, what was he doing here? And could he stand out any more drinking red wine in a navy pinstriped suit in the middle of fresher's week surrounded by drunken students? Before Morgan could think of an excuse to approach him, both Fenik and Tristan marched across the dance floor directly to the Commander's booth. Both bouncers stationed in the room joined them. The Commander rose from his seat, downed his glass of wine in one gulp and walked out of the room, followed by both the bouncers.

Morgan wanted to know what had transpired and how did they know each other? Why would four men approach a Commander in Chief of the British Intelligence Agency and ask him to leave? Morgan needed answers. She tried a jokey approach with Jono and Jake, but if they knew anything they didn't give anything way. She would need to find a way to ask Tristan, but she didn't see him again.

The busy night continued and her shift ended around two-thirty in the morning. Morgan turned her phone to silent as she walked down the pedestrian street to the main road where her uber was waiting. Her phone signal must be low, as her phone alerted her to a missed call from Aunt Winnie and a voicemail presumably from her. Distracted by her phone she didn't notice that her uber wasn't the only one waiting for her. In a split second Morgan felt a hand around her mouth as she was pulled off her feet into an alley. Her senses heightened as her body tensed in fear. She had been trained how to defend herself, but in the moment, all her training escaped her as the fear gripped her.

Whoever it was, was much taller than her, their grip was strong and then she heard a familiar voice. She instantly recognised him; it was the Commander in Chief.

"You stupid girl, do you not know how important this operation is. You've been here two weeks and you've delivered nothing. You cannot be that incompetent. What are you hiding?" Then a piercing pain scorched through Morgan's neck and she blacked out.

Ten minutes later Jono and Jake stood next to Tristan as he locked up and rolled down the shutters. Fenik had already retired to his flat above the bar. The heavens had opened minutes earlier, so all three had stayed inside to see if it would pass. The rain continued to pour down hard, so they decided to exit quickly. Jono was staying with Jake in a large flat above a clothes shop, in the city centre. The pair ran one way and Tristan ran the opposite; towards the nearest car park.

Suddenly, Tristan smelt blood and Morgan's scent. He followed her scent to an alley just off the main street. Slumped on the cold wet pavement behind a commercial bin was Morgan. Two perfectly formed puncture marks visible on her neck.

A Vampire had bitten her and he had a pretty good idea which one. Tristan would have put money on it being the one that he had forcibly removed, from the bar earlier that evening. At least she was still breathing. Vampires rarely acted so rash nowadays, preferring to play their political games rather than getting caught out in public.

As Tristan bent down to scoop her up in his arms, she woke up muttering only his name, before passing out unconscious again. He carried her to his car as if she was as light as a feather and drove to her house. When he pulled up outside he realised it was gone three in the morning and he had no idea which room was hers. She was still passed out in the passenger seat, so he did the only thing he could think of and drove her home to his parents' house.

CHAPTER 5

Becoming Immortal

As Silas sank his teeth into her soft flesh, he eagerly anticipated the warm blood, to taste better than drinking a large glass of Barolo wine, sat in a quiet vineyard in Italy at dusk. But he choked in shock, as the taste was bitter like 100% dark chocolate. He spat her blood out of his mouth in disgust.

The usual torrent of poignant memories that should flood into his mind upon her taste didn't appear. She was passed out in his arms, completely lifeless like a patient under general anaesthetic. Whilst Silas contemplated taking another bite, a deluge of rain pelted down upon them, washing away the blood he had spat on the pavement and from around her neck.

His thirst to know everything she knew overtook his better judgement; he braced his fangs and took a second bite. It was as disgusting as before, but he clamped down waiting for her thoughts to merge into his mind, but they didn't come.

He spat the remaining blood in his mouth onto the ground and placed her limp body behind a commercial rubbish bin. She wouldn't remember anything in the morning and his bite mark would fade in a few hours. He had nothing to fear by leaving her in the street to wake.

Dripping wet and furious, he left her lifeless body in the street and walked in search of someone to enhance his mood. Any vagabond would do. Three streets west sheltered in a shop doorway was a sleeping old man. He bent down next to the man, as if he was leaving money in his hat. Then bit down ferociously tearing the flesh and sucking all the blood from his body. His limp body convulsed as his organs gave up functioning. Silas removed a small dagger from a Swiss Army knife and then slashed the man's throat to cover up the brutal neck wound.

The vagrant's entire life's memories flooded into his psyche and Silas' loathing for mankind grew. Now his appetite was sedated and the repulsive taste of special agent Morgan Hudson was eliminated from his mouth. Silas' frustration for not being able to read Morgan's thoughts increased. He had never come across blood that tasted like that. He had always been able to read victims thoughts, when he chose too. He needed answers.

He walked the short distance through the town to his hotel room, making small talk about the shock weather with the receptionist. Once alone in his room he accessed his work laptop through a secure VPN network and typed out a message to his secretary. He notified her to amend his diary as an urgent family issue needed priority and he would be leaving the country for a couple of days.

On his secure personal phone, he booked the first available flight to Rome from Manchester airport, leaving the UK at nine that morning. He repacked his overnight bag, checked out and made his way to the car park to drive to the airport. He needed very little sleep to function and he could rest in the airport lounge. He parked in short stay and took the convenient bus ride to terminal one.

After the necessary check in and security measures, he made his way to the first class lounge and ordered a large glass of Chianti. He boarded the plane appearing outwardly like a respectable business man, whilst inwardly seething that he had been reduced to visiting his sire to ask for assistance. He had a tumultuous relationship with Padre Ivan. Ivan Rossi was the Vampire that had turned Silas to an immortal. In tradition Silas called him Padre (Father). Ivan was an ancient Vampire and resided in Italy, hence the Padre term of respect.

Silas had been a poor farmer from Sardinia in the late 1600s, before he met Ivan. His entire village had perished due to widespread disease and poverty. As a religious man, he could not end his own life and have a hope of his soul going to heaven. He begged a travelling noble man to put him out of his misery. The noble man had been Ivan. He had promised Silas that he would give him riches beyond his wildest dreams.

In exchange, Silas had to swear eternal loyalty and allow Ivan to do unthinkable acts of pleasure to him. Silas was a greedy man. He knew lying with a man was against the will of God, but God had forsaken him. Leaving him to watch his family starve to death, so he agreed.

He travelled back to Rome with Ivan's travelling group. They fed and clothed him and Silas was very happy with the choice he had made. That was until the second night at Ivan's villa. A servant sent for Silas informing him his oath needed to be fulfilled that night.

Silas had entered the bed chamber of Ivan late in the evening. The light from several candles burned bright, flickering around the ornate wooden four poster bed, casting shadows on the stone walls.

Ivan was a handsome tall man with oily black hair, olive skin and a defined jaw. Standing in front of Silas with just his breeches on, Silas could see his strong physique and chiselled muscles. Ivan had instructed Silas to remove his clothing and stand at the foot of the bed. He had done so, without protesting.

With immense speed Ivan had appeared behind him, smelling his hair and naked flesh. Ivan had tied his wrists and ankles to the posts of the bed so he was stood in a star formation unable to move. Ivan held a leather whip in his hand. It was not a flagellum, used for punishment. This was a soft leather whip with a large leather handle, unlike any whip Silas had seen before. Ivan had whipped Silas' naked back and rear with the whip. He had been whipped as a child, when he had been caught stealing grapes from a vineyard. This was a different type of flogging and hadn't cut as deep into his flesh. He had been grateful for that.

Ivan had offered him a sip of wine from his goblet and even now Silas remembered that being the best wine he had ever tasted. Sweaty and aching from the pain, Silas had welcomed being released from the restraints. He lay face down on the bed. It was the most luxurious bed Silas had ever felt, adorned with soft fabrics.

He had felt the weight of Ivan, as he climbed onto the bed and lay naked on top of him. Silas had smelt his sweat and the sweet earthy smell of wine on his breath. Ivan had whispered into his ear that he needed to fulfil his promise or he would not execute his. Silas lay in silence, completely still. The thought of gold, servants and food piled high on a banquet table manifested in his mind.

The pain had been nearly unbearable. He had grabbed at the fabric on the bed and bit down into it, to stop himself from screaming out. He had not wanted the servants to appear in response to his cries. Ivan had enjoyed his pain though, his panting had grown harsher and thrusts had come quicker, until he had reached climax.

When it was over Ivan had offered him a goblet of wine and told him to drink every last drop. As he had put the goblet to his lips, he could tell the liquid was different, this was not the wine he had been offered earlier, but he had obeyed. He remembered the taste had been foul and it had taken him a moment before he realised what the liquid was. It was blood. Immediately after he had drained the goblet, he had felt the most immense pain in his neck, as Ivan had bitten him.

The next thing Silas remembered was waking in a shallow unmarked grave. The dirt filling his open mouth, but strangely he didn't seem out of breath and wasn't choking. His immediate thought, had been that Ivan had tried to murder him rather than pay his debt. He dug at the earth until he was free and only noticed he was fully clothed after he had marched across the field and entered the villa through a side entrance.

The sun had risen in the sky, but there were very few servants around, so he had guessed it was early morning. He had marched into Ivan's bed chamber to find him writing at his desk. A beaming smile had radiated from his mouth and he stood, hand out, in a welcoming gesture. Silas had confronted him outright in a blaze of anger, before Ivan had explained the truth. Silas had been born again and was now an immortal. He would live forever and accumulate vast wealth and knowledge, just as he had promised.

The plane touched down outside Rome and as Silas rented a Maserati MC20 coupe, in his native Italian tongue, he allowed a rare smile to cross his face. One of the few joys in his life was speaking Italian again. How he longed to live back in Italy, where the women were prettier and the wine delectable. However, he had been assigned by the high council of Vampires to infiltrate the UK police force and report back.

He only had two years left in the UK and it couldn't come soon enough. He hated the weather and the crude language. At only one hundred and thirty years immortal he was a young Vampire and had no choice but to obey the council. He needed to prove himself worthy to become a council member himself. The council was made up of the eldest and most influential members of Vampire society and headed up by Alexander Vladislav.

Working for the council had its perks, an additional salary, land and respect. He couldn't stay in anyone position long as he didn't age, so he received a new assignment every ten to fifteen years, usually in a different country. He had bought back his family land in Sardinia and had a villa built.

He intended to retire there once his service was complete.

Lycan's had thrived in the UK, loving the colder weather and it was feared they were behind the alarming Vampire deaths. The recent increase had been unexpected and he had personally been tasked with solving the case. It was extremely difficult to kill an immortal and the only method Silas was aware of was by severing the head and burning it. But these recent deaths were different.

The bodies were intact, with the pathologist in all cases ruling the deaths as the result of an overdose. The blood had coagulated but their bodies were in perfect condition, apart from the fact that they were dead. Only three days ago, he had received a call from Demitri Vladislav, cousin to Alexander, who was a descendant of the first Vampire, demanding a swift resolution. It had been because of that call, that he had directly intervened in the operation and attacked the undercover agent Morgan Hudson.

His smile faded as he turned down the single lane to Ivan's villa. It was a huge single story villa set in acres of land, with the original building dating back to late Roman Empire. At the gates he pressed the intercom and announced himself. It seemed his arrival had been anticipated; Ivan had spy's everywhere. The electronic gates swung open and his Padre's latest man servant welcomed him inside, like the prodigal son returning home.

He led him inside his father's newly restored villa, down one familiar terracotta corridor to another, until he reached his father's study. He knocked and waited for a response before opening the heavy wooden door. Ivan greeted his son with pride, hugging and kissing both cheeks, as per Italian tradition. He opened an ornate glass decanter on his large wooden desk and poured two glasses of red wine into crystal cut glasses. He offered one to Silas as he gestured for him to sit down in the opposite chair.

As Silas raised the glass to his lips, he smelt the sweet smell of Borolo wine before he took a large mouthful. His father had excellent taste in wine. Ivan had said living for over a thousand years enabled you to source the very best vineyards and forced you to demand the best. Whilst he didn't know exactly how old his father was, he knew that he was classed as one of the oldest immortals and was a close confidant of Alexander Vladislav. Ivan knew everything but rarely intervened directly and seldom left Italy.

Ivan spoke affectionately to Silas, in his native Italian, "It has been too long, since you graced this villa with your presence. What brings you here now? I can tell something is troubling you my son."

Silas explained the events of that morning and asked Ivan if he had ever experienced this himself. Ivan sat in contemplative silence before reaching for his phone. He appeared to be typing an email or a lengthy text message, before he placed his phone back down on the desk and responded to Silas.

"I have not come across this before myself, but I have heard rumours. I have messaged Alexander Vladislav's daughter Anastasia, to arrange an audience with him to discuss it. Stay the night; enjoy the sun and the wine, until I can have an answer for you."

Silas had not been prepared for his short comings to become public knowledge, he asked Ivan, "Is that not too hasty, to make Alexander aware?"

Ivan never appreciated his actions being challenged. He rose from the desk and in response he simply stated, "I am aware of the task you have been set. These deaths in the UK are disturbing and a quick resolution is needed. If our powers are waning and other creature's powers are growing the council needs to be aware. Alexander is the oldest of our kind, if he has not come across this before, we all need to be concerned." As he sat back down in his chair he dismissed Silas with a wave, as if Silas was a child, or worse a servant.

Silas left the study and disappeared down the corridor to his father's library. He selected an Italian version of Robert

Stevenson's 'Strange case of Dr Jekyell and Mr Hyde'. Book in hand, he went in search of the solace of the olive grove. He spent the rest of the day basking in the warmth of the sun, loosing himself in the written word.

As the sun started to set, a young female servant hurried towards Silas. She notified him, that his father requested his presence. He could hear the blood pulsing through her veins, she was human. Her cheeks blushed, as she stared at Silas lying on the ground in the olive grove topless. Silas rose immediately, donned his shirt and followed her back to the villa. Vampires couldn't sweat, but if they could his palms would be damp. He was nervous to hear the outcome from Ivan and Alexander's meeting.

As he entered the study Ivan was sipping from the same crystal cut glass as this morning and the decanter was now empty on his desk. He ordered the young servant to pack him an overnight bag before gesturing for Silas to sit down, "Alexander wants to speak with you directly this evening. My private jet is being prepared as we speak, collect your belongings and meet me in the courtyard in ten minutes." Silas nodded, before turning to obey Ivan's request. He had never met Alexander before, but his sadism and astuteness were legendary. Silas was apprehensive to meet him.

As instructed, Silas reconvened in the courtyard and climbed into the back of his father's chauffeur-driven black Rolls-Royce Phantom. The Phantoms massive size and excessive cost made it a statement collectable. His father liked to collect cars and had exceptional taste, although rarely drove himself. It was exquisite inside and out, but Silas couldn't help thinking that his father was just showboating.

They sat in silence on the short drive to the local airstrip, where a small private jet was having the final checks made before flying. An attractive brunette, dressed in a long emerald, silk, side wrapped dress with gold strappy high heeled sandals, greeted them at the top of the stairs and served them a glass of red wine. She appeared overly affectionate with Ivan and Silas noticed his father's hand slip onto her bottom.

Silas had never been on the private jet before and he wondered how long Ivan had owned it. The flooring was a luxurious cream carpet and four seats faced towards each other with a table in between, like at a dinner party. The seats were made of plush brown leather and through an open door at the back of the plane, he could see a large bed and presumably a toilet. Silas sniggered, his father clearly got bored whilst flying. He wouldn't put it past him to have joined the mile high club with Miss Hostess.

The plane took off quickly after they arrived and Ivan proposed a game of chess to pass the time. It was rare for Silas to beat Ivan at chess but he had relished the few occasions when he had. He agreed and the next three hours flew by. Just before landing, Ivan had put Silas in check mate and Silas had to concede defeat.

As they disembarked the plane, Silas noticed a black Mercedes Maybach with tinted windows pull up on the tarmac. A chauffeur exited the vehicle and held open the rear door. An extremely attractive, slender blonde woman, in her early twenties emerged from the car. She greeted Silas formally in Latin, but Ivan who clearly knew the bombshell, was greeted with, "Ciao bello." and received an additional trio of kisses. Ivan introduced the beauty as Anastasia, one of Alexander's daughters.

Ivan and Anastasia spoke in Romanian throughout the car journey and Silas; who had never been great at learning new languages, understood less than half of the conversation and had no idea what was being discussed. He had a sneaky suspicion that this had been intentional. After an hour they slowed down, making their way to a standstill inside a stone courtyard, outside an elaborate stone walled mansion. In certain lights it could be considered a castle, as it had a large stone wall surrounding the main dwelling.

It was now late in the evening and extremely dark, but

Vampires are not affected by the lack of light and the trio could see clearly without torches. Ivan and Silas followed Anastasia through the countless corridors until she opened a wooden double door at the end of a long passageway. Sat at the back of a large stone walled ballroom, lit only by candle light, on what can only be described as a red velvet throne, was a tall handsome man surrounded by a handful of females.

The man on the throne had dark olive skin, a sculptured beard and a bald head. He had an athletic figure with rippling muscles, appearing to be early thirties. He was dressed in a maroon silk shirt, black chinos and a large gold chain adorned his neck. If this was Alexander he was not what Silas had expected. He wasn't really sure what he had expected, but this man looked like a billionaire playboy model that could grace any catwalk in Milan fashion week.

Ivan led the way, he stopped just short of the man, bent down on one knee and the man held out his hand for Ivan to kiss. Ivan sidestepped to the left and Silas copied his actions. Then he spoke in perfect English and from the presence he commanded it was clear he was Alexander. "Now formalities are over, clear the room," he waved at the surrounding women, "I have questions for our young guest."

Once Alexander, Ivan and Silas were alone, Alexander rose from his seat and greeted Ivan like a brother, hugging and kissing him on the cheeks. He looked at Silas before uttering, "Appearances must be upheld." Turning back to Ivan he continued this time in Italian, "You must join us in the French Alps this December, no excuses."

Ivan responded, "It would be an honour." Alexander then marched towards thick red drapes behind the throne and disappeared through a hidden door. Ivan and Silas followed. They had entered a much smaller room with a large fireplace and multiple antique navy plush chairs. Alexander opened an antique globe drinks cabinet next to the roaring fire and poured three glasses of wine from a glass decanter. He passed the glasses around and sat in the grandest looking chair. Ivan and Silas took up the remaining seats. Looking directly at Silas he asked in Italian if Silas was fluent. Silas confirmed Italian was his native tongue and so the rest of the conversation continued in Italian.

"Tell me in your own words the events of this morning," Alexander commanded. Silas relayed the incident in full detail. Alexander appeared deep in thought with a pensive gaze. "Do you know our history and the story of creation?" He asked Silas.

Silas shook his head and Alexander continued, "You will likely have heard the Christian story of creation, with Adam and Eve. Many have heard the story of their children Cain, Abel, Seth and two daughters, but few have heard the true story and realise the significance. It is widely believed that through Seth's lineage humanity was founded. This is factual. The scriptures also detail that Cain killed Abel and God punished Cain for this. But what is not public knowledge is why, and Gods true punishment.

Abel was partnered with Cain's twin sister Aclima and they had a son Caleb. Cain was envious of Abel's relationship with Aclima and forced himself upon her making her pregnant. Abel and Cain fought and Cain killed Abel. In retaliation God cursed Cain."

Alexander then stood up and retrieved an old looking book from a shelf on the wall behind him. As he sat back in his chair, he flicked through the first few pages. "The Bible states the words of God in Genesis 4:10-12 'The Lord said, what have you done? Listen! Your brother's blood cries out to me from the ground. Now you are under a curse and driven from the ground, which opened its mouth to receive your brother's blood from your hand. When you work the ground, it will no longer yield its crops for you. You will be a restless wanderer on the earth.'

However the words were misinterpreted, or rather humans could not comprehend the true curse. Cain was made an immortal, who would live forever with his shame, only blood would provide nourishment, never food.

Full of vengeance Caleb was given powers by God to protect himself and those powers heightened with the power of the moon and from him all Lycans are descended.

To ease Aclima's suffering God made her and her unborn daughter Witches. God gave her female lineage powers to protect themselves. Their blood would taste bitter and they could protect their mind from Cain's descendants.

Over the centuries Witches powers have diluted, Lycans are coupling less thus producing fewer heirs and Vampires are failing to sire. It appears this Witch doesn't even have the powers to fend you off. Keep an eye on her and focus on the task you have been set. Judgement day may be upon us."

Silas had been listening intensely but didn't understand the reference to judgement day. He toyed with asking Alexander but thought better of it, however Ivan then spoke. "Surely Alexander, you are not referring to the second coming of God."

Alexander stared into the distance as if he was trying hard to remember, "I met him once. Jesus that is, I thought him a charlatan, but perhaps he was not. The first Ecumenical Council who wrote the Nicene Creed deciphered ancient text that decreed, 'He (Jesus) shall come again in glory to judge the living and the dead,' the dead he referred to was Vampires, however the council ruled to omit the second sentence of the text. I was there and kept the original scroll. It was interpreted as, 'When the gifts from God are no longer required, Gods creations will cease to be differentiated.' - That is when judgement day will commence."

After a brief pause he added, "Obviously it goes without saying that this conversation is confidential and you will not discuss it again. I do not want to incite panic, there are few left who know the truth." He then turned to Ivan asking him to stay a while. Ivan accepted the invitation and offered Silas the private jet back to England. Silas took that as his cue to leave, placed his empty glass on the fireplace, bowed his head and disappeared behind the curtain covered door.

His mind was racing with the knowledge he had just learnt, did God really exist? Would he be judged for the crimes he had committed in death? He shuddered at the thought of what Gods vengeance would be. He decided to focus on the task at hand. He needed to find out everything about Morgan Hudson and solve this rising death rate mystery. He boarded the plane bound for England and sat in contemplation throughout the journey, plotting what move to make next.

CHAPTER 6

The Truth

Tristan turned down a small lane just wide enough for a large car. He drove up to the gates, beeped the fob on his key and the automatic gates opened into a large driveway. A converted stables with an open side acted as a garage and already housed his father's navy Bentley, his mother's pristine white Range Rover, his sister-in-law Hannah's rather dirty black Range Rover and his pride and joy; a lime green Lambourgini Aventador. There was just enough space for him to park his khaki Land Rover Defender on the end.

Still passed out in the passenger seat, he scooped up Morgan like a sleeping baby cradled in his arms, shutting the car door with his foot. He walked towards the side door of his parent's large manor house, to his private entrance.

Many people thought it unconventional to live with your family past the age of mid-twenties. But Tristan's family were close and the house was large enough, that he had the whole top floor to himself. The top floor consisted of a basic kitchenette, a large bathroom, lounge area, which he used mostly for gaming and a large bedroom.

His parents slept on the second floor and Hannah and his nephew Jacob, had a smaller cottage in the grounds behind the main house. Hannah kept horses and had converted her garage into a stable preferring to keep her car with the rest of the family's.

Tobias, Tristan's older brother lived a mile down the road, in the next farm house. The land had been in the family for generations with the oldest living son inheriting the land and houses. Vincent Lucas, Tristan's father had been an only child so he had lived in the farm house his entire life, including being born there.

Vincent had made a few alterations as his children had grown up, converting the barn into a garage and building Timothy a cottage in a sympathetic style to the larger farm house when he married Hannah. Timothy was Tristan's older brother by one year and had been murdered eleven months ago.

The pain the family felt was still very raw and Hannah often didn't leave the cottage for days. Marisa, Tristan's mother delivered groceries and meals every other day. She took Jacob for walks in his pushchair to give Hannah a rest from the tantrums of a two year old. Tobias' wife Charlotte came every day to tend to Hannah's two horses; whilst she was still in mourning. Tristan felt very fortunate that he had such a close family and couldn't imagine life without living so close and being involved in each other's daily lives.

He climbed two sets of stairs before arriving at the third floor, which opened into a small kitchenette. The ceilings were high even though they were in the eaves of the roof space and several skylights filled the room with moonlight. Tristan walked through the lounge area past a complex games console wall, with a seventy inch flat screen TV in the centre and a large navy L shaped leather sofa. He placed Morgan on his super king sized bed.

He had a large bedroom but minimal furniture with just a bed, side table and fitted wardrobes down one wall. Off the bedroom was a large en-suite with a free standing bath in the centre of the room and walk in shower on the far wall.

His mother had redecorated the whole suite just three years earlier, when Timothy moved out and Tristan moved upstairs. She decorated it to her monochrome tastes, to match the rest of the house. The walls were the colour of clotted cream with black skirting and door trims. Tristan who had no interest in design liked the minimalist look, insisting only on the slouchy sofa and a large shelving unit filled with every console developed, to make it a bachelor pad.

Tristan looked down at Morgan, completely vulnerable on the bed. He couldn't undress her that wouldn't be right, so he tucked the duvet over her fully clothed. Vampires had a property within their saliva when they bit someone, which caused amnesia of the event, so when she woke up she wouldn't remember what had happened and how he had helped her.

Tristan contemplated where he should sleep, before grabbing his summer duvet from the wardrobe and heading out to spend the rest of the night on the sofa. He wisely decided that Morgan was already going to freak out when she woke in a strange bed, without rolling over to his morning breath.

Tristan woke up at ten to the sound of his alarm beeping in the distance, he held out his arm trying to feel for the button, when he remembered he was on the sofa and who was in the bedroom. He rushed into the room, forgetting to put on his trousers, which were now crinkled in a heap on the floor. Morgan was sat bolt upright in bed with the covers pulled up to her chin. Her eyes were wide open when he entered. She screamed "Where am I? And what are you doing here?"

Tristan explained he had found her unconscious in an alleyway near the pub, as Morgan instinctively felt her neck. The bite marks were completely faded now and Tristan was surprised by her actions, when she suddenly blurted out, "He bit me, he bit me and he left me there." Morgan could see a door ajar in the far corner of the room and could see enough of the room inside to realise it was a bathroom. She ran to it in search of a mirror.

Tristan was shocked. How was it that Morgan

remembered? Staring into the mirror feeling her neck, Morgan couldn't see a wound that would explain her memories from earlier that morning. She needed answers. Morgan made her way back to the bed, curling back up in the same spot under the covers.

"Tell me I am not going mad. Did I have blood on my neck when you found me? Did you clean it off?"

Instead of answering her question, Tristan responded with another, "Did you see who it was?"

Without thinking Morgan immediately answered "Yes," but caught herself just before she said his name. Instead amending her response to, "the man from the bar you escorted out."

Tristan clinched his teeth and let out a low growl, before sitting on the end of the bed and started to explain everything that had happened that night.

"You don't live in the world you think you do," he began, "that man was a Vampire. I don't know why he came to the bar last night but it must have been to provoke me. Maybe he's been watching me, maybe he saw me at your house the other night and he attacked you to get at me. I'm so sorry.

Vampires can read your memories when they drink your blood and he was clearly after information. They don't usually attack people and leave them in such public places. To be honest, I'm shocked you remember. I've never known anyone to remember being attacked. It's a security measure they have in their saliva that makes you forget. How do you feel?"

Morgan insisted she was physically ok, but mentally it might take some time and then she stared straight into Tristan's eyes before asking how it was he knew all this.

Tristan wasn't looking forward to this bit, should he tell her or should he lie? He liked her and she was special to him, that much was evident, but could she be trusted to keep his families secret. He had never told anyone before. He made a split decision to tell her everything, hoping that he wouldn't regret it.

"I'm not human, I'm a Lycan," he confessed, looking back at her puzzled face he added, "You probably know it better as a Werewolf."

Morgan recoiled further back into the pillows on the bed away from Tristan.

"Are you really expecting me to believe that on the full moon you turn into a wolf man."

Tristan laughed, "Not exactly, myths and legends all have a basis in fact, but the stories often got distorted through the years. I can turn into a wolf whenever I want. The full moon only heightens my strength and plays a key role in ceremonies."

Staring at Tristan like he was a madman, Morgan didn't really believe him, so she told him to show her. Tristan rose off the bed and leapt into the air, landing as a fully grown large grey and white husky type wolf. He shook his body and tail until the fur magically disappeared and he turned back into his human form. His naked human form.

Morgan let out a yelp of shock and scrunched her legs into a tight hold underneath the covers. Morgan threw a pillow at him and told him to cover up. He smirked and walked over to the wardrobe, picking out a pair of running shorts to wear.

It really wasn't the time but Morgan couldn't help notice how incredibly muscular Tristan's body was, his torso was covered in dark hair but beneath it clearly visible was an incredibly defined six pack and his manhood appeared to be perfectly sized. Standing fully naked in front of her, he was clearly not lacking in confidence.

Morgan blushed and found his assuredness very attractive. Once dressed, Tristan walked back and sat on the end of the bed and asked Morgan if she had any further questions. She simply stated, "I want to know everything to know about Vampires and Lycans, leave nothing out."

Tristan was impressed with how well she was taking the information. He explained that Lycans aged like humans and could be killed as easily as humans. Although, Lycans had a great sense of smell and immense strength just like a wolf. Silver burned the skin which is where the myth that silver bullets killed them came from. The moon was sacred to them and when the full moon was visible in the sky they drew extra strength from it. All babies born to Lycans are male, so all females are created during a special commitment ceremony in front of the light of a full moon; the Lycan version of a wedding.

Then he moved onto explaining Vampires. "Vampires and Lycans are sworn enemies. Vampires are immortal and do not age, it's rumoured the oldest Vampire is over 3,000 years old. To kill a Vampire you need to sever the head and burn it, although I don't know anyone who has ever managed it. Vampires are strong, fast and barely eat or sleep. They are fully integrated in human society, holding many positions of power and are governed by the oldest family of their kind, the Vladislav family in Romania. The daylight and bat assumptions are a complete myth."

Morgan listened intently before asking, "And that's everything, there are no mermaids or wizards like in Harry Potter?"

Tristan looked uneasy. "Every great story has a basis in fact," he repeated, running his hair through his hands, "Mermaids don't exist, as far as I'm aware, but then again I don't really like the sea, but female Witches exist. They don't carry wands around, or go to a special magic school but they are in tune with nature and the weather. They cast spells and make potions; some meddle with love lives or can see into the future. I think they all have different gifts and specialties. They are often described as Hippies.

They are the opposite to Lycans as you have to be a women to be a Witch, the men in the families don't become Wizards. We all keep to ourselves and don't interact much with each other," pausing for a second before adding, "Until recently."

Morgan didn't pick up on the pause or what the

inference might mean, as she was lost in thought, her mind was racing. Without knowingly doing so, Tristan had just described Aunt Winnie and half the residents of the commune. Morgan stood up, still slightly dizzy from the attack and the information overload. She explained to Tristan that she needed time alone to process and asked if she could have the rest of the week off work. He agreed and showed her the way down the stairs to the front door.

    Luckily, they didn't run into any family members and Tristan offered her a lift home. Morgan was in a daze and didn't have chance to appreciate the beautiful house or grounds that Tristan lived in, or panic at the perfect opportunity she had missed to snoop around the family home.

    The wind was blowing a gale outside so Tristan held her close, as he walked her to her front door and she assured him that she was ok. Once inside she dragged her suitcase out from under the bed, threw in some essentials and headed for the train station, to catch the next available train to Great Yarmouth. Once on board, she stowed her luggage, found a seat and text Aunt Winnie to give her notice of her impending arrival.

    Noticing the red dot on the voicemail app, Morgan listened to a short message from Aunt Winnie who seemed flustered, but was checking up that Morgan was well after she had a bad dream about her. She then messaged Steve, notifying him that she was really ill and would need to take the night off work, so there would be no recording tonight. Three and half hours later, after one transfer and one Uber ride, Morgan arrived at the caravan site ready to confront Aunt Winnie.

    Aunt Winnie greeted Morgan warmly, enquiring if her mission had now finished and asking how long she planned to stay? Entering the caravan Morgan took a deep breath before asking Aunt Winnie to sit down at the dining table.

    Morgan began, "Aunt Winnie I need you to promise

to tell me the truth?" She paused for a response and Aunt Winnie nodded her head with a puzzled look on her face, before continuing in her interrogation, "Are you a Witch?" The puzzled look disappeared from Aunt Winnie's face and a wave of relief and pride beamed from her wide smile before responding.

"I can't tell you how long I've wanted to be able to talk openly with you." Once she started talking, she didn't stop. She apologised that she had never been frank with Morgan, but she had obeyed her sisters (Morgan's mother's) wishes and raised Morgan without the knowledge of the magical world.

Morgan's mother, Belinda had shunned the magical world when she turned nineteen and opted for a normal life without magic. She had met Morgan's father and vowed to never introduce Morgan to magic. Aunt Winnie was the only person from the magical world that Belinda had stayed in contact with, on the promise that she never did or acted in a magical way in front of Morgan or her husband. When she had died, she felt that she would be betraying her memory if she went against her wishes, so she had hidden everything from Morgan.

As Morgan listened intently, not wanting to interrupt in case she missed any new information about her parents, Hermes jumped onto her lap and began purring. She had so many questions buzzing around her head that she needed to ask. Why did her mother shun magic? What magic powers did Witches really have? Had her father ever known? Did that mean she was a Witch? She blurted them all out at once. Aunt Winnie answered them one by one, explaining that not all Witches have a specially defined gift.

Belinda had hated not having a special ability and was jealous of anyone that had one. The more jealous she became, the more she hated anything magical. She left the commune at nineteen, when their father had passed away. She went to University and socialised with average humans, outside of the magical community. When she met Morgan's father she was happy and no longer jealous. So she shunned magic and withdrew from the magical world.

Aunt Winnie explained that she herself had no unique powers, but loved to use magical potion books to create antidotes to ailments or mood changers and grow the very best flowers. The majority of Witches could use potion books and achieve results, even without special abilities.

Witches senses were more heightened than humans and they could draw on these senses to predict the weather or season changes. As far as Aunt Winnie was aware Simon, Morgan's father, had never known of Belinda's magical past. Morgan had never displayed any special powers as a child, So Aunt Winnie wasn't aware if Morgan had any powers or any magic running through her veins, but offered to help Morgan to find out.

"I want to find out, is there a test I can take?" Morgan asked eagerly. Aunt Winnie shook her head and explained there was no test, but she had collected some ingredients that afternoon to make a cold remedy potion for Mr Hanley, who lived two caravans down. Aunt Winnie suggested Morgan could make the remedy, to test if she had the magical ability for potion making. Morgan decided to try.

Aunt Winnie was ecstatic, she stood up, lifted the foam seating on the bench she had been sat on and lifted out an old looking wok, placing it on the gas hob. She then disappeared into her room and came back with a very old brown leather book. She laid it on the dining room table, opened the cover and placed both hands above it hovering in mid-air and clearly stated, "Cold remedy." The pages of the book flapped without assistance and opened on a page labelled cold remedy.

Morgan was wide-eyed and in a state of amazement. How many times had she seen this book and not known what it really was. She had definitely eaten food cooked out of that wok.

Aunt Winnie then instructed Morgan to prepare the ingredients in the recipe and follow the instructions. Morgan emptied Aunt Winnie's wicker basket of thyme, fresh ginger and garlic flowers. She then opened the fridge bringing back orange juice to the table. Morgan opened the far left top cupboard, closest to the door and grabbed the table-salt and a jar of honey.

"There's one ingredient missing, what's Echinacea Angustifolia?"

Aunt Winnie smiled as she replied, "The purple daisies outside the front of the caravan, I grow them for this specific recipe." Morgan opened the door and walked to the front of the caravan, collected four stalks as the recipe stated and returned.

Using a measuring jug, Morgan added precisely 250ml of orange juice and turned on the gas stove. When the first boiling bubble popped, she added five heads of garlic flowers, one spring of thyme, a teaspoon of salt and four purple daisy stalks. Using the grater she added two peels of the fresh ginger. She grabbed a wooden spoon from the draining board and stirred clockwise three times and then anti-clockwise three times. She then added the purple petals from two of the daisies and a tablespoon of honey.

The boiling bubbles immediately disappeared and the colour deepened. Morgan looked at Aunt Winnie for reassurance. Aunt Winnie smiled and handed Morgan a flowery teapot. She used a ladle to decant the mixture from the wok into the teapot and held it by the handle as she followed Aunt Winnie to Mr Hanley's caravan.

Aunt Winnie knocked three times on the caravan door and a very sickly and snotty looking Mr Hanley answered the door. He thanked them immensely and promised to return the teapot when he felt better. When they returned Morgan asked, "So how do we know?"

"We will find out tomorrow, if Mr Hanley is recovered," said Aunt Winnie, manner of factly; as if that was obvious.

Morgan was sure she had drunk Aunt Winnie's special orange juice more than once and asked her, "Did you make me potions as a child?"

Winnie smiled, "I have always helped those in need when I could. My potions can't cure cancers or prevent old age but they can mend broken bones and ease suffering." Aunt Winnie seemed very proud of her hay fever treatment, commenting, "Over half the commune asked for my honey and camomile tea this summer; as the pollen count has been the highest it has been for years."

Morgan spent the rest of the evening guessing who in the commune was magical, with Hermes snuggled up on her lap. Aunt Winnie divulged tales of their magical mishaps, having grown up with most of them on the commune. Turns out Mr Hanley's late wife was a Witch and he had embraced the community, continuing to live in the commune after her death.

It wasn't until Aunt Winnie was making pancakes for breakfast the next morning that she wondered, why Morgan had suddenly guessed about her magical background. Morgan had turned a shade of green when she asked, so Aunt Winnie demanded to know immediately.

Morgan doctored the story somewhat as she retold the events of the following day. She explained that she had been attacked in an alleyway and bitten on the neck. A new friend had taken care of her and he had explained she had been attacked by a Vampire and that he was a Lycan. In explaining this hidden world of Vampires, Lycans and Witches she had guessed Aunt Winnie was a Witch.

Aunt Winnie had sat down, looking very pale at the part of the story where Morgan was bitten. "Was it terribly painful?" She asked. Morgan confirmed that she passed out from the pain and didn't wake for several hours.

"Who is this Lycan? I haven't met many but maybe I have heard of his family," she continued. Morgan shook her head and confirmed she would rather not say, but added that she had not addressed her suspicions of Aunt Winnie to him, so there was no need for her to know his name. Aunt Winnie huffed but nodded in agreement before adding, "Was he kind to you? I have heard many conflicting stories about Lycans." Morgan affirmed that he was without giving away any other information.

Out of the corner of her eye, Morgan saw Mr Hanley waving through the window, as he walked up to the door. She opened the door and there stood Mr Hanley with a beaming smile, fit as a fiddle, waving Aunt Winnie's flowery teapot. He thanked them both and went about the rest of his day.

"Well then," said Aunt Winnie triumphantly, "That's a good start. The potion clearly worked. You must have magic running through your veins."

Morgan didn't know how to feel, shocked, happy, dismayed, maybe a little of all three.

CHAPTER 7

Anticipation

After breakfast, Morgan checked the train timetable and pre-booked a seat on the early afternoon service. She wanted to ensure she made it back to Nottingham, in time for her shift at Wild. She needed to talk to Tristan. Aunt Winnie wasn't very happy about Morgan leaving to go and associate with Lycans, but she knew once Morgan's mind was made up, it couldn't be changed. She asked only that Morgan call her every day, to let her know she was ok. Morgan agreed and booked an Uber for later. They spent the rest of the morning together, taking a walk on the beach. They continued discussing Aunt Winnie's magical upbringing, whilst the sea and sand mixed together between their toes.

On the train ride back to Nottingham, Morgan weighed up the pros and cons of telling Tristan about her links to Witchcraft. It would be very tricky to tell him without confiding in Tristan about Aunt Winnie and she didn't feel that was her secret to share. So she decided against it for now.

Her mind wandered to how many of the staff at Wild were Lycans. Fenik and Jono's stature and close bond with Tristan must mean they were. Nathanial definitely wasn't if his story about asking for a job was true and Morgan had no clue about Summer or the other women she had met briefly. Although she remembered that Tristan had said that all

Lycans were men and you had to marry into the family before you transitioned. She concluded that the women at the bar were regular humans, as none wore wedding rings.

Morgan arrived home to an empty house, so she decided to relax on the sofa whilst watching some reality TV until her shift began. The next thing she heard was the slamming of the front door and a howl of laughter which startled her awake. She checked her phone for the time and saw it was ten o'clock. Morgan cursed under her breath as she jumped over the sofa, shouting, "Hello, sorry I'm late for work," as she squeezed past Molly, David and Phil in the corridor to get to her room.

Morgan ordered an Uber and scrambled to get ready as quick as possible. She selected a pair of high wasted vertically stripped skinny jeans from her wardrobe. They reminded her of Beetlejuice and then picked out her cropped Wild T-shirt from a stack of fresh laundry. She applied her make-up, going a little heavy on the eyeliner and a shade of deep purple lipstick to compliment her purple hair chalk, which she topped up. Morgan heard the car pull up before her phone alerted her and she ran for the taxi.

As she ran from the taxi to the entrance, the bouncers were already outside, managing the flow of people into the bar and waved her inside ahead of the queue. Having no personal belongings with her other than her phone and keys, Morgan turned her phone off silent and shoved both into her pockets, whilst heading straight down the stairs.

Even for a Saturday night the underground bar was very busy. Tristan had even rolled up his white shirt sleeves and was serving, behind the bar. As his eyes locked onto hers, she saw an instant flash of concern upon his face before she smiled in return. His facial expression mirrored hers, as he smiled back.

Once the immediate rush of orders calmed down, Tristan nestled slightly closer than necessary into her ear as he spoke, "What are you doing here? You didn't need to come in. Are you ok?" She turned to face him before responding, "I'm ok, I just want to get back to normality." As soon as she said it Morgan worried that might sound odd on the recording to HQ, but she was certain that Tristan wouldn't approach the supernatural topic of conversation in a crowded bar. She would deflect any chat of that nature to after work, when she could switch off the recording.

There was something about Tristan that made her feel at ease, too at ease, where she could forget her true reason for working at his bar. Maybe it was that he had fully opened up to her and shown his vulnerable side. But she still couldn't deny that he was somehow embroiled in selling drugs and the devastating consequences that came from that; along with a suspicious death of a fellow agent. Morgan just couldn't comprehend how the man, who had eaten a takeaway with her housemates or cared for her after her attack, could lead a double life as a drug dealer. She convinced herself that it must be down to his family and he was just a victim. She would need to get closer to him and his family to prove this hypothesis.

Even when the demand for drinks reduced to a steady level, Tristan remained behind the bar for the full shift and Morgan wondered if that was because of her. As the comedy songs started to play and the lights came on, Morgan switched her mobile back to silent mode. She made a beeline for Tristan, who was now chatting with the Cane twins in the furthest booth from the bar. Before she reached him, Tristan had turned around and walked towards her. As he reached her he placed his arm over her shoulder and tilted his head to lock eyes with her, saying, "Let me drive you home. I won't take no for an answer." Morgan agreed and allowed him to lead the way to his car.

Morgan studied him as they walked. He kept turning toward her as if to speak but then deciding against it. He seemed nervous. Morgan Hudson would probably be reacting the same way, if she was alone with an attractive man who had days earlier poured out his life story. But Morgan Fletcher was assertive and ballsy. Being Morgan Fletcher gave Morgan the confidence to act as brazen as she would inwardly want to be. So she took his hand and intertwined her fingers in his, pulling gently on his arm with her right hand, beginning a conversation.

"Thank you, I have to admit I ran from the taxi when I arrived, not only because I was late but because I was scared. I wasn't looking forward to making the dash to the taxi again, past that alleyway."

Tristan looked down at her warmly and squeezed her hand ever so slightly. "You don't have to arrive on your own again. I will pick you up before your shifts. I feel awful that he attacked you to get to me. I just don't understand how he knew." Morgan looked puzzled and a bit worried her cover was about to be blown when she asked, "Knew what?"

"That I like you."

He had responded so quickly that Morgan was taken aback and fell out of character, amazed that Tristan actually liked her. He was staring at her now and they were stood motionless in the street. How would Morgan Fletcher react? She thought. She closed her gapping mouth and snapped back into her new identity. She tilted up on the balls of her feet and landed a kiss on his cheek, before adding, "I like you too." A wide smile spread across Tristan's face and he continued leading the way to his parked car.

As they approached his car, he beeped the fob and they both climbed into the front seats. His stereo blared out heavy metal music. Tristan started head banging, singing along with the chorus, before turning to Morgan, apologising and turning the volume down low. "What sort of music do you like?" he asked.

"Most types to be honest, apart from Jazz, I like songs with good lyrics." It was the truth. There was no reason to lie or make up a different persona for Morgan Fletcher.

For the rest of the short journey to Morgan's house, they

discussed their favourite songs, surprisingly learning that they both had a soft spot for the same pop artist. As they pulled up outside her front door, Tristan turned off the engine and turned to Morgan asking, "Would you go on a proper date with me this evening?"

Morgan smirked as she responded, "What do you mean by proper?" Knowing full well her answer would be yes to whatever he suggested. Very confidently he replied, "Dinner, would you like to go to a restaurant with me, as a date?"

Trying to play it cool, Morgan nonchalantly replied, "Alright then." Tristan grinned adding, "It's a date then, I'll pick you up at eight." He then undid his seat belt, leaned in towards Morgan and kissed her on the mouth. He held it for just a second and then returned to his side of the car. Morgan must have been blushing. His lips were soft and he smelled divine. Looking over at him now with purple lipstick on, she chuckled and wiped the smudged lipstick off his lips with her thumb. She quickly exited the car and hurried to her front door. Once inside her room, she collapsed face down on her bed.

It took her a minute to realise that he didn't like her, he liked Morgan Fletcher. She was about to get caught up in a complicated mess, if she didn't control her feelings. But then again, what was different between her and Morgan Fletcher. She dressed more edgy, but Morgan had tailored the wardrobe selected for her to be more to her taste and she actually came up with the hair chalk look herself. She didn't usually wear make-up because it had never mattered to her before and she wanted to be taken seriously in the agency. Her hair was her own, it wasn't a wig and lots of people dye their hair.

Being Morgan Fletcher gave her the confidence to act with the attitude she had deep inside. She decided to relish in it, regardless. No one had ever said they liked her before and she had never been on a date.

She woke the next morning extremely excited and

raring to start the day. She jumped out of bed and grabbed her running gear. The weather was glorious for an October morning, the sky was clear blue and the temperature was mild. Whilst out on her run, she wondered where Tristan would take her tonight and what sort of cuisine it would be. She knew he liked Chinese, maybe he would take her to a Chinese restaurant in town or maybe a steak house. She hoped it wouldn't be Italian, if it was she would have to have a pizza because the idea of slurping spaghetti and getting pasta sauce all down her was a high possibility.

Then it suddenly hit her, a wave of panic flooded through her and she ground to a halt mid run. What was she going to wear? She tried to think back to un-packing Morgan Fletcher's case. She couldn't remember seeing anything suitable. There wasn't a single dress. Surely you should wear a dress to a posh restaurant she thought. Her mind was racing and she was now spiralling with anxiety. So many thoughts rushing through her head all at once. What if it wasn't going to be a posh restaurant? What if she wore a posh dress and then he took her to a chain pub. Surely that wasn't his style, he was a stylish sophisticated guy and he had money. She would have initially described him as a playboy, but since she had spent time with him he didn't give her that impression anymore.

She convinced herself that he must know how to wine and dine a woman. She decided that she would ask Molly to help her choose an outfit. It seemed the most logical solution. Resigned on her decision she turned around and ran home at full speed, hoping to catch Molly before she made plans for the day.

She ran straight up the two flights of stairs to Molly's attic room and knocked on the door. A sleepy sounding, "Come in." Echoed back in response. Morgan opened the door. Curled up in bed was Molly. She had an eye mask still over her left eye and soft rollers in her hair. She was staring at Morgan with one eye.

Morgan blurted out, "I have a date tonight with Tristan

and I have nothing to wear. Will you help me?"

Molly leapt out of bed, flung her eye mask to the floor and embraced Morgan in a big hug. "Yay, a shopping trip! Of course I can help. Get dressed and be ready to leave in forty minutes. I'll book an Uber." And with that she ushered Morgan out the door.

Morgan had left her towel in the bathroom drying on the radiator, so she made her way down one flight of stairs and got straight in the shower. Wrapped in a large black towel as a toga, Morgan descended the stairs to her room to get ready. With the weather being nice, she decided to choose a black cut out crop T-shirt which had buckles on the shoulder and yellow tartan straight leg trousers. She reapplied purple hair chalk to her fringe and applied her make-up just as she had been shown. She heard the doorbell ring and the sound of feet hurrying down the stairs. She grabbed her handbag and her pleather jacket and met Molly at the front door.

Molly was dressed in light blue skinny leg jeans, a beige cashmere one shoulder jumper and beige kitten heels. She had perfect wavy locks and pristine make up. Morgan had to admit she looked stunning and she had thrown this together in forty minutes. Morgan was convinced she had chosen exactly the right person to help her, but had to admit they must look like an unlikely pairing of friends.

Once in the taxi Molly explained that they were heading to Meadow Hall in Sheffield, as it had an excellent selection of shops in one vicinity. Molly then demanded to know every detail from last night and how Tristan had asked her on a date. Morgan had always been the tomboy, with very few girly-girl friends, but she had to admit it felt nice conferring with a friend and bonding over the same anxieties. They gossiped the whole drive with ease.

Molly knew the entire layout of Meadow Hall and led Morgan from shop to shop. She loaded Morgan's arms with outfits to try on, before shoving her in a changing room and demanding to see each outfit. The only problem was Molly's interpretation of Morgan's edgy, slightly punk style, mixed with attending a posh dinner, was creating some questionable ensembles. In one store she made Morgan try on a black, pleather, boobtube, floor length dress with a side split and an electric pink tartan trouser suit, with a silver sparkly bralette.

Morgan was reaching breaking point, so she suggested grabbing lunch to take a break. They walked to the food court area and each decided on what to have for lunch. Not knowing what she would be eating later, Morgan opted for a chicken salad from subway and Molly chose sushi. They ate together in the communal dining area. "Let's loosen up a little," said Molly pulling out two small bottles of white wine from her bag with two plastic cups. "I got us these. Do you have an idea of what you want to wear, or who you would like to look like?"

"Not really, I'll know when I see it. What would you wear?" Morgan asked in return.

"I know you're playing hard to get, but I would go ultra-sexy. He's on the hook now. You might as well look like the bait." Molly responded.

Morgan smirked, "Ok then, dress me how you would dress, ultra-sexy!"

They finished their lunch and their wine before Molly led her, to her favourite shop. She headed straight to the dress section and picked out a black tailored satin lapel blazer dress. Molly then headed to the back of the store and asked Morgan her shoe size, before selecting a black patent, strappy high heeled stiletto. Morgan apprehensively entered the changing room and slipped on the blazer dress and heels. She looked into the mirror, amazed at the person staring back at her. This was it! This was the dress.

She opened the curtain to show Molly her appearance, with her new found confidence. Molly clapped before verbalising, "It's perfect!" Morgan got dressed back into her old clothes and paid for the outfit and shoes at the counter.

"Now for the underwear," Molly stated, as she led the way to Ann Summers. Of course Morgan knew what sort of shop Ann Summers was, but she had never actually been in one. They both had a giggle at the explicit underwear, that there really was no point in wearing; it exposed everything. Molly showed Morgan knickers that were gusset-less and bras with slits to expose the nipples. At the back of the store were the sex toys and even Molly blushed at a huge black double ended dildo.

Molly finally found the section she had been looking for and handed Morgan a box containing a sticky push up skin coloured bra. She then grabbed a black lace thong from a rail and ushered Morgan over to the counter to pay. As they left the store it was clear Molly was on a mission, with a clear goal insight; make Morgan body ready.

"Have you shaved or waxed recently?" She asked Morgan.

"Define recently," Morgan replied, fearful that the next thing Molly would plan for her was waxing.

"Do you wax?" Molly asked impatiently. Morgan nodded. "Your legs seemed fine when I saw them in the changing rooms, was your lady garden waxed at the same time?"

Morgan blushed. She had never been so open about intimate areas of her body before with anyone. "Yes, about two weeks ago," she confirmed.

"That should be fine then, come this way I know a brilliant spray tanner. I'm sure they can squeeze us in," and off she marched, linking arms with Morgan.

Morgan had never had a spray tan before. Molly had arranged it all selecting a light all over body mist spray for them both and now Morgan was alone in a room with a pair of paper pants. She begrudgingly undressed and carefully shuffled into the paper pants. She heard a knock at the door before a beautician entered the room and ordered her to stand in the pop up tent booth, on the opposite side of the room.

The beautician was extremely friendly and eventually put Morgan at ease, making jokes and small talk. Morgan waited a few minutes to let the tan dry, as instructed, before getting dressed again and meeting Molly outside.

"Next is nails," she explained excitedly. Morgan was amazed at the level of preparation it took for one date. She was extremely glad she had roped in Molly for assistance.

Morgan opted against false nails much to Molly's protesting, insisting it was too much maintenance and she would look silly as they grew out. This seemed to convince Molly, but she insisted on a manicure and a deep burgundy red nail polish with a matt finish.

It was nearly four in the afternoon and shops were starting to close. Molly ordered an Uber and they travelled back home, discussing how Morgan should wear her hair for the date. Morgan needed to wash her hair, so she took a second shower. Afterwards she descended the stairs in a slightly damp towel; still wet from its earlier use.

Molly had been waiting for her in the kitchen/living room and asked if she could style Morgan's hair. This truly was turning into a pamper day. Morgan agreed and she sat cross legged on her bed as Molly combed and blow-dried her hair. She had brought an assortment of products down from her room before spraying potions and rubbing creams into Morgan's hair. "No hair chalk this evening," she insisted.

Morgan unpackaged the stick-on bra from Ann Summers and turned to Molly with a puzzled look, before asking for help. Molly showed her the principles of application on her own clothed body, before confirming she would help if needed. It was still too early to get dressed so Morgan applied her make-up alone, before putting on her PJs and entering the kitchen/living room for some company and much needed distraction.

The lads were all playing video games on the sofa and the banter provided good entertainment. Just before eight Morgan slipped back to her room and got dressed. She entered the communal space, nervously clutching her handbag from earlier that day. Molly was her biggest champion and prompted the boys to turn around and praise her until she spotted Morgan's bag.

"You can't use that bag, don't you have another?" She asked.

"No, I only have this and my rucksack."

Molly looked appalled and jumped over the sofa and flew up the staircase. Moments later she returned with a small, black, patent clutch that matched Morgan's new shoes perfectly. "Borrow this," she said handing Morgan the bag.

Morgan had just enough time to swap over the contents, before the doorbell rang. Molly squeezed Morgan's hands, smiling as she gave her a final pep talk.

"Be confident, there's nothing more attractive. You've got this." Molly then left the hallway and entered the kitchen/living room, shutting the door behind her.

Morgan was alone now in the hallway. She had decided earlier that day to not record the date. She convinced herself that the supernatural world was likely to be a topic of conversation and she didn't need the pressure of her first ever date, being live streamed back to HQ. She took a deep breath and opened the door.

CHAPTER 8

A Week Of Firsts

The first thing she saw was his baby blue eyes transfixed on hers, followed by his wide grin. He looked different, more relaxed. His hair was floppy and a little messy, his usual smart trousers and black shoes were replaced with dark denim jeans and white trainers. Rather than a shirt, he was wearing a white cotton T-shirt and a brown pleather jacket. He looked sexy.

Tristan stood in the doorway, mesmerised by Morgan's appearance. As soon as he thought that he was starting to figure her out, she just kept surprising him. He had agonised over what to wear tonight, to make her feel the most comfortable. He had no idea what sort of outfit she was going to wear. He had opted for a casual look, hoping that it would put her at ease. He needn't have worried, she looked stunning!

He greeted her with, "Wowza, you look gorgeous," and he meant it. Morgan beamed from the compliment and Tristan turned back to the pavement. Morgan couldn't see his car, so she followed him down the road, until they reached a lime green sports car. Tristan beeped the fob and stepped into the road towards the passenger side and lifted the door upwards. Morgan was slightly taken aback. She had never seen doors that opened that way. This must be an expensive sports car, she thought. Her instant reaction was to tease him, "Are you trying to impress me, with your fancy car?"

He smirked and answered coyly, "Never, it's not my style, I just love this car," before adding, "Did it work?"

Morgan smirked and shook her head. Tristan knew full well it had impressed her. It was his signature move, to turn up in a flash car to a date, but rarely had he been called out for it. This was one of the reasons he was falling for Morgan. He loved her attitude and how different she was to anyone else he had ever dated. Once Tristan was in the driving seat she asked, "So where are we going?"

He smiled again and replied, "It's a surprise."

As he started up the engine, Morgan's favourite pop album played on the sound system. It made Morgan smile that he was trying to seduce her. Tristan was good at the seduction game. She would need to play him twice as hard at his own game, or she might end up losing herself.

Tristan began polite chit-chat and asked Morgan about her day. Not wanting to let him know exactly how much effort she had put into this evening, she told a white lie about the events of her day and asked him about his. They appeared to be travelling in the opposite direction to Nottingham city centre. Morgan recognised some of the roads from her drive from Tristan's house to hers the other morning.

Morgan suddenly panicked. Surely they weren't driving back to his house for a takeaway, or worse, dinner with his parents. She had made all this effort getting ready and it was hardly the ideal outfit to wear to meet the parents. Then suddenly at a familiar T junction, he turned left off the main road. The signpost read 'Rempstone and Wymeswold'. Morgan relaxed, they weren't going back to his place.

Conversation had now changed to Morgan's degree and Tristan asked lots of open ended questions. He genuinely seemed interested in her course. He started to slow down and signalled left into what appeared to be a small quirky pub car park. Tristan helped Morgan out the car and offered her his arm, to walk down the slopping path towards the rear entrance to the building. He opened the door and a friendly male bartender greeted them warmly with a smile.

Morgan deduced that they must have only just opened, as they were the only three people in the building. The bar was in the middle of a smallish room, with tables all around it. Two small rooms with three tables in each were off to the right and to the left was a bigger room with more tables. It had old flagstone walls, adorned with beautiful artwork and the tables had cute farm animal sculptures made out of wire on them. Looking back around the room again, Morgan noticed that none of the tables had cutlery laid out. That seemed odd.

"This way Mr Lucas," said the bartender as he lifted up the bar hatch and led them around to the larger room on the left. He showed them to the middle table, holding out the chair for Morgan. Morgan noticed that this was the only table in the room, which had been set with cutlery. Once seated, the bartender handed them a leather padded clipboard, which on inspection listed a seven course taster menu and announced, "The pre-ordered bottle of Veuve Clicquot will be delivered to your table shortly, would you like any water for the table or anything else?"

Morgan shook her head and Tristan said, "Just the Champagne will be fine."

When the bartender was out of earshot, Morgan leant across the table and whispered, "Why are we the only ones here?"

"I thought it would be more private if we were alone, in case you wanted to discuss things that we wouldn't want anyone else to hear. Plus I thought it might impress you to hire out the whole restaurant." He shot her a cheeky grin as he said it.

Morgan straightened up before replying, "Impressing me will depend on the quality of the food."

"Not the quality of the conversation?" Tristan retorted in jest.

Morgan smirked, "No just the food, I only accepted this

date because it's a free meal and I'm a poor student."

Tristan laughed. No one made as much effort in their appearance as Morgan had tonight, to be only interested in a free meal. "I'm in luck then, the chef is excellent."

Just then the bartender returned with a bucket on a stand, filled with ice. He popped the cork on the bottle of Champagne, filled both glass flutes already on the table and placed the bottle back in the bucket. Then he disappeared in the opposite direction, presumably to the kitchen, based on the tantalising smell that wafted through the restaurant as he opened the door.

Morgan picked up the menu again to study it. She didn't recognise half the words and had certainly never tried these dishes before. Seeing the puzzled look on her face, Tristan said, "I never know what I'm eating when I come here, but it tastes great."

Just then the bartender returned, announcing that the first course was sweetbreads with chorizo and red pepper. He laid a beautifully presented plate in front of Morgan, which looked like a tiny posh chicken nugget on mash. Morgan couldn't resist asking, "What is sweetbread?" She wasn't fussy or afraid of eating anything, but she preferred to know exactly what, she was eating so that she could make an informed decision.

The bartender replied, "This particular sweetbread is a gland from a lamb reared just over those hills." He pointed out of the window, past the car park and then returned to the bar. Morgan grimaced as Tristan tucked into the plate of food, remarking that it was the best bit of gland he had ever eaten. Morgan laughed and he urged her to try it. She picked up her knife and fork and took a small bite.

"You're not wrong," she remarked, "It's really tasty. I wish I hadn't asked."

"Trust the chef, that's what I always do," Tristan replied.

"If I don't know him, then how can I trust him?" She questioned.

"Then trust me, you know me."

Morgan smiled coyly, "Do I?"

"What do you want to know?"

"Everything," she stated, "start with your childhood, what were you like at school?"

The rest of the evening passed by with great food and even better conversation. He made her laugh with anecdotes of his friends and brothers. Not wanting to turn the evening solemn or divulge too much about Aunt Winnie, Morgan decided against telling Tristan about her parent's death and her new life on the commune. Instead, she only referenced her earlier childhood memories.

Morgan over-indulged in the cheese trolley, so when the last course arrived she was so full that she had to apologise to the bartender and offered him her dessert. He gladly accepted and then left them alone to continue their conversation. Tristan tucked into the dark chocolate and hazelnut soufflé. After a couple of spoonful's he held out his loaded spoon across the table for Morgan to take a bite. It looked so appetising that Morgan gladly accepted, licking the excess chocolate from her lips. For the first time that evening, Morgan noticed Tristan's eyes wonder down to her breasts and he shuffled in his seat and offered a cheeky smile when he noticed that he had been caught.

The conversation took a more sexual turn, with Tristan asking Morgan what her biggest fantasy was. Whilst she paused to think, she started playing footsie with him under the table. A trick she had learnt on a previous undercover mission, to distract the mark whilst planning your next move. She rather enjoyed watching Tristan's reaction. She didn't really have any sexual fantasies. She had only kissed a few men. Truth be told she was still a virgin, but she didn't want him to know that. Her focus had always been on her career and she had never given much thought to finding a partner. Aunt Winnie was single and she had always seemed happy.

She had watched enough movies to make something up but she didn't want to lie to him. Instead she suggestively replied, "I can't make it too easy for you, you will have to figure it out yourself." She shuffled back in her seat and crossed her legs over exposing her bare legs. She saw Tristan's eyes glazing upon her bare flesh and took the opportunity to change the topic of the conversation to life goals.

Tristan happily spoke about growing his family nightclub business and wanting to step out of his older brother's shadow. He then returned the question to Morgan.

"My career goals are obvious but in all honesty, I have always wanted my own family. To be a unit. Us against the world." She was speaking truthfully from the heart and if her profiling was right, she knew coming from a close family, he would more than likely want the same.

His expression softened and all his bravado was gone.

"I've grown up in a very close family. My brothers both married the love of their lives and I'm still single, waiting desperately for love to happen to me. Hopefully, both our lucks might be about to change?" He said it with such care and meaning in his voice, Morgan couldn't look away from his eyes, losing herself in them. This was definitely a moment, like she had seen in movies. They just stared at each other in silence for at least a minute, before the bartender interrupted them by clearing away Tristan's plate.

Tristan checked his watch, "It's getting late, I should get you back home, so you can rest before Uni tomorrow." He held out his hand and Morgan rose from the table, she took his hand in hers. They left the restaurant hand in hand. Morgan caught a glimpse of their reflection in the window, they looked good together. She couldn't help but smile.

Tristan had to park at the end of her street due to the amount of parked cars, but like a gentleman he helped her out of the car and walked her to her front door. Morgan fiddled in her bag for her keys, stalling on purpose. Tristan seized the opportunity he lifted her chin with his right hand and placed his lips straight on hers. Moving his hand down her body to her bum, where he gave it a squeeze and pulled her closer to him. Morgan could feel his firm body pressing against hers and she felt powerless in his embrace. He parted her lips slightly with his and she allowed his tongue to fill her mouth, caressing it with her own. She started to feel dizzy and if he had suggested staying over tonight, she would have been too weak to resist. However, he was a perfect gentleman and walked back to his car.

Morgan allowed herself one last glance at him before entering the house. She felt so conflicted. She was falling hard and deep for this man, but he was a suspected criminal. She was going to need therapy after this mission.

Monday at University was just like any other, apart from Morgan's constant phone checking. She didn't want to be the first one to message. It wasn't until she was walking towards the bus stop, that she saw him. Tristan was leaning against a tree nearby. He waved as he ran over to her and put his arm around her shoulders. "I was just with Fenik and he said you would be finishing Uni about now." Morgan couldn't hide her smile, this felt so right and natural.

He continued, "Me and Jono have Wednesday off this week and my brother has a foam party planned at Wild in Loughborough, want to come? You can bring your housemates. I will hire a minibus?"

"Yeh ok, that sounds great." Morgan stopped walking and indicated this was her bus stop.

"Ok, see you on Wednesday," Tristan confirmed. He lent down and planted a kiss on her lips, before walking in the opposite direction back to the bar.

When she returned to the house, wonderful smells were floating out of the kitchen. David was cooking a chicken curry from scratch for everyone. She unloaded her belongings into her room, before joining everyone. Not having seen any of them since Sunday evening, she downloaded the events of the date. Phil was mostly interested in what make and model the sports car was. He started bringing pictures up on his phone and asking Morgan if she recognised any of them. When she confirmed it looked like the fourth picture he showed her, he got very excited and proceeded to rattle off facts about the car. Molly seemed particularly interested when he mentioned the price tag.

Then Morgan explained her brief meeting with him after University and that they were all invited to join him for a night out in Loughborough on Wednesday. Phil looked absolutely devastated that he had to decline. He was going back to Newcastle, as his father had secured him a ticket to a football game. George was refereeing in a Uni rugby match, so was a no. David had a coursework deadline, which he doubted he would finish in time to join, but said he was a maybe. Molly jumped at the opportunity and wanted full details about Jono, before running through options of what to wear. Panic hit Morgan again. She had only bought one outfit on Sunday and couldn't wear that again. Molly seemed to read her mind and told her to join her upstairs to plan.

Molly had an extensive wardrobe and whilst she was a size smaller than Morgan, some of her dresses were stretchy and might fit. Neither of them knew the vibe at the Loughborough Wild, so they both went for a classic night-out look. Molly chose a short skimpy Barbie pink metallic halter dress, exposing a lot of back flesh. After trying on a couple of Molly's dresses, Morgan selected a plain black velour asymmetrical dress with one full sleeve. She thanked Molly and took the dress back to her room.

That night she checked her phone before she went to sleep and saw a message from Tristan. He wrote, *'Night x'* she smiled and replied *'Night x'*. She woke the next morning to a voice note from Steve saying, "Good work Morgan, I can see you are getting closer, keep it up, the Chief is still pushing for answers."

Morgan cursed. She had momentarily forgotten that they would be monitoring every interaction on her phone and that included reading all her text messages. She decided that she needed the freedom to conduct her own investigation slightly off the radar. She was certain her Tristan was not involved in murder. She got dressed for her morning run and tucked her bank card into her sleeve zip pocket.

There was a newsagent on the corner of Faraday Road and it had a cashpoint outside. She withdrew a few hundred pounds. She would fill an expense report in later and explain the funds as food and University supplies. In her lunch break she nipped into the town centre and bought a sim card along with a basic phone. She transferred a few people's numbers into the new phone, including Molly, Aunt Winnie and Tristan. She then typed a generic message that she would be using this number moving forward.

Tuesday and Wednesday came and went uneventfully. Morgan couldn't wait for them to be over. Tristan had messaged her new phone to say *'be ready for nine x'*. Molly and Morgan were dressed and ready by eight. They decided to have pre-drinks whilst they waited.

Molly opened a bottle of Prosecco and Morgan retold the story of Jono making his own version of her Wild T-shirt creation, which made Molly howl with laughter. David was still working hard on his coursework in his room, so couldn't join them. Morgan's new phone buzzed, Tristan had messaged to confirm that they were outside. Both girls downed their glasses and left the house.

A large minibus was waiting on the other side of the road and Tristan slid open the door as they approached. Morgan made the introductions and both girls climbed in. Tristan was wearing navy chinos, brown suede shoes and a bright white shirt. Jono was more casually dressed in Jeans and an AC/DC T-shirt.

The chat was friendly and free flowing on the journey to Loughborough. Jono had brought a hip flask of Whiskey and passed it around the group of four. Morgan declined, but Molly took full advantage.

The taxi stopped right outside the door to the nightclub. A long line was forming outside. Arm in arm with Morgan and Molly, Tristan and Jono marched straight up to the front of the queue. The bouncers stood aside and let them through. They walked into a small red hallway with a ticket booth on the left and a cloakroom on the right. A woman in the booth waved at Tristan and he nodded in acknowledgement as he walked straight up the vertical staircase. They climbed the stairs in couples and walked through black double doors into the nightclub.

The first room was small, with a bar to the right and a DJ booth to the left. The DJ was playing cheesy eighties music. A round podium was directly in front of them and people were dancing already. Tristan continued straight through the room, to another set of smaller doors. They walked through a busy corridor into a much larger room. The space was three times the size of the smaller room. The DJ in this room was playing hip hop music. It had a large dance floor surrounded by booths with the DJ in the centre, very much like the underground bar in Nottingham. The bar was to the right and Tristan walked straight over ordering a bottle of Tattinger Champagne and four Sambuca shots. Then he pointed to an empty booth at the back of the room, to signal where to bring them.

Tristan led Morgan by the hand to the booth he had pointed out. Molly and Jono joined them and within a few minutes, the bartender arrived with the drinks. Molly raised her glass and started a toast. "To new friendships." Whilst staring seductively at Jono. She squeezed up next to him in the booth, shamelessly flirting. The conversation flowed between the foursome and before long; Molly led them all to the dance floor.

Morgan took a bathroom break and when she re-joined the dance floor, Molly and Jono had disappeared. Morgan insisted on finding them. After scanning the room and deducing they were no longer here, she led the way to the corridor. She glimpsed Molly's metallic pink dress through the dim lighting, pressed up against the corridor wall. Her legs were wrapped round Jono's waist, passionately embracing. Morgan turned to Tristan, who had also spotted them. She giggled then pushed Tristan back into the larger room.

They re-joined the dance floor. Now alone they started kissing whilst dancing and Morgan allowed Tristan's hands to explore her body. Morgan spun around, so she could wiggle her rear into Tristan's crotch, whilst he kissed down her neck and collar bone from behind. Morgan felt tingles running up and down her body, as if Tristan's touch was inducting a current of electricity all over her skin. All the hairs on her arms had stood up. She could feel Tristan's erection caged within his trousers as she pressed up against him.

Suddenly Tristan pulled away. Morgan turned around to see why. A tall man with blonde hair and facial features similar to Tristan had his hand on his shoulder. Morgan knew from the background information that this was Tobias, his older brother but she had to play dumb until she was introduced. Tristan introduced them and Tobias nodded before walking away. The greeting seemed a little cold. Tristan whispered in her ear, "Ignore my brother. He is suspicious of new people. He will warm to you." Morgan nodded and they picked up where they left off, dancing sexually and kissing passionately.

Molly and Jono found them on the dance floor a little after one and they all retired back to the booth for another round of drinks. Molly cuddled up to Jono and spoke seductively into his ear. Looking very excited at what was being said, Jono whispered in Tristan's ear, before standing up and offering Molly his hand. She followed him but not before leaning into Morgan's ear, "I'll see you at home tomorrow for a de-brief. Jono lives in Loughborough, so I'm going back to his," and with that they left. Tristan and Morgan just laughed. They stayed a little longer and had another drink, before Tristan offered to book an Uber.

They kissed the whole car journey back and as they pulled up outside Morgan's house, she didn't want it to stop. Why did it have to? She thought to herself. "Just the one stop now," She said to the taxi driver and grabbed Tristan by the hand, dragging him out of the taxi. Tristan made no objections, he stood behind her, kissing her neck and fondling her breasts, as she lead him into her room. Once inside there was no stopping his advances and Morgan let him take the lead, hoping instinct would not out her as a novice.

She turned on her desk lamp so that there was a dim glow throughout the room. She let him slide her dress down to the floor and they both laughed as he saw her stuck on bra cups. He indicated he didn't know what to do with them. Morgan ripped them off her skin and threw them to the ground. Tristan cupped her breasts in his hands. He moved his head to her breasts and started kissing, first on her skin, before he then placed her nipple in his mouth. He licked her nipple with his tongue, until it was perfectly erect. Morgan found herself groaning in passion completely swept away with desire.

He then kicked off his shoes and unbuttoned his shirt to reveal his chiselled chest. He had a small amount of dark hair on his pecks. She suspected he waxed the rest to show off his toned abs, as a small amount trailed from his belly button down under his waistband.

He intertwined his fingers in her silken black thong and pulled her underwear down her legs. He knelt on the floor and kissed her inner thigh all the way up to her entrance. He smirked when he saw the panther tattoo. A wild cat and a wild dog were natural enemies but not tonight, he thought. He looked up at her with his puppy dog blue eyes. The bed was directly behind her, so he pushed her gently back. He spread her legs open and she wrapped them around his neck.

He then devoured her with his mouth, sucking, blowing and licking. Morgan had never experienced anything like it. It felt wonderful. Her core temperature started to rise and tension rose within her until a scream burst from her throat in ecstasy.

Tristan appeared above her on the bed, panting with a large smile on his face. He kissed her even more passionately than he had all evening, allowing her to taste herself. His body was pressed against her naked skin and his glistening chest was hot and damp with sweat, in contrast to his trousers, which felt cool on her legs. In his passionate caresses, he made her feel safe and loved.

She ran her fingers through his hair, as his hands slowly trailed up and down her body. He started to fiddle with the button on his trousers, but cursed as he couldn't manage it one-handed. He sat upwards, straddling his legs either side of her body. She moved his hands and undid the button on his trousers. Biting her lip, she lowered his zipper.

He climbed off the bed to remove his trousers, revealing his white Calvin Klein briefs, before removing them as well. His manhood was now visible, large and erect. He picked up his trousers, pulled his wallet out of his back pocket and removed a condom. He ripped it open with his teeth and rolled the condom down his engorged penis.

Morgan watched him intensely, trying not to let her mind wander to whether it would hurt and if she would bleed, giving away her secret. As soon as he locked eyes with her again, all her concerns melted away and she was lost in his kisses.

As he lowered himself onto her body, she felt his penis throbbing at her entrance. With a slow thrust of his hips, he was inside her and she felt satiated. Each movement he made penetrated deeper inside her. She felt no pain. It was just the opposite, it was pleasurable. As he moved in a rhythmic motion, the tension she felt before began to rise again and she felt herself panting as heavily as he was.

She had to pause from kissing him, to focus on her breathing until she finally reached orgasm. His climax followed shortly after hers. She felt his entire body tense as he groaned in pleasure. If he suspected that she was a novice he didn't let on.

He raised himself off the bed, removed the condom and sat back to kiss her again. Morgan had sat upright to watch him, but now rose from the bed herself and grabbed her PJs from under her pillow. She got dressed, before excusing herself to use the bathroom.

As she had feared, there was a small amount of blood. She took a moment to process what had just happened and the realisation hit her. She had lost her virginity to a mark she was investigating. She was falling madly in love with a suspected criminal and she couldn't stop herself. She rationalised that all she had to do was prove his innocence and hope that he loved her enough in return, to forgive her deception.

By the time she returned, Tristan was tucked up under the covers with his eyes half closed. She climbed into bed and he snuggled up next to her, spooning her. He whispered, "Goodnight," In her ear and shortly after she heard his breathing slow, as he lightly snored. She turned off her alarm and drifted off to sleep, safe in the warmth of his embrace.

CHAPTER 9

Suspicion

Tristan woke up first. He could tell Morgan was still asleep by the sound of her breathing. He carefully pulled himself up into a sitting position and just watched her. Flash backs of last night swam through his mind. Last night had been good. He had never felt so content in someone's company. Usually he would be making up any excuse to leave in the morning, but not today.

Suddenly out of nowhere, Nu-metal music blasted through the walls and Morgan woke with a fright. Morgan looked confused and Tristan offered to investigate. He climbed out of bed and put on his briefs before disappearing out the room. The volume level of the music reduced, although the damage had been done and Morgan sat upright in bed. Tristan returned, explaining that George didn't realise anyone was home, as he usually had the house to himself on Thursday mornings.

Morgan looked at the time on her new phone and rolled her eyes. It was eleven. She had missed a morning of lectures. Although she knew Steve would never find out, she did feel guilty. She had never even been late for a commitment, let alone just not shown up. She rationalised that the most imperative mission objective, was to infiltrate the Lucas family and she was definitely getting to know Tristan on a personal level.

Tristan started to get dressed and asked, "Did you need me to leave, so that you can get ready for uni?"

"It's ok, there's no point going now. I only have morning lectures on a Thursday."

Tristan leaned in and landed a quick kiss on her lips before asking, "Does that mean you have the rest of the day free?" He winked at her as he said it. Morgan just looked up at him, biting her lip in contemplation, imagining a repeat of last night before confirming, "I'm all yours."

Pulling on his trousers he told her, "Get dressed, let's go to mine for the afternoon." Morgan grabbed a black Led Zeppelin T-shirt, her blue ripped denim jeans, some underwear and headed for the bathroom to take a shower. She used a shower cap, hoping that she didn't have to wash her hair. When she returned to her room, it was empty and she could hear talking in the kitchen/living room. She quickly applied her make-up and gave her hair a hasty brush. She sat on the bed and put on her trainers, before joining the boys in the communal room.

George and Tristan were racing each other on some car game, deep in conversation, so Morgan grabbed herself a can of pop from her shelf in the fridge. She joined them on the sofa, just as Tristan won the race. He punched the air in satisfaction. George pleaded with him to make it a best of three games, but Tristan jumped over the sofa explaining that the taxi was waiting outside. Morgan followed him, grabbing her bag on the way out.

The taxi dropped them off on the main road and they walked the short distance down the lane to the gate. Morgan hadn't appreciated the size or the beauty of his parent's house the last time she had visited. As the house came into view she took it in, in all its glory. Tristan typed the code in the keypad and the gate swung open.

As they walked through the courtyard Morgan heard a

car door shutting and a petite woman with Mediterranean features appeared, laden with shopping bags. Morgan recognised her as Tristan's mother from the background intelligence. Tristan jogged towards her and offered his assistance. His mother turned and they came face to face.

Tristan made the introductions and his mother smiled warmly before speaking directly to Morgan, "This shopping is all for our Halloween party on Saturday night. I just love Halloween. You must come." Morgan looked at Tristan seeking some reassurance, before responding, "I'm actually working Saturday night."

Tristan smiled before adding, "I think I can let you off work for the night, to make my mother happy."

"Excellent, that's settled then," his mother said. She looked triumphant and very pleased with herself, as she opened the front door.

Morgan followed Tristan inside, through a beautifully monochrome decorated hallway and into a large modern farm house kitchen. Tristan placed the bags on the kitchen island, kissed his mother on the cheek and took Morgan's hand. He lead her through a door off the kitchen. They entered a utility room with a hanging drying rack and ironing board set out. Next to a back door was a set of stairs and Tristan explained that it was his private entrance and staircase.

They climbed the stairs and it opened straight into a small kitchen. Tristan immediately opened the fridge and started reeling off the possibilities for lunch before saying, "Let's order pizza." Morgan gratefully nodded. She needed some bread to soak up the alcohol still in her system.

Tristan showed Morgan the lounge and went into detail about his games console collection. They sat down on the sofa and the conversation turned to the Halloween party. "How big is this party going to be?" She asked.

Tristan grinned before confirming, "Big, my mother goes all out."

"It's in the house though, right?" Morgan queried.

Tristan shook his head before explaining, "My mother hires a company to put up a marquee and has catering staff for the event."

Morgan was impressed, but now daunted about what to wear, "What's your outfit going to be?" She asked.

He teased, "That is top secret I'm afraid." He leaned over and starting kissing her. They continued heavy petting until Tristan's phone rang. It was his mother telling him to collect his takeaway from the kitchen. Tristan took a minute to straighten out his clothes, re-adjusting his underwear to try and hide his erection.

They spent the next few hours eating pizza, whilst Tristan tried to teach Morgan how to win at car racing games. It felt so natural and easy to be in each other's company. Morgan felt he was the best friend she'd never had. Tristan's winning streak was interrupted by his phone ringing. He pulled his mobile out of his pocket to see that it was Jono calling. Moments later Morgan's phone rang and it was Molly. Clearly they had both just parted company and wanted to gossip about the evenings events. Tristan indicated he would take his call in the bedroom and Morgan curled up on the sofa to take Molly's call.

Tristan re-entered the lounge after his call finished, grinning like a Cheshire Cat. Morgan continued talking on the phone until Molly took a breath. Seizing her opportunity, Morgan managed to explain that she was at Tristan's and would catch up with her later. Tristan winked as he remarked, "Jono had a good night. I've told him to invite Molly to the Halloween party." Morgan smiled. It meant that she could go shopping with Molly and that she could help her pick out the perfect outfit.

"Molly was also giving a glowing report," she retorted, biting her lip to tempt Tristan into kissing her again.

Reading her body language he curled his finger and beckoned her to join him in the bedroom, as he walked backwards through the doorway. They spent the rest of the afternoon in bed, exploring each other's bodies. Morgan learnt how much she enjoyed her nipples being caressed and how much Tristan liked her to fondle his testicles. She had always been curious about how many times a man could ejaculate in quick succession. It turned out that Tristan had great stamina.

As they got dressed, Tristan caught Morgan off guard as he announced, "I like your tattoo." Morgan blushed as she explained it was a teenage act of rebellion and she had no plans to get anymore.

Tristan drove her home before her shift at Wild. He left her to shower and change, whilst he chatted with her male housemates in the communal area. Once she was ready, he drove her to Wild in time for her shift. They walked into the bar hand-in-hand, which definitely caught Fenik's attention. Fenik smirked, as she walked upstairs to the staff room. She could hear him taunting Tristan downstairs.

Once she was downstairs in the underground bar, Morgan turned her work phone off silent and placed it on a low shelf out of sight. Hoping that it would record only the loud music and she would be free to have conversations, when she left the bar area.

The shift was uneventful. Morgan missed the camaraderie she had built up with Jono, who had now returned to working in the Loughborough club. Tristan didn't appear from his office until the lights came on and helped Morgan with the clean-up, before driving her home. Not wanting to miss any more lectures, Morgan explained that she needed to sleep alone tonight. Tristan acted out being wounded with an arrow in the heart, before kissing her goodnight and driving away.

Friday's lectures dragged on slowly, as Morgan was desperate to see Tristan again. Whilst she waited for him to pick her up for her evening shift, she gossiped further with

Molly about Wednesday night and made a plan to go shopping on Saturday, for the perfect fancy dress costumes.

Friday was busy in the bar, with lots of students dressing up for Halloween. Tristan worked on the underground bar with Morgan for the whole night. In between serving customers he took any opportunity to touch her and repeatedly brushed himself up against her as he squeezed past. She loved every second of his attention, the blurred lines between Morgan Fletcher and Morgan Hudson had completely disappeared.

As the lights turned on and the bar was vacated, Tristan led her upstairs to his office. They started making out before they even reached the office door and Morgan unzipped his trousers as he fiddled with the key. He bolted the door before leading her through into the second room. Morgan sat on the edge of his desk, pulled back his briefs, exposing his manhood and pushed him backwards onto the leather chair. She dropped to her knees and started licking and sucking his penis, as he had tutored her.

It didn't take long for Tristan to lift up her chin and motion for her to stand. He stood too, kissing her passionately. He turned her around and bent her over the desk. He pulled up her skirt and pushed her thong to the side. He entered her from behind and had to steady himself on the desk to prevent climaxing too soon.

As her breathing grew coarser he tugged at her hair, gently at first, then a little harder. Her breathing turned to panting as she reached the peak of her desire. He exploded into her, which tipped her over the edge into orgasm. The sex was fantastic. In truth she had never realised it would feel this way, but their closeness was more than just the physical act. She felt truly connected to him and she was certain that he felt exactly the same way.

She fell back down to earth, when she checked her phone

before bed and was faced with reality. Steve had messaged, asking for a report of the investigation so far. She had to give him just enough to satisfy him, without giving away that she was more involved with Tristan than she had led on. Rather than go straight to sleep, she stayed up for two hours perfecting the report. Detailing her suspicions about the Cane twins and admitting that she had been invited to a Halloween party at the Lucas house on Saturday night.

She woke in the morning to a response from Steve, congratulating her on her success. She felt like a fraud. The last thing she ever wanted to do was play Steve for a fool, but the Chief Commander was no innocent party. She had more than just Tristan to protect; she had Aunt Winnie and her own secrets.

Molly joined Morgan for her morning run on Saturday and they discussed costume options. Molly insisted they had to go all out, but remain sexy. Molly wanted to go in PVC to show off her figure, but wanted to avoid the obvious options of cat women or bat girl. Morgan had loved experimenting with make-up recently, so intended to pick an option that allowed her to put her new skills into practice.

Once showered, they headed out to the bus stop. They were venturing into Nottingham town centre. They grabbed a light lunch and a pumpkin Frappuccino at Starbucks, whilst researching potential costume ideas on the internet. Molly was against a homemade design, insisting they looked tacky and you could always tell.

They visited the first of three fancy dress shops in town that Morgan had found on the internet. The first Molly described as only selling children's fancy dress. The second had clearly already been ransacked in preparation for this evening. The third was harder to find and they ventured further out of the centre than either of them had ever been. Morgan found a skeleton halter neck catsuit in her size, which fit perfectly. It was black with glow in the dark skeleton bones in a spray paint design and had long gloves that finished just above her elbow in the same design. She bought white and black face paint to complete the look.

Molly however, was still not happy and decided to try a sex shop for a PVC outfit. She had decided to be Trinity from the matrix and purchased some large space-age black sunglasses from the shop before they left. The shop assistant gave them directions to an independent sex shop a few streets away, but he warned them it was rather risqué.

As soon as they entered the shop, they both had to stifle a giggle. The shop was sadomasochist focused. Chains hung down from the ceiling and even the shop assistant was wearing PVC lederhosen. Molly asked where the PVC outfits were and the man pointed to a rail at the back of store. They had lots of styles in multiple sizes and Molly consulted images on her phone, before choosing the exact one she wanted. She tried it on with the glasses for the full effect and even Morgan had to admit she looked amazing. Happy with their purchases, they returned home to get ready for the party.

Morgan watched multiple videos on the internet, before committing to a Skeleton make-up design and trialling it on her own face. She settled on a Day of the Dead style with a white face, black eyes and a skeleton smile across her cheeks.

Tristan was helping his mother set up the party. So Jono arrived in his blue BMW M3 at eight to take them. Jono hadn't changed into his outfit yet. He said he wouldn't fit in the driving seat. When he saw Molly he howled like a wolf with delight and Morgan's eyes widened. Jono was clearly aware that she knew his secret. He winked at Morgan when Molly was distracted. Molly was focused on twirling around to show off her full costume. Jono embraced her in a long sensual kiss and then opened the car door for them both to climb in.

As they arrived at the house, the driveway was full of cars. Morgan recognised several of the bars bouncers at the gate, letting taxis in to turn around. Strip lighting lit a path around the house to a gigantic white marquee. Jono left them both at the entrance, as he needed to change into his costume. Morgan and Molly looked at each other, amazed by the scale of the party. A DJ was playing music in the far left side of the tent, behind a large black and white dance floor. Several large round tables were laid out to the right adorned with black candelabras, fake cobwebs and spiders. A large buffet table ran the length of the right side of the tent wall and was filled with delicious looking food.

Waitresses dressed identically as Wednesday Addams, were handing out canapés and Champagne flutes. Decorations filled every space and from the ceiling hung lit candles, which gave the illusion that they were floating. A Wednesday Addams passed by with a tray of Champagne and Molly grabbed them both a glass. Another Wednesday passed by Morgan, with cream cheese stuffed jalapeño's. The canapés looked like mummies with pastry bandages and she grabbed one for each of them to try.

Molly spotted Jono before Morgan did. He was walking towards them in a blow-up suit that had the illusion of a green alien, carrying a man. He was laughing hysterically and next to him was Tristan dressed as Beetlejuice. He was wearing a black and white pin stripped suit, with a crazy white wig that gave the appearance he was half bald. His cocky swagger gave away how impressed he was with his costume choice. He greeted Morgan with a passionate embrace that made her fall backwards. He caught her in a swooping motion, like a dramatic stage kiss and led her to the dance floor.

The DJ gave a shout out to officially open the buffet and then Morgan's all-time favourite Halloween track started playing. People piled onto the dance floor and started forming rows to perform the popular dance routine. The night continued and everyone was having a great time.

As Morgan excused herself to use the ladies room, she spotted a familiar face walking into the garden. If she wasn't mistaken, Cordelia Levingstone from the commune was at the party. She was dressed in an extravagant female Dracula costume, with a top hat and cane. Her long dark wavy hair and disdainful facial expression was undeniable. She always looked like she had a bad smell under her nose, leading Morgan to believe she had a superiority complex. Morgan paused for a moment, before following her. She knew her make-up would make her unrecognisable, especially as Cordelia wouldn't have expected to see her, but she didn't want to risk getting too close.

She followed her out of the marquee and into the grounds, towards the posh portaloo cabin. She slowed her pace to allow a significant gap but she couldn't get a clear view of her face in the dim lighting. Cordelia climbed the steps to the portaloo cabin and disappeared out of sight. Morgan hid behind the cabin, positioning herself with a clear view of the entrance back to the marquee. In a matter of moments, Cordelia reappeared and walked back towards the entrance, when a tall man in a Bane costume approached her. Together they changed direction and began walking in the direction of the house.

Morgan couldn't hear what was being discussed. As they approached the house, an older man dressed in a tuxedo with slicked back luminous green hair and scary make up joined them. Morgan only just recognised him as Vincent Lucas, Tristan's father. The exchange looked heated and the man dressed as Bane punched the wall of the house, next to Cordelia's head. She stood her ground defiantly, not even flinching. Morgan could see clearly now that it was definitely Cordelia, but what was she doing here? She wondered. If Morgan wasn't mistaken, Cordelia had rolled her eyes into the back of her head, so only the whites of her eyes were showing and she floated a foot from the ground. The Bane character and Vincent Lucas stepped back, clearly in shock. Cordelia's eyes returned to normal and she landed back on the ground. She glared at them both, before marching back to the marquee.

Vincent and Bane walked in the opposite direction, towards the back of the house. Morgan thought it safe to come out from her hiding place and re-entered the marquee. What she couldn't have known was that Bane had doubled back and saw her sneaking out of hiding. He growled under his breath and made it his mission to find out who she was. He didn't have to wait long.

As she entered the marquee she saw Cordelia striding across the tent and out the other side, presumably to leave. Tristan was still on the dance floor, dancing and laughing with Jono. Molly was stood to the side of them with a woman in a black leather cat woman costume. As Morgan joined them, the lady in the cat woman costume signalled over to someone behind Morgan and the man dressed as Bane joined the group. Tristan introduced them as his brother Tobias and his sister-in-law Charlotte. He introduced her, as his girlfriend. Charlotte seemed happy to meet her, but Tobias treated her with just as much coldness as the other night in the club. Tobias excused himself and his wife quickly. Tristan didn't appear to notice Tobias' distain and started caressing Morgan's neck from behind.

The music stopped and the DJ handed a microphone to Tristan's mother, who was dressed in the smallest red metallic hot pants Morgan had ever seen. She had ripped fishnets, a white baseball top and jacket. Her hair was in blonde pigtails and it must have been a very good wig, as it looked realistic. Vincent Lucas' attire made sense now. They were Harley Quinn and the Joker.

Marisa, Tristan's mother, thanked everyone for attending and then turned to Vincent. She proceeded to thank him for indulging her, with her love affair with Halloween. She gave the microphone back to the DJ and led Vincent over towards Tristan. She greeted Morgan with continental air kisses, due to Morgan's elaborate make-up. Then Marisa encouraged Tristan to introduce Morgan to his father. Tristan put an arm around his father's shoulder and proudly introduced Morgan as his girlfriend. His father looked surprised at the label. Leading her to believe this was a rare and unexpected introduction. Marisa however, clapped and hugged Morgan again, clearly happy by the news.

Once the shock had worn off, Vincent seemed genuinely interested to get to know Morgan. He asked how they met and what Morgan was studying at University. She didn't feel like she was being interrogated. More like a father taking an interest in his son's life. Jono and Molly joined them and Jono introduced Molly to the hosts of the party. Tristan's parents treated Jono like a son, embracing him and Molly like they had done with Tristan and Morgan. The party continued into the early hours of the morning. Morgan had a great time, laughing and dancing the whole night, but she couldn't shake off the feeling she was being watched.

CHAPTER 10

Detective Morgan

Morgan had an important paper due by five on Thursday, so the week passed extremely slowly. There were no visits from Tristan and a limited amount of time spent away from the library. Luckily Phil and David had papers with the same deadline, so they all travelled together to and from campus.

Over a quick dinner break on Tuesday evening, Molly told Morgan that she had switched her major to International Media and Communications Studies. She was loving her new course and saw a future for herself in social media. Molly was toying with not telling her father until graduation day, in the hope that he would still be proud of her. But she wanted people's opinions on whether that was a good idea or not. Morgan thought for a moment before responding, "If I was a parent I would want to know, but I would be proud that you had decided what you wanted to do in life and that you had a goal. From everything you have told us about your father, he wants you to be happy and have a focus. Surely he would be delighted you had found a passion for something."

Molly thanked Morgan for her input, but was still deliberating, so changed the conversation to her love life. She was still in regular communication with Jono. He was in the process of moving to Nottingham, to work full time at Wild. This news cheered Morgan up immensely. She had missed his energy in the bar.

Morgan handed her paper in Thursday lunchtime after her morning lectures and it felt like a weight had been lifted off her shoulders. She went home, with a plan to sleep until dinner time, but Tristan had other ideas. She saw his car parked outside her house, as she turned into the street. Morgan peered in the window and saw that the car was empty. As soon as she opened the front door, Ed Sheeran - Perfect, started playing and she couldn't help but smile. She entered the kitchen/living room. Tristan was alone. He was wearing David's cooking apron behind the island, transferring steaks from a pan onto plates. She could see that he was topless, but it wasn't until he stepped to the side to gesture for Morgan to sit at the island, that she realised that he was completely naked under the apron. As his eyes met Morgan's, he gave a devilish grin and she could see that he had set the island with cutlery. The dinner looked and smelled amazing. Steak and chips was one of Morgan's favourite meals. Tristan explained that Molly had helped him to set this up and they had the house to themselves, for the next few hours.

Morgan leant in for a kiss and squeezed Tristan's bare bum. He took that as a sign to play dirty. He lifted her off the ground by grabbing her bum and sliding her legs to lock around his waist. As they kissed, intertwined in each other, he walked over to the sofas, gently lying her down. He whipped off the apron, to reveal his erect penis, as Morgan wriggled out of her jeans and pants. They had quick, hot, passionate sex right there on the sofa. Morgan climaxed so intensely that she clawed at his back. She had missed not seeing him the last few days and her body had clearly yearned for his touch. Once sexually satisfied, her tummy rumbled reminding her that dinner was waiting for her on the counter. They both got dressed and sat at the island, to eat the meal that Tristan had prepared. It was delicious, even though it was now lukewarm.

They spent the rest of the afternoon curled up on the sofa together watching a box set. It felt like heaven to be wrapped up in his arms, safe from the realities of life. Tristan had spare clothes in his office, so when it was time to leave for work they drove straight to Wild. Tristan had a few business meetings, so he didn't join Morgan behind the bar to serve. He established himself on a booth closest to the bar. That way he could watch Morgan working.

A mixture of people she did and didn't recognise joined Tristan at the booth. First there were the Cane brothers and Matthew Negus, then a couple of much younger men that she had never met before. One had dreadlocks with baggy trousers, which showed his briefs when he walked and the other was dressed in an Adidas silver tracksuit, with a shaved head. They didn't dress like any of Tristan's other friends and quite clearly were not dressed for a business meeting. Morgan had to admit that most business meetings were not conducted at night in a club. She grew intrigued as to the business being discussed.

Morgan continued serving, but took every opportunity to look over at the booth. The strangers eventually left looking rather smug. Tristan stayed at the booth talking to his friends. Towards the end of the evening, Tristan came over to the bar and told Morgan to come up to his office when she was finished, before he disappeared. She hadn't been her usual jolly self, too intrigued with finding out what business Tristan was up to. Jono teased her that she was pining after Tristan. As soon as the lights turned on, signalling for everyone to leave, Jono told her to go to him without finishing the clean-up routine. She thanked him and discretely fetched her phone, sliding it back to silent, before heading upstairs.

Expecting Tristan to be alone, she opened the office door without knocking and walked in on a scene that she wasn't expecting. The unfamiliar men from earlier were sat on the left sofa, opposite Tristan. They were stashing small clear packets of round blue pills into two rucksacks, whilst Tristan was counting wads of cash into a suitcase. Fenik and Matthew were stood up opposite Morgan with their arms folded.

Everyone stared at Morgan when she entered the room.

"Sorry to interrupt, you said to come straight up. I didn't realise that you were busy."

Tristan signalled for her to join him on the sofa, zipped up the suitcase and handed it to Fenik. Standing with his hand stretched out, Tristan ended the meeting by announcing, "Our business is now concluded gentlemen, get in contact with Matthew when you sell out." The men rose immediately and shook Tristan's hand before Matthew escorted them out.

Tristan locked the office door and Fenik unzipped the suitcase. They both walked over to the sofa that had just been vacated and lifted it from either end. They then rolled back the rug to reveal a rough patch of carpet which had been cut. Fenik removed it, to reveal a hidden iron safe in the floor. Fenik stood up and turned around to face the wall. Tristan then used his body to hide the combination code from Morgan's view. They both emptied the stacks of money into the safe and then returned the room back to its original layout. Tristan unlocked the office door and Fenik left holding the empty suitcase.

As soon as the door closed, Tristan apologised for what Morgan had witnessed and kissed her. Anger had been building up in Morgan, but she didn't want to explode in front of Fenik. She didn't kiss him back; instead she remained as stiff as a board. Sensing Morgan was not her usual self, Tristan stepped back, not sure what he had done wrong. She unleashed upon him, "What the hell was that Tristan? You're involved in drugs?"

"It's not as bad as it seems," he insisted.

Morgan continued to talk louder than usual, trying to assert dominance over the conversation, "Not as bad as it seems, either you are a drug dealer or you aren't. It's quite simple! Which is it?"

Tristan started to stutter trying to find the right words to calm the situation down. Morgan wasn't impressed with his delayed response. Her mind was racing, she began punishing herself for getting emotionally involved, how stupid was she? She screamed at him, "My parents were killed by a meth addict, do you not know what damage drugs can do to families. Do you have no remorse?"

Tristan's expression changed and he went to move towards Morgan, before thinking better of it and retreating. "They're not that type of drug. I promise you. They're energy boosts, filled with caffeine to keep students awake. It enables them to party hard and still attend lectures."

Morgan looked at him like he was telling her that pigs could fly. Her tone was of disbelief and disgust as she challenged him, "So you're telling me that they are completely legal?"

"I mean they aren't government approved, but I assure you that there is nothing in them that's illegal." He seemed genuine, but Morgan was too riled up to stop the interrogation.

"Would you take one right now?"

"Yes, if I had any left but I just sold them all."

"How did you even get involved in this?"

"That's a much longer story," Tristan insisted.

Morgan sat down, crossing her arms and legs before responding, "I've got all night. Start explaining."

Tristan joined her on the sofa and held his head in his hands as he started explaining, "My brother was murdered last year in a hit and run. The police never gave us any answers and there were no leads. Then one day a Witch named Cordelia knocked on the front door and told us that she had a premonition of a supernatural war that would be a massacre for Witches and Lycans.

Vampires outnumber Witches and Lycans, but if we joined forces, together we would have the numbers and the power to defeat them. Vampires are just as strong as Lycans, but harder to kill. They have political power and enormous wealth. We needed a plan that meant we could go under the radar for some time, before the Vampires got suspicious.

Cordelia had a plan. She had created a caffeine supplement using magic that didn't harm humans only boost energy levels. If a Vampire drank a person's blood that had this supplement in their system, it would kill the Vampire and make it appear like an overdose.

I don't understand the magic or the chemistry behind it. She needed us to be the distribution network through the nightclubs. The money we are making from it is being invested into opening more clubs across the UK, to widen the distribution. I promise you that no one is getting hurt, other than Vampires." As Tristan finished he grabbed Morgan's hands, hoping that she believed him.

"I saw the Witch at your parents Halloween party, she was arguing with your brother and father. If you're working in partnership, what were they arguing about?" Morgan demanded.

Tristan was taken aback and looked slightly confused. He answered anyway, not wanting to challenge how Morgan knew, "She said that we're not working hard enough with the distribution network and she wants faster results. Tobias and my father don't like being accused of falling short on a deal. She tried to threaten them by showing the strength of her powers and warned them against making her an enemy."

Morgan's whole body relaxed in the seat. That did sound exactly like something Cordelia would do. She was a few years older than Morgan and had always been tyrannical. She was the daughter of the owner of the commune land and threatened more than one child with becoming homeless if they didn't let her join in games when they were young. Morgan was desperate to know if Aunt Winnie knew about this plan, or if it was something Cordelia had concocted on her own.

She had no reason to doubt Tristan and seeing Cordelia at the party did support his story. Morgan's mind was racing and she was now suspicious of Chief Commander Silas Nicolescu's involvement. "She said that Vampires were involved in your brother's murder, did she tell you who or why?"

"No, she only saw a shadow, but they bit him and took

some of his blood with them in a test tube. Why take it and not drink it, if it wasn't to study Lycan blood?" He looked genuinely emotional retelling the story of his brother's death and Morgan's fears melted away. She held him close, as she felt him choke back tears.

A knock at the door, followed by Fenik saying, "I'm going to bed now boss. I'll leave you to lock up," ended the embrace and the conversation.

Tristan rose, covering his face and disappeared into the other room. He returned quickly with his coat and Morgan could see that his eyes were slightly pink. He unlocked the office door and waited for Morgan to collect her belongings, before leaving the bar. Tristan rolled down the automated shutters, using the internal keypad and they left.

Tristan kept the car running outside Morgan's house, so she took that as a sign that he didn't want to come in. She kissed him goodbye on the cheek and headed inside.

She woke the next morning to a message from Steve, *'I need you at HQ Monday through to Wednesday next week, when it's half term. Monday 0930 in my office. The Commander wants an update.'* Morgan smiled, this was perfect timing. She wanted to read the reports on Timothy Lucas' murder and see if she could find out more. She wasn't keen on seeing the Chief Commander again, but he wouldn't know that she remembered the attack, so she had the upper hand.

By Friday night, the heated argument between Morgan and Tristan had been forgiven and forgotten. The usual flirty banter between the two continued throughout her shift and he asked her back to his, which she gladly accepted. They spent Saturday in bed, enjoying each other's company and neither wanted to leave when it was time for work. Morgan stayed over again that night and it wasn't until late on Sunday, that she told him that she would be travelling home for a few days as it was half term. Tristan offered to drive her but she dissuaded him, explaining that she had already purchased her train ticket and had coursework to complete on the journey.

Morgan woke early on Monday and packed a few essentials into a single suitcase. She dressed as Morgan Fletcher in a skull hoodie, baggy black trousers with chains and Dr. Martens. She took the first train to London and arrived at eight-thirty. She caught the underground line that stopped the nearest to her apartment and walked the short distance home. Once inside she showered and changed into her standard office attire.

By nine-twenty she had greeted Martha and was waiting in Steve's reception room. Steve opened the door at precisely nine-thirty and welcomed Morgan inside. He returned to his seat behind the desk, but Morgan stood until he gave her permission to be seated. Steve began, "I've been re-reading your reports. I can't help but think you are holding back. You're recounting the events and facts but you're not telling me your hunches. I value your assessment of these people and what you think is going on. Who do you think is the ring leader? This will help you to decide who to focus on and who to spend more time with. For example, the Halloween party, you were introduced to more of the family. Did anyone act suspiciously or give you a funny feelings?" Steve stared at her, waiting for a response.

"Something about Tobias Lucas put me on edge. He was very cold towards me. I don't think he trusts me," she replied.

"Could he be on to you?" Steve responded with concern, evident in his voice.

"No absolutely not, I just think he's suspicious of anyone who's new to the inner circle."

"Tread lightly with the brother but try and get invited to a family dinner, you need to get closer to Vincent."

"Yes sir," Morgan responded. "I have another line of enquiry that I would like to explore. Tristan opened up to me about his brother's murder. I would like to review the case. I believe it could be pertinent to our investigation."

Steve sat back in his chair as if to assess Morgan's intentions, "Of course, let me know if you need anything from me. The Chief Commander is due in the office Wednesday at one. I want a detailed report on my desk by five today. Include everything you have seen and feel about the inner and outer circle. We will review tomorrow."

Morgan stood and nodded, leaving his office. She grabbed a hot chocolate from the office machine and said hello to a few agents she knew on a superficial level, before settling down to an empty desk. She entered her ID into the computer and searched the database for information on the hit and run of Timothy Lucas. It took no time at all to review the local police investigation. Morgan downloaded a copy of the report and the forensic photos to a USB flash drive.

The photos were horrific. Timothy had been on a Triumph speed motorbike. His body was in the middle of a junction on a country road, with tyre marks visible on his torso over the leathers. The bike was a metre away from the body and black paint had transferred onto the side of the blue bike. The road markings indicated that the bike had been travelling at speed and he had tried swerving to change course several times. The photographs showed large puddles on the ground, indicating bad weather. The brakes on the other vehicle were not applied sharply enough to leave tyre impressions, which proved negligence if nothing else.

Emergency services had not been called until a passing motorist called in the incident at ten. The pathologist ruled that he died instantly after the incident, from internal bleeding and head trauma. However Morgan noted that this contradicted the statement from the paramedics, who said that his helmet visor was open when they arrived on the scene. The police statement from the witness who called in the incident also stated the visor was up and they only checked for a pulse on his wrist. Morgan listened to the 999 call recording, which supported this account.

The report stated that the weather had been

horrendous, with high winds and rain. Timothy was an experienced rider and had been coming home from a meeting in Coalville that had overrun. Weather had been ok when he left Coalville at eight in the evening and called home to say that he was on his way back. The police report stated that the widow was inconsolable and blamed herself for going to bed after the call, not realising her husband had not made it home.

The tyres and paint colour had been matched to a Ford Raptor truck. With the help of a hidden county council park camera, detectives had tracked down the truck via the number plate, to a vehicle reported stolen that day from a car park in Nottingham. From there the case had gone cold. Footage from surrounding areas had been collected, but no links to the stolen vehicle had been made.

Morgan stretched her legs by walking over to the machine for a cuppa soup. She settled back at her desk and watched the footage meticulously. The car park was very busy, but Morgan created a detailed spread sheet and logged each person that entered. She noted down what vehicle they drove and what time they exited. By three o'clock she decided to take a break and grabbed a much needed sugar hit from the vending machine.

She started on the report for Steve and emailed her analysis across just before the deadline. Morgan went into detail about her thoughts on all the main characters in Tristan's life that she had come in contact with. Notably her uneasy feeling about the Cane twins, Matthew Negus and Tobias Lucas. She outlined her next objective to get closer to Vincent Lucas and a few ideas she had to achieve that.

Morgan included her friendship with Jono and that she had introduced her housemate Molly to him. She detailed their new relationship and how she was using this as another way in to the inner circle. She felt guilty in exploiting her friendship, but she would not share any intimate details. Morgan of course, could not mention the supernatural discovery she had made. She chose to withhold the energy supplement information for now, choosing to believe Tristan that they were linked.

Morgan left the office at five-thirty, but took the USB flash drive home with her. That evening she continued to analyse the grainy car park footage. It wasn't until ten that she made a discovery. A brunette woman in a black raincoat walked into the car park at three-ten behind a family with a twin stroller. It appeared as if she was with the group but having studied the day's footage, she did not arrive with them. The family then leave in a BMW Mini at three-twenty.

Morgan knew that three adults and two child's car seats would have difficulty fitting in such a small car. Morgan recalled the Carmichael family who lived on the commune. When Morgan moved to live with Aunt Winnie they had a daughter who was three, they then unexpectedly had twins. They had to change their small hatchback to a people carrier, because they couldn't fit three car seats into the rear seat.

After logging everyone who came and went that day from the car park, Morgan was convinced that this mysterious woman was the phantom driver of the truck, which didn't leave the car park until four-thirty. Now she had a figure to retrace the steps of, she trawled through the town centre footage, which had been collected and linked to the file. It took another two hours until she spotted her.

The woman walked out of Marks and Spencer's, before disappearing off camera and then reappearing behind the couple as she walked into the car park. The strange thing was that she never entered the shop. Morgan watched all the footage from that day and then she saw it. The handbag she was carrying was a black Hermes Birkin, or a very good copy. Twenty minutes before the suspect walked out of the shop, a blonde woman in a beige raincoat walked into the shop with the same bag. She followed the blonde women through the town until she captured a good angle of her face for photo recognition software. She set the program running through every database on the system and crashed out, asleep on the sofa. When Morgan woke the next morning she was intrigued to see the program had come back with a classified notification.

Morgan could think of only three reasons for a classified file, an undercover agent, an informant or witness protection. She was happy with the progress she had made on the case and wanted to call Tristan with the news, but she couldn't. Morgan could never explain without outing herself and she wasn't ready to do that just yet. Maybe if she could solve his brother's murder and out the Chief Commander, he could forgive her. She wanted desperately to believe that their love could survive her deception.

She got ready quickly, choosing a grey trouser suit and then hurried into the office. Morgan went straight to Martha to check when Steve had a spare ten minutes. She was in luck he was free in fifteen minutes. She hung around Martha's desk, listening to the latest ideas for the office Christmas party. The door to Steve's reception opened, agent Mark Travis exited and nodded politely at them both. Morgan slipped through the door before it had chance to close and knocked on Steve's office door. "Enter," came back Steve's voice.

Steve immediately looked up as Morgan entered, clearly intrigued to see who his unannounced visitor was. Morgan explained her findings in regard to the open Timothy Lucas murder case and she opened her laptop to show the classified profile, facial recognition software had detected. Steve seemed genuinely interested and impressed in Morgan's findings, agreeing with her that it was suspicious that the profile was classified.

"Leave it with me, I will do some digging and find out why it is classified," as Morgan turned to leave he added, "I read your adjusted report, it's much better. Thank you. Be ready for when I call you into my office. I have a feeling the Commander will want to speak to you in person."

CHAPTER 11

Deep Undercover

Steve sat forward in his office chair and typed in his authorisation code into the facial recognition software. 'Access denied' flashed across the screen. He sank back into his chair and rang through to Martha. "Martha Hi, please call Luke from IT and have him come to my office as soon as possible." He sat mulling over the reasons as to why his access was denied and why the program didn't identify who placed the block. The only reason he could think of, was that the classified block was put on by someone of higher rank than him. It was rare that a senior officer would do such a menial task and it intrigued him. But who and why would they need to hide that they had placed a block on an agents profile. More importantly why was an agent stealing a vehicle and involved in cold blooded murder.

Within the hour, Luke from IT arrived and Steve explained the issue. Luke paired his laptop and spent fifteen minutes trying to lift the block, with no success. However, he could confirm the block was placed by Chief Commander Silas Nicolescu. The reason for the block was listed as 'undercover agent'.

Steve believed that he was a good judge of character and he had never liked the Commander. There was just something off about him, along with the fact he never seemed to age.

He always wondered how someone so young could hold such a senior position. Steve was suspicious by nature, which had made him a great detective and he was now very interested in the Commanders ascension to power.

Steve started jotting on his notepad, everything he knew of the Commanders previous roles and then used his computer to fill in the blanks, building a timeline. There were definitely some dubious promotions. He worked in various roles across Europe for most of his career, so it was difficult to pinpoint all of the positions he had held. His last post before being made Commander was in organised crime. Steve began searching for the undercover agent within that team.

He opened the employee database, where you review applicants for new roles, filtered out men, women older than forty and narrowed the search to organised crime employees. There were sixteen women in active service, with one on maternity leave.

Steve searched through the personnel files until he found her. She had a short brown bob, but it was definitely her. Her name was Irina Smirnov and she was a transfer from Russian Intelligence. Based on the dates in service, she joined the team after the Commander left organised crime. So the Commander would never have come into contact with her. This made it even more intriguing that he manipulated her file. Steve print-screened her profile and transferred it across to an empty USB flash drive.

Morgan was clock watching, the seconds hand ticked round and another minute passed. It was four-thirty and it wasn't respectable to leave the office until it reached five. All of a sudden, she saw Chief Special Agent Steve Rush stride through the main office. He walked straight over to the hot desk she was using and loudly announced, "Tomorrows meeting has been moved to eight-thirty, my office, be punctual."

He discretely slid a USB flash drive under her notebook,

whilst looking Morgan straight in the eyes. She understood the importance, "Yes Sir." She waited till the clock struck five and then packed her belongings into her laptop case, including the flash drive.

With nothing in the fridge to eat, she stopped off at her local convenience store to purchase dinner before heading home. As soon as she locked the front door, she turned on her laptop and opened the USB flash drive. It was an agents profile, her hair was different but it was her, the mystery woman who Morgan believed had committed the hit and run on Timothy Lucas.

Steve had uncovered her. Her mind started to race and anger was boiling over within her. Why would an agent murder someone in cold blood? She wanted to throw something in anger. Suddenly her dirty water glass from the previous day flew up into the air and smashed against the wall.

Morgan was startled. Had she done that? Whilst she stood there is disbelief, her phone rang, it was Aunt Winnie's personalised ringtone. She answered automatically, still slightly in shock. Aunt Winnie's voice bellowed through the speaker, "Are you ok? I got a sudden feeling that I had to call you? Heightened instincts are a Witches talent."

Morgan composed herself before answering, "Yes. I'm ok. I'm at home. I just found something out that made me really angry. I can't believe I'm saying this, but a glass flew into the air and smashed right in front of me."

There was a pause before Aunt Winnie responded, "It sounds like your powers are awakening. Powers are linked to your emotions. Try and avoid extreme emotions in public until you can control them. Telekinesis is one of our powers. You can practice by focusing on an object you wish to move."

Morgan thanked her Aunt for the advice and spent the rest of the evening trying to make objects around her apartment move, to no avail.

Her dreams that night were filled with visions of Irina. In one vision, Irina was nervous, constantly watching over her shoulder as she went about her daily life. At night she roamed the cobbled streets, until she decided on a victim to bite. In Morgan's dream, Irina was a Vampire. The dream repeated over and over through the night. Each time Morgan saw more details, the train station, tartan kilts in the windows of shops and a castle on a hill. Until she realised that Irina was in Edinburgh. Morgan had visited as a child with her mum and dad. She remembered the castle clearly.

Silas sat at his black marble desk in his home office relaxing in his black leather Chesterfield office chair, with a glass of Chianti. He pondered the approach he was going to take in tomorrow's meeting with Steve Rush and Morgan Hudson.

Steve was competent, but dull and lacked any original thought. However, Morgan still intrigued him. An agent was an odd line of work for a Witch. They were usually very in tune with nature, a bit hippy and stank of incense. Morgan didn't come across like that. Although, he conceded he had only met her a handful of times.

Since returning from Europe, he had read her background file and entrance transcripts a couple of times. She was an orphan and had gone to live with a relative as a child, so it was possible that she wasn't aware. What interested him most about Steve and Morgan was that over the past twenty-four hours they had both accessed agent Irina Smirnov's profile. Had Morgan worked out she was a Vampire? Or had they deduced that she was the one who murdered Timothy Lucas?

If they connected his blocking of her profile to the murder, they may realise that her actions were based on his orders. Silas was sure that he would find out tomorrow, he could read simple minded people easily. He drained his glass of wine and rose from his chair. Silas marched out of the study and across the vast open-plan living area of his rented house in

Weybridge Surrey, located an hour outside of central London.

The house was a perfect reflection of Silas' character. It was cold and bleak, made out of raw polished concrete with vast black framed windows. When approaching the house, a black dyed moat greeted you, with a concrete bridge leading to the enormous black front door. It was an impressive entrance. The house was cube shaped, with a flat roof. It had been built partially underground, so only the top floor was visible. The layout was open-plan and inside all the walls were polished concrete. A huge black marble island housed all of the kitchen appliances and a large white marble dining table mirrored the island. The only pops of colour came from the sofa and the odd piece of mounted artwork. Silas had rented it fully furnished, so could take no credit for the decor. Best of all, it was secluded and allowed Silas to live peacefully, away from prying eyes.

Just before midnight, his driveway camera sent him a notification of a car approaching. He had hired some evening entertainment and dinner, in the form of a high-class escort. She parked her black Porsche Taycan, then sashayed across the bridge to the front door. She didn't have to knock as Silas was waiting, ready to open the door as she approached. He had hired Rachael before, she knew the drill.

No pleasantries were exchanged. She undid her Burberry beige Macintosh and allowed it to fall to the floor. She strode up the stairs to the bedroom in just her black lace underwear, suspenders and Louboutin heels.

Everything in the bedroom was cream and it had plush thick carpet. Velvet curtains hung all around the room like wallpaper. Rachael knelt on the floor at the foot of the bed, head down and hands palm faced up, as if begging. Silas drew back a curtain to reveal a wall of sex aids. The wall held every toy imaginable including whips, chains, latex gear and clamps. He reached for the leather paddle and ordered his victim to climb onto the bed on all fours. Silas liked to inflict pain and humiliate, it helped him to climax.

Once he was finished with the paddle, he tied her ankles

together with leather shackles. He reached over and bound her wrists to her ankles, so she was face down on the bed. He repeatedly spat on her whilst hurling insults, before he entered her anus forcefully from behind.

Rachael knew not to fake screams of pleasure. Her client wanted her to feel pain. Silas knew if she faked the scream and hit her twice as hard the next time. He was rough and sadistic, but he paid well. In her line of work, there were worse clients. She had prepared in advance, using lube and a butt plug. As he reached climax he bit down on her neck and salivated over the thick warm gushing blood.

In that moment connected to her thoughts and memories, he found peace away from his own mind. He stopped himself before he drank too much blood. She was too good to waste and disposing of a body was an extra hassle that he didn't need.

Rachael passed out on the bed and he was secure in the knowledge that she wouldn't remember the biting when she woke. He undid the shackles and went back downstairs to work in his study.

Just before six he heard the tapping of heels on the marble flooring, before the front door locked shut. Rachael had left. Silas went upstairs to wash and change for the days meetings. He selected a grey tweed double-breasted, three-piece suit, with a white shirt and brown leather brogues. His driver arrived at seven and Silas strolled across the bridge to meet him. He continued his work in the back seat, whilst the driver drove him to the office.

Morgan was startled awake by the alarm that morning. She felt restless, like she hadn't slept at all last night. She showered and changed, selecting a plain navy suit and a red silk shirt from her closet.

Before getting on the underground, she grabbed a caramel Frappuccino and a blueberry muffin from her local coffee shop. She arrived at the office at eight-ten and headed straight for Steve's office. Martha let her into the waiting room, but stated that Steve had not yet arrived.

Steve appeared ten minutes later. He signalled to Morgan to wait in his reception. He unlocked his office, placed his bag behind his desk and hung up his coat, before joining Morgan back in the waiting room. "The meeting is in the Chief Commanders office," he stated, before marching out, past Martha towards the elevator.

The Commanders office was on the sixty-first floor. Morgan had never been there before. As they walked off the elevator, the Commanders PA greeted them warmly, before asking them to wait on the black sofa to the right of the elevator. They both sat down in silence.

At precisely eight-thirty the Commanders PA rose from her seat and knocked on the Commander's door. Morgan heard, "Allow them in." Before she saw the PA gesture them over, holding the door wide open.

Steve rose from his seat and strode across the lobby. Morgan followed, closing the door behind her. The Chief Commander was writing in his notebook and didn't look up to acknowledge them until the door latched closed.

"So update me? I want to know everything." He stared at Morgan and blatantly ignored Steve's presence in the room. Steve and Morgan were still standing, as the Commander had not notified them to sit.

Morgan repeated the information she had written in her report. The Commander stared at her, hanging on her every word. When she finished he asked, "How would you describe your relationship with Tristan Lucas?"

"We're more than friends now. He has introduced me as his girlfriend to his parents." She maintained eye contact as she spoke and tried not to blink too much.

"Are you in a sexual relationship?" He asked, as he licked the corner of his mouth.

Morgan struggled to keep her composure. "Not yet," she

lied, trying to steady her speech pattern. To make her story more believable she added, "It is heading that way." She hoped she sounded convincing.

Silas paused before responding. He was assessing her body language and any tell-tale signs of lying. Why would anyone introduce a partner to parents these days without being intimate? Maybe he thought they'd had the best night of his life and she had just bewitched him. The thought made him chuckle to himself. If she was making up her answers, she was a good liar.

"I want to know your plan for getting closer to the family."

Morgan repeated what was in her report nearly verbatim, whilst keeping eye contact with the Commander. When she had finished he finally acknowledged Steve and asked if he had anything to add. Steve supported Morgan's assessment and confirmed he did not. The Commander studied them both, before dismissing them from his office and turning his attention back to his computer screen.

In the lift Steve hand signalled for Morgan to return with him to his office. Morgan fell in line and followed him. Once alone in Steve's office, he mocked the last hour's events in a rant, before adding, "He was the one that put that confidentiality lock on her profile. What we need to discover is why would an officer of his level, who supposedly has no connections to Irina Smirnov, do that?"

Morgan took his statement to be rhetorical, as she wasn't able to enlighten the situation.

"This must remain between us two, no communication in writing on this matter. Only face to face, in private. I will continue investigating, you concentrate on the mission."

Morgan agreed by nodding and Steve dismissed her from his office.

Once back at her desk, she checked the train timetables to Nottingham and booked the three-fifteen from St Pancras.

She spent the next few hours replying to emails and tidying up her inbox. Morgan grabbed a light lunch and coffee from her local cafe on the way home. She packed her belongings and transformed back into Morgan Fletcher in time to catch her train.

Tristan had been texting her all day, but she kept the conversation light hearted. She wasn't ready to tell him about her discovery just yet. He agreed to meet her at the train station as it would be dark on arrival. She had missed him. More than ever she wished she was Morgan Fletcher. Life would be so much simpler.

As the train pulled into the station, she saw Tristan standing on the platform waiting for her, in casual jeans and a bright red Adidas hoodie. She ran off the train and jumped into his arms. He caught her effortlessly and they kissed each other passionately. When they finally parted, he grabbed her case handle. He began pulling it for her and placed his left arm over her shoulder. They walked back to the car like two teenagers hopelessly in love. Tristan drove back to his house, picking up a family KFC bucket on the way home.

They spent the evening catching up and kissing on the sofa. At eleven, Tristan rose from the sofa and peered out of the skylight. He turned to Morgan asking, "Will you follow me? No questions asked?" Morgan nodded.

Tristan led the way down the stairs, out the door and into the field adjacent to the house. Once they were standing in the middle of the field, out of shouting range from the house, Tristan turned to Morgan and held her hand. The full moon was high in the sky, casting a beautiful blue glow around them.

"I love you Morgan. I want you know that. In the light of the moon, I pledge myself to you and only you."

Morgan's heart was so full it nearly burst. It was so romantic! He loved her and she knew that he meant it. Her response escaped from her mouth before she had a chance to process it, "I love you too." She kissed him and he spun her around like a princess at a grand ball. They kissed passionately and any clouds in the sky vanished. The moon was alone in the sky, shining brightly upon them.

Neither of them were conscious that they had begun to levitate. They were three foot off the ground before either of them noticed. "What the hell?" Shouted Tristan suddenly. He clung onto Morgan, who was now as white as a sheet. Her secret was exposed!

Aunt Winnie had said no extreme emotions. Panic hit her! What else could she do except tell the truth. If he accepted her, it was one step closer to him knowing the real Morgan. Whilst nervously biting her lip she looked at him and focused on returning to the ground. They landed gently back on the grass, before she said, "I think I'm a Witch."

Tristan looked at her in disbelief, but didn't let go of their embrace. She felt safe in his arms, safe enough to tell him the whole story. Morgan explained that when he told her about the supernatural world, his description of Witches resonated with her and her upbringing at the commune. Her Aunt had confirmed her suspicions when she went to visit and ever since she had been trying to work out if she had any powers. She admitted to knowing but not liking Cordelia, which is why she had followed her into the garden and witnessed her disagreement with his family.

Morgan was subconsciously biting her lip again, waiting for him to speak. As if understanding her nervousness, he answered her unspoken question, "This changes nothing between us. I just wish that you had confided in me sooner. You can tell me anything."

If there was ever a moment to tell him the truth about Morgan Fletcher, now was the time. She looked into his gorgeous eyes and felt the love of his embrace. But she couldn't risk it. Not yet. She couldn't tell him. She was too afraid. They walked back to the house and fell asleep cradled in each other's arms.

Morgan woke to the smell of bacon frying. She tiptoed

out of bed and followed the smell to the kitchenette. Tristan was placing bacon into bread rolls. He turned to greet her as she approached, remarking, "Super-hearing, you can't sneak up on a wolf." He chuckled as he said it and Morgan knew that her admission last night hadn't changed a thing. They spent the day in their PJs, swapping childhood memories and silly anecdotes.

CHAPTER 12

Self-Discovery

Saturday's shift started like any other. Morgan was serving on the underground bar and Tristan was conducting another business meeting in the booth closest to the bar. Tristan's meeting ended and he stood up to shake hands with his guests before they left. Tristan remained at the table with the Cane twins and Matthew Negus. They appeared to be having a good evening, as every time Morgan looked over they were laughing.

The dance floor was fairly empty and Morgan had a direct line of sight to Tristan. He caught her looking at him once or twice and winked in her direction. She blushed at being caught and started to clean down the bar, emptying the drip trays attached to the pumps. The next time she looked over to the booth, a group of attractive women had joined the men.

A stunning dark skinned, leggy woman was sat next to Tristan, openly flirting. She was playing with her long braids and touching his arm, as she whispered in his ear. Jealously rose deep from within Morgan's gut. She was now staring at the pair. Tristan was smiling and it appeared to Morgan that he couldn't keep his eyes off of the mysterious woman.

Morgan was seething and her mind was racing. Why was he even entertaining this woman's affection? Morgan didn't understand the logic, he knew she was watching and yet he was openly flirting with another woman. Her jealousy was bordering on anger. As the unknown woman took a sip from her glass, she touched Tristan's cheek and in that split second, Morgan's emotions erupted.

The glass the woman was holding shattered in her hand. At the same time, hives started to appear on the woman's face and arms. Clearly feeling the irritation on her skin, the woman furiously started scratching. Tristan instinctively looked over at Morgan. She was glaring at him and did not look happy. He suddenly assessed the situation objectively. From Morgan's point of view, he was sat at a table with a group of attractive women and he was sat next to one of them laughing.

There was no way Morgan would know that the woman was Matthew's cousin, who was adopted into the family and brought up as his sister. She knew all about Lycans. Tristan had always known that she had a soft spot for him, but he had never crossed that line, in fear of Matthew's wrath more than anything.

Naomi, Matthew's cousin excused herself from the table and headed towards the door, presumably to the bathroom. Tristan crossed the dance floor over to Morgan. He placed his hands over hers and said, "I think you need to calm down. Come to my office." She followed him up to his office, breathing deeply.

He unlocked his office door and held it open for her. Once inside, he took her hand again as they both stood, "Nothing was going on. She's Matthew's cousin, who was brought up as his sister. I've known her since we were infants and nothing has ever happened between us."

"I didn't mean to, but when she touched your face, I just lost control." The guilt and embarrassment rose up in her cheeks until she was red faced.

"She said that I had an eyelash. I know it might have looked a little flirty, but honestly there has never been any attraction. Besides, Matthew would kill me."

Morgan's emotions switched from embarrassment to

anger and she raised her voice when she quickly responded, "So if she wasn't Matthew's family you would have tried it on with her?"

Tristan hadn't expected that retort, his attempts to calm her were backfiring. Her mood swings were giving him whiplash. She had gone from jealousy, to embarrassment, to anger in the space of minutes.

The energy in the room felt charged and the plant pot in the corner of the room suddenly caught fire. The whole plant was engulfed in flames, but the flames were localised to just the fern. Tristan grabbed her by the arms gently and looked directly into her eyes as he replied, "I didn't say that. What's wrong with you? You're very emotionally charged tonight. You need to calm down. I love you."

Morgan broke down in tears and held her head in her hands. She didn't know what the matter was. Her emotions were so up and down it was like she was a teenager again. The fire burnt itself out and the fern disintegrated into ash. She sat on the sofa with tears rolling down her cheeks. She just couldn't get it together.

Tristan sat next to her and she cuddled into him. "Let's look at the positives. I reckon you're going to be a pretty powerful Witch, when you learn to control those powers. I'm glad you're on our side," he joked. His smile brought her joy and she laughed along with him. "Are you feeling calmer now?" He asked.

"Yes, but can we just go home now? I'm exhausted and I don't trust myself around people."

"Of course, grab your things." Tristan grabbed his jacket from the other room and locked the office as they left.

They went back to Tristan's house. Once in bed she curled up in a ball and Tristan spooned her from behind. It only took minutes for her to fall fast asleep.

When she woke in the morning, Tristan was still

spooning her from behind and she felt loved. She gave herself a talking to, telling herself to not get so emotional today. She wriggled out of Tristan's arms and tiptoed to the bathroom. When she returned Tristan was awake. His hair was tousled and he had morning breath, but she didn't care. He looked gorgeous. She climbed back in bed and kissed him. Kissing led to sex and they made love all morning.

At midday Tristan went to make them a cup of tea, but realised that he was out of milk. He descended the stairs to raid his parent's fridge. His parents were in the kitchen making lunch and he stopped to chat with them before returning upstairs.

When he reappeared with milk and a packet of chocolate digestive biscuits in hand, he explained that his mum was hosting a big family dinner tonight. "I'd love you to join us?" He asked. Although she was nervous, she knew his family meant a lot to him. Plus she had told Steve that she would get to know his family more, so she agreed.

Morgan messaged Molly to tell her the news and that she wouldn't be home this evening for dinner. She asked Molly to check her shelf in the fridge for anything that might have gone mouldy. It was a while since she had been back to the house for more than just a quick change of clothes.

By six-thirty they were both dressed and ready for dinner. Tristan had told her to dress comfy and casual, but attending the dinner party in her sweatpants wouldn't give a good impression. She had deliberated between dressing in her style, or dressing more like Morgan Fletcher. If she dressed as Morgan Fletcher, she could focus on playing the character, rather than getting nervous at the gravitas of spending the first evening with his family.

However, she wanted his family to get to know the real her. She had agreed with Tristan in advance, that they wouldn't mention her being a Witch just yet. She decided to go as a hybrid of the two Morgan's. She chose to wear her denim jeans and a plain grey T-shirt. But she applied her now signature pink hair crayon through her fringe and applied her make-up, going light with the eye liner.

Tristan led her into the large cream dining room. Tobias, Charlotte and their two boys were already seated around the white-washed oak table. Tristan introduced the boys. Both were the spitting image of Tobias. The eldest was approximately ten and called Zachary. The younger was roughly five and named Nathan.

Nathan was picking his nose and eating it, whilst Zachary was playing his Nintendo switch, occasionally growling when he made a wrong move. Charlotte smiled warmly, but Tobias appeared to be grinding his back teeth.

Tristan pulled out a black velvet chair next to Charlotte and Morgan sat down. Tristan sat next to her and poured them both a glass of red wine from an open bottle on the table. Hannah and Jacob arrived next, choosing to sit at the end of the table, where the highchair had already been placed.

A few moments later Vincent arrived in the dining room, carrying a large serving dish with a roasted leg of lamb. It smelled delicious, as he placed it in the centre of the table. Marisa followed behind greeting Tristan and Morgan, as she placed roast potatoes and cauliflower cheese either side of the lamb.

Vincent started carving the meat and Marisa disappeared again, returning moments later with two gravy boats. She left the room a third time and returned with a large dish full of roasted vegetables. There were carrots, broccoli, parsnips and pumpkin puree. The lamb was beautifully pink and there was a moments silence as everyone started filling their plates.

Marisa started the conversation as she passed around a pot of homemade mint sauce, "It's so lovely that you could join us Morgan on such short notice."

"The pleasures all mine. Thank you for the invite," she replied politely. Everyone at the table, apart from the children, were looking directly at her and she felt quite self-conscious. She had always been a messy eater and readjusted the size of the food on her fork before taking a bite.

Vincent spoke next, addressing Morgan, "Tristan tells us you are living in shared housing, away from home for the first time. How are you finding your new life in Nottingham?"

Morgan responded politely and explained she was enjoying the change. A loud burp came from the other end of the table and Hannah apologised to the group for little Jacob's behaviour. Nathan was laughing and the boys started a burping competition, however Tobias ended it with a stern look at his sons.

Tobias decided that it was his turn to quiz Morgan. "Where are you from originally, I can't place the accent?"

"Chelmsford originally, but then I moved to Great Yarmouth," Morgan replied.

"Why did you decide to go to Nottingham University?" He asked next.

As confidently as she could, Morgan answered, "It had the best course for me."

Tobias had prepared a barrage of questions and started firing them out one by one at Morgan. So what made you want to go University as a mature student? What were you doing before? How do you plan to use your degree after you've finished University? Do you plan to live in Nottingham after University? What's your back up plan if physiotherapy doesn't work out?

She answered them one by one as they were asked until he said, "Are you close to your parents?"

"They were killed in a car crash when I was eleven, but we were close." As Morgan responded the atmosphere in the room changed. She looked to Tristan for support, to stop this endless grilling. She knew the impact that statement would have around the room. From the look on everyone's face, she could tell that they were reflecting on their own recent tragic loss. The room went silent.

Charlotte who sat next to her, grabbed her hand and said, "I'm so sorry for your loss. I'm very close to my own parents and I couldn't imagine the pain at such a young age." Marisa excused herself on the premise of filling up the gravy boats and Vincent offered seconds of Lamb around the table.

Tobias remained quiet for the rest of meal and Tristan started a light hearted conversation. Hannah eventually joined in the discussion, over homemade lemon meringue pie. They retired to the lounge for coffee and Hannah sat next to Morgan on the cream sofa.

Hannah tapped Morgan on the arm and quietly shared her heartfelt sympathies for the loss of Morgan's parents. Hannah appeared on the verge of tears and was completely sincere. Morgan longed to share her discovery, but she couldn't, not yet.

Apart from Tobias, who clearly had a vendetta against her, Morgan thought Tristan's family were really quite lovely. Marisa passed around mugs of coffee and a plate of shortbread biscuits. The children were playing together on the carpet.

Suddenly, Jacob snatched a toy from Nathan, did a backwards somersault and transformed into a small grey wolf, snarling at Nathan. Hannah ran forward and scooped up Jacob protectively in her arms. Tobias stood up defensively and Marisa's eyes widened in panic. Everyone was staring open mouthed at Morgan. After a few seconds their faces turned to confusion at Morgan's failure to react.

Tristan interjected, "Morgan is aware of our abilities." Relief passed across the women's faces, but concern and anger rose in Tobias'.

"You've only been dating for two minutes. How do you know you can trust her? How naive are you?" Tobias exclaimed.

Tristan stood up and squared up to his brother. Vincent rose from his seat and demanded his sons sit down. They both obeyed their father.

"I'm sure Tristan had his reasons," Vincent said calmly,

looking to his son for clarification.

They had agreed not to discuss it and Morgan believed that Tristan would protect her secret, but she owed his family the truth.

"A few weeks ago a Vampire bit me and left me in the street outside the bar. Tristan found me and brought me back here. When I woke up he explained everything about the supernatural world. It led me to realise something about myself, which I have only just shared with Tristan. I'm a Witch. I'm still learning about myself and I have very little control over my powers. Last night I had several embarrassing public outbursts myself."

Marisa dropped the plate of biscuits on her lap and everyone looked shocked at Morgan's admission. "I knew it! She's in league with Cordelia. It's a trick. You've been enchanted Tristan," bellowed Tobias.

Both brothers stood again and Vincent leapt in-between them, with his hands on both son's chests.

Morgan pleaded, "I knew nothing about Cordelia until I saw her at the Halloween party and I spied on you in the garden. I do know her but we have never been friends."

Tobias stormed out of the room and Charlotte made her excuses before hurrying after him. Hannah politely said goodbye and carried the now human Jacob home in her arms. Marisa was the next to make her excuses and ushered the young boys into the kitchen, to help her wash up.

Vincent, Tristan and Morgan were left alone in the living room. "I'm sure you can understand our concern. We do not usually mix with other supernaturals," stated Vincent.

Tristan spoke first to defend their relationship. "Father you told me, that when I find love I should grab it with both hands and never let go. I've found true love with Morgan. Will you accept us? Tobias will follow your lead."

Vincent placed his hand on Tristan shoulder and looked at them both. "You have a good heart Tristan. I will support your judgement, but it will take more than my cautious approval to win over your brother. He does not trust Witches." With that he left the room and they were alone.

The minute Morgan had left his office last week, Silas had ordered the IT department to activate the tracker on Morgan's agent phone, even when it was switched off. She had barely returned to her shared housing. She had spent all her time at the Lucas family home, yet she had not submitted any sound recordings of her week, other than when she was working in the bar.

The music echoed so much down the speaker that the audio was hard to listen to and any conversation was unclear. She logged in everyday as required, but gave no hint that her activities were pertinent to the investigation.

It was Saturday night and he watched the tracker all evening from the comfort of his home office. She travelled from the bar in Nottingham back to the Lucas family home slightly earlier than the previous night. By midday on Sunday the tracker had still not moved and the phone had not been turned on to record.

He decided to act. He grabbed his long leather coat, from the coat stand at the front door and removed his Ferrari car key from the rack. He pressed the garage unlock button on the control panel and the garage door automatically opened. He entered his rosso corsa Ferrari FF and drove it out onto the driveway, before locking up the garage and the house.

Silas drove the one hundred and forty-five miles to Morgan's accommodation, without stopping. He drove at speed and arrived in just over two hours. He parked slightly down the street, but so the front door of the house was fully visible and waited.

After a couple of hours, the only activity he had witnessed was a petite blonde arriving back from a supermarket, laden with shopping bags. No one else had entered or left. The sun had nearly set and Silas decided to approach the house.

He knocked on the door and the petite blonde answered. "Good evening," he greeted her, "I was looking for Morgan. I'm her uncle and was just in the neighbourhood, so thought I would pop in for a visit. Is she here?"

Molly was lured in by his charming smile. "No she's at her boyfriend's house, having dinner with his family right now. I'm on my own. Everyone else is busy tonight." Her words were music to his ears. He pushed his way through the door, slamming it shut and bit down on her neck, until she went limp in his arms.

The blood was a benefit, what he wanted was her memories. When he finished with her, he laid her on the sofa and turned on the TV. She would wake believing that she had fallen asleep watching a soap opera. He let himself out the house and returned to his car to ponder his next move.

Morgan had quite clearly been hiding a lot of information, most notably her intimacy with Tristan Lucas. Was she playing both sides of the investigation, with her own ulterior motives in mind? Or had she genuinely fallen in love with this Lycan? Either way he was seething that a Witch had gotten the better of him and lied to his face.

CHAPTER 13

A Brash Move

Silas returned to his car and flicked through the file on the passenger seat. Morgan's next of kin was listed as her Aunt, a Winifred Morgana. He programmed her address into his sat nav and followed the route that it directed.

He arrived in just under three hours and parked his car on a secluded side street nearby. The address was clearly some sort of Caravan Park. He waited until midnight to make his move. The campsite was surrounded by a tall hedge. He jumped over it with ease. Silas stealthily walked the parameter, hiding in the shadows to avoid cameras. Vampires had excellent eye sight so his vision wasn't impaired by the dark.

There appeared to be a loose sense of order to the numbering of the static caravans. It took a minute for him to get his bearings and head in the right direction. He approached a row of older looking caravans at the back of the park. His destination, number two-hundred and thirteen had a little picket fence and flowers had been grown all around the static caravan, a metal mail box said 'Morgana' on the side.

The lights were off, so Silas quietly walked around to the back of the caravan to see if he could peer into any windows. He couldn't see anything, so instead he placed his ear to the rear window and listened. He filtered out the sounds of the night. An owl was hooting in the distance and a mouse ran out from under the caravan. He could hear a single heart beating the other side of the window.

The caravan was old, with rust in several places. It didn't appear to have an alarm system. He felt around the window ledge and gave the seal a pull. The window creaked and budged slightly. He used more force and it came away in his hand. Silas placed the window under the caravan and leapt through the hole.

The woman asleep in bed woke up startled. He lunged at her, roughly biting her neck until she passed out in his arms. Silas carried her out of the door and jumped over the hedge behind the caravan, carrying the woman like a new-born. He followed the hedgerow back in the direction of his car.

After climbing over a stile and jumping over a fence, Silas eventually came to a built up area with houses. They were the same design as the ones he parked near and it only took him a few moments to get his bearings. He located his car and placed Aunt Winnie in the boot. He laid the back seats down in order for her limp body to fit inside when he closed the car boot. Silas set his sat nav to home and began driving.

It took him slightly longer to return home as he didn't want to arouse suspicion by speeding. His guest was still unconscious. Silas threw her onto his shoulder and carried her into the house. The pantry would be the perfect place to house her. It had no windows and was under the staircase. As a Vampire he took little enjoyment from eating and didn't need food for sustenance, so the pantry was empty.

He dumped Winifred on the floor and headed upstairs for restraints. His personal sadism collection would be useful. He used a ball gag to ensure she couldn't chant any spells and used rope to tie her ankles and hands. He secured an eye mask over her eyes with brown parcel tape. He was a fan of parcel tape. He loved the screams as he ripped it off, pulling all the hairs off a victim's skin. He tied a rope around the double door handles to the pantry, making it a secure prison. He hadn't slept a wink in days, so decided to rest for a few hours upstairs before work.

Morgan woke in the middle of the night with a sickening feeling. She had been having an awful dream where Aunt Winnie had been attacked in the alley outside Wild. It was a flashback to her attack and Chief Commander Silas' face loomed over her as if she was a victim again. She felt the fear, the pain and a cold chill.

Tristan stirred next to her, so she settled back on the pillow and tried to fall asleep. Her dreams were haunted all night. She tossed and turned, eventually sneaking into the living room at five with her mobile. She called her Aunt Winnie but there was no answer. She played a game on her phone to pass the time. She called Aunt Winnie every thirty minutes until Tristan woke at eight.

Aunt Winnie was usually an early riser. It was Monday and she always took part in sunrise yoga. Morgan was concerned, but she got ready for University and Tristan drove her to her lecture. At lunch she called again, with no luck.

She messaged Tristan to confirm that she was getting the bus home with David and Phil. Once home she tried repeatedly to get hold of Aunt Winnie, but she received no response. She hadn't copied any other people from the commune's numbers over into either of her phones. So she went on the internet and found the holiday park customer services number. It was after six so she left a voicemail, with her new personal number, asking them to call her back. Michelle Murphy ran the reception team, she was conscientious and hard-working, so Morgan was confident she would hear back tomorrow.

That night her dreams haunted her again. Over and over she saw the Commanders face and felt the cold damp floor of the alley beneath her. It was like she was reliving the attack with all her senses. She smelt the same damp musk odour, tasted blood in her mouth and felt rain on her cheeks. She woke in a cold sweat at four in the morning and decided to make a cup of coffee. She opened her laptop and started on her next assignment, trying to busy her brain.

She heard movement in the house around seven, so she packed away her laptop and headed for the bathroom to take a shower. She went to University on the bus with Molly and George. They were having a lively discussion about a reality show love triangle. Morgan was extremely tired so didn't join in the conversation that much, but nodded in the right places.

Morgan's phone rang just after her first lecture had started. Embarrassed she excused herself, explaining it was a family emergency. It was unmistakably Michelle's voice, but she started babbling so fast that Morgan could only understand every other word. "Slow down please, I can't understand you. Did you say Aunt Winnie is missing?"

Michelle slowed down but Morgan could still hear the panic in her voice. "We think she's been kidnapped, the window was removed from her bedroom and her bed is unmade. No one has seen her since Sunday evening."

Fear hit Morgan in a huge wave. "I'm on my way, don't touch anything." She hung up and ran for the bus. Once aboard she rang Tristan, briefly explained the situation and asked him to meet her at her house, as soon as possible.

Tristan arrived ten minutes after she got home. In that time she had changed into jeans, trainers and a hoodie. She had filled her rucksack with road trip snacks, her laptop and both phones. She programmed Aunt Winnie's postcode in the Lamborghini sat nav and Tristan set off at speed, breaking every speed limit.

They arrived in less than three hours and Morgan instructed Tristan to pull up in the staff car park by reception. His car was too low to drive on the rough dirt track on site. Morgan led the way to her Aunt's caravan on foot, running all the way.

There was a small group around the caravan including

Cordelia, who stood in a protective stance, with her palms open when she saw Tristan approach.

"He's with me Cordelia. He's here to help me my find my Aunt. What do we know?"

Cordelia continued to glare at Tristan as he joined Morgan at the rear of the caravan. Michelle and Mr Hanley explained what they had found and showed Morgan the window that had been removed. Tristan knelt down next to the window and addressed the group, "Do you mind if I sniff around?"

Morgan indicated for him to do so. He smelled the rim of the glass window on the ground first and then around the open window. Tristan jumped effortlessly into the opening and Michelle let out a gasp. He sniffed the bedding and turned back to Morgan. "It was a Vampire. I can smell the undeniable stench."

Michelle gasped again, holding her head in her hands. Mr Hanley looked very concerned and placed his arm around Michelle's shoulders.

Cordelia appeared next to Morgan. "I can try a locate me spell, but it would work better if we knew who took her so I can visualise them. Any ideas?" She asked, directing her question at both Morgan and Tristan.

Morgan looked at Tristan, now was not the time to worry about giving away her undercover secret. Aunt Winnie's life meant more to her than that and if it was the Commander then this was her fault. "Could it be the Vampire that attacked me?" Morgan asked Tristan.

"It could be, the scent does seem familiar but I can't be certain."

Morgan opened her laptop and entered the employee database. She typed in the Commander's full name and his profile appeared. She showed Cordelia his image and she nodded. Cordelia drew a pentagram inside a circle on the ground in white chalk. She stood in the centre of it and started chanting. Her eyes rolled back into her head and she levitated three feet off the ground.

Morgan closed her laptop and zipped it back in her rucksack. Tristan jumped back through the gaping hole in the back of the caravan. "What did you show her?" He asked Morgan.

"His image, I've been doing some investigating of my own. His image haunts me in my dreams." She remembered the dream she had on Sunday night and wondered if it wasn't at dream at all, but a message from Aunt Winnie. She tried to recall the details.

Tristan hugged her from behind, clearly feeling guilty about Morgan's admission. Cordelia came out of her trance and requested a pen and paper. They entered Aunt Winnie's caravan and Morgan hurried to fetch what Cordelia needed. Tristan went to sit at the dining table opposite Cordelia, but the look of wide eyed disbelief she gave him caused him to back off and he retreated to the doorway. He wasn't afraid of her, but he was trying to keep the peace.

Morgan sat next to Cordelia who began to sketch. First a square building with lots of windows and what appeared to be a moat around the outside. Next was lots of lines, it looked a bit like the London underground map. When she finished Morgan was still none the wiser as to what Cordelia had drawn. She looked confused at Cordelia who explained, "It's an aerial road map. We need a map to compare it to. Do you have one?" Morgan shook her head.

Tristan piped up, "I have one in the car. I'll go get it." Tristan ran at full speed back to his car and retrieved the map from his car boot.

"Let's start near London," Morgan advised. She knew the Commander must live somewhere local to the office given he was in the office most days. Tristan pulled out several pages to separate them and all three of them poured over the maps, looking for a match to Cordelia's sketch.

After twenty minutes Tristan said, "I think I've found it. I think it's Weybridge. Look at this line here where it intersects this one. It's a match for the M25 crossing the M3 and down here you can see the M25 meeting the A3."

Both Cordelia and Morgan studied the two maps and agreed. Morgan pointed at two shaded blobs on the sketch, "The two reservoir's match too. What now?" Both Tristan and Morgan looked to Cordelia for answers.

"We need to get to Weybridge before I try more magic."

"We came in Tristan's car but it's only a two-seater," Morgan replied.

Cordelia placed a dot on the map and a dot on the sketch in the same spot.

"Meet me here, as fast as you can," Cordelia said, pointing to the dot on the map. She left the caravan with the sketch. Mr Hanley had finished boarding up the broken window and Morgan used her own keys to lock up the caravan.

As Tristan started the engine of his car, Cordelia zoomed past them in a retro lime green VW Beetle. She turned the corner, drove off the park and onto the main road a lot faster than an old car should. Morgan would not have been surprised if magic was assisting her speed.

As soon as they were on the main road Tristan opened up the engine as Morgan programmed the sat nav using the map coordinates. Tristan put some music on to pass the time, but Morgan was lost in thought and guilt. She would never forgive herself if Aunt Winnie was hurt because of her. Aunt Winnie must be petrified.

Just before the sun rose that morning, Silas showered and changed into grey suit trousers with a white shirt, ready for a day at the office. His guest would still be out cold from the attack, but he couldn't help taking a peak at her before he left for work. He undid the rope and opened the pantry door. She was in exactly the same spot on the floor that he left her in a few hours earlier. Silas watched her for a few moments contemplating what he would do to her later. There was no point doing anything whilst she was unconscious. He enjoyed fear in his victim's eyes and painful screams too much. He secured the door again, before leaving the house.

Silas struggled to keep focused in his boring and predictable meetings that day. His mind was plotting all the fun sadistic torture he could perform to extract information from the Witch. As he left the office for the day, he took a banana and an apple from the fruit bowl in reception. He would use them as rewards for good behaviour, to assist in his interrogation.

Silas arrived home at eight. The Witch would be awake now, scared and hungry. He took a bottle of still mineral water out of the fridge. He placed his suit jacket on the door handle and untied the rope around the pantry door. He approached Aunt Winnie.

"How do you like your stay?" He asked mockingly.

Knowing she couldn't respond with a ball gag in her mouth, his question was rhetorical and he laughed. "There's no point in shouting. We are completely alone. I will remove the gag if you promise to speak only when spoken to. Any hint you are casting a spell and I will snap your neck in an instant." He leaned forward and untied the gag. "I will reward answers with water and if you please me I will bring you food."

Aunt Winnie was terrified, she had only caught a glimpse of her attacker, but when she woke she had spent all her energy trying to send the image to Morgan and her friends. She knew he was a Vampire and would think she did not remember the attack, so she would need to play dumb. She also figured it was too much of a coincidence that Morgan was attacked by a Vampire whilst befriending a Lycan and now she had been kidnapped in the dead of night. She would need to be smart with her answers, if she was to survive this. She had very few powers, but he clearly didn't know that and she hoped she could use that to her advantage.

Silas began his interrogation, "You're here because your niece Morgan Hudson interests me. Does Morgan know she is a Witch?" Aunt Winnie stayed silent.

"Dying today will not save your niece!" Silas reminded her.

Aunt Winnie's throat was so dry, that when she spoke her voice was quiet and hoarse, "Her mother didn't want her to know." Silas bent down and poured water into Aunt Winnie's mouth. It was cool and refreshing. Aunt Winnie savoured it, licking her lips to get every drop.

"What are her powers?" He asked eager to know the answer.

"She doesn't have any. You have to practice and be in tune with magic for it to develop," Aunt Winnie answered.

Silas bent down again and tilted more water into Aunt Winnie's mouth. "Is she in love with a Lycan?" The question threw Aunt Winnie off guard and of course her immediate reaction served her well. Her body shook at the thought of an interracial relationship. She had never heard of such a thing. Silas saw her subconscious body reaction and believed her when she replied, "I know nothing about any Lycan."

This kidnapping was proving to be pointless, so Silas changed his line of questioning. "What do you know about the recent Vampire murders?"

"Nothing, why would I?" She responded truthfully. Aunt Winnie wasn't a Witch of great power and therefore wasn't a member of the Witch council. She knew nothing about the alliance. Silas believed her, but he had been lied to by a Witch before.

He was getting bored with this interrogation. He decided to push his luck and assert his dominance. "How many Witches are in your coven?" He asked in a disgusted tone, "Tell me truthfully, or I will rip your head off your shoulders."

Aunt Winnie had a split second to answer, did she exaggerate or underplay it. She decided to underplay it, hoping that if he returned to the commune, he would do so unprepared. "There are a few families that live at the holiday park all year round. Morgan and I are the last of our great family," she answered.

"How many is a few? Your answer will determine if you leave here today," Silas asked menacingly.

She pleaded with him to set her free before answering, "Five families are left." She bent her head low and started to sob. It wasn't hard to act frightened and dismayed given her current situation. He tilted her head back and tipped the remaining water into her mouth. He then fitted the ball gag back into place.

"I'll return with food soon." Silas thought he would give her hope. It would make her more amenable to his desires later.

He didn't believe that there were only five families, but it did confirm that there was an active coven living at that holiday park. She wasn't just a lone Witch. Silas needed to report back to Alexander and start his own investigation into the coven.

Silas locked up the pantry again, put on his suit jacket and marched to his home office to call Ivan. The phone rang several times before Ivan's distinct voice answered, "Ciao mio figlio." (*Hello my son*)

Silas answered in his native tongue. "Padre, I have discovered the location of a coven of Witches. I can easily insert a human plant to feedback numbers. Will you seek Alexander's approval?"

"I will," Ivan answered, "Good work Silas. Ciao."

Silas didn't need Ivan's praise but he enjoyed it all the same. Ivan was well connected and loyal. He had intervened several times on his behalf to ensure his assignments suited Silas' ambition; especially as Silas wasn't good at learning languages. He didn't want to look a fool in front of the council members, by being assigned to a country where he couldn't speak the language. Being immortal meant you had to make allies. Ivan had taught him that. Silas was keen to make

Alexander an ally.

An hour passed before Silas received a text message from Ivan with one word *'Procedere'* (*proceed*). Silas smiled a devious grin and set to work, organising an undercover operation on a suspected meth lab at the holiday park. By one in the morning he had compiled a brief, fake witness statement's and arranged a meeting at ten with Steve Rush to assign an undercover agent to the mission.

Now it was time for some fun. A wide sadistic grin spread across his face. He walked towards the pantry and removed the rope. The Witch was lying on the floor, trying to sleep. He marched into the room and lifted the Witch with ease over his shoulder. She was startled and her body tensed in his arms, but she remained silent. He carried her upstairs to his bedroom. He threw her down on the bed. Her breathing was heavy. He couldn't risk her casting a spell and had to leave the ball gag in place, but he was desperate to see the fear in her eyes.

He ripped off the parcel tape, ensuring it ripped out clumps of hair from her scalp. He pulled back the eye mask and her green eyes locked onto his. The panic in her eyes was delectable. She watched him walk around the room. He moved the curtain wall behind the bed, where a headboard would usually be. Behind the curtain was an elaborate metal frame complete with restraints. He looked back at his victim to ensure she was watching. She was, her eyes were wide and tears had started to form.

He dragged her by her hair, from the middle of the bed to the wall. He flipped her over and untied the ropes binding her hands. She tried pitifully to fight him but his superior strength dominated over her. She managed only a few scratches before he smacked her across the face so hard she was knocked unconscious.

She was only out cold for a few minutes, but in that time he had managed to attach her upright to the wall contraption. He used a spreader bar to keep her legs wide apart and he had ripped her clothes off her so she was completely naked.

As she slowly regained consciousness and lifted her head, Silas watched her from across the room. He had moved the bed to the side and was enjoying the view. He wondered whether Alexander or Ivan had ever kept a Witch captive. It took Aunt Winnie a matter of moments to assess the situation. This Vampire was sadistic and thrived on pain and fear. She needed to be strong and resilient.

Silas opened the curtain where he kept his whips. He reached for a red leather flogger and thrashed it against his guest's breasts. He saw her body tense and heard muffled whelps of pain, as she tried to hold back her screams. The gag prevented any loud cries of pain, which frustrated Silas. When her chest was red raw, he selected a brown leather riding crop and whipped it against her thighs. When he was bored with that, he moved onto a bamboo cane, hitting it against her shins until they bled. Aunt Winnie kept her eyes tightly shut, even though he shouted at her to open them. She knew that he wanted to see her fear and that was the only power she had in this situation.

After an hour of torture, Silas was enraged. Without hearing her screams or seeing the fear in her eyes, he could not get aroused. This had never happened to him before, he felt impotent. He slapped the Witch unconscious again with one simple swing of his palm. Silas removed her from the restraints and dressed her in a black towel dressing gown, so she didn't get hyperthermia. He tied up her wrists and ankles again. Then he carried her downstairs, locking her in the pantry.

Silas spent the rest of the early hours in his study, reading human anatomy and medieval torture books. He was devising how best to cut out a tongue, so the victim stayed alive and how to force eyelids open, so a victim had to watch. He settled on slicing the eye lids off. Silas would need substantial pain killers and some medical equipment to ensure the Witch stayed alive. At six he left his study, showered and dressed for the day. He left the house without checking on the Witch.

When Silas arrived at the office he called special agent Vincenzo Leonardo and ordered him to his office immediately. Vincenzo was a low level, young Vampire at just thirty years old, but was excellent at languages. He had just been stationed in England under Silas' watch and inserted into Steve Rush's team. Silas had taken an instant dislike to him, but enjoyed making him carry out menial tasks, where he could assert his own dominance. Silas spoke in Italian and handed Vincenzo a shopping list, warning him to be discrete and make the purchases untraceable. He was to deliver the items to Silas' address tomorrow evening. Vincenzo nodded and left Silas' office to carry out his assignment.

The coordinates led Morgan and Tristan past a library, through a small high street, then into a residential area. They pulled up outside a gate to a medium sized country park. Cordelia's car was already parked up across the street. Tristan exited the vehicle first and assisted Morgan.

The VW Beetle was empty so they walked through the old Victorian black gate into the park and surveyed the grounds. It was a wide open space with trees around the edge. In the centre of the lawn was Cordelia, sat crossed leg with her arms stretched up to the sky, looking like she was conducting a yoga pose.

As they approached they could see Cordelia's eyes were closed and she was chanting. When they were approximately two metre's away, Cordelia spoke without opening her eyes. "Morgan do as I do and take my hands." Morgan obeyed. "Picture your Aunt in your mind. Our words will be stronger together. Chant after me to form a round," Cordelia instructed. "Someone cherished was taken, please let their life not be forsaken. Drawing on all our senses long forgot, to guide us to her spot. We call upon our ancestors from the past, to help us in this spell we cast." Morgan closed her eyes and repeated after Cordelia three times.

Tears started to stream down Morgan's face and the heavens opened. Rain poured down from the sky, even though no clouds were visible. Tristan and Cordelia looked up at the sky, realising this was no normal weather pattern. The sun was still high in the sky and a rainbow formed. "Follow that rainbow!" Cordelia exclaimed, pointing in the direction of a row of houses and ran towards her car. Tristan and Morgan followed.

They reached the car in a matter of moments and Tristan followed the arch of the rainbow, behind Cordelia's green Beetle. It led them out of the small town centre into a more rural area. The houses were large with gated entrances and spaced further apart. Soon they were far from houses and heading towards farmers' fields. It was early afternoon and the sun was low in the sky, blinding them as they drove. The rainbow disappeared behind a large hedge and Cordelia stopped abruptly. It was a good job Tristan had fast reflexes and sports car brakes, otherwise he would have crashed into the Beetle. Cordelia exited her car and signalled for them to follow. As a threesome they walked the length of the hedge until they came to an iron gate.

Tristan pointed to a camera above the gate watching the road. He mouthed, "Wait here," and ran back to his car. When he returned he had a black woolly hat in his hand. "I'll jump the hedge back there and cover the camera lens with this hat. You can then climb the gate." The women nodded and within a matter of seconds, Tristan had jumped over the hedge. He placed the hat over the camera and made a bird tweeting sound as a signal, in case the camera had listening capabilities.

The women started climbing the gate and Tristan helped Morgan over the other side. Cordelia gave him a look that warned him from offering her any assistance. Tristan led the way down the sweeping hedgerow until it opened into a large driveway. An impressive square house lay beyond a concrete bridge. What appeared to be black water in two ponds separated the driveway from the house. "She's inside, I can sense her pain," announced Cordelia.

Tristan could see the doorbell camera and knew they were being filmed. They needed to act quickly. It was still daylight and as no one had come to greet them, he was willing to take the gamble the house was empty, apart from Aunt Winnie. Tristan ran at the front door with his full force. It tore off its hinges and slammed to the floor with a deafening sound. Tristan landed on top of the door, as it slid across the concrete flooring. If anyone was inside, the element of surprise was definitely gone.

Morgan shouted, "Aunt Winnie," as loud as she could, several times.

Tristan shouted, "Quiet!" So he could use his sensitive Lycan hearing to listen for any clues of Aunt Winnie's location. He heard a distant rhythmic banging, like a door being hit. He followed the sound towards the staircase. He spotted a door with a rope wrapped around handles. He untied the rope and ripped open the door. Morgan and Cordelia were right behind him. Lying by the door on the floor was a red headed woman bound and gagged in a black dressing gown.

Morgan screamed out, "Aunt Winnie," and ducked under Tristan's arm, to hug her Aunt. Aunt Winnie was crying tears of happiness as Morgan embraced her. Tristan bent down and carefully untied the rope restraints, to free Aunt Winnie's limbs. Morgan unbuckled the ball gag and threw it to the ground in disgust. Tristan helped Aunt Winnie to her feet but she felt too weak to walk or speak and she collapsed in Tristan's arms. He scooped her up and carried her as they all fled the house.

When they reached the gate, Tristan placed Aunt Winnie on the ground and ripped apart the iron metalwork with his bare hands. He jumped up, snatching his hat back off the camera, before picking up Aunt Winnie and heading for the car. He placed Aunt Winnie on the back seat of Cordelia's car and instructed Morgan to ride with Cordelia back to the commune. Tristan confirmed he would follow behind them. Cordelia set off at lightning speed and Tristan only just managed to keep up with them.

Silas returned to his office after his last appointment of the day. It was a particularly dull meeting with the finance department about extending the budget for undercover operations. He checked his mobile phone to see several home alarm alerts. He checked the live stream and saw nothing unusual on the gate or front door cameras.

Silas played back through the footage, to the time the alarm notification sounded and swore loudly at the scene unveiling before his eyes. He picked up a glass award for excellence from his bookcase and threw it at the door. It smashed through the wooden panel leaving a gaping hole. He heard the award smash into pieces on the reception floor, followed by a woman's shriek. Silas grabbed his briefcase and stormed across the reception area to the elevator in a fit of rage. No one dared to approach him. His fury was etched into his face.

CHAPTER 14

Fire And Ice

Cordelia called ahead to her mother, to request she cast strong protection spells all around the complex. As it was winter the park was closed to holiday makers and this made it easier to cast additional enchantments. The gates that were usually open were now locked and security was stationed at the entrance. Ralph, the guard, opened them as Cordelia approached. She wound down her window and told him Tristan would arrive soon. Ralph waved Tristan through when he arrived moments later. Tristan parked at the reception car park and followed the VW Beetle on foot.

Cordelia drove to the clubhouse and abandoned her car outside. Tristan caught up quickly and assisted Aunt Winnie out of the car. She leaned on him and Tristan supported her weight. Cordelia unlocked the main door and ushered them inside. Aunt Winnie had no shoes on and winced as she stepped on the gravel. Tristan offered to carry her, but she declined with a shake of her head. Once inside Cordelia locked the door behind them and proceeded through the arcades to a door marked staff only. She unlocked the door and held it open for her guests.

It was a narrow terracotta hallway with a steep staircase. Morgan switched on the lights as she entered first. Tristan supported Aunt Winnie as she slowly climbed the stairs, following Morgan. Cordelia brought up the rear, locking the door behind her. Once upstairs they were greeted with two doors. Cordelia shouted, "Knock on the door to the left." Morgan knocked and Frank Levingstone opened the door with a worried expression on his face. He was a portly bald man roughly in his seventies. He always had a cheery disposition, however he took one look at Aunt Winnie and worry lines appeared on his forehead as he ushered them inside.

Morgan had never been inside the Levingstone's home. It was a vast open plan space, clearly modernised recently. The left outer wall was completely glass, enabling you to see beyond the holiday park and over to the new glamping site. A grey, fully fitted kitchen with breakfast bar was directly in front of them and to the right a comfy lounge area.

Tristan helped Aunt Winnie to the sofa and Cordelia disappeared through a door to the right. Cordelia returned quickly with a pile of her mother's clothes. Morgan and Cordelia helped Aunt Winnie to the bathroom, where Morgan stayed to help her get dressed.

Frank Levingstone, Cordelia's father made coffee for everyone in the kitchen and Cordelia raided the fridge, fixing together a cheese sandwich. Tristan assisted Aunt Winnie back to the sofa and she thanked everyone for their kindness. Aunt Winnie ate the sandwich slowly savouring every mouthful. The colour started to return to her face. She even managed a smile, as Cordelia explained how they had found her and how instrumental Morgan had been in her rescue.

The front door opened and Maura Levingstone, Cordelia's mother, entered the apartment. She was an exact replica of Cordelia just an older version. Although on closer inspection her facial expressions appeared softer, but that might have been Morgan's interpretation of her character.

Maura had always been extremely friendly. She ran first to Cordelia and hugged her daughter. She then rushed over to Aunt Winnie and embraced her tightly, as tears started to run down her cheeks. They had been lifelong friends, growing up together on the commune. Frank returned to the kitchen to make another round of drinks and Maura composed herself.

"We have put all manner of enchantments on the site parameters, doubled security and alerted everyone that they must travel everywhere in pairs," Maura explained. "We have had the window replaced in your caravan and moved its location to under the large oak tree in the centre of the park. We have added additional charms to the caravan and installed a loud panic alarm in the bedroom. You're more than welcome to stay here though. You can sleep in the bed with me and Frank will take the sofa."

Aunt Winnie looked grateful and welled up with the love she was receiving but declined the offer. "I would prefer to stay in my own home, but thank you for the offer." Aunt Winnie turned to Morgan before asking, "Are you able to stay with me tonight?"

"Of course," Morgan replied, taking her Aunt's hand in hers and giving it a light squeeze.

"Are you ready to explain what happened?" Cordelia asked. Aunt Winnie explained to the group all she could remember, including the interrogation questions and the answers she gave. She omitted the details pertaining to the torture she endured, simply stating, "He tied me up and whipped me, before leaving me alone in that room." No one pressed her for more details.

"Did you get a good look at his face?" Morgan inquired.

"Yes," Aunt Winnie confirmed resolutely.

"Can I show you an image, to confirm if it was the Vampire who attacked me?"

Aunt Winnie nodded and Morgan opened her laptop, showing the Commander in Chief Silas Nicolescu's photograph. Aunt Winnie shuddered and closed her eyes. Morgan closed the laptop. Aunt Winnie confirmed, "That's him." Tristan let out a low growl under his breath and Morgan hugged her Aunt tight.

"I would like to go home now and rest," Aunt Winnie

announced. Tristan helped Aunt Winnie down the stairs and together, the three of them walked towards the large oak tree. Morgan had a sense of being watched and looked up at the large clubhouse windows. The glass was tinted and appeared to be one-way, as Morgan couldn't see through it. Cordelia stared down at the unlikely threesome, watching intensely. She knew Morgan wouldn't be able to see her, but she stepped back automatically when Morgan glanced up.

Cordelia had always thought Morgan was non-magical. It happens occasionally in magical families and the gene can skip multiple generations, especially when Witches marry into non-magical families. However, the level of magic Morgan had shown today, by summoning the rainbow from her tears was beyond anything Cordelia had witnessed or could manage herself. Cordelia wondered how much Morgan was aware of her powers.

Cordelia left her parent's apartment, to enter her own next door. Her parents had renovated their home a couple of years ago, splitting it into two apartments to give Cordelia her independence. She lit the log fireplace and searched through her bookcase, looking for a particular book entitled 'The Twelve Elements of Nature'. When she found it she removed it from the shelf and settled in a large pink bean bag by the fireplace.

The book was very old and the pages were delicate. Cordelia had read it before but a long time ago. The introduction described the twelve elements and a chapter was devoted to each one. Water, Wind, Earth, Fire, Thunder, Lightning, Ice, Fog, Time, Force, Light and Movement. The last chapter was titled, 'Harnessing the power of all twelve'.

Most Witches only possessed the power of one element. Cordelia like her mother was a Wind Witch. She could summon the wind at will and distort the air to make her fly. She had never managed more than the height of a caravan, but she was very proud of her abilities. A rainbow requires both water and light. Cordelia skipped ahead to the last chapter and settled in to read that first.

As the threesome approached the caravan, Aunt Winnie signalled for Tristan to stand back. "You will need to be invited in," she warned. Aunt Winnie unlocked the door and entered the caravan. She turned to Tristan and loudly announced, "Tristan welcome into my home." Aunt Winnie held out her hand and as she touched him, a gust of wind rushed past him. He entered the caravan unharmed and turned to see Morgan following him inside.

"What would have happened to me if you hadn't invited me in?" Tristan asked.

"The power of the wind would have sought to prevent you from trying again," replied Aunt Winnie. Tristan looked confused and Aunt Winnie just winked at him.

"I need to rest now, but I would appreciate it if you both stayed in the caravan tonight." They both nodded. Aunt Winnie opened the door to her bedroom and disappeared from view.

"How about I make us something to eat?" Morgan suggested.

"Perfect I'm starving," replied Tristan.

Morgan opened the fridge and found a large stone-baked margarita pizza. It had gone out of date the day before but didn't look spoilt. She unwrapped it and placed it in the oven to cook. Tristan sat on the bench seating in the lounge area and turned on the small TV. He typed in his Netflix password and asked Morgan, "What sort of movie would you like to watch, comedy or action?"

"I've had enough action for today, let's have a comedy. What about a romantic comedy?" She offered up a couple of choices for Tristan to pick. When the oven timer rang, Morgan sliced the pizza and they spent the evening cuddled up together watching movies.

Morgan's old bedroom had a single bed so she converted the dining room table into a double bed and pulled extra bedding out of the bench seats. They snuggled up together and Morgan fell asleep first, safe in Tristan's arms.

The next morning Morgan and Tristan woke to knocking on the dining room window. Tristan opened the curtains to see Cordelia carrying a tray laden with pastries and fruit. Morgan opened the main door and let her inside. The enchantments didn't strike fellow Witches, so she walked in without Aunt Winnie needing to invite her.

Aunt Winnie had been awake for a while but didn't want to disturb Tristan and Morgan. Upon hearing voices, she joined everyone and they all started eating the breakfast Cordelia had kindly brought. In between mouthfuls of croissant, Cordelia inquired if Morgan was planning on staying for a while, "I would love to help you explore your powers and share with you the insight of our history."

Morgan looked first at Aunt Winnie and secondly at Tristan before confirming she would stay a while. "Tristan, there's no need for you to stay, you can go back home and I will catch the train at the end of the week," Morgan stated. Tristan nodded in agreement.

Tristan left after breakfast and even Aunt Winnie gave him a hug goodbye. Cordelia offered to loan Morgan some clothes for the rest of the week, as they were about the same size. After checking that Aunt Winnie was comfortable being left alone, Morgan followed Cordelia to her apartment.

Once inside Cordelia's bedroom, Morgan selected a few plain T-shirts, a pink knitted jumper and a pair of jeans from the wardrobe. Morgan took a shower in Cordelia's bathroom and got changed, whilst Cordelia made them a hot chocolate. Cordelia lit the fire and they both relaxed on pink beanbags.

Cordelia had decorated the apartment like a Moroccan tent. The rooms were bold with rich colours on the walls and ornate fabrics hung from the ceiling. The living room was fuchsia pink with a rich purple patterned rug. There was no sofa only a selection of pillows and bean bags. The air smelled of cinnamon and Morgan saw an incense stick burning on the windowsill. Cordelia explained she had returned from backpacking last summer and fell in love with Africa. It had been her inspiration for the décor.

"How much do you know about magic?" Cordelia enquired.

"Very little. I only found out a few weeks ago," Morgan admitted.

"Witches' powers are a gift from God. Did you know that?" Cordelia asked. Morgan shook her head. Cordelia continued, "The ancient scriptures say magic was a gift given to Aclima, daughter of Adam and Eve after she was attacked by her brother Cain. All her female descendants would be given the power to protect themselves. Witches draw on the elements for their power. Over time, some Witches have been unable to call upon their gifts and our power has weakened. Your Aunt for example has no active powers. My mother and I are Wind Witches. We can manipulate the wind and call it when needed, to protect ourselves or to fly. Most Witches can only call on one element, but you called on two when you created that rainbow yesterday; water and light."

Morgan had been listening intently and scrunched up her face in confusion. "But wasn't it the spell that cast the rainbow?" Morgan queried.

"No, it was your tears. I could feel the energy radiating from you. Have you ever made anything else happen that you can't explain? When your emotions were heightened," Cordelia inquired.

Morgan thought for a moment before responding. She told Cordelia of the levitating when she was happy, the smashed glass when she was angry and the jealous incident in the bar, leading to the plant bursting into flames.

Cordelia looked gobsmacked. She counted on her fingers as Morgan spoke, "That's water, light, wind, movement and fire. That's five elements." Morgan could hear the excitement in Cordelia's voice as she asked Morgan, "Can we try practising together, to see if you can call the other elements?" Morgan nodded and set her empty mug down on the floor. Excited, Cordelia grabbed both Morgan's hands and pulled her up, as she stood. "Follow me."

They left the apartment and headed down the stairs. Morgan followed Cordelia to the outskirts of the glamping site, to a small stream. "Stand in the water," Cordelia instructed. Morgan pulled a face at the thought of getting her feet wet. She decided to remove her shoes and socks before she entered the water.

"Focus on a powerful positive memory and how you felt in that moment. Let it consume you. Then imagine turning the water to ice," Cordelia said eagerly. Morgan closed her eyes and concentrated hard on the moment Tristan had told her he loved her. She tried to imagine the water around her turning to ice. Morgan could swear she felt the water getting colder and opened her eyes in excitement, but the water was still liquid. She shrugged her shoulders and looked to Cordelia for encouragement.

"Ok maybe start smaller, what about imagining the water turning to mist and then fog," Cordelia suggested. Morgan tried again, concentrating on how happy she had been in that moment and imagining the water around her turning to fog. She heard Cordelia gasp loudly and she opened her eyes to see mist all around her.

Morgan felt euphoric. She continued to focus and the mist continued to rise, before thickening into fog. The fog engulfed the air around her until she could no longer see Cordelia. Morgan felt determined and powerful. She settled the fog and fixated on a droplet of water on a nearby water reed. As the water droplet ran down the stem it froze into a tiny icicle.

Morgan couldn't explain how she was doing it, but she believed she could and therefore she could. The water all around her was turning to ice. She stepped back out of the stream to the other side and watched as the stream froze solid. Cordelia was jumping up and down. She shouted over excitedly, "You're doing it!"

Morgan wondered what else she could do. She focused on a large boulder in the stream and imagined it rising up above the water line. For a split second, she thought she saw it wobble. Morgan persevered, visualizing the rock rising up to eye level. Suddenly, the boulder started to rise. It left the water and was hovering in the air at chest height. With a sharp turn to the left Morgan directed the rock to smash into the frozen water, five metres away. The boulder smashed through the thin layer of ice and sank beneath the water.

"You're incredible!" Cordelia shouted. Morgan couldn't contain her happiness. She was ecstatic, but extremely tired. She focused on reversing the temperature of the water to melt away the ice and walked back through the stream. Morgan sat on the grass bank to put on her socks and shoes.

"How do you feel?" Asked Cordelia. Morgan explained she felt drained, but amazed at what she had accomplished. Cordelia agreed Morgan should rest and offered to visit later, as she had some books to loan her. They returned to the holiday park and parted ways.

After explaining the morning's events to Aunt Winnie, Morgan went for a nap in her old bedroom. Hermes had made himself scarce whilst Tristan was around but reappeared as Morgan returned from the stream. Hermes curled up on the end of Morgan's childhood bed and they fell asleep together.

When Morgan woke it was dinner time. Aunt Winnie was cooking a spicy red lentil dhal and the smell was amazing. Aunt Winnie explained that Maura had dropped off bags of groceries earlier that day and they had done a yoga class together. Morgan could tell that Aunt Winnie was starting to get her carefree mojo back and suggested sunrise yoga on the beach tomorrow. Aunt Winnie's face beamed with joy and she agreed.

After dinner, Cordelia arrived with a selection of ancient-looking books. The three of them sat together at the dining table and Cordelia opened up a large leather-bound book with a tree on the front. Cordelia pointed to the intricately designed pages as she spoke. "This is a book about our heritage. Aclima's daughter Una, had twelve daughters. Each one possessed the power of a different element. I am descended from Augusta, the Wind Witch on my mother's side and Ursula, the Water Witch on my father's side. I have taken after my mother's line and I can harness the wind. Your grandmother, Glinda and her mother before her could control ice. You are both descendants of Bronwyn."

"I don't remember her well," said Aunt Winnie, "but my father's grandmother could click her fingers and a flame would balance on her thumb."

"She must have been a descendent of Seraphina, the Fire Witch," Cordelia remarked. "Males born to Witches carry the gene but they don't possess any magical powers. They can pass them down to their children though, even when the mother isn't magical but it is rare."

"My sister and I never inherited any active magical powers," Aunt Winnie declared.

"Maybe that was because ice and fire are opposite elements. Look here," Morgan interrupted, pointing at the opposite page. The page had an almost circular shape on it but with 12 points.

"What kind of shape is that?" Aunt Winnie asked.

Morgan took out her phone and checked the internet. "A twelve-sided shape is a type of polygon called a dodecagon." Each point was labelled with an element and lines connected the opposite elements. Ice was opposite Fire. Earth opposite Movement. Time opposite Wind. Water opposite Fog. Force opposite Lightning. Light opposite Thunder.

The threesome sat and conferred for a few moments before Morgan asked, "How is it that I appear to be able to call on several elements?"

Both Aunt Winnie and Cordelia shrugged, "No idea," confirmed Cordelia, "I've never read about it in my books, but

I think I know who would have the answers. Agatha Harkess is the head of the Witch Council. She lives on an Island off mainland Scotland. Will you travel with me to meet her?"

"When?" Morgan asked.

"Tomorrow?" Cordelia replied excitedly.

"Will she be available tomorrow?" Morgan queried, hopeful for some answers.

"She'll make time to meet you. Trust me," Cordelia smiled.

"Aunt Winnie will you come with us? I don't want to go without you." Morgan used all her charm to convince her Aunt that she needed her by her side. When in truth she just didn't want her Aunt left alone. It worked and Aunt Winnie agreed.

"How will we get there? It will take all day," Morgan complained.

Aunt Winnie and Cordelia smiled a mischievous smile like they knew a secret they weren't willing to share. Morgan grew suspicious and asked, "What are you not telling me?"

This time Aunt Winnie led the explanation. "We can apparate there. All we need to do is create a portal and cast the right spell." Cordelia stood up and headed towards the door, as she opened it she said, "Be ready to travel at ten tomorrow. Meet me by the stream we were at today. I'll make sure Agatha sets the portal up at her end in time," and then she left.

It was late now and both women got ready for bed and hugged goodnight before entering into their own bedrooms.

CHAPTER 15

Sisters Bound Through Magic

The next morning Aunt Winnie woke Morgan up with a cup of tea before the sun rose to do yoga on the beach, as they had planned. The sea was freezing but Morgan enjoyed the familiarity of the wet sand between her toes. Aunt Winnie seemed to be back to her normal carefree self and they ended up having a water fight using their feet.

When they returned to the caravan, they took it in turns to shower and change. Aunt Winnie went first, then proceeded to make scrambled eggs and toast for them both, whilst Morgan got ready.

Just before ten, they left the caravan to meet Cordelia at the stream. When they arrived Cordelia was setting up the portal. She had used broomsticks to create a pentagram star on the ground and rope to create the outer circle. Cordelia beckoned them to join her in the circle and they all held hands as Cordelia started to chant.

Aunt Winnie whispered, "Close your eyes and empty your mind. Listen to the words."

Cordelia repeated her chant three times. "I call upon the powers given to Witches at creation, to change our location to our chosen destination. Witches of Skye hear our spell, move what is mortal through this portal."

Morgan felt a strange tugging sensation and then heard

a loud pop. When she opened her eyes she stared around in disbelief. She was still holding hands with Aunt Winnie and Cordelia, but the stream was gone. The pentagram was made of broomsticks but the circle was now made of red ribbon. They were stood on top of a cliff very close to the edge and Morgan could see the sea in every direction. Seagulls flew overhead and she could hear the crashing of waves below. Cordelia let go of her hand first and addressed a group of Witches behind Morgan.

Morgan spun around to greet them. Agatha introduced herself first. She was younger than Morgan expected maybe late thirties, with blonde curly hair and a strong jawline. She spoke with a Scottish accent and had an attractive smile. Brianne appeared to be Aunt Winnie's age, with long, dark, wavy hair, rosy cheeks and red lips. She embraced Aunt Winnie like they were good friends. Meredith was very striking and clearly the youngest of the group. She was easily six feet tall and towered over the rest of the Witches. She had short blonde spiky hair and bright green eyes. She was curt with her greeting and had a soldier-like stance.

After the introductions, Morgan, Aunt Winnie and Cordelia followed the group of Witches down some stony steps to a medieval stone castle. The gates were open and inside was a flurry of activity. Children were barefoot, running around and laughing. A group of females of varying ages were sat in a circle floating objects in the air. The youngest looked no older than five. Morgan's amazement must have been visible on her face. Agatha approached her, explaining the castle was a safe haven for all Witch families, where they could live openly.

Brianne led the group through a series of dark hallways until they came to a medium-sized circular room on the ground floor of the turret. It had small ornate windows all around. Candles lit the room from the ceiling and on closer inspection, Morgan realised the candles were hovering in the air. The floor was covered in red blankets and bean bags were placed in a circle. On the wall in red paint was a pentagram.

Everyone took a seat and Agatha began to speak. "Welcome sisters. Cordelia was cryptic in her message last night. Why is it you have travelled here today?" Cordelia relayed the events of the past few days. She detailed the events of Aunt Winnie's kidnap and rescue, including Tristan's assistance. The next-to-know explanation as to who Tristan was, made Morgan realise that this group of Witches, were involved in the drugs and distribution operation. Cordelia then moved on to Morgan's abilities and what she had witnessed the previous day at the stream. When Cordelia finished speaking all three women were smiling.

Agatha spoke first, "Morgan am I right in thinking you have only recently discovered Witchcraft and your talents?" Morgan nodded and Agatha continued. "This is extraordinary. I have heard of Witches who can call upon multiple elements, or who have special gifts, but it is rare. I have never heard of a Witch who can call upon so many."

Morgan didn't know how to feel. The women in the circle genuinely appeared proud and excited about Morgan's abilities. It made her feel a sense of pride in herself yet she didn't know why. It wasn't like she had worked hard and trained for these abilities.

Agatha continued, asking Morgan, "Will you stay a few days with us? We have Witches of all talents here who can help you hone your powers and teach you to call upon them at will."

Morgan looked to Aunt Winnie for reassurance, she smiled in response. Sensing Morgan's reticence, Agatha added, "Of course, you are all welcome to stay." Cordelia, Morgan and Aunt Winnie all smiled and thanked their hosts. Brianne clapped her hands together and said, "Perfect," before ushering everyone to follow her out of the room and back towards the courtyard.

They joined the group levitating objects and Brianne introduced them to Mary. Mary was close in age to Morgan and had a South African accent. Her hair was a gorgeous tightly curled Afro and she had a wide smile. Mary introduced herself, explaining that she was a descendent of the Witch Selina and had the power of telekinesis, she could move objects at will. Mary introduced the young girl in the group as her daughter Maya. Mary asked Maya to demonstrate floating a spoon in the air. Maya did as her mother asked, raising the spoon above her head until it was at Morgan's eye level.

"That's incredible to have that much control," Morgan said as she stood in amazement. Maya beamed at the compliment. Her smile matched her mother's. Agatha asked Mary if she would spend some time with Morgan, to help her harness the gift of movement. Mary agreed obligingly and Morgan took a seat in the circle. Aunt Winnie joined in too, eager to witness what Morgan could achieve. Cordelia excused herself as she had council business to discuss with Agatha.

After a couple of hours, a bell rang signalling lunch and Mary led them to a large dining hall. A buffet-style lunch had been prepared. Morgan and Aunt Winnie followed Mary, queuing up to grab a tray. They both selected a chunky slice of freshly baked bread and a hearty bowl of vegetable stew. They sat in the middle of a very long dining table and everyone seemed keen to talk to the visitors.

In total, there were sixty families that lived on the island. Some lived inside the castle and others had homes a short walk away. Morgan could feel a sense of community and friendship. It was lovely.

During lunch, Mary introduced them both to an elderly Witch named Elspeth. She was blind and used a stick to navigate her way around the castle. Morgan thought it rude to ask how old she was but was desperate to know. Elspeth asked Morgan to join her after lunch was finished. Morgan and Aunt Winnie followed her to what must have been the castle's chapel. The windows were beautiful, with ornate stained glass designs featuring several women. The floor was a mixture of fabrics and bean bags as the council chamber had been. Elspeth muttered something under her breath and clapped her hands before sitting in mid-air. Morgan looked sideways to Aunt

Winnie, who just smiled.

"I am a descendent of the Witch Allegra. I possess the rarest of Witches' talents, that of time. I was never blessed with children, so my line ends with me; unless you possess that talent also. Magic has a way of surviving and I foresaw your arrival. I have been waiting for you," her expression changed to a devilish smile before she continued. "Premonition is not so rare a talent, many Witches possess it. Time is not the power of premonition. With Time you must be careful. You can alter the past, but you can never go to the future, because quite simply it hasn't happened yet. The future is constantly changing, affected by the many decisions every person makes each moment. The further you go back the harder it is and you cannot take anyone with you."

She paused for a minute before pulling out three objects from her pocket. A piece of bread from lunch, a fork and a spoon. She handed them to Morgan. "I took these from the hall at lunch. Try holding them and concentrate back on when you were eating. Imagine you are back there. How did it smell? How did you feel? How did it taste? Call upon Allegra to guide you through time and space."

"How would I do that?" Morgan asked.

"Close your eyes dear, focus and say in your head or aloud, 'I call upon my sister Allegra to empower me, help me, I implore thee'. It is a simple chant. It can be adapted for any of the sisters to help you. If you have the power to call upon them," Elspeth replied.

Morgan did as instructed and repeated the words in her own head as she focused on being back in the dining hall. When she opened her eyes, she was sat in the same room with both Aunt Winnie and Elspeth staring at her. "Did it work?" Aunt Winnie asked.

"No," Morgan admitted, disappointedly. Morgan looked to Elspeth but she didn't look downcast, in fact, the opposite.

"I believe you will be able to call upon Allegra one day. When you need her the most, she will aid you. Now I need my afternoon nap, so I will leave you," and with that, Elspeth rose from her seated position, with the help of her walking stick and left the room.

Morgan and Aunt Winnie followed the corridors back to the courtyard, where Mary introduced them to Brianne's granddaughter's, nine-year-old twins, Cassie and Sophia. They were identical in every way, from their rosy pink cheeks, straight auburn hair and a multitude of freckles. However, Mary explained that they were very different in their abilities. Sophie had taken her powers from her mother's side, through the Witch Lucinda and could call upon thunder at will. Cassie had taken the powers from her father's side of the family, through the Witch Lenora and could cause lightning to strike. Although Cassie admitted that she couldn't make it strike exactly where she wanted just yet, but she was hopeful with practice she could.

Morgan and Aunt Winnie followed the twins out of the castle grounds back up the stony steps to the cliff. The twins held hands, as they gazed out towards the sea. Together they made the sky turn a dark purple-grey. Morgan heard a loud rumble of thunder in the distance, followed by a bolt of lightning that shot out of the sky and struck the water. The sisters cheered, high-fiving each other and the sky returned to normal.

The sisters spent the rest of the afternoon trying to teach Morgan how to harness their talents but with no joy. Morgan thought she managed a weak rumble of thunder at one point, but the twins dismissed it as being their tummies rumbling for dinner. The group made their way back to the castle to find an empty courtyard. The twins led the way to the dining hall and they found it full with everyone enjoying dinner.

After they finished eating, Agatha asked Morgan and Aunt Winnie to join them back in the council chambers. Everyone sat in the same circle as that morning. Agatha explained Cordelia's vision and how they had worked together to create a potion that would not harm humans, but could kill a Vampire if they fed off a human who had ingested it.

Morgan then disclosed her role as an undercover agent, who had been placed in the Lycan's bar. With everything Morgan had now uncovered, she was certain that her mission had been sanctioned by a Vampire. That Vampire was high up in the department and was convinced Vampires were dying as a result of drugs being distributed at the Lycan's clubs. Morgan explained that she was certain that Vampires did not suspect Witches were working together with Lycans.

Morgan detailed her attack and how she had grown close to Tristan Lucas. Explaining it had been he who had introduced her to the supernatural world and led her to discover her own magical abilities. Morgan believed that her Aunt was kidnapped because she had discovered that the Vampire had authorised the murder of Tristan's brother. It was evident now from his interrogation of Aunt Winnie, that the Vampire was now aware that Morgan was a Witch. It wouldn't take long before the Vampires realised Lycans and Witches were working together.

"Whilst it is regrettable that they may know we are working together, it only proves Cordelia's vision is true and that we're right to work together. Do you believe you can trust these Lycans?" Agatha asked.

Morgan answered truthfully, "Yes. With my life."

Agatha studied Morgan before responding, "Good. It may come to that." She took a long breath before continuing, her face twisted into an ugly sneer, "This Vampire is likely to be working for Alexander Vladislav, the head of the Vampire council. He is ancient, calculating and extremely arrogant. He will reach out to me I am sure. I believe we should wait to see what move they make first and continue with our current plan. Morgan, you need to encourage the Lycans to increase distribution. Can you end the investigation into them to take away the heat of law enforcement?" Morgan nodded and with that, the meeting ended.

Brianne led them further into the castle and showed them to a large room with three single beds. "We thought you would all be more comfortable together," she said before pointing over to a door in the corner, "The bathroom is just through that door and extra clothes have been placed on the beds. Breakfast is served in the dining hall from six. I will be leading sunrise yoga at seven-thirty for those of you who are brave enough to withstand the morning Scottish air." Brianne closed the door and left the group to relax.

Morgan and Aunt Winnie told Cordelia how they had spent their day and the Witches they had met. Aunt Winnie expressed an interest in staying longer in Scotland but admitted she might wait until the summer. The castle really was snug and warm but the outside air was very fresh, especially when the sun went down.

Morgan left the room to call Tristan. He must have been busy at the bar as she couldn't get through. She sent him a goodnight message instead. They changed into the night clothes provided and Morgan fell asleep as soon as her head hit the pillow.

All three woke up to the sound of a distant bell ringing. Morgan checked her phone and saw it was six. She had a soppy response from Tristan and smiled as she read her message. Cordelia gave a sarcastic glare, clearly aware of why Morgan was smiling. Morgan blushed and they took it in turns to use the bathroom.

Aunt Winnie decided to skip breakfast and went to join Brianne for yoga instead. Remarking that yoga fed her soul, which was more important than her stomach. Cordelia and Morgan had breakfast together sat next to Edmund and Rihanna.

Edmund was the first man Morgan had seen whilst at the castle. He was Rihanna's husband and his mother had been a Witch. They were in their late sixties and moved to

Scotland from London when they retired. They had both been teachers and met during University when backpacking in a gap year. They believed magic had a way of drawing magical blood together.

Morgan was intrigued by them as they were the first magical couple she had met who held regular jobs, breaking the stereotype that all Witches were hippies. They explained they wanted to make a difference in the world and they had worked in a disadvantaged school in a rough area of London. They had adopted three magical children, whom they discovered in foster homes. Although Edmund had no magical powers, he felt he could sense when magic was near and he was drawn to it.

Rihanna went on to explain she was a descendant of Agnes the Earth Witch. She offered to show Morgan some of her powers after breakfast. Cordelia, Morgan, Edmund and Rihanna left the castle grounds, down the hill, towards the gardens. Rihanna demonstrated how her magic worked in multiple ways. She held a lump of solid soil in her left hand. Focusing on the lump of soil, Rihanna clicked her fingers and the lump of soil disintegrated in her hands. The soil was so fine it fell through her fingers onto the ground.

Next, she knelt on the ground next to the stone wall around the garden. A wooden spoon in the ground said raspberries. She placed her hands over a patch of dirt and closed her eyes. Slowly she rose to a standing position. Miraculously out of nowhere, a raspberry bush grew from the ground, covered in fruit. The bush grew to be half the size of Rihanna. When she opened her eyes again she looked satisfied with her creation and pride flashed across her face when she saw Morgan's astonished facial expression.

"I have one more ability to show you, but you will need to follow me out of the garden, further down the hill where it is safer," Rihanna instructed and led the way down the hill. She asked everyone to stand back and she stood with her legs apart in a wide stance, with her fists clenched at her side. Rihanna closed her eyes again and shook her clenched fists once in the air. As her arms moved, she let out an aggressive shout and the ground trembled under Morgan's feet.

Morgan watched intently, not sure what was about to happen. The ground in front of Rihanna split in two. A large crack formed three meters in front of her. Rihanna opened her eyes and looked relieved. "I tried to only show you a little earth tremor. I'm glad it didn't go too far."

The group were extremely impressed. They spent the rest of the morning back in the walled garden, as Rihanna showed Morgan how to focus on growing seeds that had just been planted. Cordelia and Edmund made themselves useful by harvesting the crops. By lunchtime, Morgan had managed to grow two cabbages and a bunch of carrots. They carried the crops to the kitchen to be used for dinner.

Morgan was on a high and couldn't wait to tell Aunt Winnie when they met for lunch. Aunt Winnie had spent the morning catching up with Brianne. They had been at summer school together in Wales, back when Witches ran exclusive holiday camps. Aunt Winnie spent lunch telling Morgan all about the mischief they had got up to and what fun it had been.

After lunch, Morgan went in search of Elspeth. Morgan found her, in her bedroom resting. She offered to read to her but Elspeth said she wanted to hear more about Morgan's life and instead asked Morgan to tell her about her life as an agent. Morgan started with her first undercover mission. An hour later she had told Elspeth her entire life story and how she'd fallen in love with a Lycan. Elspeth didn't judge, which surprised Morgan.

"You don't seem shocked by my relationship with Tristan," Morgan challenged.

Elspeth took her time before answering as if she was remembering. "I have dabbled in time travel for the sake of my curiosity; especially when I was younger. I once went back to the 17th century, when Vampires were leading Witch hunts to murder Witches. Hundreds of Witches were brutally murdered. Lycans, Humans and even some sympathetic Vampires who wanted to live in peace helped Witches to hide. We did not always live such separate lives. Lycans and Witches still marry humans. I myself fell in love with a human, but he couldn't accept me for what I was."

"I'm sorry to hear that," Morgan said, thinking of the pain Elspeth must have gone through.

"Thank you dear, but it was more than ninety years ago now, several lifetimes. Fight for your man and your love. Love is worth fighting for," Elspeth replied.

"Ninety years ago, how old are you?" Morgan blurted out.

Elspeth chuckled at the directness, "On my next birthday I will be one hundred and eight. Now leave me to take my afternoon nap. Come back tomorrow morning to practise some more."

Morgan did as she was told and went in search of Cordelia. Together they spent the rest of the afternoon with Mary and Maya practising levitation. Morgan was starting to feel tingling in her hands as if the magic was trying to obey her commands.

After dinner, they went to the library and spent time reading through the handwritten spell books collated together over centuries. Morgan wrote down some simple spells to try at home.

The next morning after breakfast, Morgan visited Elspeth as promised and they spent the morning practising time travel, but to no avail. After lunch Morgan, Cordelia and Aunt Winnie said their goodbyes. They departed the castle and ascended the stony stairs on the cliff. They stood on the pentagram portal in a circle and held hands, just as they had before. Cordelia repeated the following words three times, "Reverse the spell that was cast, take us home fast, by way of witchcraft."

CHAPTER 16

Confession Time

When Aunt Winnie and Morgan were settled back in the Caravan, Morgan booked her train ticket to return back to Nottingham. They spent the evening practising the spells Morgan had written down. Morgan impressed herself, she was getting pretty good at potion-making. In her laptop bag, she packed the three potions she had mastered. A mending bones potion, a garlic salt that cured a common cold and a fish bone tea that enhanced brain function temporarily. She thought the latter might come in useful for pre-Christmas exams, given how many lectures she had missed.

The next morning Morgan joined Aunt Winnie for one last sunrise yoga on the beach before making her way to the train station. Morgan tried catching up on University assignments on the train journey, but began day dreaming about the future instead.

Morgan considered how life would look if she continued as an agent, but she couldn't get past how she would explain that side of her life to Tristan. Even if he did accept her, would his family? She then imagined her life if she chose Tristan over being an agent, working in the bar full time, but that didn't make her happy either. She had been exposed to a whole new supernatural world and she had powerful abilities that she owed to herself to explore. Was a supernatural war with

Vampires really on the horizon? Would she need to use her powers to prevent a massacre? The journey was over in a flash and Morgan nearly didn't hear the tannoy as it announced they were approaching Nottingham station.

Tristan was waiting for Morgan on the platform with a huge grin on his face. He was dressed casually in jeans and a polo shirt. He stood out on the platform, as everyone else was wrapped up warm in coats. Morgan remembered Tristan had said he rarely felt the cold. The wolf blood in him kept him warm. Morgan hugged him tight and felt him squeeze her just as tightly back. "I've missed you," Tristan confessed, as he let go of her and they walked along the platform to the car park.

Morgan couldn't hide her smile as she climbed into Tristan's Land Rover Defender and asked, "What have you got planned for us this afternoon?" Tristan flashed Morgan a devilish smile before starting to drive out of the car park.

"Church," Tristan said as he winked at Morgan.

"Church?" Morgan repeated thoroughly confused.

"I plan to worship you all afternoon," he cheekily responded. It only took Morgan a second to understand his sexual innuendo and she started to get excited in anticipation.

Tristan drove back to his parents' house and they ran like children at the end of the school day, up to his third floor living quarters. As soon as they reached the top stair, Tristan pulled off his polo shirt and unzipped his jeans. Morgan followed his lead, removing all her clothes including her underwear. They left a trail of clothes on the way to the bedroom. By the time Morgan reached the bedroom she was fully naked. She laid on the bed on her side, propped up on one arm and seductively beckoned Tristan to join her, with her index finger. Tristan took a moment to imprint Morgan's image to memory, before leaping on the bed to kiss her.

Morgan was clearly no expert in the bedroom. She allowed Tristan to take the lead and took his direction well. He hadn't let on that he thought her a novice. In fact, he liked it! He liked that she hadn't been with lots of men. The mere thought of her with another man-made bile rose in his throat. She was growing in sexual confidence and he enjoyed being her teacher, rewarding her for good behaviour.

"Tell me where you want me to touch you," he teased.

Morgan bit her bottom lip, an act which drove him wild with desire. "Here," she said, pointing to her breasts. Tristan was surprised and delighted she had not gone for the obvious answer. He happily obliged, taking her nipple into his mouth and sucking. Whilst he teased one breast with his tongue, he gently squeezed the other, until he swapped sides.

When he was satisfied she was aroused, he asked again, "Tell me, where do you want me to touch you?" But she didn't reply. It was like she couldn't allow herself to say the words. So instead he teased her by placing a finger in her mouth. "Here?" She didn't respond. He moved his hands down her body until he met her breasts. He groped both and teased, "Do you want more of this?" But she still didn't utter a sound. Tristan then trailed one finger from her belly button down to her moist centre, before taunting, "Or maybe here?"

Morgan bit her bottom lip again and nodded. Tristan savoured the look of wanton desire in her eyes. He slipped a finger inside of her and started moving it in a circular motion. With his thumb he found her clitoris and mirrored the movement of his other finger. Morgan started to make small groans of pleasure, so he slid another finger inside her, stretching her ready for his desire.

He loved watching her writhe whilst he pleasured her. He was pushing her to the brink, but he didn't want her to bubble over. He wanted to make that pleasure happen whilst he was inside of her. He loved the feeling of her exploding on his cock. It was indescribable.

His penis was now rock hard, desperate to join in. He pulled out his fingers and swiftly replaced them with his member. He kept his thumb circulating on her clitoris and with a few thrusts she lost control and came all over him. Her body shuddered and her insides pulsated around him. It nearly sent him over the edge, but that would have been an embarrassing outcome. He wanted to put in a good performance.

He only managed ten minutes more, before he let his desire take over him. He would make it up to her, he assured himself. She just drove him so wild. What he couldn't manage in stamina, he would make up for in orgasms. After fifteen minutes recovery time, he felt ready to go again. He rolled her over and entered her from behind. She felt wet and tight, and moaned at all the right moments. They were both soon lost to desire again. He collapsed on top of her, but was careful not to let his full weight rest on her. He kissed her on the cheek and rolled off her, whilst tucking her body into him.

That evening in between playing video games, they deliberated how to increase distribution of the energy pills and reach a wider demographic. Tristan suggested Morgan could circulate pills at University, but Morgan fiercely opposed the idea. In the end they decided the best course of action was to increase marketing to the three clubs through socials and events. Morgan agreed to poster the University campus with marketing material and Tristan resolved to meet with more dealers to spread distribution further across the country. They went to sleep that night happy and blessed to be back in each other's arms again.

Morgan's Monday morning alarm woke her up with a fright and she reached across the bed to feel for Tristan, but the bed was empty. She opened her eyes and scanned around the room, but he was nowhere to be seen. Morgan opened Tristan's wardrobe and selected a plain white T-shirt and slipped it on, along with her knickers. She wandered out of the bedroom and into the lounge in search of him, but he wasn't in the apartment.

Morgan glanced out of the window and saw Tristan jogging across the driveway in running clothes. Morgan knew he would want a shower straight away, so she decided he could join her in there. She undressed and started the water running in the shower. Within a few minutes Tristan was in the bedroom and as he removed his earphones he heard the water running. Tristan smiled at the thought of joining Morgan. The door to the bathroom was open, so he took that as an invitation. He undressed and slipped into the shower behind her.

He kissed her on the neck and down her collarbone as she washed her hair. Tristan squeezed shower gel onto his hands, frothing it up before cupping her breasts and covering them in bubbles. Tristan pressed up against her and Morgan could feel his erection pressing into her bum cheeks as he became aroused. She turned around and they started to kiss as the warm water ran down their faces.

Tristan pushed Morgan back gently, so she was pressed up against the wall. He placed his hand between her legs and let his fingers tease her until her breathing pattern changed. "Not yet," he whispered in her ear as he withdrew his fingers and slid his erect penis inside of her.

Tristan lifted Morgan's legs up around his waist and she locked her legs in place behind his back. His natural rhythm took over as he thrust inside of her. It wasn't long before they climaxed together. Morgan felt exhilarated. This was excellent way to start the day.

As Tristan placed Morgan back on the ground, he had to help steady her. Her legs had turned to jelly beneath her. Tristan gave Morgan's bum one last squeeze, before grabbing the shower gel and washing himself clean. Morgan kissed him on the shoulder blade as she exited the shower and grabbed a towel.

Morgan was grateful that she had left a few clothes at Tristan's, after wearing other people's clothes all week. She changed into her own spare underwear, black jeans and grey punk-rock T-shirt. As Morgan applied some make-up in the bathroom, Tristan left the shower to get dressed.

He heard an alarm and went over to Morgan's phone on

the bed side table. It wasn't making any noise. Tristan knew it wasn't an alarm he had set on his phone but he checked anyway. His phone wasn't ringing. Tristan listened hard and followed the sound to Morgan's laptop bag. He searched in the bag and found a second mobile phone. The phone battery was dying, causing the phone to alarm. Tristan was confused. Why did Morgan have two mobile phones? He decided to leave the phone where he found it. He would ask her about it another time. When they were both ready, Tristan grabbed his car keys and drove Morgan to University.

After a long day of lectures, Morgan caught the bus home. As she walked from the bus stop to her shared house her phone rang, it was Cordelia.

"Hi, I was back in Scotland this morning making more of the energy potion. What's the plan for increasing the distribution? I can deliver two suitcases a week if you set a portal up in Nottingham," Cordelia enquired.

"I can do that, anything to help. Tristan and I have a plan. Tristan's going to meet with some more," Morgan paused trying to think of the right word to use, she was walking in public after all, "associates soon, to extend the reach."

"That's great. My gut is telling me we need to move quickly. That Vampire will want to take his revenge soon."

"I agree. I need to find a way to end the investigation into the Lucas family without having to debrief in London in case I run into him."

"Well I'll leave that up to you to figure out. Set up a portal on Sunday at five, somewhere secluded but in open space. Meet me there."

Morgan agreed and hung up the call. What Morgan wasn't aware of, was that Tristan had planned to surprise Morgan by meeting her off the bus. He was a little late and as he parked up ready to surprise her, he caught the tail end of her phone conversation. He held back and got back in his car.

What had she meant by end the investigation into his family? Were the Witches running an investigation into him? But then Morgan didn't know she was a Witch when she met him and why would she need to debrief in London? Tristan started the engine and drove instinctively back home in a daze.

Once inside his apartment he opened his laptop and ran an internet search on Morgan Fletcher. Apart from a couple of social media pages, nothing of note appeared. Tristan flicked through the pictures on social media scrutinising them. There was nothing from recent months.

Morgan had confided in Tristan, that her parents had been murdered in a car crash by a meth addict when she was eleven, so he searched for any newspaper reference that year. Bingo! He found a reference to an orphaned Morgan Hudson, following a car crash that killed both her parents. He read the article and knew it was Morgan's story. Why had she changed her name? Fletcher wasn't even her Aunt's surname. It made no sense. Tristan had an uneasy feeling in the pit of his stomach. He knew his Morgan, she wasn't a liar. Nevertheless, he slept poorly that night. He woke the next morning resolute in confronting her that evening.

Morgan woke to the sound of her alarm, alerting her to go for a run before University. She rolled out of bed and got dressed in her running clothes. She popped in her earphones and set her phone to play the latest episode of her favourite podcast. As Morgan turned the corner on her street, a small beige pug appeared out of nowhere yapping at her ankles. It was dragging its lead which proceeded to wrap around her legs causing her to stumble and nearly fall over. A young woman was running up the road carrying a black pug waving frantically and shouting, "Come back Frank." The young woman apologised and scooped up the dog, as Morgan untangled the lead from around her feet.

The rest of Morgan's run was uneventful. She returned

home to shower and change before catching the bus to University. She was a little disappointed Tristan hadn't responded to her usual *'Good Morning Babe'* message, but she figured he was probably still asleep.

After morning lectures Morgan met Molly in the cafeteria to eat lunch on campus. Nottingham University was always celebrating cultural events from around the world, to make international students feel welcome. It was Thanksgiving this week and a full turkey roast dinner was being served. Unusual dishes were on the menu such as, marshmallow sweet potato mash, creamed corn and pumpkin pie. Morgan and Molly piled their plates high and sat down on the bench seating together.

Molly and Jono were now dating. Last night Molly had stayed at Jono's new place in Nottingham. They'd had their first argument and Molly wanted Morgan's opinion on it. It was a really trivial matter which had been blown out of proportion. On recounting the events, even Molly agreed it sounded silly now. Morgan helped Molly write out an apology message to send to Jono. Morgan checked her own phone and noticed a message from Tristan, confirming he was free to come over to her house that evening. Morgan smiled and couldn't wait for her afternoon lectures to end, so she could race home.

By four-twenty Morgan was turning the key to her front door, when Tristan appeared behind her with his hands in his jacket pockets. He didn't have his usual cheeky smile on his face and Morgan was instantly worried. She froze in place waiting for him to speak, or crack a smile. "We need to talk," was all he said.

Morgan felt like her world had come crashing down around her. She felt bile rise in her throat, making her want to be sick. Dread washed over her in waves, as she opened the door and held it open for Tristan. She opened her bedroom door and Tristan followed behind her, with a continued solemn expression.

Morgan removed her coat and sat on the edge of the bed.

Tristan remained standing, next to the closed door. He wasn't making eye contact with her and when he spoke he looked at the floor.

"Are you lying when you say that you love me?" He spoke quietly and Morgan could hear the emotion in his voice, like he was holding back tears. Morgan answered honestly and immediately, "No, of course not. Why would you think that?"

Tristan looked up and made eye contact. Morgan could see a small teardrop in the corner of his right eye. "Why are you doing an investigation into my family? And why have you lied about your real surname?"

Morgan gasped in shock. How had he found out? Morgan stumbled over her words as she tried to explain. "Please don't be mad. It's not how it sounds. I'm an undercover agent working for the National Drugs Intelligence Unit. I was undercover but I messed up. I fell for you." Morgan watched Tristan for his reaction.

He was clearly shocked as his eyes widened. "You're an undercover cop? Were you ordered to get close to me?" His voice was raised now and Morgan could tell his heartache had turned to anger.

"I was, but when I got to know you I fell in love with you. I haven't faked anything." She hoped Tristan would believe her.

"Have you been feeding information back on me? What mark did you score me for my performance in bed?" He asked mockingly, with disgust in his voice.

"I haven't. I promise. I wouldn't do that," Morgan pleaded.

"How can I believe anything you say?" Tristan reached for the door handle.

"Please don't go Tristan," Morgan begged, standing up and reaching for his hand.

Tristan looked at her in disgust, shaking off her gesture. He opened the door and turned to leave before saying, "It's over Morgan. We're done." He slammed the door behind him as he left. Morgan was left alone in her room devastated. She held her head in her hands and sobbed. This was all her fault. She should have come clean with him and told him the truth. She had no idea what had sparked his suspicions. The weather had turned and rain poured down, creating a soothing pitter-patter on her glass window. She stayed in her room and cried herself to sleep. She was still fully clothed, clutching a T-shirt and a pair of socks Tristan had left under a pillow on his side of the bed.

Morgan woke the next day just before her alarm sounded. She looked in the mirror and prodded her puffy red face and swollen eyes. She looked as bad as she felt. Morgan decided a run would do her good. It would clear her mind and perhaps the fresh air would reduce the puffiness of her face. She couldn't bear to listen to any soppy love songs or chat today, so she left her headphones at home.

After a quick stretch to warm up, Morgan ran at full speed, jumping over puddles that had formed overnight. As she turned into the next street, Frank, the small beige pug she had met the previous day, had escaped his owner again and was running up the street towards Morgan. His owner, a young woman was running after him, shouting his name and dragging her other pug behind her. Morgan ran towards Frank and grabbed his lead before walking in the direction of his owner to hand his lead back to her. She thanked Morgan who waved as she carried on with her run.

Morgan ran a little further than usual, so when she returned home she had to rush around to get ready for University. The fresh air had reduced the redness of her face, but she applied a thick layer of make-up anyway. She wanted to save any embarrassing chats about whether she was feeling ok. She missed her usual bus to University, so had to take the later one which got her there with seconds to spare. She was the last student to slip into the lecture theatre and sat on her own at the back.

The lecture started and Morgan sat confused. They had

covered the human cardiorespiratory system in yesterday's lecture. At first Morgan thought they were recapping the previous lecture, but she was getting a serious case of déjà vu. Her lecture lasted all morning and she drifted off thinking about how she should have handled the situation with Tristan differently. She replayed the conversation over and over again in her head. She simulated different things she should have said and imagined how different his reaction would have been.

Before she left the lecture theatre she checked her phone, hoping to see a message from Tristan. Instead was a message from Molly asking to have lunch in the cafeteria. Morgan agreed and walked across Campus to meet her. Morgan surveyed the lunch options, whilst she waited for Molly to arrive. It was the same offering as yesterday. Morgan assumed the food would be the same all week to celebrate Thanksgiving.

Molly arrived in good spirits and Morgan didn't think Molly had noticed how down Morgan was. Morgan hadn't eaten since yesterday lunch, so she forced herself to start eating. Morgan stayed fairly quiet and Molly filled the silence, detailing the latest argument she'd had with Jono. Morgan tuned back into what Molly was saying and had a sudden feeling of déjà vu again. "Didn't you resolve this argument yesterday?" Morgan asked.

Molly looked confused, "What do you mean yesterday? It only happened last night when I stayed over at Jono's," Molly replied.

Morgan stopped and looked around the room. They were sat at the same table as yesterday. At the end of the long bench they were sat on, was a couple of skater boys with beanie hats and baggy trousers; the same as yesterday. Behind Molly on the next table was a couple passionately kissing; the same as yesterday. Morgan looked at Molly's confused face before asking, "What day is it?"

Molly pulled a face as she responded, "Tuesday."

Morgan dropped her fork on the table. She had gone back in time. It was Tuesday and if it was Tuesday then Tristan hadn't ended their relationship yet. "I've got to go. I'm sorry," Morgan said suddenly. She ran from the cafeteria, leaving her dinner tray and Molly at the table. Morgan ran outside and steadied herself on a low wall outside the cafeteria. She threw up the lunch she had just eaten. She thought about last night. She had dreamt of turning back time and she had fallen asleep hugging Tristan's clothes.

Morgan thought back to what Elspeth had said about time travel. You need three items and you need to concentrate hard. Her magic had always shown itself when her emotions were overwhelmed. She must have done it. She must have turned back time. She had a second chance to fix things with Tristan, but she had no idea what to say. There was no guarantee she could ever turn back time again, so she only had one shot to fix this. She didn't know what to say to him, but she knew she had to approach him and confess before he challenged her.

Morgan took out her phone and called him. The phone answered. Before he had time to speak Morgan blurted out, "Tristan where are you? I need to see you now."

"I'm at Wild," he responded. Morgan hung up and started running towards the bar.

She managed to get there in ten minutes. The run allowed her to calm her thoughts. When she arrived, the bar was open for lunch service, so she walked in and proceeded up to Tristan's office. She banged on the office door and Tristan answered it with a puzzled expression on his face. "What's with the urgency? I thought you had lectures this afternoon."

Morgan couldn't hold back her emotions any longer. As she entered the room and closed the door, she blurted out, "I love you more than anything, you know that right?" She paused, waiting for Tristan to respond. He nodded. "What I'm about to tell you will shock you but you have to believe me and hear the whole story," she paused, waiting for him to promise. He nodded again. "Sit down," Morgan instructed, as she grabbed his hands and sat next to him on the sofa.

"We didn't meet by chance. I orchestrated getting a job here because I work for the National Drugs Intelligence Unit as an undercover agent. I was assigned by the Vampire that attacked me to investigate why people were dying from drug overdoses in the midlands." Tristan went to speak but Morgan put her finger over his mouth, to signal that she needed to finish speaking first.

"He attacked me because he thought I wasn't reporting back quickly enough. But by attacking me he started a chain of events which he could never have predicted. You explained a world to me I never knew existed and that I actually belonged to. I fell in love with you and I stopped reporting back the day I got a new phone. I switched sides and I would never betray you or your family. In half term I went back to London and started investigating your brother's murder. I found who did it. It was an ordered hit by the Vampire who attacked me and kidnapped my Aunt. His name is Silas Nicolescu and he's the Commander in Chief for the National Drugs Intelligence Unit."

Tristan sat in disbelief, stunned with the revelations he had just heard. Morgan's timing could not have been better. He had planned to question her that evening about what he had overheard, but she had been honest and beaten him to it. He had to admire her for that. She was as honest and as truthful as he knew her to be. He knew in his heart she loved him and he loved her, but the fact their love story wasn't as organic as he had believed, did sting a little. She had stopped playing a part a long time ago and he thought back to when she changed her phone. It was before they had sex for the first time. She had started to dress more casually, wearing jeans and trainers more. She had been exactly the same person around her Aunt and Cordelia as she was alone with him. Surely they would have noticed if she was playing a part and not being herself. She was from the supernatural world and she had shared her magical self-discovery with him. And most importantly she had used her skills to investigate his brother's murder to get justice for his death. He had no words, so all he could think to do was hug her. Morgan hugged him tightly back.

As Tristan pulled back from the embrace, he looked Morgan in the eyes before saying, "Thank you for being honest with me. I love you." Morgan had tears rolling down her cheeks. She reached up and kissed him on the lips. Tristan kissed her back and they hugged tightly again.

Morgan didn't know if the tears were from exhaustion or happiness, as she wiped her face on her coat sleeve. "Let's go back to mine," Tristan stated, grabbing his coat from the back of his office door. He locked up as they left the room, hand in hand.

That night Tristan asked Morgan to tell him all about her life as an agent. Morgan went into detail about her time in training camp and her previous undercover missions. Tristan eventually asked how she had discovered his brother's murderer and Morgan opened her laptop to detail the steps she had taken. She showed him the security footage she had spent hours watching and ended with showing him the file Steve had given her for agent Irina Smirnov. Morgan could see Tristan was grinding his teeth and holding back his rage.

When they went to bed that night Tristan couldn't sleep. He kept replaying the security footage over and over in his mind. When he finally fell asleep he was haunted by the night he had kicked the Vampire out of his bar, moments before he attacked Morgan. When he woke that morning the only thing on his mind, was revenge.

CHAPTER 17

The End

Tristan was quiet that morning as they got ready together. Morgan didn't want to press him. She knew his mood wasn't about her. He was reflecting on all the information she had given him yesterday about his brother's murder. Tristan kissed her goodbye as he dropped her off at campus for her morning lectures. Morgan wasn't quite sure why she was keeping up the pretence of University. She needed to arrange a meeting away from the office with Steve and end the investigation into the Lucas family. Tristan hadn't challenged the absurdity of it either, but Morgan knew his mind was focused on other things. She carried on with the charade, but sat at the back of the lecture theatre and made notes on what she planned to say to Steve.

As Morgan walked through the front door of her shared house that evening, Molly was just leaving to go out for dinner with Jono. Molly was dressed in a gorgeous, long, navy blue, velour dress and Morgan could tell she had put a lot of effort into curling her usually straight, blonde hair. Morgan wolf whistled at Molly as she slid past her in the hallway and Molly cheekily replied, "If you like the dress, you should see what I've got on underneath. Don't wait up for me!" Molly winked and walked across the street, to where Jono was now holding the passenger car door open for her. Morgan shouted, "Have fun!"

Tristan arrived after dinner but was still very quiet. He wasn't his usual jokey self and didn't join in with any of the boys banter. Morgan pulled him aside in the kitchen and asked if he wanted to talk, but he shook his head. Before nine Tristan excused himself, saying he was really tired and needed a good night's sleep at home. He kissed Morgan passionately goodbye, reassuring her he just needed sleep. Once home, Tristan called each one of his closest friends and explained that he had found out who murdered his brother. He formulated a plan to get revenge and murder Silas. He asked his pack of friends to meet him at nine the next morning.

By nine that morning, Jono, Matthew, the Cane twins and Fenik had arrived at Tristan's parent's house, where he was already waiting in the car. Jono and Fenik joined Tristan in his Land Rover Defender. Matthew drove the Cane Twins, in convoy with Tristan, down to Silas' house to confront him.

Morgan had decided that she would not keep up the pretence of being a University student anymore. After breakfast she planned to call Steve to arrange an offsite meeting. She had allowed herself a lie in and woke up naturally at eight-thirty. Morgan entered the kitchen/living room, believing she would be alone in the house, but Molly was standing by the toaster in her nightie. Molly jumped when she saw Morgan walk in.

"You gave me a fright! I thought I would I be on my own this morning."

"Me too," Morgan confessed. "Did you not stay at Jono's last night after your hot date?"

Molly's face said it all. "No," Molly replied clearly disappointed, "Jono got a call from Tristan at ten, just as we were finishing dessert in this gorgeous little restaurant. Jono went bright red, like he was really angry and he actually broke the wine glass he was holding. It just shattered. After that call he said he needed to be up early to be at Tristan's for nine, so needed to drop me home straight after dinner."

"Did he say why he needed to be at Tristan's for nine?" Morgan asked, checking her watch for the time.

"He didn't really go into detail, but said he needed to pick up Fenik from the bar before heading over to Tristan's. After I questioned him further, he told me that they were driving to Weybridge. So they will probably be gone for the whole day." Molly pulled a face showing she was clearly not impressed with the lack of details Jono had given her.

Morgan froze in place. Tristan was going to Weybridge with a group of his Lycan friends. Morgan knew what Tristan was planning. Revenge! She bolted from the room giving Molly no explanation. She hastily booked an Uber to take her to Tristan's. Whilst she pulled on the first pair of jeans and hoodie she could lay her hands on, she repeat dialled Tristan's number. But he didn't answer.

It wasn't yet nine, so she tried calling Jono and Fenik, but neither of them answered. The taxi arrived quickly and she ran out of the house to meet it. Morgan begged the driver to go as quickly as possible, but by the time she pulled up at Tristan's house it was nine-fifteen and his Land Rover was not on the drive. Morgan pressed the gate buzzer, but no one answered. Morgan had to think quickly.

She looked over to Tobias and Charlotte's house further down the road. She could see smoke coming from the chimney. She instructed the taxi driver to reverse down the narrow lane, back onto the main road and drop her off at the alternative address. Morgan ran from the taxi to the front door and knocked on the door furiously. The taxi left and after a few agonising minutes, Tobias opened the door. He was dressed in a black tracksuit, as if he was about to go on a run. After seeing Morgan alone on his doorstep, his expression immediately turned from surprise to concern.

Morgan rapidly explained the situation and Tobias grabbed his car keys, before showing Morgan which car was his. Morgan jumped in the passenger seat of the navy BMW seven series parked on the drive. Tobias sped out of the

THE UNDERCOVER AGENT AND THE LYCAN

driveway as Morgan programmed the sat nav to Weybridge. On the journey, Morgan confessed how she had found out about Timothy's killer and how Silas her Chief Commander, who was also a Vampire, had ordered it. She divulged how she had used magic to find her Aunt after she was kidnapped by the same Vampire and that's where she believed Tristan was going to seek revenge. Tobias listened calmly to it all, without asking any questions.

When Morgan finished speaking, Tobias finally asked. "Do you know who he has gone with?"

"I know he's gone with Jono and Fenik, but I don't know if anyone else has joined them."

Tobias put his foot down on the accelerator pedal and Morgan felt the car jerk forward. She glanced at the speedometer and could see the needle was over 100 mph. "Why did you ask that?" Morgan queried.

Tobias took a deep breath before replying, "Because this Vampire is surely expecting us to take revenge. He won't be alone. Three Lycans are no match for a coven of Vampire's. I don't know anyone who's killed a Vampire. I can't believe he's being so reckless. My father told us stories of Lycans that had managed to kill a couple of Vampires, but you'd need a whole pack."

"How many is a pack?" Morgan asked concerned.

"Six or more."

Morgan had a sinking feeling in the pit of her stomach. They sat in silence until the sat nav cut out in the middle of Weybridge town centre and Morgan had to relay the rest of the directions based on memory.

The roads had been fairly quiet and the two car convoy had made it to the Vampires house in just over two hours. Tristan pulled up to the side of the country road, as he had previously, out of sight of any cameras. Matthew pulled in behind him and everyone exited the cars. "Time to transform," Tristan instructed, as he started removing his clothes.

The others copied and one by one, they all transformed into Wolves. As Wolves they could use pack telepathy to communicate, as well as through howling. Tristan assumed the role of alpha male and directed the pack around the side of the Vampire's property. Tristan started to dig under the hedge, making a hole large enough for him to crawl through. He appeared on the driveway, hidden from the house by the brick garage. He waited until all six of them were on the driveway, before showing himself to the house. Tristan instructed the others to wait behind the garage for his signal, to use the art of surprise to their advantage. Tristan howled loudly and stood firm on all four paws in the centre of the driveway.

The front door opened and Silas appeared in a black shirt and suit trousers. "I was wondering how long it would be, before you turned up for revenge," Silas said in a mocking tone, as he cracked his neck from side to side. Tristan howled again and the remaining five Wolves slunk out from behind the garage, forming a V behind Tristan. Silas laughed. "I'm glad you didn't come alone. That would have been too easy."

Silas stepped forward. Behind him appeared Irina Smirnov and Vincenzo Leonardo. At the sight of Irina, Tristan let out a deep growl and pack telepathy told the rest of the Wolves, she was the one who had murdered Timothy. The rest of the pack growled in response. Tristan could barely contain his anger. He assigned the Cane twins to take out Irina. Fenik would join him to tackle Silas, leaving Matthew and Jono to attack the other Vampire.

Tristan made the first move and the Wolves followed his lead. They swiftly ran towards the Vampires, who had an advantage as they were positioned behind the black moat. The Wolves leapt in unison over the water. Vincenzo stood his ground, managing to grab Matthew and spun him into the moat, but Jono caught him off guard and tackled him to the ground. Irina ran around the side of the house and the twins gave chase. Silas jumped, meeting Fenik and Tristan mid-air.

Silas tried to grab them both, but missed. Silas was now on the driveway and the Wolves on the other side of the bridge. Tristan instructed Fenik to jump again from the side, to make it appear he was assisting Matthew, whilst Tristan walked slowly and confidently over the bridge.

Silas' sole attention was focused on Tristan. The divide and conquer tactic worked. Silas sprinted at Tristan, he grabbed him and lifted him off the ground but Fenik predicted his attack and managed to lock his jaw around Silas' ankle. Silas let out a piercing scream. Whilst he tried to shake off Fenik, Tristan wriggled out of Silas' grasp and began tearing at Silas' arm.

Matthew was now out of the moat and joined Jono in tackling Vincenzo. Jono had chewed off Vincenzo's right foot and hand. Jono was stood on top of Vincenzo's chest, with his jaw around Vincenzo's throat. Matthew was gnawing off Vincenzo's left hand. Jono's white fur was covered in thick red blood, as he finally managed to rip open Vincenzo's throat, severing his wind pipe. Vincenzo stopped resisting and his body started convulsing, as blood gushed from his throat. Matthew assisted Jono, in severing the head completely from the body.

Irina had climbed half way up the drain pipe on the side of the house and was taunting the twins. She had no intention of fighting them, but was trying to distract them long enough for Silas and Vincenzo to appear.

Tobias recognised the cars on the side of the road before Morgan. He did an emergency stop, pressed the cars automatic window button down and listened. He could hear a commotion and a mixture of growls. Morgan pointed to the Vampires house just up ahead and Tobias made a quick decision, to ram the security gates with his car. He pressed his foot hard on the accelerator pedal, turned off the front airbags and held his arm out to protect Morgan. They burst through the newly repaired metal gates, straight into the driveway.

The scene before them made Morgan hold her breath. Silas was in the middle of the driveway, a large brown Wolf was gnawing at his ankle, whilst Silas had both hands round the throat of another Wolf. Morgan recognised the colourings as Tristan. The appearance of the car didn't appear to distract anyone, so both of them exited quickly. Tobias transformed into a large white Wolf and ran for Silas' other leg. Tristan lost his fur and returned to his human form before Morgan's eyes. He was choking to death.

Morgan felt a moment of helplessness and despair, before she gathered her thoughts. She looked up to the sky and stretched out her arms as she screamed. "I call upon my fellow sisters to empower me, help me, I implore thee." The sky turned grey, thunder rumbled in the distance and a bolt of lightning struck the ground in front of Silas. Morgan knew her ancestors had heard her plight. Morgan raised her left leg and stomped as hard as she could on the ground. The earth in front of her began to crack open, forming a cavern all the way up to the bridge between Silas' legs. Silas let go of Tristan and his body dropped to the ground. Both Wolves jumped back and Tobias dragged Tristan's body away from the Vampire.

Silas jumped to one side of the cracked earth and started to walk towards Morgan. She stood her ground. She was ready for the fight and now confident in her abilities. Morgan turned her head to stare at a large oak tree, on the other side of the hedge perimeter. Using only the power of her mind, she uprooted the huge tree from the ground until it was hovering in the air. Gesturing with her hand she hurtled it towards Silas. The tree collided with the Vampire, knocking him to the ground.

Jono and Matthew had now joined the others on the driveway. Feeling the ground tremor and hearing a deafening sound. The twins had also made their way to the front of the house, to find out what was going on. Irina climbed the drainpipe to the roof and skulked to the front of the house, watching from above. Curiosity had gotten the better of her. Everyone watched intently as Morgan used her magic effortlessly.

Silas crawled out from under the tree, snarled at her and jumped on top of it ready to lunge. He had pure hatred in his eyes. Morgan used her hands to gesture a powerful gust of wind, to force him backwards. As much as Silas tried to walk forwards, he was rooted to the spot. Morgan suddenly flew up into the air, more than ten feet off the ground. She clicked her fingers and Silas burst into flames. His scream was haunting. The tree beneath him was untouched by the fire. As Silas screamed in pain, he tried to pat down the flames. Morgan clicked her fingers again, turning the flames to ice. Silas went rigid and Morgan could see his eyes wide in fear as the ice prevented him from blinking.

Morgan gestured with her hands once more and Silas' body rose into the air. Morgan could feel power surging through her body, like an electrical current. She felt uneasy with the magnitude of power and hesitated before making her next move. She descended herself back to the ground.

She glanced over to Tristan's naked limp body, being cradled by a now naked, human Tobias. The others remained as Wolves. They were staring at her and Silas' frozen body hovering in mid-air. Anger took over and she screamed, "The end." Morgan dropped her arms down dramatically and Silas' frozen body fell from the air, shattering on impact with the ground. To ensure he could never resurrect, she clicked her fingers again and his remains burst into flames. The ice melted away and he had turned to ash on the ground.

Irina looked on in disbelief at what she had just witnessed. Never had she heard of a Witch so powerful. She quietly ran from the rooftop, jumping over the perimeter hedge. She kept running as fast as she could, without looking back. She needed to tell the council what she had witnessed.

Morgan ran to Tristan. Tobias had put him in the recovery position. Purple bruising had already appeared around his throat.

"Is he?" Was all Morgan managed to say.

Tobias confirmed, "He's alive, just weak. His ribs and clavicle bones are broken."

Morgan looked towards Tobias as he spoke, horrified at the injury's he was describing. Tobias placed a hand on her shoulder before adding, "We heal quicker than humans. As long as it's just broken bones, he will heal."

The other Wolves disappeared, only to reappear in human form with clothes on moments later. Jono handed Tobias a pair of boxers and a plain white T-shirt, before walking over the bridge towards the house. Jono pulled a lighter from his pocket and set fire to the remains of the other male Vampire. Matthew joined him over the bridge and entered the house. He came back moments later, letting everyone know he had removed the memory card and battery from the surveillance equipment.

Morgan sat on the ground next to Tristan for what seemed like an eternity, before she heard a faint groan. Tristan opened his eyes and Morgan burst into tears of joy. Tristan looked at all seven faces staring down at him and asked, "Did we win?"

"Course we did," replied Jono immediately, "You should've seen Morgan, she was amazing. She obliterated that smarmy bastard."

Tristan managed a smile and attempted to sit up, but Morgan could tell from the wincing sounds, it was a painful undertaking. Tobias held out his hand, for Tristan to brace himself as he stood. Tristan accepted it and the brothers exchanged a heartfelt stare. Tobias stepped forward and gently embraced Tristan in a big bear hug. Morgan was the only one to see Tobias wipe a tear from his eye, as the rest of the pack relayed the details of the fight.

Jono and Matthew beamed with pride, recounting how they had taken down the male Vampire together. The twins were frustrated that the female Vampire had gotten the better of them. Everyone was impressed with Morgan, patting her on the back as if she was one of the pack. Tristan dressed slowly in the clothes Fenik had retrieved from the car, leaning on Morgan to steady himself. Morgan stretched up and gave Tristan a kiss on the cheek, before asking quietly, "Are you ok?"

Tristan flashed Morgan his cheeky grin as he responded, "Yes, I'm fine. I just wish I had seen you in action." He bent his head, to kiss Morgan properly on the lips and Morgan placed her arms around him, carefully.

"Enough of that, let's get home," said Tobias in a stern tone. Morgan went to pull away, but Tristan continued kissing her passionately, ignoring his brother.

When he eventually pulled away, Tristan cheekily responded, "I nearly died. I think at the very least, I can enjoy is a kiss with my girl."

Tobias just shook his head and everyone headed towards the entrance. Tobias climbed into his car and turned it around on the drive. The tree was still lying across the driveway, so it took him several reversing attempts to manage it. Morgan joined Tristan, Jono and Fenik in the Defender and they all waved to Tobias as he drove off. Jono offered to drive, so Tristan and Morgan sat together, cuddled up in the back seat. Every now and again Morgan heard Tristan wince from pain. They drove back slowly to Tristan's house, in convoy.

Morgan started to digest the events of the fight in her head. She had called upon so many elements. She started to count them in her head. With what she had conjured up in Scotland, the time travel earlier that week and during the fight she had successfully used every element's ability. Morgan smiled to herself, wondering what that meant.

CHAPTER 18

New Beginnings

As Jono pulled up outside, Tristan's whole family was waiting ready to greet them. Marisa and Hannah had tears streaming down their faces. They hugged everyone as they exited the cars. Hannah whispered, "Thank you," in Morgan's ear as she embraced her. Marisa gave Morgan a tight squeeze before letting go. Even Vincent, gave Morgan a sideways squeeze.

Marisa started fussing over Tristan, but he politely declared, "I need to rest. I just want to go upstairs with Morgan. Tobias can explain everything in detail." Morgan put Tristan's arm over her shoulder and helped him inside. Once upstairs, Morgan helped Tristan to get undressed and into bed. She suddenly remembered the mending bones potion she had made with her Aunt and fed Tristan a large spoonful.

When Tristan woke the next morning, Morgan was asleep next to him. He watched her sleep. After a short while, Morgan woke to see Tristan staring at her. "How do you feel?" She asked, hoping that the potion had worked.

"Fit as a fiddle," he replied. To prove it, he lifted Morgan on top of him and started kissing her. Morgan giggled and kissed him back. This led onto more physical pursuits and Tristan proved beyond doubt that his body was fully healed. They spent the rest of the day in bed, only leaving the bedroom to get snacks.

By Saturday lunchtime Marisa had insisted the couple join the family for dinner that evening. Tristan knew she would not be convinced he was healed, until she could see for herself, so he agreed. The couple arrived hand in hand in the dining room that evening, with not a scratch on either of them. Marisa looked satisfied, but a little put out that she hadn't been needed to nurse her son.

They were joined for dinner by the entire family. Vincent placed a large haunch of Venison down in the centre of the table and proudly announced it was courtesy of Zachary's hunting skills. Zachary beamed at the compliment from his Granddad, as Marisa placed the accompanying vegetables on the table. As Vincent sliced up the meat Morgan couldn't help but notice how bloody it was. Charlotte who was sat opposite her smiled before saying, "You will need to get used to your meat on the rarer side, now you are part of the family."

Morgan gave a happy smile at the thought of being accepted into the family and looked at each member individually. None of them had heard Charlotte's kind words. Each one was happily tucking into the delicious spread, comfortable in a Witches presence. Tobias' attitude towards Morgan had softened and he greeted her with a smile each time she caught his eye. He didn't berate her with questions like at the last meal. The feeling in the room was much more relaxed and Morgan began to feel like part of the pack. Morgan gave a happy sigh of contentment and started to load up her plate.

After the main course, Tobias helped his mother carry out the leftovers and serve apple crumble with custard for dessert. Tristan's nephews were intrigued with Morgan, asking her over and over what magic she could perform. In the end, Morgan clicked her fingers to extinguish the candles on the table and then ignited them again with another click. The boys were stunned into silence and spent the rest of the meal trying to click their fingers, in the hope of performing magic.

After dessert Tristan excused them both and they

returned upstairs to his apartment. The conversation turned to the topic of Morgan's future. Tristan seemed nervous to ask what Morgan was planning to do, after she ended the investigation into his family. She confirmed she wasn't quite sure and hadn't planned that far ahead. She had decided to travel to London on Monday, to talk with her boss. Tristan leaned across the sofa and grabbed Morgan's hand, before asking her, "Move in here with me? You can work at the bar full time or until you find something else you might prefer. You don't need money. I can provide for you. I just want you with me, always."

Morgan couldn't help but beam with happiness at the declaration of love. She nodded, as she tried to gather her thoughts, "I will ask for a sabbatical from work, to give me time to decide if I want to end my career for good. I would love to move in here and work in the bar until then. I don't expect to be a kept girlfriend." Morgan noticed a twinkle in Tristan's eye, as if a light bulb moment had just taken place. Tristan rained down kisses on her. Blissfully happy, they took their celebrating to the bedroom and remained there until lunchtime the next day.

After they both showered and dressed, Tristan drove Morgan back to her student house to pack up her belongings. Morgan was careful to separate her belongings with that of her alias. It didn't take long to pack her possessions into Tristan's car, but Morgan found it more emotional than she realised to say goodbye to all her house mates. They had been her first friends in Nottingham. Morgan had decided to tell them all she was quitting University and moving in with Tristan. She didn't want to lie, but thought the full truth a little too complicated to share with everyone. Molly cried as she hugged Morgan goodbye. Morgan promised to keep in touch with everyone and Tristan offered free drinks at the bar whenever they visited. It was an odd feeling to leave the house one final time. It was the end of a chapter and Morgan felt excited for the future ahead.

Morgan only remembered her scheduled rendezvous with Cordelia from a reminder she had set up on her phone. Tristan helped her collect sweeping brooms from the stables and a horse lead rope to use as the perimeter of the circle. They found a secluded spot in the fields behind Hannah's cottage and Morgan created the pentagram just in time. Moments later Cordelia appeared smiling, holding two worn suitcases. She greeted both of them with a smile. Her feelings towards Tristan seemed to have greatly improved. Morgan hadn't spoken to Cordelia since the incident, so she invited her inside the house to discuss the events which had unfolded.

Cordelia was furious to have only just found out, but then became astonished as Morgan explained the details of how she destroyed a Vampire. Before she left, Cordelia promised to inform the Witches council and ensure everyone was ready for the retaliation which would surely follow.

The next day, Morgan found herself staring up at the tall ministry building in London. She took a deep breath before she walked through the revolving door. She wondered if this would be the last time she would enter the building. She thought back to the first time she had entered. The pride she had felt. The excitement had made her tingle all over. But now it was time for a new beginning, one of love and self-discovery. The future possibilities made her smile.

Morgan unlocked her agent phone and scanned her electronic pass on the turnstiles to gain access to the elevators. She took the elevator up to the fourth floor, making a beeline for Martha at her desk. Martha looked up briefly from her screen to give Morgan a disapproving look, which Morgan could only ascertain was in reference to her attire. Morgan had taken the first train that morning, so bypassed her apartment and her office apparel. It wasn't long before Steve appeared at the doorway and invited her into his office.

Morgan was now stood opposite Steve in a black hoodie, denim jeans and Dr. Martens. Steve took the opportunity to review her attire before instructing Morgan to sit. Steve had always been a stickler for etiquette and Morgan's hands started to sweat. She felt uncomfortable at the oversight she had made, in her haste to get this conversation over with.

"Before you brief me on the latest on the case, I want to update you on our mutual investigation. I did some more digging and found more condemning evidence against the Chief Commander. I took my findings to the Commissioner and he sanctioned an internal investigation. However, the Chief Commander has disappeared. He clearly has spies within the department and I am now focusing my efforts on uncovering them. Agents have been to his rental property and made some disturbing discoveries." Steve pulled a disgusted face and Morgan saw his whole body shudder.

Morgan tried to hide her fear at being discovered. She had been in no fit state mentally to remove any evidence that might have remained. Morgan thought back to the last memory she had of the house and the driveway. The uprooted tree had been left across the driveway.

Steve took a sip from his water bottle on the desk and continued talking, before Morgan had a chance to think of what to say next. "The driveway showed signs of a struggle, or maybe a freak weather accident. But what we found inside his bedroom was more disturbing. Sadistic torture implements, multiple blood and DNA samples have been identified. He clearly left in a hurry as personal items had been left. However the contents of the fridge had been emptied, so I think abduction unlikely. Perhaps he double crossed the wrong people, or perhaps he was just trying to cover his tracks. I am in no doubt he was a corrupt agent and I will do everything in my power to bring him to justice. I wanted you to be aware. It goes without saying this is classified information."

Morgan nodded in agreement. Amazed at how well the conversation had gone. Her involvement hadn't been discovered and her secret was safe.

"Now, you called this meeting Morgan. What did you need to discuss?" Steve relaxed back into his swivel chair, placing his elbows on the arm rests.

Morgan took a deep breath and began her rehearsed speech. She handed over her investigation reports, confirming that she had never witnessed any criminal activity whilst undercover.

"I have my suspicions this mission was about something else, other than drugs. The Chief Commander pushed for this undercover operation. I have been going through the case notes and the background intelligence is weak. I wouldn't be surprised if it was forged. I see no reason to continue with the investigation. I will close it down and you can make your exit. If that's all, you can leave. I expect you in the office next Monday."

Morgan felt a wave of relief wash over her, before her nerves began to build again. "Sir, there is one more thing. I intend to put in for a sabbatical. This undercover mission has put my personal life into perspective and I need to spend some more time with loved ones. I need a life outside of the agency." As Morgan looked up to read Steve's face, he was staring at her, assessing her.

"I can't say I'm not disappointed. I planned on you being instrumental in my investigation into the Chief Commander. But, mental health and family must always come first. If you believe this is the best course of action for you, then I respect it. I will grant your sabbatical, but don't be a stranger."

Morgan left Steve's office and headed for a hot desk to apply for her sabbatical. True to his word, within the hour Steve had approved it. Morgan handed in her agent equipment before leaving. It was a strange feeling, leaving the building. Morgan expected to be sad and maybe even shed a tear, but she didn't feel upset. She felt alive.

Tristan drove down to London that afternoon and loaded his car with Morgan's personal belongings. Morgan managed to hand in the keys with the letting agent before they closed. She was ready to start her new life as a Witch, in love with a Lycan.

By the time they arrived back in the midlands it was late so they ordered a takeaway. After dinner they watched a movie on the sofa and Morgan started to fall asleep, snuggled up to Tristan.

"Don't fall asleep," he whispered, "I have a surprise for you." Tristan had been waiting for full darkness to fall. He took Morgan's hand and grabbed her jacket from the back of the door. He instructed her to put it on, as he led her down the stairs. Hand in hand, Tristan led her to the field behind Hannah's cottage, where they had greeted Cordelia the night before. The full moon was visible in the night's sky and cast a beautiful glow over the ground.

"I planted a surprise this morning, after you left. Can you make the seeds grow?"

Morgan tilted her head in surprise. "I can try," she offered, shrugging her shoulders. Morgan bent down and placed her hand on the dry soil, as Rihanna had shown her. Out of the ground started to shoot thorny stems with small white buds, which developed into beautiful white roses. The full moon shone brightly on the white petals. The fragrance emanating from them as they bloomed open, reminded Morgan of rose Turkish delight. It brought back a distant memory of eating the sweet treat with her Father at Christmas. It had been such a long time since she had been reminded of her Father, tears started to form in her eyes. She tried to discreetly blink them away, so Tristan wouldn't think she was unhappy. The memory was actually one of Joy.

It wasn't until she looked again that she noticed the roses had been planted in a strange pattern, not rows as you would expect. Morgan thought how long it must had taken Tristan to complete the task in the hard winter soil and she reached for his hand.

"Tristan, they're beautiful. Thank you."

"I have one more surprise for you," he said. Landing a soppy kiss on her lips and hugging her tight. "Can you fly up and look down on the field."

Morgan was intrigued but doubtful of her ability to control her power. She focused all her energy into her hands, closed her eyes and imagined she was floating. Morgan felt a surge tingle through her fingers and toes. When she opened her eyes, she was indeed hovering above the ground, but only by a foot. She closed her eyes again and focused. She pictured the first time she had levitated, when Tristan had told her he loved her. It was such a powerful memory. It gave her the power, to believe she could do anything.

When she opened her eyes again, she was higher than Hannah's cottage. Morgan looked down at the field in front of her. Her mouth fell open as she read the words the roses spelled out. MARRY ME. Tears of happiness sprang to her eyes and she lowered herself to the ground, to embrace Tristan. He was now on bent knee, holding open a velvet, red ring box. Her face was beaming and her response obvious, but she shouted, "Yes!" In that moment she was the happiest she had ever been. Tristan loved her, as much as she loved him.

Morgan dived on him to hug him, before even looking inside the box. As she pulled back, their eyes met and they passionately kissed. Morgan eventually realised she had not looked inside the ring box. Eager to see the ring he had chosen she carefully took the box from Tristan and held it up to the moonlight. It was stunning. A single flawless, round, light pink gemstone stood proud on a rose gold band.

"I tried to find a gemstone as unique as you are and the only one I came across was one named after you! The gemstone is called Morganite."

Tristan took the ring out of the silk cushion and slid

it onto Morgan's finger. It fit perfectly. Any negativity or backlash from being an interracial relationship, they would face together. There was no need to dwell on those thoughts tonight. Tonight was about celebrating the love of two people and celebrating is what Tristan planned to do. Tristan swept Morgan off her feet and carried her back up the staircase to the third floor. By the time they made it to the bedroom he was rock hard. He carefully placed her on the bed and started undressing.

Morgan was in a devilish mood and decided to tease him. She removed her clothing to reveal silk lacy black underwear. She sat at the edge of the bed, took his engorged member in her mouth and caressed it with her tongue. She used her hands, like he had shown her to massage the shaft, as she sucked on the tip. Morgan felt his legs start to quiver and heard his breathing pattern shorten before he let out a small throaty groan. Wanting to tease him further and prolong his orgasm Morgan stopped and shuffled back into the centre of the bed.

"Not yet Mr Lucas. My turn now," she teased.

"I could get used to taking orders," Tristan responded, as he climbed onto the bed and removed her silk knickers with his teeth. She helped him shimmy them down her legs and then pulled up her knees, opening her legs wide, to indicate exactly where she wanted him. As he lowered his head in between her legs, he muttered, "Ahhh, there's my favourite pussy." A reference to her panther tattoo.

He truly was a master at oral pleasure. Morgan experienced a multiple orgasm, which raised her from the bed, writhing in ecstasy. Satisfied that Morgan was wet and ready for him to enter her, Tristan lowered himself onto her body. His penis slid into her opening, as if they were made for each other, a key to her lock. He started moving rhythmically, whilst Morgan ran her finger nails lightly over his back. Just the way he liked it.

Just as his desire was about to take over him, Morgan attempted to roll him over. Her attempt was pitiful against his strength, but it gave him a moment to calm his desire. He took her lead and rolled over. She was now on top and they were still intimately joined. Morgan unclasped her bra from behind and flung it to the ground. Her breasts were now free to bounce up and down as she rocked her hips forward and back. Tristan lay back on his pillow, with his hands behind his head, enjoying the view. His desire quickly took over and he sat upright, taking her right breast into his mouth, whilst gently squeezing her left. He licked his tongue over her nipple, until she started to moan. He could feel her tense up internally around his pulsating member. Seizing his opportunity and unaware how much longer he could be teased for, he rolled them back over. Morgan was now lying on the bed and he resumed pounding her with his throbbing penis. Desire took over them both and they came in unison as Morgan screamed in bliss. She quickly crashed from exhaustion and Tristan watched her sleep, before succumbing himself.

The next morning Morgan woke with the biggest smile, remembering the events of the previous night. She turned towards Tristan, who was lying asleep in the bed next to her. She watched him for what felt like an eternity, before he eventually began to stir. He opened his eyes and immediately locked onto Morgan's deep emerald eyes.

"Are you nervous to tell everyone?" She asked immediately.

Tristan stretched his arms as he responded calmly, "No."

"Good. Let's call Aunt Winnie."

Tristan laughed as her excitement was infectious. "We're not even dressed yet."

"She won't know that. It's a phone call." As she responded, Morgan had grabbed her phone and started dialling.

CHAPTER 19

The Gathering

    Irina ran as fast as her legs would carry her, across the fields behind Silas' house. She didn't care who saw her. In the distance she saw a residential area. She ran towards it, slowing to human speed as she approached the first street. Irina used her heightened senses to assess her surroundings. It was a quaint suburban village. No one was around. The first car she spotted was an old blue Fiat. She crossed the street and sidled up to the driver's door. Irina took another quick look around, before she punched her fist straight through the window, pulled up the latch and opened the door to let herself in. She pulled the wires from underneath the steering wheel and hot-wired the ignition to start. Within seconds she was driving away from the scene of the crime. As she drove she punched the rest of the window away, as if she had just wound it down.

    Irina drove into Greater London and abandoned the car on a random back street in Hammersmith. She took the underground to Southwark and walked the short distance to a pay as you go gym. She flashed her ministry badge as she marched through reception to the changing rooms. In front of her was a row of changing cubicles and a bank of lockers. She made a beeline for the last cubicle, grabbing the rubbish bin en-route. She closed the curtain and stood on the bin, to enable her to lift the polystyrene ceiling tile out of the way. She reached inside the ceiling cavity and withdrew her emergency bag. Inside the plain black satchel were multiple fake IDs, pre-paid credit cards, a wad of cash in various currencies, several pre-paid phones, a long auburn wig and a pair of fake designer sunglasses. She replaced the tile in the ceiling and climbed down from the bin.

Irina strode out of the changing rooms past reception and out the front door. She took the underground to St Pancras station and purchased the next available ticket on the Eurostar to France. She paid in cash, but made sure that she was caught on camera. Once on board, Irina headed straight for the bathroom. She closed the door discretely and immediately set to work on changing her appearance. She scraped her hair into a low bun and applied the auburn wig. She turned her beige rain mac inside-out to display a navy blue mac. Irina removed her black suit jacket, ditched it in the bin and put on the sunglasses. Before she left the toilet, she took a moment to check her appearance in the mirror. She was unrecognisable. She smirked at her own brilliance. She had always enjoyed being a master of disguise.

When she disembarked in Paris, Irina strode off the Eurostar as Miss Lucile Kingston. She rented a car and made her way across the German border. Once in Austria, she abandoned the rental car, hired another under a second alias and continued on to Romania via Hungary. She abandoned the second hire car at the side of the road and walked a short distance to the train station. She took the train into the capital city and from there took a taxi to Alexander's residence. Demitri greeted her as she exited the car.

"To what do we owe the pleasure?"

"I need to speak with Alexander urgently."

She brushed past him with a mixture of disgust and contempt. She had always found Alexander's lackeys to be desperate hangers on, with no intelligent thought. She loathed having to report back to a man, even if he was ancient and wise. She hated being a pawn in someone else's game. She took all the risks, whilst he sat in his ivory tower giving orders. She would never have agreed to a life of immortality, if it meant working for a man for eternity. She had agreed to three centuries of service and she was eleven months away from fulfilling that agreement. She had signed the deal in her own blood, all those years ago on the premise that once her service was complete, she would be free to live the rest of day's as she wished.

She had been to Alexander's castle only a handful of times, but remembered the way to the great hall. The walk was imprinted on her memory. She was much more confident this time versus the last. The previous time she had to explain how her cover had been blown and how she had failed at her assignment to murder a high-ranking political figure. This time, although she was not delivering good news, she had information that Alexander would want to know.

As she entered the great hall through the double doors, with Demitri close behind her, she surveyed the scene in front of her. Alexander was sat on a throne in the centre of the giant room. He was wiping blood from his mouth with a white handkerchief, now soaked in deep red blood. Four dead humans lay on the ground at his feet. Two were male and two female, all in their early twenties. One had a fancy camera around his neck and Irina assumed they were unfortunate tourists.

Demitri smirked as he saw Irina's expression. She corrected herself and removed the disdainful grimace, which had crept upon her. Gluttony and male bravado did not impress her. She was just as strong and quick as a male Vampire. She believed whole heartedly that she was quicker than Demitri. She found that intelligence played a major part in how quickly you saw a danger approach. She wagered that living as a man servant would have dulled his senses. Why Alexander felt the need to display his prowess in front of others was beyond her.

Irina marched forward and forced herself to kneel in

front of Alexander until she felt his hand on her head permitting her to rise.

"How lovely of you to visit us today. What news from the UK do you bring?" Alexander asked.

"I witnessed a pack of Lycans and a Witch join forces. They murdered Silas and Vincenzo. The Witch had power like I've never seen before. My cover is blown and I will need a new assignment. I thought you should know about Silas and the young one."

Alexander's face switched in an instant to an evil twisted grimace.

"An alliance between supernaturals is unheard of. I will need to see for myself. You understand."

Before Irina had a chance to refuse, Alexander had risen from his throne and bitten down onto her throat, hard. She stopped herself from screaming in pain, she wouldn't give him the satisfaction. For a Vampire to feed on another was a despicable violation of privacy. When Alexander's vice like jaw let go of Irina, she dropped to the floor like a sack of potatoes, weak from the loss of blood. She clutched at her throat.

"Fetch Irina a glass of our finest," Alexander ordered, as he disappeared behind a curtain to his private study for contemplation.

Alexander poured himself a glass of red Barolo wine from his globe drinks cabinet, before sitting in his navy wingback chair by the fireplace. He liked to watch the wood logs burn to ash. A constant reminder of how he would die one day, burnt to ash. He liked to stare death in the face.

He took his encrypted mobile phone out of black chino pocket and dialled Ivan. Ivan answered immediately and after exchanging pleasantries, Alexander notified him of Silas' murder. Ivan went silent.

"Ivan, we will take vengeance. But first I need you with me when we confront the vermin. It appears that Witches and Lycans are working together. We cannot have this! Together they have proven they can take us down, even if it is one by one. Balance must be restored. Vampires are the only true righteous species to rule this world."

"I am in your service Alexander. Let me know when and where."

"Soon, I will reach out to the leaders and arrange a gathering. Ciao." Alexander hung up and moved to his writing desk. He opened his ink pot and dipped his quill. On pure white parchment he began to write a summons to Agatha and Vincent, the heads of the Witches and the Lycans in the UK. When he had finished, he melted the red wax on the fire and used his gold signet ring to apply his crest to seal the letters. His crest was a capital V overlapped with an A. He sent for Demitri and when he arrived, he handed him both scrolls. He told him to task his two best Stultum to hand deliver these invitations. "When they return, I will grant them immortality." Demitri nodded and left the room.

Alexander poured another large glass of wine and returned to his thinking chair by the fireplace. In truth he was horrified by what Irina had witnessed. He had not seen powers in Witches like this for over two millennia. He wanted to know what other secrets were being hidden. Alexander took out his phone again and called Anastasia. He instructed her to arrange a conference call for nine that evening with every European countries head Vampire. Most held positions of importance within the government or Special Forces and all were loyal to him above the council.

After hanging up on Anastasia he left his study in search of Bella. He marched across the great hall, striding over the corpses as he went. He turned left and walked down a series of corridors, until he reached a winding circular staircase that led to the furthest turret. He knocked before entering and a soft voice uttered, "Come in father, I'm just having my supper."

Alexander opened the heavy oak door and saw Bella straddling a naked young male, who was tied by all four limbs to an old wooden four poster bed. He had a gag in his mouth and was lying deadly still. As Alexander entered the room, he could tell the man was deceased. Bella had slit him from sternum to navel and half his organs were visible on his torso. Bella's hands and mouth were covered in fresh blood and she was eating his liver, whilst they were still conjoined.

"So theatrical Bella," Alexander said pride evident in his voice. Bella was his greatest creation. Her mother had been a beautiful brunette Witch, who had reminded him so much of his human mother, that he had imprisoned her over a millennia ago. He had raped her repeatedly and she had died giving birth to Bella, his one and only true daughter. Alexander had been intrigued when the Witch got pregnant not realising it was even possible. It became evident soon after birth that Bella was a hybrid, although arguably more Vampire than Witch. The difference between her and a sired Vampire was that she enjoyed and needed food to survive, as well as blood. She grew as a human would until she matured at eighteen years old. By this time she had blossomed into the spitting image of her mother, with dark brown eyes and long wavy, chestnut hair. Her cruel nature outmatched even his. From her mother she had developed a sixth sense that could extract a person's greatest fear and then she used it against them. She said a person tasted sweeter with higher levels of cortisol running through them.

Alexander found her magnificent. He had spent the years following her birth trying to create siblings. But every human he experimented with died before giving birth and the Witches either committed suicide or never fell pregnant. She was truly one of a kind and he kept her true identity a secret. He knew even amongst Vampires her existence would not be celebrated.

"Bella, when you have finished your supper I need you to call a council meeting for tomorrow morning."

"Yes father," he heard over the sounds of masticating, as he left the room.

Anastasia appeared in Alexander's study at eight forty-five precisely, laptop in hand. She logged into the secure video call and stood behind Alexander as he opened the meeting. All the country leads had accepted the urgent invitation and Alexander began his address.

"I have disturbing news to report. We have seen an increase in unexplained Vampire deaths in the UK over the last year. One of my best subjects was assigned to uncover the truth. However, he has been murdered by a pack of Lycans working together with a Witch. She had greater powers than I have seen in over two millennia. I want in-depth reports on all known powers held by each coven, along with the latest report on both Witch and Lycan numbers and location settlements across your regions. I am dealing personally with the UK situation."

Germany efficient as always raised the question notification on the video call. Alexander opened up the floor for Greta to speak, "Are the council aware?"

Alexander snarled before responding, "The elders will be told what they need to know tomorrow morning. All reports are to be addressed to me and me alone." No further questions were asked. Alexander closed the call. Anastasia shut the laptop and left the room, understanding she would need to collate the reports as soon as they arrived.

Alexander stewed in his study, seething with rage all night, until Anastasia returned at one in the morning with the latest report on species numbers. It would take longer to assess the level of powers Witches were displaying, but that didn't bother Alexander. That part he was keeping to himself anyway. The council did not need to be made aware of every development. It would cause hysteria amongst the truly dull-witted archaic members of the council.

The council was made up of eleven members of the richest and most prolific Vampire families, with Alexander as the head. He disliked the majority of them, but only saw one as a threat. Vladimir was head of the Popov family. He had taken over from his sire, a couple of hundred years ago, when he had been mysteriously assassinated. Vladimir had radical ideas and wanted to overturn the status quo. He had no respect for tradition and Alexander hated him with a passion. Unfortunately, he had gathered quite a following, especially amongst the newly turned.

By eleven, the large round table had been reinstated in the great hall and all evidence of his earlier indulgence had been removed. Wine goblets had been arranged on the table, along with three glass decanters filled with the best wine from Alexander's private collection. He enjoyed showing off his wealth and playing host. Every occasion with an audience, was a chance to display his dominance and power. He sat in the most ornate chair around the table waiting for his guests to arrive. When Bella led his visitors through into the great hall, he rose from his seat but remained fixed at the table. He signalled each guest to their seat with a hand gesture. Everyone had arrived apart from Vladimir Popov. He was late!

"Welcome friends. As clearly not everyone can afford a watch, I suggest we start. Time is money after all." Several members of the council nodded in agreement and disapproval. Alexander was just about to start the meeting, when singing could be heard echoing in the distance. It progressively got louder until Vladimir appeared in the great hall. Alexander stayed firmly seated as he announced, "I'm so pleased you could join us, you nearly missed the meeting."

Before Vladimir even reached the table, Alexander began. "As you are aware, we assigned Silas, son of Ivan to investigate the increase in Vampire deaths in the UK. It has just come to my attention that Silas along with a young Vampire have been murdered by a pack of Lycans and a Witch that have joined forces. I have written to the head of the Witches and Lycan councils in the UK and demanded a meeting. I will personally ensure that fraternising is ended by any means necessary. I will be in England as long as required."

"I don't mind volunteering to join you. I have not been to the UK in years," Piped up Vladimir, a mocking cheer to his tone.

Alexander struggled to hide the contempt in his voice as he responded, "That will not be necessary. The council will need you here."

A few murmurs were heard around the table, before one member raised his glass and made a toast, "I would like to thank Alexander for handling the matter personally and I would like to toast to Alexander's success." Alexander graciously nodded and then continued the meeting with the trivial nonsense they discussed at these gatherings.

Morgan was stocking the upstairs bar with crates of beer and cider, as Fenik unloaded the delivery truck on this cold December morning. Tristan was running between floors, transferring the crates to the downstairs bar. A meek, skinny teenager with dark sunken features shuffled into the bar. Morgan clocked him first, shouting over, "Can I help you? We're not open." In a shaky voice the stranger responded, "I am meant to deliver this to the head of the Lucas family." He held up a rolled piece of parchment in reference.

Fenik had now entered the bar and placed two kegs of beer on the ground as he snatched the parchment from the stranger's hand. As he did so, he took a pronounced sniff and walked backwards slightly, as he shouted Tristan. Tristan appeared seconds later at the top of the staircase and pulled the same revolted face, as if a disgusting smell had drifted into the bar. Fenik handed the parchment to Tristan before barking, "You can go back to your master now. You have completed your errand."

The boy turned and walked out of the bar, relief visible on his face. "What was that about?" Morgan asked mystified by what had just transpired.

Fenik answered her as Tristan stared at the seal on the parchment. "He's a Stultum, a Vampire wannabe but he's still human, which is why we let him go."

Morgan thought about the concept of a Vampire wannabe for a second, before grabbing a bottle of pop from the bar fridge and unsealing the cap. She bent down and opened the old suitcase at her feet which Cordelia had delivered. She took out a single tablet and dropped it into the bottle. Then she ran out of the bar after the messenger. She spotted him in the distance and caught up to him in no time, shoving the drink into his hand she said, "For your trouble." As she turned to walk away she saw the surprised lad take a sip.

When she entered the bar, Tristan was reading the open parchment. "Quick thinking," Fenik said, with an impressed smirk across his face.

"The arrogant son of a bitch wants a meeting between the three leaders on Monday morning at two."

"Where?" Morgan asked.

"Stonehenge. It was once a site for all supernatural meetings. It holds significance for us all. You should reach out to Cordelia, I'm sure the Witches will receive an emissary as well."

Morgan took out her phone and called Cordelia. Cordelia said she would reach out to Agatha and get back to her.

The next morning, a boat with a single female passenger pulled into the small harbour on the Scottish island, inhabited by Witches. Meredith with a group of three other Witches was there to greet the boat. The passenger was shaky as she disembarked and placed the scroll in Meredith's hands.

"This is for Agatha, the leader of the Witches council. Are you her?"

"Go home Stultum and tell your master you completed your errand."

The woman didn't need telling twice. She climbed aboard the boat and instructed the captain to take her back to the mainland. Meredith and the group of Witches made their way back to the castle and Meredith handed the scroll over to Agatha.

Cordelia rang Morgan at noon and confirmed the Witches had also received the summons. Agatha had requested that Morgan join the Witch party and would need to arrive with them. It was imperative that the alliance between Lycans and Witches was kept a secret. Morgan agreed to travel via portal to Scotland to join the others, before they travelled to Stonehenge.

When the couple returned home, Tristan gathered his family and passed around the summons. Tempers boiled over and Tobias punched a hole in the living room door. Eventually it had been settled that Tobias would lead the meeting as head of the family. Tristan, Fenik, Jono and Matthew would join him. Vincent had conceded that he would stay at home and guard the family in case the Vampires were planning an ambush. Tristan followed orders and called the pack to notify them. They would drive in convoy to the gathering. The plan was to arrive a couple of hours early to transform and scout the parameter.

As soon as the pack of Lycans had left for the gathering, Morgan used the portal to meet with the other Witches. Agatha explained the plan and Morgan relayed the Lycan's strategy. The five Witches, Agatha, Meredith, Cordelia, Mary and Morgan travelled by portal to a small village, local to Stonehenge. Agatha had called in a favour with a nearby coven to set up a portal ready for their arrival. An elderly Witch greeted Agatha warmly and handed her a set of car keys. Agatha thanked her and took the keys, signalling for the group of women to follow her.

Agatha drove as close to Stonehenge as she could, before exiting the car quickly. They were all on high alert. "Be extremely vigilant ladies," she warned.

The group of women moved towards the magnificent structure and it appeared they were the first to arrive. Within minutes a solitary man walked towards the landmark. Morgan recognised him instantly as Tobias, flanked by two large wolves. Morgan tried not to give away that she recognised them as Jono and Tristan. Fenik and Matthew must still be patrolling the parameter she mused.

At precisely two, five figures walked slowly towards the monument. A man led the group followed by three women and another man. Morgan recognised one of the women as Irina. The Wolves recognised her instantly and growled as she passed them. Within seconds the two absent wolves joined the gathering.

Alexander began, "Thank you for accepting my invitation. I thought it high time that we met and reinstate the old council gatherings." He turned to Agatha, saying her name and nodding.

She in turn said, "Alexander," and nodded.

Alexander then turned to Tobias and said, "I was expecting Vincent, I hope he is well?"

"My father is very well, thank you for enquiring. I have taken on the lead role in our family affairs. My father thought I should learn diplomacy. I'm Tobias." Tobias made a point not to nod.

"Welcome," Alexander said through gritted teeth. The lack of customary manners clearly aggravated him. "It has come to my attention that two of my subjects were brutally attacked at home, by a Witch and a pack of Lycans. I have gathered us tonight to understand why. I wish us to live in peace and harmony."

Agatha jumped in immediately, knowing that Tobias might slip up with his hot-headed male temper. "That Vampire attacked a Witch and imprisoned another. He received a fair punishment. I assumed he was a rogue Vampire working alone, as I know you would not purposefully upset the equilibrium we have reached." She was calm and firm as she spoke. Morgan was impressed with how fiercely she stood up to the Vampire.

"I am shocked by these accusations and will of course

investigate. You have my word."

He said all the right words, but Morgan didn't trust anything that he said. He spoke with an arrogant tone and a fake smile. Morgan looked behind him and assessed the group of Vampires. The fact he had arrived with three women surprised her.

Alexander had made a beeline to assess Morgan as soon as he saw her. She was standing at the back of the group shielded, but he noted that she was assessing the group of Vampires.

"Forgive me, where are my manners? I have brought with me, my daughters, Bella and Anastasia, Irina my informant and Ivan my close friend and Silas' father." He signalled to each Vampire as he introduced them. Bella stepped forward and started to skip towards the outside of the tall stones. The wolves growled and watched her every move, as she skipped around the monument whilst muttering. Her behaviour was truly bizarre and Morgan couldn't help but stare at her. Alexander appeared not to notice her odd behaviour.

Tobias took his opportunity to speak. "Whilst we are trading niceties. That Vampire murdered my brother." He pointed to Irina and she had the audacity to smile.

"Do you have proof? I would gladly review it," Alexander proposed.

Tobias stumbled. He had proof, but not proof he could share without giving away the alliance and Tristan's relationship.

"Ask her," was his reply.

Alexander turned to Irina and asked if she had committed such a heinous crime. Irina responded, "Not to my knowledge."

The wolves growled loudly in response to her blatant lies.

"You understand without proof I cannot pass a sentence."

Agatha grew tired of the niceties and interjected. "Why have you really gathered us together?"

When Alexander replied he answered calmly and sternly, whilst staring into Morgan's eyes so intensely that Morgan thought he was seeing her soul.

"I came to seek justice for a grieving father and to ensure that fraternising was not taking place."

"What fraternising are you referring to?" Agatha enquired.

"Fraternising between Witches and Lycans."

Morgan noticed Agatha turn to look at Meredith for a split second longer than necessary, before she responded to Alexander. "I would never associate with Lycans and this is the first time I am meeting with that pack. I will ensure my house follow the rules if you ensure yours do the same. Are we agreed?"

"We are," responded Alexander.

Meredith had taken her cue from Agatha, and drew a pentagram encased in a circle on the floor in white chalk. When Agatha finished speaking she stepped to the side, into the circle. The rest of the Witches followed suit and held hands. Morgan joined in, consciously trying not to look over at Tristan. In an instant they had disapparated through the portal to Scotland. The Lycans were now alone with the Vampires. Alexander spoke first.

"Do you agree to maintain the equilibrium we have upheld for centuries?"

"Lycans do not make promises with Vampires or Witches. You stay away from us and you won't force us to retaliate."

Now was not the time to get revenge on Irina. Tobias leapt into the air and transformed into his Wolf form. His clothes shredded and fell to the ground. He joined the pack and ran into the distance. The Vampires were left alone at Stonehenge.

As they descended the stony steps to the castle Morgan pulled Agatha aside for a private chat. "Agatha we may have an issue keeping that promise to Alexander. Tristan and I are engaged." Agatha didn't look shocked or concerned.

"Everything that Vampire said tonight was a lie. We don't need to make peace with our friends Morgan." She paused before continuing and took Morgan's hand in her own, "Although, before you give up on being a Witch. Would you do something for me? Would you visit the sisters at the Holy Mary Convent in Corcaigh, Ireland? They can help you harness your powers and train you to use them at will. Maybe you won't want to give them up when you see what you could be losing."

"Why do you think I will lose anything?"

"Because when you marry a Lycan under the full moon you become a Lycan. It is ancient magic and I have no evidence to suggest the ceremony would work any differently on a Witch to a human."

"My powers are at their strongest when I am with Tristan. I don't believe I will lose them but I will consider your suggestion." Morgan returned home later that morning via a portal. Tristan was waiting for her in the field behind Hannah's cottage.

CHAPTER 20

The Visit

With no one left to torment, Bella returned to the group of Vampires. She was the only one brave enough to question Alexander, "Why did we just let them leave?" Alexander snapped out of his gaze to respond. When he replied he spoke calmly and firmly.

"I wanted to get the measure of our opponents. Tobias is a typical Lycan, unintelligent, hot-headed and impulsive. He will die fighting a losing battle. Agatha is different. She's a natural leader and her fellow Witches will follow her to the end. She has secrets and I want to know what they are." Alexander addressed each member of the group individually and gave them their orders.

"Anastasia, hurry the country leaders along with the report on Witches' powers. I want to know if it's just that one Witch who has immense powers, or if there are more.

Irina your cover is not completely blown. I want you to insert yourself back into the agency and smooth over Silas' disappearance.

Ivan, I know no one better to retrace Silas' steps. I want to know everything he was up to. Why did he kidnap a Witch and what was his plan?

Bella, it is time we returned home."

"But father I want to stay. I never get to have any fun. Let me go with Ivan."

Alexander stood for a moment, not wanting to show open favouritism that could highlight his weakness; his feelings for Bella. To him, everyone was indispensable, except her. He valued her life, nearly as much as his own. He pondered if that's how all parents felt. "Very Well," he responded.

Anastasia hid her jealously well. Alexander always showed favouritism to Bella and allowed her to speak to him with such disrespect. Over the years Anastasia had made peace with being treated differently. She had her own ways of rebelling against her father. Ways that provided much more amusement.

Morgan and Tristan spent the next few weeks working at the bar and doubling their efforts to distribute the pills. The week before Christmas, Morgan decided to visit the Convent. She rang Agatha, who made the arrangements for her. Morgan kissed Tristan goodbye and promised to return before Christmas Eve.

Morgan was met at the portal by two nuns. They introduced themselves as Sister Mary Faustina and Sister Mary Rose. They both wore the full traditional habit which hid a lot of their physical features, although Morgan could tell that Rose was a red head from her eyelashes and eyebrows. Faustina was much younger than Morgan expected. She appeared to be in her early twenties. It shocked Morgan that someone so young would take a holy vow. Rose on the other hand looked exactly like you would expect a nun to look. She was much older than Faustina, certainly over seventy. They both seemed excited to have a guest.

"We don't get many visitors these days," Rose confirmed, "Our convent is quite secluded and since the school closed we only have each other for company. Agatha tells us you spent some time in Scotland recently. How is Elspeth?"

"You know Elspeth?"

"Oh yes we know Elspeth she regularly visits. Not as regularly as we would like but often. The last time was 1999 I believe. She spent the millennium with us. That was a special night." Rose looked off into the distance and smiled as if she was remembering a great event.

"She was well the last time I saw her," Morgan confirmed.

"Good," Rose answered with a warm smile. She had many wrinkles and a fair, freckly complexion, but her cheeks matched her name and her face lit up when she smiled. Faustina appeared to be studying Morgan. She was much quieter a plain Jane in comparison, with no blemishes or remarkable features.

It was only as Morgan approached the convent, that she took the time to appreciate her surroundings. It was a beautiful old stone building located on the top of a large hill. As she span around to take a look at the view, she smelled the salty sea air and heard the seagulls shrieking. Morgan smiled she enjoyed the sea air. A path that led to a beach was visible to her right. A nearby green house and allotments were visible behind the convent as she neared. No other buildings were in sight.

They entered the convent though a small wooden side door which led to a small cloakroom filled with outdoor wax jackets, fishing gear and wellington boots. Morgan followed Rose through the room and into a large kitchen. But this wasn't a regular kitchen. Several nuns wearing aprons were preparing food. One was stood over the sink washing dirt from carrots. Another was gutting fish. The third was focused on several chopping boards, as knives independently cut up a selection of vegetables. In place of an oven sat a large cast iron cauldron. The liquid inside was bubbling but there was no visible heat sauce. Morgan's jaw dropped.

Rose laughed, "Not what you expected?"

"You're all Witches!" Morgan exclaimed in surprise.

"Not every nun is a Witch but most. Magic is a gift from

God for Aclima's female descendants to protect themselves. Have you not put two and two together to realise that faith and magic are intrinsically linked?"

"Not until now." Morgan felt a little foolish. She had been intrigued by Agatha's request, but had simply thought that she wanted her to have time away from Tristan. Believing that she needed time alone to meditate and think independently.

Rose led Morgan through the kitchen to a hallway and from there into a room set up as a classroom. It had old-fashioned wooden school desks that opened and a chalkboard on the wall. Each desk was engraved with a dodecagram star. (Twelve-pointed star) Old books lined the numerous bookshelves and small cauldrons hung on tripods next to each desk.

"Many years ago the convent ran a school for young Witches. I enjoyed the days of teaching. Agatha was my best student. Present company excluded of course," Rose said as she looked at Faustina. "Sister Mary Faustina only came to us a few years ago. Agatha came here at five years old. Agatha was so talented she could already use her gift at will, but she was determined to learn everything about casting."

"Has Agatha explained to you my situation and why she asked me to come?"

"She has," Rose confirmed and Faustina nodded.

"You have a rare talent to be able to access so many active powers, but they are worthless if you cannot control them. We can help." As Rose spoke she perused the bookshelf and selected an old red, leather-bound book from the middle shelf. She placed the book on the closest desk and her hands hovered over it, just as Aunt Winnie had done. She directed the book to, "Open at chapter ten." The book did as she commanded and fell open on a chapter titled 'Multiplication'. Rose instructed Morgan to sit at the desk and to read the chapter. Faustina gathered items from around the room, placing them on the desk. When Morgan had finished reading the chapter she studied the items on the desk in front of her. An old sand timer, a lead pencil, a stick of white chalk and a fake potted plant.

Morgan focussed on the pencil first. She held it in her hand and stared at it intensely, willing with all her might for it to multiply. Then, barely moving her lips as the book instructed she muttered the word, "Harbeh." Morgan heard a faint pop sound and in her hand were two identical pencils. She continued to stare determined to push herself to do it again. She repeated the word and now four pencils appeared in her hand. Rose clapped and Morgan heard Faustina inhale loudly.

"Excellent work and on your first attempt," congratulated Rose, "Many of our casting spells contain words from ancient languages long forgotten by the world."

Faustina had gotten over her shock and was flicking through the pages. She turned the book around, Morgan read the title, 'Molecular Structures'. "Could you try this one?" Morgan placed the pencils back on the desk and read the chapter. When she felt confident with the instructions, she placed one pencil upright in the ink well on the desk and held both hands an inch above it. She muttered under her breath the word, "Kebhedhuth." Nothing happened. Rose corrected her pronunciation explaining the H's were silent. Morgan tried again but it appeared that nothing had happened. This time Faustina reached for the pencil and tried to lift it from the well but it was stuck.

"Amazing!" Faustina exclaimed, "Try yourself?" She instructed Morgan.

Morgan went to move the pencil but it felt so heavy that she couldn't lift it.

"You have changed the molecular structure of the lead in the pencil," Rose explained. "Now try and use the power of force to lift that pencil."

Morgan wanted to impress them, but the only time she had ever been able to control her powers was when thinking about Tristan. She knew her abilities were linked to emotion, so she thought back to the night Tristan proposed. How happy she had been. She focused on that feeling and grabbed the pencil. She lifted it with ease out of the ink well and then laid it down on the desk. The two nuns were thrilled, they both had beaming smiles.

"I want to try one more experiment before lunch. Follow me down to the beach," Rose instructed. Morgan and Faustina followed her out of the convent and down the dirt path to the sandy beach. They all took off their shoes leaving them on the grass to walk barefoot. Rose instructed Morgan to let the sea foam wash over her feet as she asked, "Can you call upon the water and the light to cast a rainbow over the sea?"

Morgan knew this would be the hardest task yet. She focused again on happy memories with Tristan. This time she chose the moment he told her he loved her, but nothing happened. She thought back to the first time she had cast a rainbow. She had been crying. Morgan thought for a moment. Whenever she had been her most miserable, the weather had seemed to feel her pain and reflect her mood. When her parents died it had rained for weeks and when Tristan ended their relationship it had rained all night. She closed her eyes and remembered the pain of that night, before she had time travelled. She envisaged she was back in bed, tears streaming down her face with the sound of the rain on the window pane.

Suddenly, she felt raindrops on her face. She opened her eyes and the sun shone brightly in the sky. The sisters were stood next to her watching. They were both completely dry. The rain falling on Morgan stopped and a rainbow arched from the horizon to beyond the convent. "Magnificent!" Rose exclaimed.

Morgan joined the Sisters for lunch in a grand dining room with a singular long wooden table. Sister Mary Faustina led grace. A nun that Morgan had not yet met served everyone fish broth from a floating cauldron. A bread basket was handed around laden with fresh bread rolls. Morgan was starving after her morning lessons and happily ate the delicious broth.

Once lunch was finished Rose led Morgan outside to the allotment. They walked through rows of planted vegetables, until they came to an archway with a closed metal gate. Above the gate in wrought iron was written, 'Poison Garden'. Morgan turned to the sisters. "You have a poison garden?"

Faustina replied, "Plants are vital to life and to Witchcraft." She pushed open the gate and instructed Morgan not to touch anything. Each plant was clearly labelled. Faustina led the way through the garden until she stopped at a leafy green bush with dark, purple berries labelled, 'Atropa Belladonna'.

"This is Belladonna also commonly referred to as deadly nightshade. It can be used to cure an irritable bowel or provide a good night's sleep, but in high doses or incorrectly used it can cause hallucinations and even death. I have been experimenting with it to enhance my visions."

"Have you always had visions?" Morgan asked curiously.

"Yes ever since I was a child. My mother thought I was disturbed. It wasn't until I grew older and reconnected with my father that I found out I am a Water Witch. It was a vision that led me here three years ago."

Faustina withdrew some gardening shears from her habit and snipped off a few springs of Belladonna. Morgan followed the nuns back to the classroom and Faustina grabbed a large green text book from the bookcase labelled, 'Herbology'. She instructed Morgan to find the chapter on, 'Atropa Belladonna'. Morgan flicked through the book until she found the right chapter. However before she had a chance to start reading Rose leant forward and closed the book giving Morgan a stern look.

Morgan knew what she wanted her to try. She held her hands over the book and said, "Atropa Belladonna." Nothing happened. Morgan was frustrated. She tried again this time picturing Tristan next to her, encouraging her. It worked, the book flicked open at the correct page. Morgan flashed a satisfied smile. She read the chapter and as she finished

Faustina placed the fake potted plant in the centre of her desk. "Bring the plant to life and then create the deadly nightshade potion to kill it."

Morgan touched the potted soil as Rihanna had showed her in Scotland. She pictured the moment the white roses had risen from the ground, before Tristan had proposed. After a brief pause the fake leaves on the plant in front of her bloomed into a real red rose. Pride radiated from her. Morgan set to work on creating the potion. With the help of Faustina she found the rest of the ingredients and then followed the steps outlined in the spell book.

"I need to boil the Belladonna leaves for an hour. How can I do that?" Morgan asked.

"Like this," Rose said as she clicked her fingers and a flame appeared.
Morgan copied her remembering the dinner with Tristan's family where she had shown off to his nephews.

"To prolong the heat without having to hold your hand under the cauldron the whole time, just whisper Exardesco." It worked and Morgan sat back in her chair thoroughly impressed with her accomplishments.

After an hour the liquid stopped bubbling and turned a deep purple. As the instructions detailed Morgan took a pipet of the liquid and carefully squirted it on the red rose, it wilted immediately. The petals fell off shrivelling into brown decaying mulch. The remains of the plant stalk turned brown and crisp. Faustina clapped fervently and Rose smiled.

"I need to start writing down some of these spells," Morgan mumbled.

"Yes you should. Feel free to access this library as much you like," Rose offered, whilst passing Morgan a plain, unused lined exercise book. Rose excused herself from the room for the rest of the afternoon and Faustina helped Morgan to search through the text books, to note down the most useful of spells. Occasionally she asked Morgan to try one to see if it worked for her.

At six bells rang nearby and Faustina explained it was the dinner bell. They packed away the books and Faustina led the way to the dining room. Seafood was on the menu again. Clearly it was in plentiful supply being so close to the Sea. After a delicious meal of crab linguine followed by apple strudel, Morgan followed Faustina to the chapel for reflection on the day.

Morgan was desperate to ask what vision led a twenty year old to join a convent, but couldn't find the words without sounding condescending, so instead she settled for, "Did you choose the name Faustina when you became a nun?"

"I did," confirmed Faustina, "I share many similarities with Saint Faustina. She had many visions sent to her by Jesus. She was young when a vision told her to join the holy order. Her given name was Helena and my parents named me Helen. The similarities were too strong for me to ignore so I chose her as my mentor, when I gave myself over to God."

Morgan spent the rest of the evening asking Faustina questions about faith and her visions. When the bells rang at ten to signal bedtime Morgan was truly exhausted and ready for sleep. Faustina showed Morgan to her room. It was a plain, small windowless room. The walls were brick and the only furniture was a wrought iron bed. Faustina pointed down the hall to the communal bathroom and said good night, leaving Morgan alone. Morgan took out her phone to message Tristan but she had no phone signal. She hadn't anticipated there would be and had warned Tristan to expect that. She closed her eyes and pictured kissing Tristan goodnight before getting ready for bed. After visiting the bathroom, she curled up in the single bed. It was only on reflection that Morgan realised that although both ladies were Irish there was a slight difference in the sister's accents. She assumed it must be a regional difference. Her last thought before she fell asleep was that she must enquire about the ladies' lives before they became nuns.

After a surprisingly delicious breakfast of smoked

kipper omelette, Morgan followed Rose back down to the beach.

"Fire can be a great offensive power in a battle against Vampires. Many are afraid of fire as it's the only true way to kill them. I want to teach you today how to really control it and harness its power," tutored Rose. She was an excellent teacher, very calm and patient. Morgan spent the morning practising how to dance flames across the water and burn driftwood to ash.

"Before the bell rings for lunch I want to show you one last fire power, the black flame. It's tricky to master and I doubt you will be able to manage it whilst you are here but please practice. I am sure it will come in handy one day soon. The black flame does not harm Witches, but it burns so fiercely hot that a single touch from a Vampire can burn them to ash." Rose stepped backward and placed her hands together in prayer. She shouted, "Purus Exardesco," and she burst into dark green almost black flames.

Morgan was startled and fell backwards in the sand, but Rose didn't appear to be harmed. She held out her hand for Morgan to grasp. After a moment's hesitation Morgan took a deep breath and touched Rose's fingertips. The flames spread from Rose's fingers to Morgan's and then slowly engulfed her whole body. She couldn't feel any heat just a warm glow and a slight tingling from her fingertips.

Rose stepped into the water and the fire disappeared from her body, her clothes un-scorched. Morgan did the same and the flames evaporated.

"That was amazing!" Morgan exclaimed.

"It's a special gift from Serephina. You can pass on the black flame to fellow Witches for protection. Agatha has the power and she is planning on using it in the war to come, but she could sure do with another to assist her."

After lunch Morgan returned to the beach and spent the rest of the daylight attempting the black flame, with no success. As she closed her eyes to sleep that night, she tried to reflect on the new skills she had learned since she had arrived. Morgan tried hard to focus on the positive results and not her unsuccessful afternoon.

The next day began the same as the last. Although she was thankful for today's breakfast of blueberry pancakes; finally a meal that was not seafood. Today she was spending the day with Faustina by the sea, to learn how to manipulate water without having to cry.

First Faustina taught her how to take a dew drop from a leaf, place it in a glass and then turn the droplet into a whole glass of water. Next, she showed Morgan how to manipulate water at will, sending jets flying through the air and twirling around her body. Finally, she demonstrated how to split the ocean. She walked into the sea and as she did so, the waves parted allowing her to walk eighteen feet into the ocean, without getting wet.

Morgan spent the rest of the afternoon practising. By the end of the day she was thrilled that she had mastered water manipulation and could even manage walking six feet into the sea before the waves crashed around her. Her failed attempts meant that she was soaking wet from the waist down and shivering, even though December was unusually mild. But she didn't care as she was bursting with pride. She couldn't wait to show Tristan her new skills. She was starting to really miss him. It was the longest she had not spoken to him since they had become a couple.

After a fish and chip supper, Morgan ventured to the convent library and perused the shelves. She couldn't decide what book to choose so instead held out her hands and said, "Salem Witch Trials." A navy, leather-bound book flew gently towards her and landed at her feet open to a page titled 'Salem Witch Trials'. Morgan picked up the book and returned to her room to read it before lights out.

As Morgan made her way to breakfast, she took a detour

to the library and returned the book she had borrowed. As she was exiting, Rose was walking past. Morgan felt like she had been caught doing something she shouldn't, so she rushed to explain. However, Rose wasn't upset with her, in fact she seemed impressed.

"The Salem witch trials are important to know about, they teach us the horrors and genocide that can be carried out due to fear. Ancient Vampires such as Alexander play on fear to gain power especially from vulnerable humans. Vampires have been behind every heinous genocide in history."

"Every genocide? Like World War Two?" Morgan inquired.

Rose nodded. "Alexander himself was named 'The Angel of Death' during World War Two. He was a prominent Nazi figure in charge of experiments. You should read more about our history in the library. The truth behind the history you think you know, might actually shock you."

"But the Nazis were defeated. So Vampires don't always win."

"Vampires make up less than 0.1% of the population. They are greedy, arrogant and egotistical. They don't work well together let alone with others and therein lies their weakness. Humans make up the bulk of the population of this planet. When Witches, Lycans and Humans work together for one goal against a common enemy, we can defeat them.

Witches worked with humans to create the atomic bomb that was dropped on Hiroshima and Nagasaki which ended the war. It was a terrible act done in the name of the greater good and one, many Witches still bitterly regret. Giving humans the power to commit such terrible crimes is something our species will have to live with."

Morgan shuddered at the thought of being responsible for so many deaths. She made a conscious decision to read up on the events of World War Two that evening.

After breakfast, Morgan followed Rose and Faustina

back to the classroom. Today's lesson started with trying to control the white chalk on the chalk board. By the time the bell rang for lunch Morgan had written the full lyrics to 'Twinkle Twinkle Little Star' nursery rhyme on the board. Morgan was growing in confidence and over lunch she convinced Faustina to take her down to the beach again to continue to practise controlling the elements. By the time the bell rang for dinner, Morgan had whipped up a small tornado out at sea, frozen an empty rock pool solid, created a mist over the whole beach and created a thunderstorm. As her confidence grew, so did her abilities.

That night before bed, she read up on the atrocities of the Second World War. Her hatred for Vampires grew, but her compassion for every other species and the importance of working together increased. Agatha may have sent her to the convent to learn about the importance of being a Witch, but her visit had also taught her the importance of standing together against evil.

CHAPTER 21

The Declaration

Alexander returned home alone by private jet. As he stepped out of his chauffeur-driven black, Bentley Continental, he wondered why Demitri had not received him at the airport. He strode into the great hall it was empty and he was perplexed at where everyone was. It was usually a hive of activity and that was the way he liked it. Alexander reached into his pocket and dialled Demitri but the call rang out unanswered. His irritation was now boiling over into anger. He turned around and headed for Demitri's quarters.

Alexander saw no one as he walked through the corridors that led to Demitri's suite. He half expected an orgy to be taking place, but the rooms were silent apart from a lone heartbeat. He marched through the rooms until he entered the bed chamber and found a single female Stultum sitting by the bed holding a corpse's hand.

She was startled when Alexander burst through the door. It wasn't until Alexander entered the room that he recognised the corpse as Demitri. His eyes were wide open, a look of frozen horror on his face. His skin was translucent white, with dark blue, almost purple veins all over his exposed flesh. He looked as if he was frozen solid.

"What happened here?" Alexander demanded.

In a shaky voice the Stultum responded, "The messenger returned. Demitri went to give him his reward. As he drank his blood he just collapsed. He's been like this ever since. The others left. I'm the only one who stayed. I alone am devout. I deserve to be rewarded."

Alexander felt a pang of fear which he quickly dismissed. How dare they attack a Vampire in his own home! His anger started to rise. He didn't know what sorcery this was but he would get to the bottom of it.

"The messenger where did they return from the Witches or the Lycans?"

"The Lycans my Lord."

"You have been tainted my child. You understand I cannot allow you to tell anyone what happened here."

As quick as lightning Alexander had approached the Stultum and snapped her neck. He could not have word of this reaching the council. Witches and Lycans would not get the better of him. Alexander took out his phone and called an old friend from the Gestapo era. Klaus had agreed to assemble a team of discreet scientists with a keen interest in investigative medicine. They would arrive by the end of the week to solve the mystery of Demitri's assassination.

Ivan and Bella took a taxi to Silas' rental property. Ivan ripped away the police tape from the wrecked iron gates and stepped onto the driveway. Bella followed behind twirling and cackling. They both stopped abruptly as the driveway opened up to reveal a large tree lying across the gravel. Ivan proceeded to examine the tree whilst Bella jumped onto the trunk and continued twirling. When Ivan reached the house he cut through the police seal around the door with a Swiss Army knife. He gave the door a sharp push with his shoulder. The front door flew open and slid across the concrete floor. Ivan stepped through the threshold and searched every room meticulously. Bella followed him inside, watching him and assessing him.

"Why so serious Ivan? Lighten up you're being boring."

Ivan didn't look at her when he responded. He was too busy riffling through Silas' office desk. "When Alexander gives you a job to do, you do it to the best of your ability."

"My father would expect nothing less from you Ivan. That doesn't mean you have to do it in silence, it's just so boring," and she rolled her eyes dramatically.

Ivan didn't acknowledge Bella's response. He sat at the desk and phoned Irina. "Irina, I need you to send me Silas' electronic diary and computer files."

Bella could hear Irina's reply with her advanced hearing. "How do you expect me to do that? Those items are in evidence."

Ivan's usually calm demeanour disappeared for a split second as he snapped, "Find a way, by tomorrow."

Ivan headed outside with a bunch of car keys he had found in the safe in the office. He entered each car and wrote down their most recent sat nav destinations. Two were of interest. One was a postcode for Nottingham. The other, the most recent was a postcode for Great Yarmouth. Ivan started up the engine and gestured for Bella to join him. He opened the glove box and saw a folder. Within it, he found a background intelligence report on an agent Morgan Hudson. This was the Witch Silas had bitten. The Witch who Silas had sent unknowingly to investigate Lycans. The Witch who Irina claims killed Silas with powerful magic and the Witch who stood in support of Agatha at the gathering. Her address matched the Nottingham postcode in the sat nav. Ivan programmed the sat nav to the Nottingham address and set off at full speed.

Irina stayed late in the office under the premise of catching up on paperwork. She waited until she was the last one on her floor. It was always eerily quiet in the office at night. Irina stood at the vending machine in the corner of the office and selected two chocolate bars, paying in cash. She walked to the floor kitchenette and made two mugs of strong coffee. She popped two sleeping tablets into one of the mugs before marching across the office to the elevator. Irina pressed the button for basement level one; 'Evidence Storage'.

Once off the elevator she sauntered up to the evidence clerk's desk and placed the drugged mug of coffee on the table. She withdrew both bars of chocolate from her pocket and handed one to Geoff the clerk on duty. She perched her bum on the corner of the desk to flirt with the clerk. Irina opened the other bar of chocolate and seductively sucked the end.

"Treat yourself Geoff. You work too hard."

Geoff thought Christmas had come early. He knew Irina professionally of course but he wasn't aware she knew his name. He was a balding, middle-aged man that had recently divorced his college girlfriend. He didn't think he had much game with the ladies, certainly not with such an attractive woman. He was convinced that she regularly went undercover, as she went missing for several months at a time. She always popped up in the thick of gritty investigations.

Geoff accepted the gifts graciously and attempted to flirt back. Within ten minutes of drinking his coffee his eyelids grew heavy. He rested his head on his arms for a moment's relief. Irina leapt off the desk and switched the mugs around. She patted Geoff down to locate his keys, finding them in his left trouser leg pocket. She used them to open the locked door to the evidence room and slip inside.

Earlier that afternoon, she had watched the colleague sitting next to her log in and memorised her sign-in information. She used it to log into the PC in the evidence room. She used the investigation number to locate the correct storage bay. She quickly strode through the racking to the correct bay and lifted the laptop from the shelf. She sliced the evidence tape with scissors from her handbag withdrew the laptop and turned it on. She inserted a memory stick and downloaded the contents of the laptop to the drive. When the download was complete she wiped the laptop and returned it to the evidence bag. She carefully copied the signature that she had sliced through. She returned the laptop to its place on the shelf and slipped back out of the evidence room.

Geoff was still snoring loudly on the table. Irina had to double back to collect his drugged mug from the desk before she entered the elevator. She pressed the button for reception and marched across the lobby with no intention of returning. Not even if Alexander demanded it.

Irina rang Ivan from the black cab she picked up outside the building. "I have it. Where do you want to meet?" Ivan gave her the address of the Ibis Hotel in Nottingham and said he would book her a room. Irina gave the details to the cab driver and offered to pay him double for his trouble. She handed him five hundred pounds in twenty-pound notes. The cab driver graciously accepted the cash and they set off bound for Nottingham.

Whilst in the cab, Irina took out her laptop and inserted the memory stick. She wanted to know what she had collected in case it had any bargaining value. She perused the internet history and cache data. She read Silas' recent diary entries and red-flagged emails. Irina then searched his recently accessed files. There was nothing of interest. Irina had never been a fan of Silas but she almost felt sorry for him. His life was all work. Boring actual police work at that. He had meeting after meeting in his diary and he seemed to complete tons of administrative work in between.

After several hours, the taxi pulled up outside the Ibis Hotel. Irina exited the cab without thanking the driver. She phoned Ivan as she entered the lobby but she needn't have bothered. She spotted Bella immediately in the hotel bar. Bella was draped over some unsuspecting man clearly seducing him with her charms. On a second glance Ivan was propping up the end of the bar, silently sipping a glass of wine. Irina joined him and before she had a chance to speak, he signalled the bartender and ordered her a glass of red Shiraz. He turned to Irina as he spoke, "It's the best they have I'm afraid." Irina handed Ivan the memory stick, grabbed the glass of wine and turned to walk away.

"Irina why did Silas order you to take down Timothy Lucas?"

Irina turned around shocked that Ivan was so blatant with his question. His code of take down was hardly subtle he might as well have just said murder.

"Orders are orders. I didn't question why."

Ivan didn't look satisfied. "Did you know who he was?"

Irina looked a little embarrassed. Truth was she hadn't known until she tasted his blood. It was different. Sour almost. She had spat it out. His memories flooded her brain and she had realised he was a Lycan and that he belonged to a prominent family. "Not until my assignment was complete." Irina walked away to reception after answering him. He didn't challenge her further. Bella and her new friend joined Irina in the elevator. Her unsuspecting dinner guest was surprised when Irina said, "Ciao Bella," as she exited.

Ivan stayed at the bar until it closed at three in the morning. When he returned to his hotel suite, that he shared with Bella he shook his head at the sight that he was presented with. Bella and her guest were in the bathtub. It was filled with bloody water. Both of the man's wrists had been ripped open by Bella's fangs. She was drinking his blood from the bathroom cups provided, using his radial artery as a wine fountain.

"Bella, we try to be more discrete in sating our appetites when in unfamiliar territory."

"I was hungry! I will clean up."

Bella rose naked from the bathtub and downed her glass of blood before smashing it in the tub. Ivan looked at her perfect womanly form. Was she trying to seduce him? He couldn't tell. She walked into the shower and rinsed off the blood before drying herself on a white towel. Bella went over to the room service trolley which had been ordered hours before and lifted off the cloche. Underneath was a plate of rare steak and veg. She picked the steak up with her hands and started eating. Ivan watched her intently as the juices dripped down her chin and onto her chest.

She was strange and erratic. Ivan didn't understand why Alexander seemed so protective over her. He made allowances for her that he would never allow with anyone else, even Anastasia. Bella yawned before asking Ivan for the credit card he booked the hotel suite with. Ivan handed it over and Bella slipped it into the dead man's jacket pocket. She removed his wallet from the same pocket and handed it to Ivan. Ivan spent the next few hours reviewing the memory stick Irina had provided. He had purchased a brand new laptop when they arrived in Nottingham. There was nothing of interest on it. He was disappointed.

Bella and Ivan left the hotel the next morning without checking out. Ivan waved down a taxi and they headed to the address of the undercover agent Morgan Hudson. It was only seven in the morning. The street was empty. Bella and Ivan stood on the doorstep listening to how many heartbeats were inside the house before they knocked. They detected three. They had no way of knowing who those three heartbeats belonged to, but Ivan was confident he could handle three humans. The only hesitation he had was if they were not human. He deliberated for a few seconds before deciding to ring the doorbell.

Bella's face lit up in anticipation. Ivan stayed focused and cracked his neck, waiting for the door to open. A petite, pretty blonde answered the door in a dressing gown. Ivan smiled thinking of all the things he would like to do to her. He put on his most charming tone when he spoke. "Ciao bella, I am looking for my niece Morgan. I was in the neighbourhood and her Aunt wanted me to drop by, to make sure she had enough food and was taking care of herself."

Molly giggled in that flirtatious simpering female way that all women did when Ivan laid on the charm. She played with her hair as she responded. "Morgan actually moved out last week but she doesn't live far. Do you have her new number? I can call her for you?"

"That would be great, thank you."

"My phones just in the kitchen, I'll fetch it."

Molly turned around and walked towards an open door. Ivan took his opportunity and sped into the house behind her. He bit down on Molly's succulent neck and carried her limp body through the open door into to the empty kitchen. Bella had entered the house behind him and closed the front door.

Ivan was careful not to drink too much blood, even though she was delicious. A young blonde was his favourite vintage. Her memories flooded his mind and he got the information he was after. The information Silas had clearly collected. He laid her body on the sofa so that she would believe she had fallen asleep. He wiped his mouth on the kitchen roll from the countertop depositing the paper in the bin.

"It's time we left Bella. I have information Alexander will want to know."

"But it's my turn. I want to taste her and there are two more upstairs."

"She is the girlfriend of a Lycan. We do not want to start a war today. We don't know who is upstairs. They may be Lycans. We must leave."

Bella was furious! She stomped out of the house in a rage. Ivan followed, carefully closing the door quietly behind him. As they walked down the street Bella picked up a handful of small stones and pelted them at parked car's windscreens. She threw the stones so hard they smashed holes through the glass. After Bella had damaged four cars in a row, Ivan grabbed her wrist. "Enough! Why don't you make yourself useful and commandeer one of these vehicles? I need to phone my pilot to arrange the jet."

Bella looked up and down the street. Two cars in front of them was a tiny old Toyota Aygo. She smirked as she strode up to the car and smashed the driver's window in with one punch. She opened the door and hot-wired the car so that the engine ticked over. Ivan was still on the phone and did not look amused. "Is this the best you could do?" He muttered in a sarcastic tone. Bella laughed as Ivan squeezed into the seat next to her. "Head for the nearest airport," he instructed. Bella did as she was told and followed the signposts to East Midlands Airport.

Irina had spent the night using Silas' access to assign herself to a mission in Scotland. She liked Scotland and it was the perfect place to hide out from Alexander for her remaining service. She had hidden out there before after the Lycan murder. When she emerged from her room to check out from the hotel there was a flurry of activity in the lobby. A housemaid was hysterical, crying and shrieking in a corner. Police were trying to take her statement and the hotel manager looked green beside her. A dead body was being wheeled out on a hospital stretcher by paramedics. Irina smirked, she would put money on that being Bella's work. She checked out and went to the bar to buy a bottle of red wine. She then headed over the road to the train station to catch the eleven-forty train to Edinburgh.

As the private plane touched down in Romania, Ivan could see Anastasia waiting on the tarmac for them with a chauffeur-driven black, Bentley Flying Spur. He exited the plane first and kissed Anastasia on both cheeks. "How is he?" Ivan enquired in his native Italian.
Anastasia knew he was referring to Alexander. "Not in a good mood," she responded.
Bella marched off the plane trailing behind them. She chose to sit in the front seat with the driver. Ivan obligingly assisted Anastasia into the rear of the car. Anastasia seductively positioned her body towards Ivan and trailed her fingers playfully up the inside of his leg. Ivan gave her a fleeting glance, before steering her hand away from his groin.

"Not now. Alexander's mood is about to get worse." Anastasia's expression turned cold, feeling spurned by the rejection. They remained silent for the rest of the journey.

The ladies led the way to the great hall and Anastasia immediately dismissed the Vampires surrounding Alexander. After Ivan bowed he requested a private audience. Alexander led him to the study behind the curtain and Bella followed them. She ignored the fact that she had not been invited. Both men sat down in the armchairs by the fire. Bella poured herself a glass of red wine, not bothering to offer anyone else one.

Ivan spoke first, "Alexander the truce is a ruse. Morgan Hudson the powerful Witch, she's engaged to Tristan Lucas, the youngest son of Vincent Lucas. I'd bet my life Witches and Lycans are working together and this is what Silas was killed for finding out."

Alexander sat silently for a moment, staring into the fire. When he spoke, he continued to look into the flames. "You're a loyal friend Ivan. I need you to keep this a secret for me. Trust me, I have a plan."

"Of course," Ivan responded as he rose from his seat, "If you'll excuse me."

Alexander held out his hand and Ivan kissed his signet ring before turning to leave. Bella took Ivan's vacant seat. When she was certain Ivan had left the great hall and was no longer in earshot, she asked her father to share his plan.

Ivan marched across the great hall at a fast pace straight to Anastasia's chambers. She was waiting for him on the bed in black lace lingerie, but her expression was menacing. Ivan grabbed her blonde hair and tugged hard. He kissed her passionately as he joined her on the bed. Anastasia used her Vampire strength to dominate him. Spinning him onto the mattress and straddling his body.

"Don't ever turn me down in front of her again," she growled.

"I'm sorry my love."

Ivan pulled Anastasia towards him and started to kiss her from her collar bone up to her ear. Anastasia melted in his arms and Ivan knew she would be his tonight. As he whispered Italian poetry into her ear she undid his shirt buttons. After a six hour marathon sex session, Ivan sat back in bed and lit a cigarette. Anastasia poured them both a glass of Alexander's best red wine and handed Ivan a glass as she joined him in bed.

"Are you aware of what he's planning?" Ivan asked.

"He's having me draw up a list from each country detailing Witch and Lycan colonies and the powers those covens' possess. He doesn't know that I know but some scientists arrived just before you. They were wearing uniforms with a Swastika on. He's planning to go to war."

Neither one of them spoke after that. They drank their wine in silence and when the sun rose Ivan dressed and left the castle, bound for Italy in his private jet.

By midday Anastasia had collated the information from the country leads and compiled them into a printed document for Alexander to read. She knocked on the door to Alexander's study and waited for him to shout, "Enter." She handed him the file along with a glass of fresh blood. Alexander nodded in thanks and dismissed her from the room. He read the report in detail before calling Anastasia and ordering her to set up a conference call with the country leads for that evening.

At seven that evening Alexander opened the conference call. He welcomed his trusted associates before declaring that they were now at war. He instructed each leader to kill as many Witches and Lycans as possible. Rewards would be given for the highest death tolls. As a special request he asked for one Witch from each coven and one female Lycan from each area to be brought to him in chains, alive. The leaders accepted the assignment and the call ended. The war had begun.

CHAPTER 22

The Vision

Morgan woke early on her last morning at the convent. Before breakfast she nipped into the empty classroom. She used the multiplication spell she had mastered to make copies of several textbooks and packed the duplications in her suitcase. She then made her way to the dining room for breakfast. French toast had been made in acknowledgement of her departure that afternoon. Morgan thanked the nuns for their kindness and the lessons they had taught her, before tucking into the soft, sweet brioche.

As Morgan stood up to leave the table, Rose requested that she meet her in the classroom. Morgan obliged. Faustina was already waiting for them and had placed the sand timer on the desk Morgan had used all week.

"We know Elspeth has taught you the principles of time travel and you have mastered the skill already, but we wanted to teach you control," Rose stated. She turned the sand timer over and the grains of sand started flowing slowly into the empty half of the vessel. "Focus, hold onto the timer. Place your other hand on the desk and hold the chalk. That way you're touching three items. Try to rewind time one grain of sand at a time."

Morgan understood the task. She did as instructed, visualising the grain of sand reversing direction. All of a sudden Faustina gripped the desk and started violently shaking. Her eyes rolled into the back of her head so only the whites were visible. Rose looked just as shocked as Morgan felt and shouted at Morgan to hover around Faustina in case she fell. It was a long ten minutes until Faustina came out of the trance. The shaking stopped, her eyes returned to normal and she stood straight, not needing to grip the desk.

"What did you see?" Rose asked immediately.

"Death!" Responded Faustina shakily. She walked backwards and leant against the bookcase. She was visibly in shock still and her voice quivered as she spoke. "The Vampires are planning to attack Witches and Lycans all around the world," looking directly at Morgan she continued, "Only united can we prevent a massacre!"

"We must inform Agatha," Rose declared to the group, as she marched out of the room.

Morgan offered to get Faustina a glass of water to help her calm down but she declined. Instead she asked Morgan to join her outside, to get some fresh air. When they were outside alone, Faustina turned to Morgan and held her hand tightly, "You must marry him and soon! It is the key. The key that will end all wars to come."

Morgan nodded, she became lost in thought. How could her marriage prevent wars? After a good fifteen minutes of fresh air, Rose joined them outside to inform them she had spoken with Agatha.

"I think it's time I returned home. Thank you both for everything."

Rose leant forward and embraced Morgan in a hug. "Don't be a stranger. Visit us again."

Morgan nodded and headed inside to collect her belongings. Faustina was waiting for her at the bottom of the stairs to take her to the portal. She reached inside her habit and presented Morgan with a beautiful gold twelve pointed star pendent. Morgan instantly recognised it as a dodecagram from Cordelia's book. "Consider this a wedding gift. Wear it always, so you'll always be in touch with your heritage, even if you are about to marry a Lycan." Morgan stood as Faustina fastened the necklace, "Thank you, it's beautiful."

As the clock struck twelve, Morgan appeared in the field behind Hannah's cottage, suitcase in hand. She marched towards the main house in search of Tristan. It was Christmas Eve and she had promised to return before Aunt Winnie arrived for Christmas celebrations. As Morgan tried to slip into the private entrance on the side of the main house, Marisa, clocked her from the conservatory and rushed out to greet her. "Do you need a hand darling?" She shouted.

"No, I'm fine honestly," Morgan responded.

"Now I know you said your Aunt is a vegetarian, but you're sure she's not a vegan? Because, I've bought a vegetarian wellington for Christmas Day and the packaging says it has eggs in it, so it's not suitable for vegans. So now I'm worried. I've never catered for a none meat eater before."

"It'll be fine, she's definitely not vegan. She loves cheese too much."

"Oh good. Come this way," and Marisa gestured for Morgan to enter the house via the conservatory. Morgan did as instructed and accepted Marisa's embrace as she passed her, kissing her on the cheek. Marisa sat back down in the conservatory with her book and Morgan made her way to the side stairs. Her mobile phone started loudly announcing all the missed communications, she hadn't received whilst in Ireland. Before checking her phone Morgan searched the apartment for Tristan but to no avail, so she sat down on the sofa and unlocked her phone.

The most recent message was from Tristan, making her aware he was Christmas present shopping this morning. He advised that he would be back just after one for a late lunch if she wanted to go out to the local village pub when he returned. Morgan responded she would love that and continued to read through her messages. Cordelia was keen to hear about the convent, so Morgan rang her and they talked for over thirty minutes about all the skills she had learned.

When Tristan returned, Morgan heard him running up the stairs before she saw him. As she locked eyes with him at the top of the stairs, his smile beamed as he announced, "You're back!" He darted towards her on the sofa, landing soft kisses all over her face. "How hungry are you? Because we could do an early dinner rather than a late lunch and occupy ourselves in other ways for the next few hours," raising his eyebrows suggestively.

Morgan giggled happily. She had missed his playful nature and how infatuated he was with her. He made her feel like the only woman alive. Morgan knew how to respond to turn him wild, "I had a big breakfast," she said and then she bit her bottom lip. Tristan scooped her off the sofa in his arms and carried her to the bedroom. They spent the next few hours worshipping each other's bodies and enjoying several orgasms each.

At three-thirty they walked the short distance to the local village pub, to enjoy home-cooked pub grub and a few pints of cider. After they had eaten, they walked back home to wait for Aunt Winnie to arrive. Aunt Winnie messaged Morgan to say she would be arriving at seven. So, shortly before seven, Morgan and Tristan made their way down to the field behind Hannah's cottage to the portal. They had taken to leaving the portal in place so that anyone from the commune could visit them. Cordelia made the trip regularly to catch up with Morgan and her training.

Just after seven, Aunt Winnie magically appeared in the portal laden with carrier bags. "So lovely to see you both!" She declared, as she placed the bags on the ground and hugged them both simultaneously. Tristan started to pick up the many carrier bags and Aunt Winnie thanked him. She embarrassingly apologised that she didn't own any luggage.

"I'm sure Cordelia would have a suitcase, you should

have asked," Morgan remarked.

"I didn't want to bother anyone. These will do, no need to fuss. Now do I look presentable enough? I wanted to save my best dress for tomorrow, but I know Tristan's parents are probably fancy folks. Oh my, look at this big house."

Aunt Winnie stood looking up at Tristan's parent's house in awe. She started smoothing out her skirt and fidgeting. Morgan could see Marisa sitting in the conservatory. When she saw the trio approaching, she leapt up and hurried to the door. For all intents and purposes this was parents meet the parents. Aunt Winnie was the only family Morgan had and she was proud to introduce her to the Lycan family she would be marrying into. Morgan found it funny that Aunt Winnie appeared more flustered at how she would match up to Tristan's parents, than worried she was walking into a house of Lycans. Lycans who she had been brought up to fear.

Vincent appeared at the door just behind Marisa and they both hurried over for introductions. Each one seemed nervously excited. Aunt Winnie introduced herself formally as Winifred, which took Morgan aback. She had never heard anyone call her Aunt by her full name. After the introductions were made, Tristan showed Aunt Winnie to the guest bedroom and carried all her bags up the stairs. Morgan followed Tristan's parents into the lounge and Marisa switched on the Christmas tree lights. Aunt Winnie separated out her belongings from the presents she had brought and followed Tristan downstairs, to join everyone in the lounge.

Vincent ensured everyone had a beverage and Marisa offered around the chocolate selection box. The conversation turned to the engagement.

"I was just so thrilled when they told us they would be getting married. We were sat having brunch in the conservatory, admiring the beautiful white roses which had appeared overnight. Isn't Tristan just so romantic? How could she have refused with that proposal? Not that he's forcing her to marry him though. It was a joint decision." Marisa's voice had sped up as she spoke, as if she was getting nervous again.

Vincent placed his hand on Marisa's knee to calm her as he spoke, "I'm sure Winifred knows how much Morgan loves Tristan and would never believe Morgan could be coerced into becoming a Lycan."

Marisa mumbled, "Of course."

Aunt Winnie just smiled enjoying her camomile tea. "Tristan is a credit to you both. He gallantly saved me from the scariest ordeal of my life and has only treated Morgan with kindness and respect. He has helped change a lot of Witches opinions on Lycans. You should be very proud."

Marisa's eyes started to well up with pride and Vincent puffed out his chest. This mutual adoration between species was a wholesome encounter to witness. The rest of the evening passed by quickly, with each parental figure trying to outdo the other with embarrassing childhood stories. As the evening drew to a close, Morgan assisted Aunt Winnie to her room to have a few moments alone. Before she left the lounge Morgan made Marisa promise she would locate a photo of Tristan, from his emo phase, much to Tristan's dismay.

Together in the guest room, Morgan checked that Aunt Winnie had everything she needed and they made a plan to do sunrise yoga in the portal field. They embraced each other goodbye and Morgan joined Tristan upstairs.

Just before eight, as the sun was starting to rise in the sky, Morgan crept out of bed, leaving a snoring Tristan. She grabbed her gym clothes and dressed in the bathroom. Before she tip-toed out of the apartment, she placed Tristan's present on her pillow. If he woke before she got back, she wanted him to be thinking of her. She was excited for him to open it. She had been working on a repair spell with Cordelia for weeks and finally she had perfected it. She found Tristan's grandfathers watch in his sock drawer. She knew how much it meant to him and he couldn't part with it even after it had been destroyed in the fight with Silas.

Morgan made her way to the field behind Hannah's cottage and saw her Aunt already in the downward dog pose. Morgan wished her Aunt Merry Christmas and followed her Aunt's lead. After twenty minutes, Aunt Winnie ended the session with, "Namaste." She then followed Morgan back to the house barefoot, to find Marisa in the kitchen. Marisa was surprised to see the early risers but passed around Bucks fizz, before returning to peeling potatoes. Both ladies offered their assistance but Marisa wouldn't hear of it and told them to return for breakfast at ten.

Morgan left Aunt Winnie in the hall and returned to the third floor to shower. Tristan was awake and wearing the watch. He was grinning from ear to ear and upon seeing Morgan he ran to her. He lifted her up and spun her around the living room. When he stopped he rained kisses down on her.

"How did you manage it?" He asked.

"A little bit of magic and a lot of help from Cordelia," she responded.

"I love you! I want to marry you as soon as possible," Tristan declared.

Morgan paused for just a second in contemplation before she responded, "Then why wait. Let's get married at New Years?"

Tristan's smile appeared to grow even wider, if that was possible. He nodded and declared what an excellent idea that was. "We can tell everyone today over dinner, when we're all together."

Just before ten they made their way down to the conservatory for breakfast. It was a large spread consisting of several types of pastries, muesli, Greek yogurt and a large fruit bowl. Hannah and Jacob had also joined them. Jacob was dominating the topic of conversation. He had already opened a Jack in the box toy. Every time the figure popped up, Jacob fell backwards laughing. His fall turned into a backwards somersault and he transformed into a wolf pup alert on all fours. He shook the fur off and returned to a naked little boy again. If Aunt Winnie was shocked she hid it well and even relocated to the floor to play with him.

After breakfast, Tobias and his family arrived laden with boxes. Everyone moved to the lounge to swap presents. The children opened theirs first and when the three of them were happily playing with dinosaurs, cars and a magician set. The adults started to take it in turns.

Aunt Winnie handed out a carrier bag to each couple. Inside were beautifully wrapped handmade gifts. Ornate bottles were wrapped in large lily pond leaves tied together with water reeds. Each bottle was carefully labelled with the ingredients and what the item was. Aunt Winnie had made everyone the same selection from homemade cold remedies, to fresh horseradish sauce and elderberry cordial. The cordial even came with a warning that if you left it somewhere warm for three months, it would turn to wine. Everyone loved the thoughtful gifts. In return, Aunt Winnie was gifted scented candles and a mulberry tree from Tristan's parents, which she thanked them for most fervently.

Hannah had also gone down the homemade route and gifted everyone a bottle of blackberry wine. Tristan had bought his father and brother rare bottles of whiskey which they both seemed delighted with.

Morgan left the room and returned with four small gift bags which she handed out to the women. Inside was a glass perfume bottle labelled moon rose. Morgan explained she had made perfume out of the roses Tristan had used to propose with. Charlotte instinctively lifted the lid and sprayed the perfume into the air. A beautiful fresh rose smell filled the room.

"That's divine! You clever thing, turning them into perfume," Charlotte voiced.

Morgan blushed at the compliment, as she responded. "I had a little bit of help from Cordelia."

Throughout the morning Marisa kept disappearing into

the kitchen to check on the dinner preparations. The rest of the presents were opened and Morgan hadn't even noticed that she had not received one from Tristan. All the presents from under the tree had been opened and Vincent loudly announced, "We have one more gift to give."

Marisa appeared in the doorway with a large circular tube. One you would expect a poster to be shipped in. She handed the tube to Tristan and joined Vincent on the other side of the room. She watched in anticipation, as Tristan withdrew the paper from inside. The paper was A1 size and Morgan didn't realise what she was looking at until Tristan held it out at full width. House blueprints.

Marisa was bursting to explain and exclaimed, "We've hired an architect to design a house for you in the field behind Hannah's cottage. This is what he's come up with initially, but you can change it to suit your tastes."

Morgan was flabbergasted and had no words to articulate her feelings. Tristan thanked his parents for the both of them and crossed the room to hug them. Morgan followed suit. Aunt Winnie exclaimed how wonderful a gift it was.

Turning to Morgan and his parents, Tristan announced, "Well, I think you've trumped my present. I have a gift for you Morgan, but you'll need to follow me outside." The whole extended family followed Tristan outside to the front driveway. There parked on the drive was a brand-new, matt grey Range Rover Sports car, with a huge red bow on the bonnet. Morgan gasped in shock and held her hands to her mouth. When the initial shock had worn off she embraced Tristan and thanked him, as he handed her the keys. Morgan jumped in the driver's seat and took Tristan for a quick drive around the village.

By the time they returned, everyone was seated around the lavishly decorated dining room table. Golden organza bows had been constructed on the backs of the chairs and a large golden glittery wreath hung from the ceiling over the dining table. Every candle was lit, providing a golden glow around the room. As Morgan took her place next to Aunt Winnie, she could see the cutlery and glassware were different to the usual Sunday dinner service. She picked up the beautiful ornate, crystal cut glass to examine it. Tristan saw her inquisitive expression and whispered in her ear, "This is the posh dinner set, for when we have guests."

Morgan smiled at the effort Tristan's parents had gone to for her Aunt. On reflection, she wondered why she hadn't received the royal treatment when she first dined with them. She leant over to Tristan and whispered in his ear, "Why weren't the posh plates used when I first had dinner here?"

Without hesitation Tristan responded, "Because my Mother already considered you family." Morgan felt all warm inside. How lovely to fit into another family so well. She congratulated herself in her own mind. She was making an excellent decision.

Tobias offered around wine as Tristan's parents brought through dish after dish of side accompaniments. There were Brussels with bacon, Yorkshire puddings, stuffing balls, colcannon, roast potatoes, carrots, parsnips, red cabbage, broccoli, cauliflower cheese and pigs in blankets. Marisa hand delivered a plate with an individual vegetable wellington on for Aunt Winnie and then Vincent arrived in the room. He was carrying the largest platter Morgan had ever seen, it held a beautifully decorated wellington. Vincent placed the dish on the sideboard at the other end of the table from Aunt Winnie. He announced this was the loin of the stag that Zachary had hunted several weeks before. Vincent sliced into the wellington and everyone apart from Aunt Winnie passed their plates around the table to receive a slice.

Marisa sat down on the other side of Aunt Winnie and explained they had chosen to serve wellington so it was less distressing for Aunt Winnie. However, she went on to say that they usually had a large slab of rare meat on the bone in the centre of the table and everyone helped themselves. Aunt Winnie tried to hide her revulsion, but she did go slightly green. Morgan stifled a giggle and loaded her plate high with vegetables.

The wellington looked superb. The glistening venison was encased in a layer of mushroom duxelle, spinach and a very thin crepe, before the pastry layer. The meat was rather pinker than Morgan's usual medium steak, but as she braved her first bite she was pleasantly surprised at how the meat melted in her mouth. The whole family split into multiple conversations as they ate their way through the feast. As the plates started to empty and everyone started to slump in their chairs, Morgan took the opportunity to stand and raise a toast to the hosts. Everyone cheered in celebration. Tristan then stood and placed his arm around Morgan. The pair looked excited to share their news with the family.

"Morgan and I have made a decision," as Tristan spoke he addressed the whole table, "we have decided to get married at New Years and we would love for you all to attend."

The women clapped and the men cheered. Aunt Winnie hugged Morgan and then swapped with Marisa who was hugging Tristan. "We don't have long to prepare. Come, let's discuss the plans in the lounge, the men can tidy away." Marisa instructed the men, including Zachary, who loudly sighed exclaiming, "It's not fair, I caught the dinner."

Hannah, Charlotte, Aunt Winnie, Marisa and Morgan made their way to the lounge.

"Have you made any decisions on the dress, or the flowers? Will you have a hen party?" Charlotte asked excitedly.

"I want to have white roses for the flowers. The rest I haven't planned yet."

They wiled away the rest of the day discussing ideas for the wedding. Marisa got out the family photo books. Even Hannah was happy to join in and reminisce. Although Morgan was happy they had decided on a date, she hadn't taken into account how much she would need to do in less than a week. The top priorities had to be to write her vows and get a dress. Before she went to sleep that night she messaged Molly to arrange a shopping trip.

CHAPTER 23

Defiance

Molly rang first thing on Boxing Day to arrange a shopping trip for the 29th. She sounded ecstatic at the prospect of helping Morgan choose her wedding dress. So much so, that Morgan hadn't the heart to tell her she wouldn't be inviting her to the wedding. She would have loved to have her there but the non-traditional supernatural elements might be too much for Molly to digest. Morgan had decided to tell her they were eloping, maybe to Las Vegas, she would worry about the photo evidence at a later date.

Morgan had skipped sunrise yoga with Aunt Winnie, preferring to stay in bed. She knew Aunt Winnie would be awake by now, so she tiptoed down to the guest room to see if she wanted company.

Aunt Winnie had clearly been up for a while as she was dressed and reading a book. She welcomed Morgan inside. "Good Morning, did you sleep well?"

"Yes thank you. I've arranged to go wedding dress shopping with my friend. Would you like to join us?"

"I would love to! Are you thinking of having any Witch traditions included in your ceremony?" Aunt Winnie enquired.

"To be honest I didn't know we had any Witch traditions. What are they?"

"Well the main traditions we could incorporate are saying your vows in a circle whilst being connected to the earth and you could wear a wicker head wreath. We could adorn it with white roses to match your theme."

Morgan looked puzzled, "What do you mean connected to the earth?"

"Being barefoot, so you can spiritually connect to the elements."

"Ok, I'm happy to take them on board. Not having to buy shoes is a bonus. Will you help me make the wreath?"

"I would love too," Aunt Winnie beamed with joy.

After a splendid buffet brunch, Morgan joined Aunt Winnie in the portal. They arrived on the edge of the holiday park just after eleven. They walked the short distance to Aunt Winnie's caravan and dropped her belongings off. They headed straight back out to the stream to collect twigs for the wreath. Arms laden with willow twigs of all sizes they made their way back to the caravan. En route they bumped into Cordelia who joined them. "So what are all the twigs for?"

"We're going to make Morgan's head wreath," Aunt Winnie said proudly.

"Oh," was Cordelia's immediate response, she looked a little unnerved, "You're going through with it then?"

Morgan wasn't shocked at Cordelia's reaction. She wasn't being mean, she was just being blunt. She had made the effort to get to know Tristan and his family. Morgan believed Cordelia had even warmed to them, but that didn't mean she welcomed Morgan transforming into a Lycan. They'd had many conversations about it. Cordelia had even been trying to search the history books, to see if a union between species had happened before. She was searching specifically for a spell to prevent Morgan turning into a Lycan. Cordelia was convinced it was an ancient magic that turned a human into a Lycan and if it was magic then it could be reversed.

Morgan had expressed her own ideas on the matter.

She didn't see why she couldn't be both. Humans didn't lose any ability, they only gained one, so why would she. Cordelia believed Morgan was just wishful thinking and wanted evidence.

"Yes and I would love you to come. We're getting married on New Year's, just before midnight."

"Then I haven't got long to search through the history books. I better get reading. I'll be there." With that Cordelia marched with purpose off to the clubhouse.

Morgan and Aunt Winnie spent a lovely afternoon making her wedding wreath. Aunt Winnie said that she would adorn it with white roses and bring it to the ceremony on the day. "It'll be your something new. I also have a long blue ball of yarn to make the circle that you can borrow. That will be your something blue and borrowed. Now you just need something old."

Morgan clasped the necklace Sister Mary Faustina had given her. "I have something old."

"Oh yes, of course you do. It really is very beautiful. What a lovely gift. I would like to visit the convent."

"You'd love it. You should ask Agatha to arrange it. Maybe you could take Elspeth too?"

"I think I will, after the wedding," Aunt Winnie said contently.

"I think it's time for me to go now. Can you be ready for nine on the 29th? I'll meet you at the portal. Molly's train gets in at nine forty-five."

Aunt Winnie nodded and Morgan headed out to the portal to return home.

At precisely nine o'clock on the 29th, Aunt Winnie appeared in the portal. Morgan and Marisa greeted her warmly. They all made their way to Morgan's new car. Aunt Winnie sat in the front passenger seat and Marisa sat in the rear. The new car smell still permeated the air, mixed with the smell of leather. It was lovely. They pulled up at the train station to find Molly waving from the entrance. Morgan pulled into the drop off zone and Molly jumped into the back seat.

"Oh, the boy did good! This car is lovely!" Molly exclaimed as she put on her seatbelt. Morgan made the introductions and Molly gave Aunt Winnie the postcode of the first bridal shop to program into the sat nav. They spent the journey catching up on the last few weeks. Molly and Jono had called it quits on their relationship. Whilst back home, Molly had ran into an old boyfriend and they had started casually dating again. However, Molly didn't think it would last when she returned to university.

Twenty minutes later, Morgan pulled up outside a very traditional looking bridal shop. The mannequins in the window were wearing large meringue-type dresses that made Morgan shudder. Had she made a mistake asking Molly to help her? She only had two days until the wedding. She didn't have time to visit every shop in the county.

Molly saw the look of horror on Morgan's face and immediately grabbed her by the shoulders to give her reassurance. "Now, trust me! You've changed your style a lot recently and I don't even know if you realise that. Look at what you're wearing today, jeans and a hoodie, no rebellious punk in sight. You might like a dress that you wouldn't have expected. This shop has every style imaginable from meringue to fishtail. Let's try one of every style and see what you prefer. We have appointments with another three shops today."

Morgan conceded and entered the shop. Aunt Winnie whispered into Morgan's ear, "I like her!" Morgan spent the next ninety minutes being pulled and wedged into every style of dress in the shop. Every time she looked in the mirror, she didn't recognise the person in front of her. Marisa clapped and Aunt Winnie gasped every time she exited the dressing room, but she hated every style. Morgan was starting to feel extremely disheartened. Molly seemed to sense her energy levels dropping and declared it was time to move onto the next shop.

Fifteen minutes later, after a couple of wrong turns, they arrived at a very unconventional bridal shop. The display dress in the small front window was pillar box red, with black lace. If it wasn't for the name above the door, 'To bride or not to bride', Morgan would have thought it was a fancy dress boutique.

The party apprehensively stepped into the shop and a very gothic shop manager introduced herself as Luna-Fox. She had neon pink hair, a long black silk lace dress with draping sleeves and a side split which flashed neon pink tights. Morgan tried to hide her amusement at the dog collar adorning her neck.

Aunt Winnie seemed open-minded but Molly and Marisa looked like they wanted to leave immediately. Morgan explained to Luna-Fox that she didn't know what she was looking for, but when she saw it she would know. She started to search through the rails. Molly joined her and whispered in her ear, "We can leave if you want? I'll make the excuses just say the word. I tried to look up alternative bridal shops and this came highly recommended, but I think maybe it's a little too much."

Morgan decided to have a little fun, payback for how uncomfortable she had felt in the last shop, being dressed up like a dolly. "I quite like it here. It's got a certain charm." Molly pulled a face, but quickly tried to hide it to not cause offense. She disappeared to the other side of the store to view a rail of white dresses. Morgan continued rifling through the dresses. Rather than a sea of white and creams like the last shop, this had much more colour. There were red, black and even a section of ombré style dresses.

Morgan tried to imagine herself standing next to Tristan in the moonlight. She closed her eyes briefly. When she opened them her hand was resting on the shoulder of a silver, silk, floor length dress. She lifted it off the rail. It was extremely light, not like the dresses in the other shop. The silver shimmered in the light, as if it was almost pearlescent. It had three quarter length sleeves and a high scoop neckline. Her favourite part was the princess floating skirt. It was simplistic and elegant. It was beautiful.

Morgan checked the tag, it was her size. She took it to the assistant and asked to try it on. Not one of her party had spotted her. She entered the changing room alone and slipped on the dress. It fit like a glove and felt beautifully soft on her skin. She emerged from the changing room and twirled around in front of the mirrors. The dress fit in all the right places and she felt like a princess. One by one everyone in the shop turned to look at her. "Wow you look stunning," Molly declared. Aunt Winnie started crying and Marisa beamed.

"Is that the one?" Marisa asked.

Morgan nodded, "Yes! This is it."

"Now what about shoes? I've been looking over here, but I'm not sure." Marisa pointed to a very gothic boot stand.

"I've got shoes covered," Morgan quickly said. Aunt Winnie whispered into Marisa ear, "It's a Witch thing, we go barefoot."

Marisa looked surprised but winked very conspicuously.

"What about bridesmaids?" Molly asked.

Apprehensively Morgan replied, "I'm not having any actually." Morgan hated lying, but there wasn't much else she could do in the situation. "We're actually eloping. We fly out to Las Vegas tomorrow."

Morgan had already briefed the others so they didn't act surprised. Molly froze for a second and Morgan didn't know how she was going to respond. "That's so romantic!" She burst out. Morgan felt a wave of relief flood over her.

Whilst Morgan returned to the changing rooms, Marisa took out her credit card and paid for the dress. Aunt Winnie stood next to her nervously.

"Oh no you mustn't, I must pay towards it."

Marisa turned to acknowledge Aunt Winnie, "Winifred I have three sons and three grandsons, the only dresses I ever get to buy are the ones for my future daughters. Anyway it's Vincent's credit card."

Aunt Winnie couldn't help but notice the reference to three sons. She smiled warmly. "Thank you Marisa, the love you already have for my niece is so special."

"We are family now," Marisa replied squeezing Aunt Winnie's hand.

Molly watched the exchange between the ladies and hoped her future in-laws would be as kind.

As Morgan left the changing rooms, the assistant took the dress and packaged it in an elaborate box, with a velvet black ribbon. Morgan went to pay but the assistant said it had been taken care of. Molly whispered in her ear, "You've hit the mother-in-law jackpot."

Morgan smiled in agreement and handed Molly the box to hold. She turned to Marisa and Aunt Winnie and hugged them tight, giving each a kiss on the cheek.

"Let's end the day with lunch, my treat," Morgan announced. Off they all went to lunch, a very unlikely looking group of friends.

On the morning of the 31st December, Morgan woke alone in bed. Marisa had insisted that Tristan and Morgan remain separate from six the night before. Tristan had gone on a stag do with his closest friends and stayed the night with Jono. Morgan checked her phone and Tristan had sent her a soppy message at three in the morning declaring his love for her. Morgan checked the bedside clock, it was seven. It would be a while before she heard from Tristan again. She decided to go for a run, before Aunt Winnie arrived at midday.

By nine that evening, the house was a flurry of activity. Cordelia and her mother had arrived. Charlotte was applying Morgan's make up, as she sat in front of a mirror in a fluffy dressing gown. Aunt Winnie was weaving fresh white roses into the head wreath. Hannah was babysitting all the children in the living room, whilst Marisa was playing hostess, organising drinks and nibbles. Agatha graciously declined the invitation, so she could declare plausible deniability if need be to the Vampires at the council. However, she had allowed Mary and Brianne to attend. Morgan assumed they were also present to report back on the events of the ceremony. The men had all taken up refuge at Tobias' house.

By eleven Morgan could hear howling in the field behind Hannah's cottage. The guests started to filter out of the house and made their way into the field. Morgan was finally left alone with Aunt Winnie. Morgan got dressed carefully, so as not to smudge Charlotte's make-up masterpiece. Aunt Winnie placed the wreath upon her head. Morgan adjusted the necklace from Sister Mary Faustina, so it was visible for all to see. Tonight she intended to blend two supernatural families. She would not forsake Witchcraft for her new Lycan family.

Aunt Winnie helped her down the stairs and fanned out her skirt as they started to walk across the driveway to the field. The gravel felt coarse and sharp under her bare feet. "Ouch. This is not going to work," she said to Aunt Winnie. "Let me try something I've been practising."

Morgan let go of Aunt Winnie's hand and focused on the ground, holding her hand flat down in the air, as if she was pushing against the earth. Slowly she floated half a foot above the ground. Her long dress gave the illusion she was just half a foot taller. Slowly and gracefully she floated to the ceremony.

As instructed, the men had set up the blue yarn circle. Tristan was standing inside it, dressed in a beautiful tailored, navy suit, with a silver cravat. Everyone was dressed in their best clothes. Unlike a traditional wedding, everyone stood around the circle. Vincent, as head of the family would be the officiator. Tristan, with help from Jono, had set up a sound system in the field. The couple had chosen a classical love song to play, as Morgan made her way from the house.

As Morgan neared Hannah's house, she could hear their special song playing. As the pair became visible to the guests in the field and the ground beneath them turned to grass, Morgan lowered herself to the ground. All eyes turned to Morgan, but she only saw the crystal blue eyes of the man she loved. It felt like an eternity to cross the field, but as she stepped into the ring and held Tristan's hand, the world turned calm.

Vincent took a deep breath and projected his voice into the night air. "We are all gathered here tonight to celebrate the special love these two share. Let them be a reminder to us all, to move past prejudice into the light. Morgan, would you like to say your vows first?"

Morgan turned to face Tristan, still holding his hand. "I have spent a long time running from who and what I am, not realising that the whole time, I was running to you. I give all that I am, to be your wife and live by your side. Only with you does this world make sense and together we can save it. I will love you until the end of time."

Tristan remained fixated on Morgan and neither of the pair really heard Vincent ask Tristan to share his vows. Tristan spoke only to Morgan, straight from the heart. "You are the most intelligent, beautiful and thoughtful woman I have ever met. I vow to be by your side for the rest of time. I will love you now and always."

When it was clear that Tristan had finished, Vincent began the ritual. "Morgan, please pass your bouquet to Marisa." Morgan did as directed using her free hand, to now hold Tristan's other hand. "Repeat after me," Vincent instructed.

Tristan listened to the vow before repeating, "In the light of the moon, I Tristan, take you Morgan, to be my soul mate. May the moon watch over us and guide us. I give my whole self to you. This is my vow."

Vincent directed, "Now you, Morgan."

"In the light of the moon, I Morgan take you Tristan, to be my soul mate. May the moon watch over us and guide us. I give my whole self to you. This is my vow."

"You may kiss the bride," Vincent finished.

Tristan leant forward and as the couple kissed, all the

Lycans in attendance howled to the moon. The couple felt a rush of wind surround them, as if an ancient magic had been awakened. Within moments of the ceremony ending fireworks burst into the night's sky, just as the clock struck midnight. Everyone looked up to watch the fireworks dancing in front of the full moon.

The night felt magical but Morgan felt no different. "Should I feel any different?" Morgan whispered into Tristan's ear. Tristan smiled and let out a small chuckle. In the haste of setting a date, he had forgotten to explain the finer details of the ceremony, "No, not until we consummate the binding." Morgan blushed in case anyone had heard them and then let out a giggle.

It was over fifteen minutes before the fireworks subsided and Vincent led everyone back to the house for a Champagne reception. Morgan and Tristan waited until all their guests had left before they returned to the apartment. Tristan carried her over the threshold and into the bedroom, placing her on the bed gently. Morgan could see raw primal desire in his eyes. He pounced on top of her and passionately kissed her. She could feel his hard penis against her. He would have loved to rip her dress to shreds, but he knew how important a wedding dress was to a woman. He pulled her close and rolled over onto his back.

Morgan was now on top and gathered her skirt up before attempting to pull the dress over her head. As she lifted the dress, Tristan began kissing her belly button then travelled lower and lower down her body. By the time she had removed her bra, Tristan was so far beneath her she was on top of his face and he was already licking her clitoris. She moaned in pleasure, urging him to continue and he placed his hands on her hips to steady her. It wasn't long before she was trembling in ecstasy above him.

He pushed himself out from underneath her and she collapsed on the bed face down. He undressed quicker than she had ever thought possible and entered her from behind. She was wet but tight in this position and he was almost overcome. He tried to pace himself to make the momentous occasion last. He tugged at her hair gently just as she liked. She began to moan again and he felt the pulsing around his pulsating cock, as she exploded with desire again. Once again he nearly lost control but he managed to gather his composure. He withdrew himself and flipped Morgan onto her back. "I want to look at you," he muttered as he caressed her neck and then cupped her right breast in his hand. His mouth trailed down her body to her free breast and he sucked on her nipple, as he gently tugged with his other hand. His cock was throbbing at her entrance and she rotated her hips to allow him access.

His rock-hard cock entered her and she gasped, she felt a wave of pleasure as he stretched her. Instinct took over and Tristan began thrusting. She was still deliciously wet. Morgan lifted her legs up to her chest to allow him to sink in deeper. His breathing changed tempo and grew shorter. He couldn't hold his climax any longer and he exploded inside her. Before he collapsed on top of her, he cupped her face in his hands and declared, "I love you."

Morgan fiddled with his hair as he lay on top of her. His breathing slowly returned to normal. It didn't take long before Tristan was ready to go again. They spent several hours consummating their union and Morgan enjoyed every second of it.

When she woke the next morning, Morgan hurried to the bathroom to look in the mirror. She wondered if she looked any different. She pondered on whether she felt any different. After spending several minutes scrutinising her reflection, she concluded that she did. Morgan heard Tristan stirring in the other room and ran back to join him in bed. "So what now?" She asked eagerly.

"Good morning wife. Could I get a coffee first?" He asked as he pulled himself into a seated position.

"We don't have time for that. Get dressed. Let's go

outside. I want to see what I can do."

Tristan smirked, he loved Morgan's go-getter attitude. They both dressed quickly into running gear and headed outside.

When they were out of view from the main house and Hannah's cottage, Tristan undressed in the field. Morgan loved his body confidence and started to get very aroused. Flashbacks of the prior evening's activities swam into her mind. Morgan tried to shake off the feeling and focus on the task in hand. She quickly undressed and neatly folded her clothes in a pile on the ground.

"So you need to connect with your senses," Tristan began, "Feel the grass between your toes, focus on your hearing and stare into the distance, it should come into focus. Your heart should start to race and thump loudly in your chest. Then I find it easier to pounce into the air as you transform. Don't worry you will land on all fours."

Morgan felt nervous. Tristan would never understand. He had been born a Lycan. He had been transforming from a baby. Tristan went first and transformed into his beautiful Lycan form. Morgan did as instructed but landed awkwardly on the ground exactly as she was, as a human. Tristan transformed back. "Let's try again. We can do it together, holding hands," he encouraged.

After five failed attempts, Morgan started to feel very disheartened. Tristan suggested they get dressed and go hunting for wild deer. Her instinct might kick in and take over. After two hours of tracking every living creature with no progress on her transformation, Morgan broke down in tears.

"Please don't cry. Perhaps you're putting too much pressure on yourself. Maybe speaking to my Mother or Hannah might help. I could just be an awful teacher."

As Morgan wiped her eyes on the back of her sleeve, the heavens opened above them. Tristan withdrew his phone perplexed at the sudden weather change. "It's not meant to rain today."

Morgan took Tristan's hand and calmly stated. "Maybe it's me making it rain." Tristan tilted his head as he took stock of what that meant. Morgan let go of his hand and stepped backwards. She held her hands to her side and pushed away from the ground. She floated into the air, just as she had done the night before. Whilst in the air Morgan looked up to the sky in anger. Anger for the upset this would cause Tristan and his family. Anger for the adventures she would now miss out on and confusion as to what this meant about her marriage. Loud thunder rumbled in the sky and a bolt of lightning struck a nearby tree. She had been convinced that she would transition into a Lycan, but also remain a Witch. She felt cheated.

Tristan shouted up to Morgan, "Morgan its ok, come back to me, it's ok. It's better even. You haven't had to change who you are to be with me. I never wanted you to have to change. You're a Witch!"

As Morgan heard Tristan's speech she returned to him on the ground. She was crying again, but she couldn't determine if they were tears of anger or of love. The shock weather stopped as abruptly as it started and a rainbow glistened in the sky. Tristan hugged Morgan tightly and she knew nothing else mattered. They returned to the house to break the news to their family.

CHAPTER 24

The Plan

Alexander sat in his study on his latest conference call, with his loyal country leaders. He spoke to each leader in their own language, partly to show off his language skills and display his superior intelligence, but mostly to restrict the knowledge of the events of the war. Not everyone was as gifted with languages as he was. Amongst the countries there were many underlying historical prejudices. The less each region knew and liked each other, the more they needed him to govern them. It also meant the less likely they were to throw a coup. Not that they would succeed, but he really didn't need another battle on his hands right now.

Lycans had been on a population expansion the last few centuries. There was a time Lycans would only have one son, to prevent fights over the estate and sibling rivalry for the alpha position. However, every region had reported significant growth in numbers. Alexander was disappointed in himself for not knowing. He had been careless and become lax. He would not let the council find out this information.

With Silas dead, Alexander had tasked Irina with leading the British takeover but she appeared to have gone AWOL. He had not heard from her in over a month. This had infuriated him before the call had even started. His scientists had made hardly any progress in the last six weeks and had now run out of subjects to experiment on.

Amelie Dubois of France had just finished telling him they had unsuccessfully attempted to kidnap the wife of the head of the Parisian Lycan pack. Alexander's mood was now abysmal. Even the news from Boris Kozlov in Russia, that they had murdered an entire coven did not improve his mood. He was sure that news of Vampire assassinations would circulate across Europe soon and he was waiting for the retaliation. He stayed in his study brooding all day, even Bella's entertaining anecdote about her Valentine's date irritated him.

Alexander decided to take matters into his own hands, to coordinate the British attack. He searched through his files for his network of contacts. He had several loyal Vampires in British Parliament, he would need to use one of them to organise systematic attacks. He chose one at random and picked up his phone. The phone call was tedious and Alexander even contemplated flying to the UK to start the war himself, but then he remembered Dimitri. It was too risky. Irina needed to step up and lead the war or be punished. He picked up his phone again. "Ciao Ivan, I have a favour to ask of you."

The last time Ivan had seen Irina she was at the Ibis hotel in Nottingham. Alexander had ordered she be found by any means necessary. Ivan called Anastasia and requested details for every systems hacker they had on the payroll. Anastasia obliged without question and by the next day, Ivan had full access to Nottingham city centre CCTV. After an hour of browsing footage, he finally spotted Irina. He watched her leave the hotel and walk to the train station. Inside the train station he watched her walk to platform two and step aboard the eleven-forty to Edinburgh. Ivan already had his pilot on standby and called him to log the flight plan to Scotland.

As Ivan stepped off the plane it started to drizzle. He hated the rain and even more so being sent to find Irina like a dopey bloodhound. However, it was always good to have someone powerful indebted to you. You never knew when a favour would need to be cashed in. Ivan had been a Vampire long enough to know it was who you knew not what you knew. As fortune would have it, he had a head start on finding her, knowing where and when to start his search in Nottingham.

Ivan requested the receptionist at the private air strip order him a taxi. The receptionist happily obliged, as she twirled her curly red hair. Usually Ivan would have enjoyed the attention, but he was here strictly on business and intended to leave as soon as possible. He instructed his pilot to be ready to leave at a moment's notice and departed for the city centre.

The taxi dropped him off at the train station, in the centre of Edinburgh. He grabbed a newspaper from the nearest shop and browsed through local news for any sign of Vampire activity. Irina hadn't been stupid enough to kill anyone, but there had been a hit and run the day before, just outside the Malmaison hotel. The victim had claimed they had passed out and woken up startled in an alley. Then semi-conscious, they had stumbled into the road and been struck by a car. The injured man later died in hospital of organ failure due to unforeseen complications. It reeked of a Vampire attack.

Ivan walked the streets close to the Malmaison hotel for the rest of the day and into the night. By eleven-fifteen the streets were filled with drunks. It was prime picking time for a Vampire. He smelled blood before he saw her. Ivan followed the smell to an alley two streets away. A female figure was pressed against a wall by a much larger male figure, or so you would first assume. They appeared to be locked in a lovers tryst, but Ivan knew better. Irina had clearly lured the man into the alley on the premise of a rendezvous, but she was now gorging on his blood.

"Hello Irina," he said, stepping out of the shadows. Irina dropped the man to the floor in shock. His head hit the cobbles with a loud crack. He would be lucky if he survived. Blood started to ooze from his skull but Irina only had eyes for Ivan, "Why are you here?"

"Really, you have to ask? A war has started and you're missing all the fun."

"I just want to be left alone."

"Insolent! Alexander wants you to lead the British troops so to speak. You can't defy him!"

"Tell him you couldn't locate me. How did you find me?"

"Don't be so stupid. You can never hide from him. You complete this task and you are free. Your service will be paid in full. Defy him and you'll be dead by the end of the year."

Ivan reached inside his coat pocket and handed Irina a phone, "Is there really a decision to make?" Then he walked away without waiting for a response. He headed in the direction of the train station. His errand was complete.

Irina stared down at the phone, enraged that she had foolishly enabled Ivan to track her. He was right. She had no choice. She opened the phone and called the only number programmed.

Her assignment was clear. She was to co-ordinate the attacks on the prominent Lycan families and the largest covens in the UK. Her individual assignment was to bring Agatha's dead body to Alexander. As assignments went, it was one of the better ones she had been given. She could organise the attacks quickly with the map and list of troops she had been given. That left her only one job to personally attend to. She could take on one Witch. It's not like Agatha was as powerful as Morgan and she had the element of surprise.

It took her a mere three hours to plan simultaneous blitz attacks. Her undercover work as an agent provided her with all the skills she needed. The plan was to take out the Lycans first, but leave the Lucas family until last. The attack on the Witches would happen at the same time as the attack on the Lucas family. She was almost sad not to be the one breaking that brute Tobias' neck. She would have loved her smile to be the last thing he saw.

Several of the Vampires she had been told to contact

had not responded. She sent them threatening messages using Alexander's name to ensure compliance. After all, no one said no to Alexander. Agatha's last known location was an island just off Scotland. Irina planned to travel there and strike before Agatha was even aware of any assaults taking place.

It was ten in the evening and Tristan's phone was ringing constantly, even after throwing it at the wall. Morgan and Tristan were otherwise engaged but the constant noise was affecting his rhythm. He finally hung his head in shame, defeated. Morgan had to stifle a giggle. Glistening with sweat, fully naked and hard, Tristan dismounted Morgan. He paced across the room and angrily answered his phone, "What?" The voice on the phone talked continuously for a few moments with Tristan making the occasional deep throaty growl. When the phone call ended, Tristan turned to Morgan as he marched across the room to their wardrobe. "Get dressed. Vampires have started the war! We need to alert everyone."

Morgan saw the fear in Tristan's eyes and obeyed without question. The pair made their way to his parent's bedroom. Morgan could hear faint snoring through the door.

"Might be best if I go in alone, I know my father sleeps naked," he divulged. Tristan disappeared into the room and within moments reappeared. He took out his phone to ring Tobias. It took several attempts to reach him and his immediate reaction was similar to what Tristan's had been. The couple made their way to the living room to wait for the rest of the family to arrive.

Tristan had forgotten to call Hannah until Morgan mentioned her. Tristan appeared torn on whether to wake her and asked his mother for her opinion. Fifteen minutes later, the adults had convened in the living room, minus Hannah. Marisa had decided to let Hannah sleep as Jacob was going through a sleep regression phase.

Tristan began, "I've just had a phone call from Fenik.

His uncle is the leader of the largest pack in Paris. His cousin just rang him. Vampires are attacking Lycans all over Paris. They just attempted to kidnap his aunt. His cousin has been monitoring Vampire activity for the last week, they're attacking covens too. Morgan you need to notify Agatha."

The family sat in stunned silence until Vincent spoke, "We have been preparing for this, Tobias you know what to do. Marisa you will need to wake Hannah, she needs to be on high alert whilst she packs for her and Jacob. Women and children are going into hiding."

Tobias stood and ushered Charlotte to leave, "You need to pack for the boys and wake them up. Get back to the main house in thirty minutes to drive in convoy to a secure location."

Tristan looked a little confused. It was obvious that he had been left out of the planning. He conceded that his father was grooming Tobias to be the Alpha and as the Alpha you had to make the decisions. Tristan hugged Morgan before saying, "I won't make you join them. If you want to fight rather than hide you should."

Morgan gave Tristan a sweet lingering kiss on the lips, "I will fight. I can make a difference. Together I know we can end this war, but first I need to warn Agatha." Morgan kissed Tristan goodbye and headed for the portal.

Agatha had been preparing for all eventualities following the council meeting and had ordered all portals to remain open to allow Witches to travel freely. Morgan arrived in Scotland on top of the cliff in the dead of night. It was freezing and she nearly slipped on the icy stone steps as she made her way to the castle. It was eerily quiet in the courtyard. Morgan used a simple locate me spell she had been practising, to guide her to Agatha's room. A ball of light appeared, hovering in the air and led the way. She knocked rapidly on the door and within minutes Agatha appeared in front of her. She took one look at Morgan in the dim candle light and asked,

"Has it begun?" Morgan nodded. Agatha invited her inside and Morgan shared with her all the information she had.

"I was afraid something had started in Europe. I've not heard from some of my contacts in weeks. We must wake the castle. I need to see for myself and alert the other covens."

Agatha knocked on the door four doors down. A slight girl Morgan had only seen but not spoken with answered. Within minutes the girl was standing in the courtyard summoning strong winds. All around Morgan, wind chimes furiously chimed. Minutes later the castle was alive with activity. Agatha asked Morgan to alert the Norfolk coven. Morgan travelled there by portal. She ran from the field to the clubhouse to wake Cordelia. She rang Cordelia several times but she didn't answer. So Morgan flew up to the window and rapped her knuckles on the glass. A startled Cordelia opened her bedroom window and leaned out.

"Get dressed. The war has started. Agatha needs you."

Minutes later Cordelia and Maura (Cordelia's mother) unlocked the front door to the clubhouse. Cordelia accompanied Morgan back to the portal field, whilst Maura raised the alarm by making the wind howl. Lights started to appear in the caravans all over the site as Witches woke up. Morgan had a momentary pang in her chest that she should collect Aunt Winnie. But she decided against it, she would be safer in Norfolk. With no active powers, she would just be putting her aunt at risk.

As Morgan chanted the spell to return to Scotland, Cordelia grabbed her hand and said, "It's good to have you back."

When they returned to the castle, every Witch on the island was now inside the castle walls. Embassies had been sent to every coven across the United Kingdom and Ireland.

"Cordelia, Morgan, will you join me?" Agatha asked.

Both of them nodded and Agatha led them back to the portal. The threesome attempted to travel to several portals across Europe but to no avail. Each time Agatha said the spell and they remained rooted to the ground. Morgan saw fear flash through Agatha's eyes. "The portals must have been destroyed," Agatha stated.

Eventually on the fifth attempt a portal opened in Siberia, Russia. Morgan and Cordelia followed Agatha as she walked towards a small traditional looking town with houses made out of wood. The snow was deep and both Cordelia and Morgan used the power of wind to float across the snow. Agatha being a Fire Witch used her own talent to melt the snow as she touched it, clearing a path to walk.

As they neared the town, Morgan could tell something was wrong. Doors were left wide open. Lights were on in the houses, but the whole town was eerily quiet. Agatha appeared to be heading for one house in particular. The door like the others was open. As they entered they saw a young girl lying face up in a pool of blood on the floor. The girl's skin was pale, with a look of horror frozen on her face. The smell of decomposition was tapered by the cold, but it was still potent. Morgan took one look at the child before turning to vomit, "Sorry, it's the smell."

Cordelia patted her on the back and replied solemnly "We understand."

Agatha's voice quivered as she spoke, "Check the rooms for others?" When they reconvened, Cordelia confirmed she had found a man dead in the main bedroom. Morgan had found no one. Agatha had gently placed the child on the sofa and covered her with a blanket. She was sat with her, holding her hand. She clearly cared for the child.

"Then maybe they got away," Agatha said more to herself than to the others. Agatha stood up and took a deep breath before continuing. When she spoke this time she was direct and in command, "We need to check each house and make a tally of the dead. Some of the coven may have escaped."

The three women separated and started to check the houses. In total eighteen men were found in the twenty houses, fourteen women and nine children. "We need to check the other buildings now, but let's do it together," Agatha ordered. The threesome walked towards the first building. The door was wide open like the rest, but the lights were off. Morgan and Agatha clicked their fingers and a flame flickered on their thumbs, lighting the way. The building appeared to be a school. Rows of old fashioned wooden desks all faced towards a chalk board. Posters and paintings adorned the walls. Morgan felt different in this building. She could feel something. "Do you sense that?" She asked the others.

"Yes," replied Agatha. "It's fear! There's someone here." Agatha then used the same locate me spell that Morgan had used and kept chanting it with different names. Eventually, a ball of light appeared in front of Agatha and started to guide her. It led her out of the classroom to a cleaning supply cupboard. The ball of light stopped and Agatha started feeling around the walls for a secret panel. Agatha passed the mop and bucket to Cordelia and felt the lowest section of panels. Under the lowest shelf of chemicals a panel popped open. Agatha swung it open to reveal a hole the size of a standard loft hatch. Agatha shouted something in Russian over and over again before making her way into the hole. Morgan followed whilst Cordelia stood guard. The dark tunnel gave them only just enough space to crawl through in single file. After approximately twenty metres of crawl space, Agatha disappeared and Morgan could hear the mumbling of several voices.

Morgan was last to exit the tunnel. It had opened up into a large room completely underground. Two adult women were conversing in Russian with Agatha and a group of terrified children were huddled in the corner of the makeshift bunker. The only light was from a few candles in the corner of the room. As Morgan's eyes adjusted to the dark, she counted the children in the corner. There were eleven seemingly all dressed as boys.

Agatha had managed to convince the women it was safe to leave the underground bunker and one by one everyone crawled through the tunnel. They piled into the large classroom. Agatha spoke in Russian but used generic hand gestures to signal follow me and led the group into the street towards the portal. As they approached the portal, Agatha explained that the group had been hiding for the last four days underground. The village had come under siege from three Vampires. The children had hidden initially at home. Then the girls had dressed as boys and ran to the school bunker.

Agatha requested that Morgan and Cordelia take three people at a time through the portal to Scotland. They did as requested and tried to use gestures to show compassion to the children, several of whom were sobbing. A young girl who looked no older than three, clung to Morgan's leg as they arrived in Scotland. She seemed fearful of everything, particularly the strange stone walls of the castle. Morgan tried to calm her but it was clear the young girl didn't speak English. Morgan desperately wanted to comfort her, so led her to the dinner hall and handed her a bread roll. The child clearly famished started eating immediately. She released her grasp on Morgan, who then fetched her a bowl of soup. Morgan asked Mary to take extra care of her. She was heartbroken for the poor child. As Morgan turned to leave the hall the child ran to her. She hugged Morgan tightly before saying, "Thank you," in broken English.

Morgan smiled down at her and gave her one last hug. The child then placed a hand on Morgan's stomach and said, "Khoroshaya mama," before returning to her soup. Morgan looked down at her stomach and wondered. She had no idea what the little girl had just said, but it sounded an awful lot like Mummy. A hand on a woman's stomach was universal in any language. Could she be pregnant?

When everyone was safe and eating a warm meal, Morgan pulled Agatha aside. "How can I help? Do you have a plan? I can help plan a counter attack with the Lycans."

Agatha ushered Morgan into a side room away from everyone. "The majority of Witches in the castle are old or children. Few of them have offensive powers. Did Sister Mary Rose show you the power of the black flame?" Morgan nodded. "We need to practise, before the Vampires are at our gates."

Morgan, Cordelia, Mary, Meredith and Agatha left the castle gates. They made their way up the steps to the portal so they had a clear view if anyone approached the castle. Agatha created the black flame and practised sending it to each of the women. Each Witch practised using it and maintaining it. Cordelia even managed letting go of the circle and maintained it for a good fifteen minutes. Then it was Morgan's turn to try to summon it. After several hours of trying and a lot of encouragement from Agatha, she finally managed it. Her fellow Witches applauded her. They were as ready as they were ever going to be.

When they returned to the castle, Agatha ordered everyone to sleep in shifts to maintain watch around the perimeter. The castle was filling up as more and more Witches arrived from small covens, who felt better protected together at the castle. Agatha pulled Morgan aside and quietly requested she use the portal to send a message to the Lycans, "Tell them we are making a defensive stand. Ensure they have put plan W into action." Morgan nodded, not questioning what plan W was. She left the castle and headed for the portal.

Tobias hitched up Hannah's horse box to her car as Marisa helped her to pack. Jacob was strapped into his car seat and Charlotte led the horses into the trailer. Tobias emotionally kissed his sons goodbye. He wiped a tear from his eye as he closed the rear car door, trying to hide his emotion from his sons. Marisa drove Hannah's car to allow her to sit in the back with Jacob. The two car convoy left the driveway and Marisa led the way to their secret location.

Marisa vigilantly watched for anyone tailing them and doubled back several times. As they entered Wales she pulled into a small lay-by and swapped her number plates. Charlotte in the car behind did the same. Ever since Cordelia had first visited them, Vincent had rented three properties in different parts of the country for six months at a time in cash. They needed a secure location that was untraceable. They arrived at the farm in South Wales several hours later. The farm was secluded and self-sufficient. A cliff face was behind the house and in front, farm land stretched for acres. Marisa breathed a sigh of relief. Her grandchildren were safe.

Vincent, Tobias and Tristan remained. Tobias and Vincent were constantly on phone calls and Tristan felt useless, "Give me something to do?" He pleaded to Tobias.

"Phone the friends that you trust and tell them to get here within the hour. Contact Morgan too and pass on a message to Agatha, plan W will be complete by sunrise."

Tristan did as instructed, glad to be useful. Morgan's phone rang out. The signal in Scotland never was any good. He just had to hope Morgan would return soon.

Within the hour, every male Lycan in the midlands has arrived at the Lucas family house. Tobias arranged everyone into eleven groups of three. He handed each member a large rucksack. He paced the driveway like a Sargent major, ready to address his troops before battle.

"Inside you will find a map to a clean water site in the UK. You need to break in unseen and empty the contents of this bag into the water. When you have completed your task send me a text message with a thumbs up. Contact your loved ones and tell them to purchase every bottle of filtered water from the nearest supermarket. Don't drink any water from the tap for the next week. We don't know what effect this drug has on Lycans. Go home, collect your loved ones and hide in an untraceable location for the next few weeks. Leave all technology behind and only use cash. Go off grid and stay vigilant." He ended his speech with a howl. Every Lycan stood in front of him joined in. The groups separated into multiple vehicles and sped off into the night.

Vincent was proud to see his son take charge. Before Tristan and Tobias dispersed, he hugged each of his sons and told them to meet him where they had the last family holiday with Timothy. It was a special place to all of them, immortalised in their memory as the last holiday with their brother. Before Tristan left he considered destroying the portal, to prevent Morgan from returning and putting herself in danger. It was extremely likely that the Vampires were already on their way to the house, but he just couldn't do it. What if Morgan needed a quick escape route? Instead he wrote a note and weighed it down with a rock just outside of the portal. He was careful with the words he chose, in case it was found by someone else. It said, *'Stay away until I contact you. Gone to ground. Plan W is in motion.'*

CHAPTER 25

Retaliation

Morgan arrived in the field hoping to see a flurry of activity or at least the house lights on, but it was eerily dark and quiet. As she stepped out of the portal, she noticed a rock had been placed on the ground and underneath it, a white piece of paper shone in the moonlight. Morgan picked it up. She instantly recognised the handwriting as Tristan's. The note read, '*Stay away until I contact you. Gone to ground. Plan W is in motion.*' Morgan stepped back into the portal and returned to Scotland. Her heart ached to be by Tristan's side, assisting him in whatever plan W was. But she had to concede that she was more useful in Scotland, protecting the innocent.

Jono programmed the coordinates they had been given into the sat nav. Tristan drove the group to the nearest Severn Trent, clean water booster station. Tristan parked the car on the last residential street on the map. Each Lycan opened the rucksack they had been given and pulled on the balaclava and gloves found inside. Jono signalled for Fenik and Tristan to follow him, as they ran cross-country to the site. Jono arrived at the gated entrance first and slipped off his rucksack. He pulled out a battery-powered angle grinder and cut through the padlock to the gates in minutes. Sparks flew as the metal grinded on metal, but his long sleeves protected his arms.

Tristan untangled the chain and the three of them entered the compound. Jono handed the angle grinder to Fenik and pulled out a hole saw drill. He swapped over the battery pack and drilled a hole big enough to fit his hand through next to the door lock. He handed the tool to Tristan and reached through to turn the lock.

Once inside, he stashed both tools back in his bag and produced a torch to light the way. He led the team over to a metal cupboard and opened the door. He appeared to be searching for something specific.

"Just pull them all out," Fenik growled, reaching forward to tug at some wires.

"No don't!" Jono instructed, "We need to pull out the digital output wires only. If you pull the whole lot out, an alarm with notify the head office control centre that there is a fault and engineers will be sent out."

Jono continued scanning the electrical panel until he found the wires labelled 'Digital Output'. He tugged hard at them, removing their connection to the panel. Then he instructed the others to follow him down to the basement level. They descended the stairs to find a vast room filled with large yellow pipes. Jono walked over to the closest pipe and took off his rucksack. He removed the angle grinder from his bag. "As soon as I cut into this pipe, a high water flow alarm will be triggered to a head office control centre. The wires I pulled out prevents them from closing the valve remotely. We will have around thirty minutes to empty the pills into the water and escape, before engineers arrive on site. The pills will be in the water network, they are undetectable. There is no stopping the water flow from entering every home that is fed from this reservoir."

"Why are we not dumping the drugs into the reservoir?" Fenik asked with a frustrated tone.

"Because the reservoirs have cameras and high security. Not to mention they are staffed 24/7," Jono replied.

"How do you know all this?" Tristan interjected.

"Because I have been working undercover at Severn Trent Water since I left Wild. I didn't go back to working at the Loughborough club."

Tristan was impressed, but a little bit annoyed that he hadn't been trusted with this information. Jono started up the angle grinder and put metal to metal. Once a square had been cut, Fenik used a crowbar from his bag to pry open the pipe. The three of them emptied the drugs into the water and ran for the stairs. They escaped without coming into contact with any engineers and ran back to the parked car.

"Have you got some place you want to be, or are you happy to come with me to Whitby?" Tristan asked. Both men agreed to stay together and Tristan sped off north.

Morgan was asleep before her head hit the pillow. She was constantly tired lately. Then again, she had been to another continent and back within the last few hours, not to mention performed extraordinary magic. Her sleep was not peaceful. Night terrors plagued her mind. Irina's face swam in and out of her thoughts. Morgan fought the vision each time. She tried to push the images away and focus on Tristan, the wedding, and other happy thoughts. It was no use. She finally succumbed to what her mind wanted her to focus on.

She saw Irina at night clad in black. The setting was familiar. It took Morgan a while to realise that she'd had this dream before. Irina was in Edinburgh. The dream started just like before, but then a man joined her. They were talking, but it didn't seem friendly. Morgan suddenly realised she recognised him from the gathering at Stonehenge. Morgan racked her memory for his name. Ivan! He was telling Irina that she was stupid and could not defy Alexander. He handed her a phone before leaving. Irina used the phone to call Alexander. Morgan could hear his voice boom through the speaker. He ordered Irina to kill Agatha. Morgan searched for clues of when this phone call had taken place. She instinctively looked up to the sky and saw a waning gibbous moon.

Morgan's eyes shot open. She leapt out of bed and rushed to the courtyard to look up at the sky. The moon was high and almost full. If what she saw was real and she whole heartedly believed it was, then Irina would be on her way. She had to stop her before it was too late. Morgan ran to the castle steps to climb the wall. She decided to stay hidden from everyone, as she didn't want Irina to be accidentally alerted. Witches were taking it in turns to patrol, but she slipped past one that was walking in the opposite direction and scanned the area beneath. She saw nothing, so expanded her search out towards the shoreline and then out to sea. The water was calm and no boats were approaching. Just as Morgan was about to run to the other side of the castle, she saw movement in the water. Morgan focused on the movement, straining her eyes to see into the distance. There was definite splashing that appeared to be getting closer to the shoreline.

Morgan scanned around the walls to make sure no one was watching her. The vision had come to her, because this was her challenge to face alone. She couldn't put anyone else at risk. She rose above the parapet, using the power of the wind to gently float down to the ground. She continued watching the spot of movement until she saw a slender figure climb out of the water. Morgan waited in the shadows, hugging into the walls to keep herself hidden.

Irina waited until the sun was setting and started swimming for the island. She had always been a competent swimmer and she thought it was less conspicuous than a boat. It was pitch black when she landed ashore. She had seen a small harbour on the map, but chose to swim to the other side of the island to attract less attention. The stone beach was deserted. She was dressed in camouflage sportswear and crawled up the terrain, hiding in the shadows. There was very little activity, just as she was expecting. High on a large hill was a castle surrounded by a stone wall. Irina was certain Agatha would be inside. Irina planned to scale the wall and find a place to hide until she found Agatha. A castle would surely have lots of dark corners. But timing was not on her side. For out of the shadows stepped Morgan.

Irina took a step backwards in shock. How had she known? Why was she not with her Lycan lover?

"Hello, Irina."

Irina contemplated running, but she had seen the power that Morgan possessed. Running would not save her. She needed to think quickly. Cunning was her only weapon. "Hello Morgan. I came to warn Agatha. Alexander wants her dead."

Morgan played along, lulling her into a false sense of security, "Warn her? Not carry out the assassination yourself?"

"I want nothing to do with Alexander. I am no longer his puppet. If you would only murder him, I would be free."

"It's an interesting idea, but Alexander is a separate matter. Today, I am here for you. I know why you really came here. No deed goes unpunished Irina. Surely you knew a Lucas would come after you for revenge one day."

"But why are you so bothered? You'd never even met him."

"True, but he would be my brother-in-law if you hadn't murdered him."

Irina visibly gulped. She racked her brain for a way out of this situation alive. "I was only following orders. Surely as an agent you followed orders without question. I was a soldier. But I'm done being someone else's disposable puppet. I want to be free of men who force me to do, what they're too cowardly to do."

"That's a good speech and you're a quick thinker, trying to play on my emotions. Problem is; I've seen everything. I saw Ivan promise you freedom in exchange for doing Alexander's biding one last time. You're here to kill Agatha, but the only person dying here today is you."

Irina had a split second to take action. She ran at

Morgan, lunging for the vein on her neck. Morgan stood still and held her ground. At the last possible moment she burst into the black flame, radiating it all over her. Morgan felt more powerful that she had ever felt before. Irina's hands had just reached Morgan, grasping at her hair ready to yank her head to the side, to expose her neck. On impact Irina let out a piercing scream as the flesh on her hands burned as hot as lava. The skin melted away before her eyes, exposing the bone, until the bone disintegrated into dust, drifting into the wind. Irina was screaming, looking down at the stumps where her hands used to be. The wind howled but the flames engulfing Morgan did not dissipate.

Thunder rumbled in the sky overhead. A bolt of lightning struck. Unlike a normal bolt of lightning, it remained transfixed in place, connecting the earth and the sky. Branches started to split off, trapping Irina in a cage of electricity.

Irina pleaded to Morgan's good nature, begging to be released. Tristan's face flashed into her mind. It steeled her resolve. Morgan used her telekinetic powers to dislodge one of the flat flint steps from the walkway and hurtled the sharp razor edge towards Irina's neck. The stone sliced her head clean off her body, as if she had wielded a sword. Irina's head dropped to the floor and rolled towards Morgan's feet.

The lightning cage vanished. Morgan walked over to Irina's limp body. She extinguished the flames on her right hand and reached into Irina's pocket, pulling out her phone. She then touched Irina's body with her left hand. The black flames danced all over the body, melting the clothes and flesh until only bone remained. Her skeleton then disintegrated to ash. Morgan stopped the black flame pulsing around her body. She picked up Irina's head by the hair and walked towards the castle gates.

The extreme weather and lightning bolt had raised alarms with those on patrol. They had gathered together on the castle walls and witnessed Irina's execution. As Morgan approached the gate, it was opened for her to enter. The Witches on the wall were staring at her mesmerized and they began clapping. Morgan didn't feel like a hero, she continued inside in search of Agatha.

Morgan heard several gasps as she entered the main hall, carrying the severed head. When she reached Agatha's table she placed the head in front of her.

"Alexander is sending assassins to kill you."

Agatha went to ignite the head with fire but Morgan stopped her, "Don't! We should arrange a meeting. Take her head to show Alexander our power. It can act as a warning, that this is the fate of all Vampires who attack Witches."

Agatha paused in contemplation, clearly weighing up the risks of meeting the Vampires again versus the bloodshed this could save.

Eventually Agatha responded, "You're right, but how do we contact them?"

Morgan withdrew Irina's mobile from her pocket and handed it to Agatha. Agatha took the phone and left the room to make the call.

Once alone in her room, Agatha called the first number in the call dial history. Alexander's distinctive voice boomed through the speaker, "Is it done?"

"No it's not," Agatha replied in her thick Scottish accent. It was undeniable who Alexander was speaking to. He took only a moment to collect his thoughts before he spoke again.

"Agatha, how nice to hear from you."

"I would like to meet, to prevent any more bloodshed. Same place, same time. Tomorrow. We need to reach a truce."

"That can be arranged. I welcome what you have to offer," and then the line went dead.

Alexander was disappointed but intrigued. Irina must have gotten herself killed or captured. Either way she was useless to him now. He valued Agatha's braveness in wanting to meet, but it would be her demise. He would have to take care of her himself. Soldiers were only as good as their leader and with her out of the way the Witches would fall.

Agatha shuddered as soon as the line went dead. His voice made her skin crawl. She would have to put on one hell of a display to get Alexander to back down. She would need Morgan's help. She went in search of Morgan to discuss tactics and to alert the Lycans.

Morgan tried several times to ring Tristan but the signal just wasn't strong enough. Agatha offered Irina's mobile, it was a satellite phone and could make calls anywhere. Morgan was reluctant to call Tristan's number in case it could be traced, so politely declined.

Instead, Morgan took the portal to Norfolk to check on her Aunt and the coven there. She intended to make the phone call to Tristan whilst she had better signal. Morgan's heart skipped a beat at the thought of seeing Tristan again. It had only been twelve hours but so much had happened that she wanted to tell him. She had avenged his brother's death and she was certain she was pregnant.

Tristan answered on the first ring, "Morgan, are you ok?" He sounded concerned. There was fear in his voice.

"I'm fine. It's good to hear your voice. Are you ok?"

"We're all fine. Plan W is complete."

"Agatha has arranged a meeting with the Vampires, tomorrow at two am at Stonehenge. Can you meet us there like before? Please be careful arriving."

"We'll be there. I can't wait to see you. I love you."

"Me neither. Tristan I… I…" Morgan stumbled over her words. She couldn't tell him about her pregnancy suspicions over the phone, so instead she told him about Irina. "Irina is dead."

Tristan was silent on the other end of the line. "Good," was his only response. When it was clear he wasn't going to say anything more, Morgan added, "I'll let you organise the others and start travelling." The line went dead and Morgan felt a little sad. Now wasn't the time to talk about babies. She was glad she hadn't mentioned it.

The Lycans were the first to arrive. Tobias was the only one in human form. Tristan stayed by his brother's side waiting for Morgan to arrive, whilst the others patrolled the perimeter.

The Vampires arrived next. The Wolves allowed them to approach from the South-East. Alexander took the lead and behind him followed, Bella, Anastasia, Ivan and one of Alexander's old Nazi friends. He wore his swastika proudly on an arm band.

The Wolves howled at their arrival, loud enough for the Witches who were waiting nearby to hear. The five Witches huddled tightly together in the portal. Morgan was concealed in the centre of the group with Irina's severed head. She used magic to disguise the scent of decay. She wanted the reveal to be a surprise.

Upon the Witches arrival Alexander took a step forward, "Agatha you arranged this meeting. Do you have news to share?"

Agatha remained where she was, but projected her voice loudly and clearly. "We have all suffered losses since the last meeting here. It is time to put an end to the fighting. We came to warn you what happens to those who attack Witches." Agatha stepped aside and Morgan strode forward with Irina's severed head behind her back. When she was an equal distance between the three supernatural groups, she released her spell and threw the head at Alexander's feet. It stopped abruptly a metre away, face up.

Anastasia let out a barely audible gasp, but Bella burst into a cackle and proceeded to sing, "Silly Irina sat on a wall, silly Irina had a great fall, all the kings horses and all the kings men couldn't put Irina together again." To the tune of the nursery rhyme Humpty Dumpty. She stopped laughing, only when Alexander turned to face her with a stern look.

The sight of Irina's head hadn't had the effect Agatha had been hoping for. It was intended to shock the Vampires into backing down, but it had just amused them. Morgan decided to take action. She said the chant and burst into the black flame and walked towards the Vampires. Tristan looked on in horror. He went to move towards her but Tobias held out his hand, barking, "She knows what she's doing."

Morgan bent down with a straight back, eyes locked onto Alexander. She touched Irina's cold face with her index finger. The flames danced down her finger and engulfed Irina's head. The skin melted away exposing the bone.

The Vampires were all silently watching, as were the Lycans. Even the Lycans patrolling had come closer. The bone disintegrated into ash. Morgan stood up glaring into Alexander's eyes. She saw a flicker of fear behind his hard exterior. Morgan stood her ground, still ablaze with the dark green, almost black flame. Agatha had ignited too and hand in hand the remaining Witches now all blazed.

The Witches walked forward together towards Morgan. Agatha reached out and held Morgan's hand so she knew they were stood in unity with her. Morgan took a step back to complete the line and then Agatha spoke, "We have our powers and you have yours. Do you really want to continue a war that will put one of us into extinction?"

In all his time as a Vampire, Alexander had never seen Witches with this kind of power. It terrified him, but he couldn't let it show. As Morgan was stood in front of him he could hear her heart beating quickly in her chest. But, his attention was diverted when he heard a faint fluttering out of tune with her heartbeat. It was faint but Alexander had heard it before, it was the singing heartbeat of a newly created foetus in the womb. Morgan was pregnant! The heartbeat was so faint that he wasn't even sure if Morgan would be aware she was pregnant. He was intrigued to what the child would be, Lycan or Witch? If it had the powers of Morgan and the strength of a Lycan, it would be the most powerful being in the world.

Unbeknown to anyone else at the gathering, two hybrids were present. It solidified his belief that hybrids were possible and Bella wasn't a one off creation. Alexander had a new mission; to track down more hybrids and harness their superior power. He would need it to win the war.

Stood in front of the five women, Alexander proposed a diplomatic truce, "I will deal with any rogue Vampires who have taken it upon themselves to attack other supernaturals. I will afford them no protection. I want only for us to live in harmony as we have done since the beginning of time. As the oldest of us here and the one who will remain long after you are all buried in your graves, I swear to uphold the sanctity of our different species and prevent any abhorrent acts that jeopardise our uniqueness." As he spoke he looked only at Morgan.

Morgan didn't know if she was reading too much into his words or if he knew her secret. How could he? But she took the words personally. He would see her child as an abomination and a reason to break the truce. Morgan remembered Agatha's words, 'we only make peace with our enemies'. The war wasn't over, but it would at least slow down the attacks and give them time.

Agatha nodded and Alexander stepped backwards. He maintained eye contact with Agatha. "It's time we left," he announced and the Vampires retreated slowly back in the direction from whence they came. When the Vampires were out of sight, the Witches extinguished the black flame.

Tristan bounded up to Morgan and affectionately nestled into her side as Morgan patted him. The other wolves approached Tobias and he signalled to Tristan they were leaving. "I'll meet you at home at midday," Morgan said, before Tristan left her side to obey Tobias.

The Witches returned to Scotland. Agatha pulled Morgan aside and congratulated her, "Well done Morgan. Your instinct was spot on. Hopefully the Vampires will be deterred for some time."

Morgan toyed with telling Agatha about her suspicion that she was pregnant, but decided against it. Tristan should be the first person to know. Instead she thanked Agatha for her support. They made their way into the castle to break the news to their fellow Witches. Aunt Winnie had arrived to see Morgan and to bring news from Norfolk. The Norfolk coven had been attacked by two Vampires earlier that evening. The coven had managed to scare them away with strong winds and a theatrical display of flying Witches, courtesy of Cordelia, her mother and cousin. Agatha requested that all covens remain on high alert and shared the protection spells to be put in place.

At midday, Morgan left the safety of the Scottish castle, to return home. As she crossed the fields to the main house, Tristan ran out to greet her. He lifted her high off the ground and spun her round like she was a princess in a fairy tale. As he embraced her, he rained down kisses on her face proclaiming, "I love you!" As they made their way inside, Morgan noticed the conservatory doors were hanging off their hinges. Tristan noticed her shocked expression and explained that the house had been broken into, but it would be secure again by nightfall. Morgan insisted that she must put protection spells around everyone's properties.

Tristan accompanied her as she cast them. As they walked over to Tobias' house, Tristan filled Morgan in on plan W. When he finished he asked Morgan how Irina had died. Morgan explained what had happened, starting with her dream. She described in detail how Irina had pleaded for her life, before Morgan took it. Tristan thanked her, knowing that Morgan didn't rejoice in taking a life, even if it was the Vampire who had murdered his brother.

On their return home, Morgan was bursting to share her other news, but she didn't know how to say the words. They had never discussed children. As they reached the portal field, just left from where they had said their vows, Morgan stopped abruptly. Tristan turned around in concern. "Are you ok? Why are you stopping?"

"Tristan, I have something to tell you! I have a feeling that I'm pregnant."

Tristan tilted his head and an initial look of shock was quickly replaced with the biggest grin. "That would be fantastic," he said, opening his arms to hug her.

"You're happy!" Morgan said, tearing up.

"Of course I am! Are you?" He suddenly asked, fearful she wasn't.

"I am. We've just never discussed it."

"Well, there's no need to discuss it now. He's already growing inside of you. What do you think of the name Tate?"

Without thinking Morgan replied, "He might be a she."

Tristan took a step back. The concept had never occurred to him. Lycan's only had sons. He had never imagined having a daughter in his wildest dreams. "I suppose," he stuttered. Morgan wished that she hadn't mentioned it. She hadn't realised the ramifications that might mean and she didn't want to put a dampener on such a happy occasion. Once Tristan had collected himself and they were walking back to the house hand in hand. He followed up with, "Either way, this baby will know nothing but love, from both sides of its family."

EPILOGUE

The following seven months passed by in a blur. Tristan and Morgan's house was nearly built in the portal field. Marisa was working around the clock on the interior design features and project managing the builders. Several storage containers were housing their new furniture.

Morgan had been unable to have any antenatal care, or scans due to the unknown nature of the baby. They had purchased home scanning equipment but none of it worked on the foetus. Its powers and gender remained a mystery. By Morgan's calculation, she was days away from being full term. The birth without drugs terrified her, but Aunt Winnie and Marisa had promised to be by her side. Aunt Winnie had made some powerful relaxation potions and a birthing pool had been set up in one of the guest bedrooms.

Mid-September under a full moon at midnight, Morgan went into labour. After nine exhausting hours Morgan and Tristan's baby entered the world. Aunt Winnie scooped the baby out of the water, swaddled it in a towel and handed it to Morgan. Morgan cradled the babe in her arms as Tristan cut the cord.

"Is it Tate or is it Theodora?" Morgan asked as she gazed down at the perfectly formed baby in her arms. The baby appeared to be the perfect mix of them both, with Tristan's nose and Morgan's petite ears. Tristan opened the towel, smiled broadly, then bent down to share the news with his wife.

AFTERWORD

Thank you for reading this story.

I hope you enjoyed reading it, as much as I enjoyed writing it.

If you enjoyed the story please leave a review on Amazon, to help others to enjoy it.

You can now follow the author on Instagram and be one of the first to hear about the launch of the upcoming sequel

@author_hannahhitchcock